The Wrong Girl

Yvonne Eve Walus

ISBN: 978-1-968061-31-9

Author's Note

Thank you for choosing to spend your time reading my book. I can't think of anything more flattering.

Table of Contents

Auckland, New Zealand
Last Week

CHAPTER 1

Last Friday morning

Madeleine Smith

Through the open door, the teenager looked asleep—eyes closed, face serene, black hair fanned out in threads of silk.

Madeleine Smith, headmistress of Arcadia High Boarding School, caught sight of the small medicine bottle tipped on its side. Three pink pills. Panic acrid in her mouth, she dashed into the room.

"Aiko? Aiko!"

No response.

The embryo-like curl of Aiko's spine almost broke Madeleine's composure. One of her students, a girl just like her own daughter, now just an empty shell.

A hollow buzz rang in her ears. She touched the limp arm, shook it. "Aiko!"

Nothing.

"Fire, ambulance or police?" said the voice in her phone. She must have dialled 111. The rectangle of the phone's frame anchored into her hand. Firm. Familiar. Reassuring.

Police? No. A visit from the police was the last thing Madeleine needed. The school's reputation was built on the premise of happiness—it wouldn't survive another fatal accident.

As for Aiko—well, Aiko didn't need the police, either.

"Fire, ambulance or police?"

Madeleine forced her brain to focus.

Wait.

Was it her imagination, or did the girl's chest rise a few millimetres?

"Ambulance," she said, her voice almost normal. "I think she's still breathing."

Yes. Ambulance. Definitely.

Aiko was alive. Everything would be all right. The school would continue to provide paradise on earth to girls whose parents could afford the luxury.

Except—

The room tilted.

What if they'd got the wrong girl?

CHAPTER 2

Later that afternoon

Constable Zero Zimmerman

Detective Constable Zara "Zero" Zimmerman of the Criminal Investigation Branch drove an unmarked white Holden. It was an old police issue vehicle, waiting to be replaced by a more climate-friendly electric Skoda, but it would have to do for her first solo mission.

The mission was a sucky one as missions went. The official objective: to investigate a near-death that would probably turn into a suicide attempt and a lot of paperwork. The undeclared objective: shut it down ASAP. But hey—the case would have to do, just like the old vehicle she had been assigned. Small steps. The New Zealand Police crawled into the twenty-first century two decades late, and the assignment of cases was less chauvinistic now, although Zero still suspected she'd landed the less-than-prestigious case strictly because of her gender.

A year ago, she would have been bubbling over with feminist indignation. Now she understood that—cliché as it might sound—every victim mattered.

"Aiko," she said the name aloud in acknowledgement. "Aiko Hamasaki."

On the face of it, Aiko Hamasaki had attempted suicide. But the cops from the Uniform Branch who'd inspected the scene earlier weren't happy with the appearances.

"Seen a few of these before," the constable had told her. "Far too many. But this one? Doesn't sit right." He wouldn't elaborate.

"Hey Google," Zero said. "Search for Arcadia High School".

"Here's what I found," came the voice of Google Assistant, which—depending on Zero's mood—sounded either metallic or melodious.

"Hey Google, let's do some reading."

Let's do some reading was a Google Assistant routine that read out her paperwork, the news, and text-rich websites while she got on with driving, walking, or chopping vegetables. She assumed the first hit would be the school website. She was wrong.

"A young teacher drowned in a school swimming pool at Arcadia High Boarding School late last night," Google Assistant read out.

"Wait, what?" Zero glanced in the rear-view mirror and tapped the indicator.

"Sorry, I didn't get that."

Zero brought the car to a stop in a patch of weeds that passed as the side of the rural road and grabbed the phone. The article was three weeks old. So no, the teacher hadn't drowned the night before. Still, a drowning, and then a poisoning?

She looked at the phone. Arcadia School's website was the third hit, wedged between articles about the hot summer taking its toll in drownings. There was also a memorial notice for Miss Parvati Patel of Arcadia High Boarding School, an article about the school's netball team—and hang on—another memorial notice?

The second memorial notice was actually a funeral announcement for a student at St Alban's Boys High. Dated the year before. The boy, name withheld for privacy reasons, had been seventeen years old. The cause of death wasn't mentioned, but Lifeline's number featured in the last paragraph.

"What the actual hell?" Zero whispered.

A suicide. Plus a drowning. Plus Aiko Hamasaki. Something didn't add up. Or perhaps added up only too well.

She put away her phone and resumed her drive. The black metal of the gate that protected Arcadia High Boarding School from the outside world loomed in the distance when Zero's phone chimed. She clicked the button on the steering wheel. "Constable Zimmerman. You're on speaker phone." A force of habit, the warning unnecessary when she was alone.

"Hi."

One word. So much suppressed guilt. "Millie."

The school gate grew bigger.

"You don't have to sigh every time you say my name."

Sisters, right? Can't live with them, can't slap them silly. Zero pulled over by the intercom pillar and waved her ID to the guard inside his booth. The gate slid to the side, and Zero motioned a *thank you* to the guard as she drove into a grove of densely green kauri trees. Then she returned her attention to her sister. "Don't be daft," she said. "I'm glad you called."

Millie snorted. "Sure. As glad as you were when I won the regional swimming gala."

Zero felt pressure in her jaw. Forced her muscles to relax. "How can I help you, Millie?"

Another snort.

"Is it about the electronically monitored bail? I know the delay is not fair."

Millie had been remanded in custody awaiting her trial, but the court date kept being pushed out in the wrong direction. The weeks morphed into long months. She should be allowed home detention.

"Millie? Would you like me to help you apply?"

"I wouldn't ask you if you were the last person on earth."

Ouch.

She needed to talk to Millie. Tell her that Dad seemed to have aged in the last few months, how fragile and sad he looked. But that barb had landed. "Look, I have to go." Zero almost said *I'll call you back*. That wasn't how it worked, though. "Bye, Sis." She clicked off.

It was official: Zara "Zero" Zimmerman—a red-haired orphan adopted first by a family of Gypsies in Romania and subsequently by a quiet New Zealand couple—now worst sister in the world. That's why she had always been the second-favourite child. Always. Even before she'd landed Millie in prison. Before she'd spear-headed her sister's arrest.

Their dad never said anything, yet he probably felt the wrong girl had been jailed.

She shook off the thought. A teenage girl had almost died today, and it was Zero's responsibility to find out why.

February in Auckland usually felt like a sauna, and this year was no exception. As soon as Zero climbed out of the air-conditioned car her skin slicked with sweat. The school path curved upwards towards the admin building and back down to the gate. A loop, convenient for vehicles, oddly fitting to the image of a very expensive and very exclusive boarding school.

A pair of glass doors whooshed apart as a woman walked through to greet her. "Madeleine Smith. Headmistress of Arcadia High Boarding School."

The voice was soothing, like an early morning by a lake. And yet something about Madeleine Smith made Zero's cop senses burn bright red. The unnaturally straight spine? The way her eyelids curtained off all emotions? Or that she hardly looked like a school principal with cheek dimples and a blouse that sparkled like the ocean on a sunny day? Nothing schoolmarm-ish about Madeleine Smith. Charming—yes. Trustworthy—maybe. Full of secrets—for sure.

"Zero Zimmerman, Detective Constable, New Zealand Police."

The handshake was firm and reassuring. If Zero had children, which she desperately and actively did *not* want, that handshake would have made her send them to a school administered by Madeleine Smith. If she had money, she'd invest it in whatever venture Madeleine Smith was running. If—

Zero Zimmerman, Detective Constable, New Zealand Police— gushing like a schoolgirl with a crush.

"Have you heard from the hospital?" the headmistress asked. Her left thumb worried the gold band on the ring finger. "They keep telling me Aiko is stable. But I don't understand what that means."

Zero did understand. The hospital had been her first stop. Aiko had ingested an overdose of sleeping pills and was in a coma. Flumazenil had been administered to counteract the benzodiazepine in the prescription medicine. When that didn't have the desired effect, she'd had her stomach pumped. She was alive. Unconscious. Not convulsing. Not responsive to external stimuli. Basically, not in any immediate danger; with the medium-to-long-term prognosis uncertain. The doctors had dissuaded Zero from interviewing Aiko's mother.

"Stable. Means her condition is not deteriorating," Zero said, aiming for gentle vagueness.

The headmistress plaited her fingers, released them, fidgeted with the wedding ring again. "Will she be all right?"

Zero side-stepped the question. "What can you tell me about Aiko, Mrs Smith?"

"Oh, please call me Madeleine, Constable. *Mrs Smith* is my mother-in-law."

Was there a flicker of a sneer above the upper lip?

"Madeleine. About Aiko—"

"I found the poor girl passed out on her bed and called the ambulance. Really can't say why they referred the matter to you. A couple of uniformed policemen were here earlier, and I told them everything I could think of."

"Hopefully we can settle the paperwork quickly. I wouldn't want to waste any more of your time."

Why was Madeleine Smith being defensive?

"Now perhaps you'd be kind enough to tell me."

"Is this really necessary, Constable? It's obvious what happened."

"It is?"

"Teenagers will be teenagers. You see it all the time with this me-me-me generation. Self-harming like cutting or purging or swallowing paracetamol—all of it attention-seeking. We're doing our best as a school to build up their confidence and a sense of selflessness, but sometimes…"

No, not defensive. Protective.

A sound cut through the air off to the side. "Baaah!"

Zero looked. A charcoal-coloured sheep emerged from the treeline, crossed the driveway, and headed for the soccer field.

"Our lovely sheep mow the lawns for us," the headmistress said. "The noise of a machine cutter would be out of alignment with the school's philosophy."

On her way over Zero had asked Google Assistant to read out the website of the "sought-after private boarding school for teenage girls." Its motto was "Through success to serenity," and the school prospectus brimmed with words like "well-being," "holistic development" and "emotional maturity." The main selling point, however, was total immersion in non-digital learning. There had also been a lot about sustainability and the environment.

Zero raised the single-use coffee cup to her lips, thinking that disposable containers were probably not aligned with the school's philosophy, either. Fair's fair, the taste of Styrofoam did nothing to improve the coffee. "About Aiko?" she prompted.

"Let's get out of this heat, shall we? I'll tell you everything you need to know for your report, then you can be on your way."

And … dismissed.

As she followed Madeleine inside, Zero glimpsed a stretch of blue ocean at the bottom of the soccer field. The air smelled of oysters and freshly watered plants. She could hear a seagull calling in the distance and the occasional bleat from a flock of sheep. There were at least ten, maybe a dozen, and they were all black.

Impossible to imagine anything bad happening in this slice of heaven. Yet Zero didn't need to imagine. It had already happened before. Twice, if you counted the incident at the sister school. In view of Aiko's overdose Zero would have to review both cases.

Before Madeleine could open the door to her private office Zero sank into one of the plush chairs in the reception area. She liked interviewing people outside of their comfort zone.

"What can you tell me about Aiko?" Answers to straightforward questions would establish a baseline of Madeleine's gestures and word patterns. Anything out of alignment later would be a red flag. The headmistress wasn't a suspect, yet Zero couldn't shake the feeling she was hiding something.

"She's a good girl," Madeleine said in a tone that discouraged anybody to challenge the fact. "Above-average grades, pleasant manner, takes part in extracurricular activities, has a close circle of friends. Now, if that's all—"

"What about enemies?"

"There's no animosity in this school, Constable. All students are encouraged to be courteous and inclusive."

"Friends she fell out with, then? Girls she used to be close to and now isn't? Girls she's only befriended recently?"

Madeleine's features hardened. "I'm afraid I wouldn't know."

It was like drawing teeth.

"In that case, who would know?"

A pause. "Aiko's teachers may be in a better position to comment."

"Who are her closest friends?"

"Bobbi Kentwood." The answer was fast. Too fast? Madeleine's knuckles paled, one of her thumbs rubbing small circles into the wrist of the other hand.

"Has she shown any signs of depression?"

Another hesitation. *Was Madeleine trying to decide what PR tack was best for the school?*

"Not to my knowledge. Nothing's been reported to me, and I don't deal with students often enough to have observed anything specific. Look, I'm perfectly satisfied that this was simply an unfortunate accident."

Another unfortunate accident, Zero wanted to say. Two accidents in three weeks. What were the odds? Instead, she asked, "What about Aiko's life at home?"

"Her home situation," the headmistress paused again, eyes sweeping the empty hall, "is complicated. She doesn't get along with her stepfather. That's the main reason she's in boarding school. Her mum is Japanese," she added as though this explained—what? That her mum was in favour of elite education? That she chose the husband over her child?

"What about her biological father?"

"He died when Aiko was little. I'm not privy to details, I'm afraid. During the entry interview, I could sense that the subject was upsetting for both Aiko and her mother, so I didn't press."

"Siblings?"

"None."

"And the nature of the trouble between Aiko and the stepfather?" Could this be the reason for Aiko's suicide attempt? Such a stereotype, a hostile or abusive stepfather; and yet it was a stereotype only because it was statistically likely.

"Again, very little was said, and not much more implied. Aiko made a comment about wanting to leave home, said that she couldn't wait to be seventeen and legally allowed to move out, but she didn't specify her reasons. She's fifteen," she added, sensing Zero's next question.

"Does she go home for weekends? Holidays?"

"Yes, and yes."

"This coming weekend was not unusual? She was supposed to go home?"

"Correct."

Had Aiko not wanted to go home so badly that she'd chosen to take an overdose? No, Zero wouldn't speculate before gathering all facts. "Let's go see her bedroom now."

"I'm sorry, why is this necessary?"

Zero gritted her teeth. "It would help if I could see," she almost said the *crime scene*, "the room where it happened."

The phrase sounded like something from a song. Madeleine must have had the same thought because the hard features softened around the mouth.

Her attitude, however, remained uncooperative. "Surely you have enough for your report now, Constable."

Zero's patience snapped. "I could come back with a warrant. Search the whole school." A bluff. Her sergeant had been clear in his instructions to move this investigation into the "Nothing to see here" filing cabinet. He would never authorise her request.

Madeleine had no way of knowing this. "There's no need for you to go to any trouble, Constable. Follow me."

Aiko's room was a small space with a large window, full of cactus plants and books. The walls were stark, devoid of decoration. On the bed, a white duvet cover with large black letters spelt out the message: "Schrödinger's cat is dead." Zero imagined Aiko's unconscious body clinging onto life on that duvet, and a surge of sadness pulled the corners of her heart all the way down.

Next to the bed, a multiple-use water bottle—a typical accessory of a typical environmentally-conscious New Zealander. What was less typical, however, was the image of Darth Vader on the bottle. A primary school kid would have such a bottle, sure. But a teenager? In Zero's days, it would have been enough to get ostracised. Perhaps this school was different? Or perhaps the hypothetical bullying explained the small brown medicine container on its side, pills spilling out onto a pink envelope.

There was an urgent tug in Zero's brain, like she'd missed something important. Was it the envelope? The pills? Something else?

Careful to preserve fingerprints though this wasn't officially a crime scene Zero opened the envelope and pulled out a folded page. A suicide note?

The words were handwritten in dark blue ink, gliding over the surface without denting the paper:

what do i
actually
mean to you?

Had Aiko written these lines? And why pen and paper rather than Snapchat? Duh! Obviously. Because no internet.

Zero turned to the headmistress. "Is this Aiko's handwriting?"

"I wouldn't know. One of her teachers will be able to assist you."

Except for the pills and the envelope, the room was surprisingly tidy. Not a single bra draped over the chair, no crumpled shirts on the floor. No discarded tissues with specks of mascara, no usual debris found in an average teenage girl's living space.

"Are the students allowed makeup?"

"As long as it's subtle. Just the essentials: concealer, foundation, neutral mascara, eyebrow filler ..."

Zero tuned out. She hadn't realised how many makeup products were essential. Her own handbag contained lip balm and a compact, and even that felt like overkill. "Where are Aiko's cosmetics?"

"In the drawers?" Madeleine pointed at a tallboy, then made a production of looking at her tiny gold wristwatch.

Zero opened a few drawers. A hairbrush, a tube of 2-in-1 shampoo-conditioner, a bottle of cider vinegar, a cake of soap shaped like Darth Vader's helmet, a toothbrush nestled with a tube of paste inside a plastic container. "Guess she doesn't use much."

That something important she'd overlooked was still bothering her. The Darth Vader soap? The cider vinegar? What?

"Do you have everything you need, Constable?" Madeleine stood by the door, her hand on the handle, borderline rude.

Zero ignored the implicit send-off. "What made you come here this morning? To Aiko's room?"

"She didn't show up for school. We don't monitor breakfast as some girls choose to sleep in, but we do take roll calls at the beginning of every lesson."

"Is that always your job? To check up on the pupils who don't attend?"

Madeleine exhaled audibly, impatiently. "Yes. The teachers all have classes to teach."

A bedside lamp shaped like a computer monitor looked familiar. "Is this a sunlight therapy lamp?" Zero asked.

"Yes."

"So Aiko *does* have a history of depression?"

"Not depression. Just an overprotective mother. Then again, show me a mother who isn't overprotective nowadays."

Certainly, any mother who felt the need to protect her daughter from the online world by sending her off to a school with no internet qualified for the adjective *overprotective*.

Zero moved to the desk. An unfinished novel, the latest by Harlan Coben, its spine still smooth and unbroken. A gold chain with a simple outline of a fish. A mobile phone. "The girls are allowed phones?"

"Only for an hour after supper, and only to call and text. This phone should have been in lock-up. Not that Aiko could have accessed the internet this way. There's no Wi-Fi at the school, and we're not in range of mobile data services."

Zero zip-bagged the phone to examine later and dangled the golden fish pendant from its chain. "Are you a Christian school?"

"We're a spiritual school, Constable. Various religions are taught as part of our culture and erudition, and we have a comprehensive set of values to guide our moral compass—"

Zero raised her hand to stop the torrent of words. "Do you know whether Aiko is religious?"

"I believe the family's Catholic."

That would be congruent with the fish symbol. If the girl took her religious studies seriously, she would have known that her church condemned suicide.

Zero picked up the thriller. Inside, like a bookmark, a glossy photo print of a toddler and a muscular man with a blond ponytail.

"Is this Aiko when she was younger?" she asked.

Madeleine glanced at the photo. "I assume so, though it's impossible to be certain at this age."

A search under the mattress and inside jacket pockets revealed nothing. The carpet's corners didn't peel away when pried. No hiding places and nothing hidden. No letters from the father, no other photos. Just schoolbooks, school supplies, clothes. A few more thrillers by popular authors, young adult "issue novels" such as *The Hate U Give* and *This is How It Always Is,* as well as several non-fiction books about topics as diverse as genetics, mythology, and gender diversity.

Zero took one final look at the room.

"Aiko didn't take the pills on purpose," she said.

A flicker in the headmistress's face. "Are you sure?"

Zero pointed to the Harlan Coben book. "Not before she read to the end." And now she also realised what her subconscious had been screaming at her earlier. The means of introducing an overdose to an unsuspecting victim. She turned to the Darth Vader drinking bottle. "We'll run a few tests before writing that report."

Bobbi Kentwood

If there's one thing I've learnt about psychologically damaged people, it's that it takes one to know one. Case in point: the plain-clothes female cop talking to Mrs Smith. Tall, pale, with lots of red hair and a fragile aura about her, like she's made of glass. I wonder whether others can see it, or if it's just me. In different circumstances I might feel sorry for her. Or at least be curious. Right now, though, the world is shrinking fast and my vision tunnels until I can see only this one thing.

Never trust anybody, my mum always says, *not even the police.*

Or perhaps, especially not the police?

The cop—I thought police officers travelled in pairs, like those people who knock on your door to help you find Jesus—is still talking to the headmistress. Must be about Aiko. Anxiety blocks my throat, makes it hard to breathe. Which is totally stupid. Mrs Smith won't know anything.

And she won't find out. Savannah will zip it, and so will I.

Breathe, breathe, breathe.

I turn from the two women and walk away, as quickly and inconspicuously as I can.

Ironically, it's a good thing we don't have the internet here. Our secret is safe—nothing on social media, no digital trail of our school lives. It's like we don't exist.

I'm used to not existing. My family certainly acts as though I'm invisible. When I'm home, my internet cuts out at ten every night. No discussion. Automatic. Would it hurt them to stop watching their stupid TV programs and tell me it's time to put my phone away? But no. It's all set to be the least amount of trouble for them. Like, they can't even be bothered to parent me properly.

I hate them. Aiko's mum may have married a monster, but I'd swap homes with her in a heartbeat.

Every day, I want to kill myself.

And the tragic thing is, I know even *that* wouldn't be enough for me to be noticed. They simply don't care what I do. That's why it's fine to sneak behind the garden shed, like this, and through a gap in the hedge, like this, into the thicket of kauri trees and towering silver ferns. The air here is green and mysterious, filled with the mating calls of wood pigeons.

Xander is waiting, his arms ripped like KJ Apa's, the floppy pale fringe a striking contrast with his dark eyebrows. He's popular. The fact that he chose me inflates my social status, and I should be happy. I'm not.

And yet I sit next to him on the damp moss, grateful that the navy blue of my school uniform won't show the stains. I want to tell him about Aiko. Don't know how. Xander hands me his phone, mobile data already switched on. Reception is weak here, in our middle of nowhere, but this part of the native bush is high enough to catch the signal in a few precious spots. Like an addict, I gorge on Insta and TikTok, while Xander's fingers unbutton my blouse and unhook the front-clasp bra.

It's a fair trade, though I would have done it even without the internet fix. I like that my body's like a magnet to Xander, I like how it's the only thing that he can think about whenever I'm around. That power is intoxicating. The only thing I don't like is that he's not Vincent.

Vincent and Xander both go to the nearby school for boys, but while theirs is a prestigious establishment that churns out future judges, businessmen and politicians, ours is a dumping ground for rich families' troubled teenage girls. I don't know what it is about Vincent—he's not nearly as good-looking as Xander—and yet it's Vincent that makes my life worth living.

Xander's hand is sliding down past my navel, and I seize it before it reaches the elastic band of my knickers. "Will you go to Vincent's party with me tomorrow?" I ask.

"I'll be there."

"I get that. Will you be there with me, though? Will you drive me? Hang out together?" Perhaps if we arrive at the party as a couple, Xander and I, perhaps that'll make Vincent notice me.

"You know I can't drive you."

Yeah. Xander is not old enough to hold a full driver licence. If he carries passengers, he'll be breaking the law.

Xander frees his hand from my grip, moves it down again, and this time I let him. Enough to make him gasp, and yet not nearly enough. I push my voice deeper into my throat to make it hoarse. "This is what you're saying no to."

"Bobbi." He sounds like he's in pain.

"Pick me up at seven?" I move my hips just right.

His eyes are vacant. When he opens his mouth, the words are barely more than a sigh. "Fuck, fuck, fuck."

"Yes," I lie. "Tomorrow."

Constable Zero Zimmerman

Zero felt a sense of—whatever the opposite of accomplishment was—as she drove back to Freemans Bay, where the Auckland City district police headquarters had recently relocated after half a century in Cook Street. Technically, she shouldn't have even caught the Arcadia High case, as it fell under the Waitemata District's jurisdiction—another confirmation that she had been handed the short straw. And now that she had it, she wasn't sure how to treat it.

The sergeant had been clear: complete the paperwork, move on. And yet, what would she put in her report? A suicide attempt or a poisoning by a person or persons unknown? Zero's intuition was screaming the latter, boosted by the matron's assertion that the poem in the pink envelope had not been in Aiko's handwriting. And yet the interviews with Aiko's teachers had failed to bring more insights.

"She doesn't have any enemies."

"Gets along with everyone. Woke and respectful."

"One of the least conflicted teenagers I've met."

It was as though Aiko had left no footprints as she moved through her school life. And yet, either the girl must have felt deeply enough to turn to the bottle of pills, or someone must have felt strongly enough to make it look that way.

Two deaths and now a girl in a coma. A girl whose religious beliefs did not align with suicide. A girl who didn't leave a suicide note. Something was wrong with this picture, or was it just Zero's wishful thinking to have landed a murder case?

As she walked past the palm trees that decorated the front of the building, probably in an attempt to make the grey blocky structure more elegant, her phone buzzed a message. *Hello? It's Emmanuelle Linden, Arcadia High's mental health counsellor. Sorry I missed your visit to the school. Can we set up a Zoom call for later tonight?*

Zero replied with a verbal and more professional equivalent of a thumbs-up, swiped into the police station, had a quick cold shower in the already-empty locker room, and got to work. She pushed aside a file labelled *Mekong Dragons*. The Vietnamese drug gang, with unconfirmed ties to 14K and the importation of pseudoephedrine, could wait.

Okay, so she wasn't exactly thinking *please-be-a-murder-case, please-be-a-murder-case, please-be-a-murder-case*. She was just being thorough.

First, she tried to trace the origin of the sleeping pills found in Aiko's room. The doctors confirmed it was the same medication as the one in her system, a strong anti-insomnia and anti-anxiety prescription medication called Temazepam, sometimes also branded as Normison. The bottle Zero found didn't have a prescription sticker on it, and Aiko had no reason to pull it off. So, not something prescribed to her—Zero had to make that assumption for now, while she waited for Aiko's family doctor to reply to her request for information under the *Health Information Privacy Code 1994*.

A quick Google search confirmed that you needed a doctor's script even if you bought the pills online, and that the total number of Temazepam scripts in New Zealand averaged over fifty-five thousand a year. She made a submission to a data warehouse called *The Pharmaceutical Collection* that contained claim information for subsidised dispensing of prescription medicine, on the off chance that Aiko had got the prescription from an emergency clinic. Of course, hackers could have got it on the dark web without a prescription, but she assumed Aiko wouldn't have had the know-how.

"Zimmerman?"

She looked up. Sergeant Sandeep Malhi, *Sandy* to his mates, stood next to her desk. What was he doing here on a Friday night? Zero had met his lovely wife and three tiny daughters at last year's Christmas party, and now she pictured the empty seat at the family table, a generous portion of dal makhana cooling in the pot.

"Sir?" Sergeant Malhi was never Sandy to her.

"Progress on the Mekong Dragons?"

Zero felt heat rise to her cheeks—blushing was the curse of redheads. "Nothing to report, sir. Still working on it."

"Right. How's the case at that girls' school going?"

Zero summarised her findings.

"Good, good. Email your report to me. Just the basics, please. Classify it as a suicide attempt."

"Sir, I'm not sure it's a suicide attempt. The other deaths—"

"Were a suicide and an accidental drowning. Tragedies happen.

It's appropriate to feel sad. It's not appropriate to waste taxpayers' money investigating them."

"But—"

"Excellent work, Detective. Keep it up."

Zero squashed down her irritation. Sergeant Malhi had a senior sergeant above him, and an inspector above that. He had a budget, deadlines, quota, and overworked staff. Her boss was just doing his job. And now she was going to do hers.

Time for the conversation with the mental health counsellor from Arcadia High. Zero followed the Zoom link on her laptop, adjusted her Galaxy buds and found herself face to electronic face with deep sadness. The woman's makeup was subtle, concealing the circles under the eyes and adding an upward curve to the mouth, but the pain etched itself into the curve of the neck and the rigidness of the shoulders.

"Good evening. My name is Emmanuelle Linden," said the voice that also had layers: warm and professional on top, hollow inside. "I'm the pastoral care dean and it's my privilege to look after the girls in Arcadia High."

Zero didn't believe in psychotherapy. A wound, in her opinion, was best left alone to heal. Scratching off the scab only led to bleeding. Her own childhood in Romania had been no picnic by any developed country's standards, and she tried her utmost never to recall even the shallowest of memories. As for blaming her parents for her life choices, she wouldn't even know which set of parents to saddle with the responsibility. Her biological mother and father? The Gypsy family who had taken her in and saved her life almost before she was old enough to remember a "before"? Or Mum and Dad, the strangers from New Zealand who had opened their home and their hearts to her? Inconceivable.

Zero angled her hands towards herself. "I'm Constable Zero Zimmerman. Thank you for setting up this call." She wished she could see the room the counsellor was calling from, but she had a background going, a photo of a single cherry blossom tree branch against the pale blue of the sky. "You're a psychotherapist at the school?"

"The term psychotherapist implies therapy. Our process concentrates on identifying opportunities that lead to good choices and good behaviour, thus nullifying the need for rehabilitation in the conventional sense."

"Meaning?"

"It's my job to help the students understand their emotional needs and manage their mental wellbeing."

Oh, to hell with the jargon. "Is it possible that Aiko attempted to commit suicide?"

She expected to waste time arguing about patient confidentiality. She expected to have to say: *In cases of suspected self-harm, either past or future, you are obliged to disclose all your notes to the legal guardians and the authorities.* She didn't expect Mrs Linden to say yes.

"Yes."

Well, then. O-kay. There went Zero's attempted homicide case. "Go on."

"The problem with teenagers, Constable Zimmerman, is that they have no perspective. The thing they fret over today, the very thing that might cause them to make unfortunate choices and—" Emmanuelle Linden caught her breath, "and ruin their life, will often become insubstantial tomorrow. Your mood at that age changes faster than the weather in Auckland. Unfortunately, teenagers don't realise it yet."

After the Zoom call, Zero sat still and pondered. Ever since she could remember, she wanted the world to be correct, for good people to be rewarded and bad people to be punished. She would tremble with indignation at every injustice. She'd abandoned her career in law when she realised that lawyers were in the business of making money, not meting out fairness or retribution.

Now she was a cop. Her job was to make sure that bad people didn't get away with doing bad things. In the case of Aiko Hamasaki's poisoning, she wasn't yet sure whether there were any bad people involved, and if there weren't, she'd be happy to write *attempted suicide* in her report. But she had to make sure. Martin Luther King said that injustice anywhere was a threat to justice everywhere, and while his cause had been a lot grander than hers, she was going to do her bit.

Doing her bit involved calling in a favour to speed up preserving fingerprints from Aiko's phone, the bottle of pills, as well as the page of poetry and its envelope. Normally, the forensic team would have been called out to the scene of the crime. In this case, Zero took the evidence to the lab herself.

"So, sure it's foul play then?" the technician asked.

"Yes." Easier to lie than to explain. "Would you be able to take the prints off the phone first? The rest can wait. Not identify them or anything," she added as she clocked the technician's grimace. "Just collect them now, so that they don't get destroyed? And analyse them when you have a moment?"

"You mean, Christmas Day?"

"Come on. You make it sound like Auckland is Crime Central."

"Certainly isn't as crime-free as it was twenty years ago."

Aiko's phone in hand, Zero hurried to the Information Technology Department. Despite the late hour, luck was on her side—Jack Jackson sat sprawled in front of his computer, looking like he was going to spend the rest of his Friday night staring at the two gigantic monitors filled with numbers and letters.

"I need you to break into this," Zero said as she placed the smart phone on his desk.

His voice was rich, the accent straight from American sitcoms, uninfluenced by Down Under vowels. She couldn't remember where in the States he'd come from. "What case number?"

"Off the record."

Jackson gave her a pointed look. "Again?"

"Yes," Zero admitted, her self-reproach rising as she remembered the first case they'd worked on together. The one that culminated with Millie in prison. "Again. Sorry. We could both get fired for this."

"Nah, not with the current staff shortages in the police force. But our next pay rise will be slashed for sure if this goes south."

"What pay rise?"

"Point. By when you need it?"

"Tonight?"

"Dream on, Zimmerman. Middle of next week?"

"Tonight."

"Will I get a kiss as a bonus?"

Zero curved her mouth. "Possibly... though not from me. Call me when you're done."

"Hang on. Tell me about the owner. Age, gender, favourite things?"

"Fifteen-year-old girl, Japanese heritage, boarding school, a bit of a nerd. *Star Wars*, Schrodinger's cat, woke."

"Piece of cake then."

"Sarcasm?"

"You're learning, Zimmerman."

Bobbi Kentwood

Because of what happened with Aiko, we—all the Year 11 girls—are supposed to see the school counsellor today. At first, we are told to gather in the school hall, where she, Mrs Linden, addresses us collectively. She starts off by saying that we all "need to improve the dialogue around mental health." But it's not a dialogue—she just talks at us about how precious life is, and something about tricks we can use to find *the little joys* in the *everyday routine*. I don't listen. Can't force myself to worry about Aiko or do a *five-minute self-assessment of my happiness levels.*

Instead, I think about Vincent.

Mrs Linden, as Vincent's mum, has that effect on me.

School is cancelled for the rest of the day. We're encouraged to stay together while waiting for our individual counselling sessions, then to start our weekend early. Go home if we can or go to the rec room and relax.

Finally, it's my turn.

"How do you feel?" Mrs Linden asks. She has a platinum blonde bob that provides a shocking contrast for her South American skin, and a face that makes you want to hug her while whispering all your troubles into her ear. I resist the temptation.

How do I feel? As questions go, this one is not very imaginative, especially coming from a qualified psychologist. Anxious about tomorrow's party. Relieved to have Savannah all to myself while Aiko is in hospital. Impatient to get home, to the real world, where I can go online and feel connected again. I wonder whether Aiko is in the news already.

"Bobbi?" Mrs Linden probes. "Talk to me."

I can't tell her about Vincent, so I tell her about Savannah and Aiko. In a round-about way. "It's not me you should be worried about. Aiko is Savannah's best friend. Savannah must be devastated."

A lie. I've been with Savannah the entire day, and she's no more devastated than I am. Thought at least she'd be tripping about the stupid thing we'd done, but no.

"Aiko is Savannah's best friend?" Mrs Linden echoes. "I thought you were Savannah's best friend."

"Yeah. Well."

My words have the desired effect. For the next half an hour, we only talk about Savannah's betrayal. "It feels like a break-up," I tell her at one point. "There's nothing romantic about our friendship, but I feel more hurt than if my boyfriend had dumped me."

A flash flickers in Mrs Linden's eyes. Empathy? Pain? Last year, when her older son committed suicide, there were rumours of a romantic relationship gone wrong. Is that what she's thinking about?

Her next words don't seem to confirm this. "Your boyfriend? Want to talk about him?"

"So not."

"Pardon, Bobbi?"

"Sorry, Mrs Linden. I meant to say, no thank you. I don't have a boyfriend. "

I'm not sure whether that's a good thing to be admitting to Vincent's mum.

"All right. How about we discuss your latest check-in entry?" Mrs Linden opens a big blue ring binder labelled *Weekly Check-In Sheets*, then reads out, "*Life is a big soup, swimming with leeks, mushrooms and people who'll tear up your heart and stitch it together, only to rip it to shreds a week later. If life is a soup, I am a fork ...*"

Those check-in forms are the school's hammer to fight bullying and its thermometer to gauge the state of our mental health. They are bullshit. You are supposed to fill in a piece of paper every week, and that will somehow protect you from mean girls who exclude you from their lunch table or make up lies about how far you go with your boyfriend.

I actually go out of my way to help them out, to make my forms more consequential. Instead of filling in highlights and lowlights, I give them streams of my consciousness. Not that they know what to do with them, of course. They have no clue.

"If life is a soup, I am a fork." My laughter sounds forced even to my own ears. "That's so funny. You have to admit that it's funny. Perhaps I should be a comedian when I grow up. I'm hilarious."

"Would you like to talk about it?"

"Being a comedian?"

"Being a fork."

I don't answer.

"You also write that you're not afraid of death. What's that about?"

I could tell her that there is nothing to be afraid of: either there is a heaven, which is a good thing, or there is nothing, which may be even better. But I still don't answer.

"It's all right to talk about suicide, Bobbi, if that's what you want. If that's how you feel sometimes. It's not a taboo topic. But neither is it a solution. You understand that, don't you?"

I'm not sure I agree with her. My nod is simply to get her off my case.

"Let's talk about it on Monday, all right? First thing in the morning?"

I nod again. Speaking to her, having her entire attention focussed on me, is a bit of a substitute for being with Vincent.

Madeleine Smith

What if they'd got the wrong girl?

The fear haunted Madeleine ever since she'd found Aiko unconscious. It intensified once the cop said Aiko hadn't overdosed on purpose. Because if not on purpose, then what? By accident? To Madeline's knowledge, Aiko hadn't been on any medication, certainly not benzodiazepine. So if this wasn't a suicide attempt or an accident, then what?

The answer came again, unbidden. *What if they'd got the wrong girl?*

They—being the Mekong Dragons, the drug gang that Madeleine Smith, the principal of Arcadia High Boarding School for Girls, had been stupid enough to do business with.

The wrong girl—being Aiko.

And the right girl … Madeleine couldn't complete the thought. Her fingers sought out a deep gash in her desk's top. The edges were still rough despite the passing of months.

At least Savannah was safe and healthy. Pissed off, to be sure, with all the energy of a teenager, but at least not in a coma.

And not a sex slave, which is what the Mekong Dragons had threatened. The pictures they'd emailed when she didn't agree to their latest business proposition … Madeleine had hoped like hell those had been photoshopped, or at least staged. The empty eyes. The needle marks. The degrading acts.

No.

She had to compartmentalise.

For what seemed like the hundredth time, Madeleine phoned the nurses' desk at the hospital. Someone—she wasn't sure whether it was a voice she recognised from an hour before—gave her the same answer as before: stable, unresponsive, we're doing everything we can.

She sent another text to Aiko's mother, short and full of meaningless phrases about prayers and support. If Savannah had been in Aiko's place, God forbid, Madeleine would have punched anybody who thought words could possibly bring her comfort, yet here she was. A child had been hurt on her watch, and that was the best she could come up with—offer clichés.

What she should do, what she should be spending time on, was figuring out the why. The simplest explanation was that the drug gang had made good on their threats. Perhaps they hurt Aiko by accident, or perhaps she was just a convenient warning shot.

But if not the gang? Madeleine had full confidence in hospitals and would leave Aiko's recovery to the medical staff; the red-headed cop, however, couldn't possibly solve the mystery without Madeleine. Or rather, without all the information.

Madeleine hadn't lied to Constable Zimmerman. Not exactly. Just—skirted the truth. When asked about Aiko's closest friends, she'd acted like a mother, not like a school principal. There was no rationale behind the decision to withhold Savannah's name. It wasn't even a decision, just a primal instinct of a mamma bear protecting her cub.

If only she could prove it was a suicide attempt. Last year, after Theo Linden's suicide at the boys' school next door, Madeleine had introduced a new mental health safeguard system into Arcadia Girls High. Every Friday, at the end of the school day, the students would fill in a short check-in report. The format was simple: describe one highlight and one lowlight of the week, name something you really want. It was the matron's duty to read the letters, compare them to those of the previous weeks, and to alert the school's mental health counsellor should any issues arise.

In theory.

Now the blue ring binder lay on her desk, centred, with label tabs showing dates from the middle of last year till today. Wait, today? Madeleine flipped to that section, the folder smooth and reassuring in her grip. Yes, even today, all students—apart from Aiko—had submitted their weekly reports.

Before today, she had never read a single one of these reports. Partly because she was so goddamned busy with everything else—Ashton and the kids and the cash-cow project, not to mention running Arcadia—and partly out of respect for the students' privacy. Now, though, she leafed through the stack until she spotted Savannah's familiar handwriting.

Under the heading Highlight, Savannah had written, "None." Under Lowlight, "Worried about Aiko." So far, so normal. Madeleine's eyes reached the What-I-want section. Her heart stood still as she took in the words.

"I want to live in Canada or Paris. Learn to speak fluent French, eat pastries every day and marry a rich guy. I want to have lots of children so that I can be a stay-at-home mother."

Savannah hadn't said she wanted Aiko to get better. Because it was obvious? Or was Savannah so self-centred she couldn't think about anybody else's needs except her own?

She flipped the tag with last week's date, found Savannah's entry by searching out her handwriting, even though by now she realised the pages within the date tabs were sorted alphabetically.

Savannah's highlight last week: "DK." Who or what was DK? Google took her to a publishing site for educational books—that couldn't be it. A boy's initials? Maybe. Privacy laws meant she wouldn't be able to ask the principal of the boys' high school for a list of names. She moved on. Savannah's lowlight: "DK." Savannah's want-section: "DK." Definitely a boy.

Madeleine moved to the first week of term. The highlight for Savannah: "Tarot." The lowlight: "Miss Patel." Shit. There was so much for Savannah and the rest of the students to deal with, and the school year had barely started. What-I-want: "For the whole week to reboot, so we can start again."

Would this week have gone any different, Madeleine wondered, if Miss Patel's accident hadn't happened? Would Aiko's day have been just another Friday, looking forward to two days of internet at home?

What had Aiko been writing? Madeleine scanned the crisp sheets of paper. The girl's highlights were invariably something to do with Savannah and Bobbi, sometimes just their names, sometimes a mention of a school project they did together, something about poetry. Her lowlights remained steadfastly empty, even the week of Miss Patel's accident, which meant either that Aiko didn't like dwelling on the negative, or that she was a secretive soul. Her what-I-want space was a mantra, a single sentence that repeated over the weeks: "I'm happy as I am." Nothing to suggest that she would attempt an overdose of sleeping pills.

Madeleine put away the folder and tackled the next task. Aiko's phone—why was it in her room, and not safely locked up in the matron's drawer? Madeleine checked her watch, then dialled the matron's mobile number.

"Mrs Moss. Sorry to intrude this late. Still no change in Aiko's condition." She allowed the small talk to continue, reassuring the other woman and making sure that the surface on which she was drumming her fingers was soft enough for the sound not to carry. Eventually, she got to the point. "We were wondering why Aiko had her phone in her room outside the permitted hours," she said. Her tone would have been equally non-confrontational had they been discussing this year's spike in summer temperatures.

"I'm not sure I understand?" The matron's tone matched Madeleine's, with an extra tinge of confusion. "I have all the students' phones right here. Including Aiko's."

After a few minutes, Karen Moss delivered Aiko's mobile phone to Madeleine's office, then withdrew, closing the door behind her without as much as a squeak. Normally, Madeleine considered students' privacy paramount. There was nothing normal about a student in a coma, however, so she powered up the phone, and was surprised to see the background photo instead of the password screen. The photo was a stock one, which was odd, because Madeleine's own daughter took great care to personalise anything in her phone that could possibly be personalised.

She looked at the phone's history. Every evening, there was a half-an-hour call to a number labelled Mum, which matched the one in Madeleine's records for Mrs Hamasaki. No texts or other calls, no browsing history, not even on weekends when Aiko would be home or at one of her friends' houses.

The conclusion was obvious—this phone was a decoy. The one found in Aiko's bedroom must have been the one she used outside the endorsed time slot.

Brilliant in its simplicity.

Madeleine wondered why her other students hadn't thought of this solution.

Or had they?

Constable Zero Zimmerman

When she got home, Zero made three lists:

- Ways in which Aiko could have taken the pills by accident.
- Reasons she might have taken the pills deliberately.

- Reasons someone might want her dead.

The first list was as simple as it was empty. There was no way you could take an almost full bottle of pills by mistake.

The list of reasons she might have taken them deliberately was broken down into giving someone a scare (so not meaning to take a dangerous dose), wanting to remove herself from someone's way (melodramatic and only happened in books), and suffering from chronic depression. Depression because of a boy, school grades, her situation at home? Zero needed to talk to Aiko's friends, her teachers, her mum.

And, finally, reasons someone might want her dead. Had she witnessed something? Stolen another girl's boyfriend? Been a bully despite the teachers' testimony? What reasons would someone consider sufficient motive to want to end Aiko's life?

Research was one of the things Zero enjoyed in life, the way others might enjoy an ice cream, or going for a run, or sunbathing. It gave her a physical sense of pleasure to consolidate information, to check the reliability of experts as well as that of the sources, to analyse until she reached a deeper layer of understanding.

You couldn't read the newspapers in New Zealand and not be aware of the teen suicide epidemic that was scouring the land. One spokesperson claimed that a young person killed themselves in this country every sixty-seven hours, in other words, on average every two and a half days. Sunday and Monday might be suicide-free, but not Tuesday or Friday. One hundred and thirty a year. More than teenage car crash and teenage cancer deaths combined. Was Aiko aiming to become one of the one hundred and thirty?

Many experts were suggesting that the approach of pretending that suicide didn't happen, of not discussing it with teens for the fear that it might give them ideas, was not working. They advocated removing the taboo around the topic, talking about depression, and following where that road might lead.

It didn't seem so long ago that Zero had been a teenager, but what she was reading now did not resonate with the teen world she had inhabited. Self-hatred? Cutting? Emailing detailed suicide plans to friends or posting disturbing messages to social networking sites? What the hell?

She forced herself to read on. And on. More sites, more statistics, more advice. "Higher minimum wages are linked to lower suicide rates"—a country-by-country study. Experts agreed that the most-at-risk teenagers came from broken families and deprived areas, where household income was low and the prospects of a decent future even lower. A no-brainer—it's hard to feel the joy of being alive when your house is cold and damp, your stomach empty, and your school shoes full of holes.

And yet Aiko's background couldn't be more different—an only child from a well-to-do family, in a prestigious school. True, she had a stepdad, not a dad, but did that matter? As an adopted child herself, Zero didn't think blood bonds were super-important. And as for the fact that Aiko didn't get along with her stepdad—was that the normal teenage rebellion, the childhood idol falling off his pedestal, or was there more to it?

She was brewing the final pot of coffee before bed, when the motion-detector light by the front door flickered. Just like everything else in this shared accommodation, the light malfunctioned more often than not. The knock that came, however, couldn't be explained by faulty wiring.

Suppressing the feeling of irritation, Zero marched along the corridor and flung open the door, her mouth already open to chastise the unwelcome guest about social graces and paying visits at eleven o'clock on a Friday night.

She closed her mouth. Opened it again. "Jackson?"

The shriek of love-starved chorus cicadas coming off the nearby manuka shrub blended with his voice. "It's not a booty call. Unless you want it to be, naturally."

Zero swallowed a sigh. "*Naturally.* Come on in."

Jackson's teeth glinted as he pointed towards the still-flickering porch light. "If I stay the night. I can fix the connection in the morning."

At that moment, one of the bedroom doors creaked to reveal Amelia's sleepy face. "Shhh," the face said before disappearing behind the white-painted wood again.

Zero cursed the Victorian design of having bedrooms by the front entrance, with the living area at the back. Without another word, she gestured Jackson in the direction of the lounge, closed the door on the cicadas and a heady garden scent. Wild jasmine, she realised. Left unchecked, it could spread and strangle native plants. Foreign, gorgeous, dangerous. A bit like Jackson.

She made a detour to the kitchen to fetch two mugs and the freshly brewed coffee pot.

Jackson raised an eyebrow. "Biscuits?"

"As long as they're considered the full and final payment for services rendered." Zero rummaged in the cupboard and found a box of Tim Tams. She hoped they weren't Amelia's.

She sat on the sofa, consciously choosing the seat opposite him. Jackson took one of the Tim Tams and bit off a corner. He turned it in his fingers and bit off the corner diagonally opposite. Zero watched him chew, intrigued. The mug full of coffee in one hand, Jackson used the biscuit as a gigantic straw to suck in some of the liquid, before he quickly crammed the Tim Tam into his mouth. He repeated the process with another biscuit, but this time he wasn't fast enough, and the thing collapsed into the mug in a soggy mess.

"Damn it," he muttered, licking his fingers. "Out of practice. Biscuits, I mean. Plenty of practice otherwise," his eyes sought hers, "if you get my drift."

"Aiko's phone," Zero reminded him. She had to keep her mind on the job, not on Jackson's fingers, lips, tongue.

Jackson slurped some more coffee, ignoring the biscuit crumbs. "Right. Here's what we've got." He stood up and placed himself on the sofa beside her, his arm touching hers, and moved the phone so they both could see. "Lots of photos, lots of texts. You can also get into her Snapchat and Instagram."

"Email?" Zero asked.

"You dinosaur. No self-respecting teenager uses that. Except for school, to communicate with teachers and sports coaches, but I don't see that here."

"Mm." Zero wasn't going to digress by telling him about the weird school with no internet. "Did you browse through the contents? Anything interesting?"

"Apart from the fact that the owner didn't spend as much time online as most girls her age?"

"Let me guess. No activity except during weekends?"

"Lots of activity during weekends, like you'd expect. Significantly less in the week, minutes rather than hours, but not none. See here? There are Snapchat streaks going back and forth between her and her friends for months."

Zero felt the straight road she had thought she was on curve dangerously towards a detour. The Snapchat streaks meant Aiko must have logged on every day for—what did Jackson say, months?

How did she manage?

Were the friends from the same school? Zero knew the photos and names didn't have to be real, but at face value all the Snapchat friends appeared to be male.

Jackson pointed. "Look here."

"What?"

One of the phone apps was for doodling and brainstorming, a simulated whiteboard on which you could write, draw, or stick pictures. In the centre, Aiko had drawn a large colourful question mark. In one corner, she'd written: "Labels negate me." In the one diagonally opposite: "If you free the boy, do you kill the girl?"

"Kill the girl?" Zero found Jackson's eyes. "What the hell?"

"Don't take it literally. Check out the music she listens to."

She did a quick scan. "Dua Saleh? Ryan Cassata? I don't know any of these artists."

"Neither did I. That's why I googled them."

"Do they all sing a certain type of music? Like punk or gospel?"

"Something like that."

"Jackson. Stop playing games. Just tell me."

"They are all transgender or non-binary musicians. Their art challenges gender stereotypes."

Bobbi Kentwood

Disaster! Vincent's party is tomorrow, and I have nothing to wear.

Of course, what I should be thinking about is Aiko. In hospital. But I don't want to. Can't. Every time my mind goes there, I yank it back. Will. Not. Think. About. Aiko.

And so I'm thinking about my outfit. My style is shorts or laddered jeans with a T and a hoodie, so I don't have many party clothes. Not the cut-off top—I wore that to the pre-Christmas party last year. Not the purple harem pants—they don't fit properly. Not the mini skirt with a white top, because only skanky girls wear that. Oops, that's slut-shaming.

This is going to be a disaster.

At least Aiko won't be there to monopolise Savannah.

Of course, now that Aiko isn't going, I guess I could wear the backless black dress. It's similar to Aiko's sexiest party outfit, but seeing that Aiko is in hospital …

Will. Not. Think. About. Aiko.

My mum knocks on my bedroom door and comes in, not waiting for a reply. I'm about to explode at this breach of my personal space, but she's wearing her fragile face, so I check my temper.

"So glad to have you home," she says, even though we've just had dinner together, the three of us at the big table covered with a freshly pressed linen cloth. My mum is like that, into family values, home cooked meals, and ironing.

I'm not sure where she's going with this, so I hedge my bets. "I missed you too." That should be safe, right?

"I'm thinking, maybe boarding school is not the best option right now? You need time to study, time to be with your parents before you leave the nest for good—"

Wait, what? What is she talking about?

"Mum, I like my school. I like my friends." It's true. I like Vincent best of all. And DK. And Xander. Also, I like Savannah again, now that Aiko is out of the picture.

Wait. Is this all triggered by what happened to Aiko? Does she think it was… *done to her*? Does she think the wrong girl got hurt by accident?

Mum gives me a funny look. "It's just that Dad's got this job offer in Invercargill, and—"

Invercargill? Is she for real? I don't let her finish. "If you and Dad want to move to the South Island, be my guests. I'll stay at the school during term and come visit you for holidays."

"Bobbi." Just a single word, but it's enough.

I understand that the battle has begun.

Chapter 3

Last Saturday

Constable Zero Zimmerman

When she'd joined the New Zealand police Zero Zimmerman had no idea how much of the work involved driving somewhere, then waiting. Her car, this time a police van with the distinctive white and blue chevron pattern, was parked outside Bobbi Kentwood's house. Or her parents' house, at any rate.

"I'd like to talk to you about Aiko," Zero typed in Instagram, a direct message to Bobbi. Teens these days—they had no clue about privacy. All Zero needed to do was follow Bobbi on social media and—*kha-boom*—they were chatting like old friends. The no-internet regulation at school, it seemed, did not have any dampening effect on Bobbi's weekend online activities.

"Why?"

"I hear the two of you are close."

"Who told you?" Bobbi's questions came thick and fast, the interviewee having turned into the one asking questions.

Zero could also play this game. "Are you close?"

"Yeah. I guess."

"Can we talk face to face?"

A full minute passed before Bobbi typed back: "Hahaha, you can't pull that one on me. Everyone knows never to meet people you talk to online."

Zero felt patience slipping away from her grasp like a moss-covered stick on a bush walk. "I'm with the police. We can talk at your house today, or at your school on Monday. Your choice."

Bobbi logged out of Instagram without replying. Zero looked up from her tablet computer. The front door, painted rich red to contrast with the navy blue of the weatherboards, swung open and Bobbi appeared. Zero could confirm her identity right away, from the many pictures the girl had posted online. Strings of yellow hair framing Bobbi's broad flattish face brought to mind images of seaweed and water nymphs.

"In a hurry?" Zero called out through her car's open window.

Something like an electric jolt made Bobbi's shoulders twitch. "You gave me a fright."

Zero was glad to hear it. "Shall we talk inside?"

The look Bobbi shot her was shifty. "Can't. Things to do."

"It wasn't a question." Zero touched her badge. "It was a request. I'm investigating the events that led to your friend's hospitalisation."

"Do I have to talk to you? Like, what are my rights?"

"No, of course not. By law, you don't have to come with me or give a statement."

"So, we're done here."

"If that's what you want. But," Zero paused, counted to three in her head. "Don't you want to help Aiko?"

An exaggerated shrug. "I'm not a medical doctor." Smart-alecky words, but grief was already beginning to draw an upside-down U-shape on Bobbi's forehead. Her sadness was genuine.

"That's not the kind of help I'm after. I need to find out what happened. If you agree to give a statement, you can have an adult present, and you can change your mind about giving a statement at any stage during the process."

"What do you mean?"

"Let's go inside and talk, kiddo. With your mum or your dad listening in and making sure you're not getting upset. If you don't like where my questions are going, we stop. We have to, by law. Okay?"

"Okay."

Once inside, they settled on a brown velvety sofa. It was like sinking into chocolate mousse. "We're good," Bobbi said. "My parents are still asleep, and they don't know Aiko anyway. What do you want to ask me?"

"Do you think she tried to commit suicide?" Zero went for shock value, watching out for Bobbi's reaction.

It didn't come. The girl wasn't taken aback or surprised. "I mean," she paused and put the nail of her index finger between her teeth. "I don't know. We all feel down from time to time. The school counsellor says it's normal." Snap. The bitten off portion of the fingernail disappeared into Bobbi's mouth. She replaced her index finger with the side of her thumb, bit down on the skin.

"Have you been seeing the school's mental health counsellor, Bobbi?"

"Yes." The snap was inaudible this time, but a drop of blood coloured the thumb.

No embarrassment, as though seeing a mental health therapist was the most natural thing in the world, which—of course—it was. Clearly, things had changed for the better since Zero was in high school. Back then, admitting to having anxiety issues or feeling depressed would have led to being bullied for sure.

The latest trend in exploring mental health issues was almost excessive and hedonistic. No wonder that one in six adults in this country had at some point in their lives been diagnosed with a mental disorder. Put ideas in people's heads, tell them that they might be depressed… the power of suggestion could never be overestimated. Harden up, that was the answer.

Except when it wasn't. Zero was a faithful disciple when it came to numbers. Numbers didn't lie. And numbers said that hardening up was not a cure for depression, nor a prophylactic against self-harm.

"What about Aiko? Has she ever visited the school counsellor?"

"Yes."

"Why? Was Aiko feeling down lately?"

"I mean, summer's over, you know? And we're back at school? So, yeah." The little finger now, its nail no challenge for the fierce front teeth.

"Did she seem more unhappy than usual the last few days? Something that seemed out of proportion, more than just your normal school-is-back blues?"

If she says 'I mean' one more time, Zero thought, *her parents have wasted a lot of money paying for her education.*

"I mean, I don't know."

Zero sighed. "Boy issues?"

"What? No!" The first false note in Bobbi's statement. "It's an all-girl school."

"So you don't know any boys?"

Bobbi deigned to offer a smile. Half patronising, half amused. "I mean, we socialise. Dance lessons every Tuesday, end-of-term school balls, sport events."

"Does Aiko have a boyfriend?"

"I mean," a long pause, another nail bitten off. "Boys like her."

"Does she like a specific boy?"

"No, she's not like that."

Not like what, Zero wondered. *Not easy with her affections, or not into boys? Worth a try.* "Does she like a specific girl, then?"

Bobbi jumped to her feet. "I don't want to answer any more questions."

"We found a poem in Aiko's room. Do you know anything about that?"

"I said, no more questions."

Damn. She never even got the chance to ask Bobbi whether Aiko took sleeping tablets. She'd asked the matron, who of course hadn't known. Or as she had put it: *not to her knowledge*. That could mean anything, really.

Back in her car, Zero added a summary of her conversation with Bobbi to her notes, then closed her laptop. Enough thinking. Time for doing. As indelicate as the timing might be, she had to speak to Aiko's parents.

As she stopped to turn into the main road, she saw a black BMW X5 with an Avis Car Rental logo. The car cruised in front of her, too fast to see the face of the driver. She got a fleeting impression of an overweight man, and mentally castigated herself for judging.

The BMW was heading to the Arcadia High Boarding School, and on an impulse Zero followed. Together they slowed down in front of the school gate—as usual, closed. The BWM drove on, while Zero stopped to have a chat with the guard.

"School employees come in every morning. Parents collect the girls on Friday afternoon and drop them back on Monday. A truck comes with groceries on Tuesdays, Thursdays, and Sundays. An occasional special delivery, usually at night."

"Are the girls allowed visitors?"

"No rule against it. But doesn't happen much."

"What about yesterday morning? Or Thursday night?" she asked.

The guard shook his head. "I was off duty, but one of the other guys would have made a note. We take a photo of every vehicle and every person entering the school. Other than parents who came to pick up their children yesterday afternoon, the only visitor was," he paused as he consulted his device, "Constable Zero Zimmerman. That's you, right?"

"Last time I checked. You have the registration number of every vehicle that came in?"

"Correct."

"What about this one?" Zero rattled off the BMW's licence plate.

The guard click-clicked the computer keyboard. "That car has never entered the grounds."

A dead end.

Madeleine Smith

"Mum. About the party."

Those four words, said in a voice steeped with entitlement, were enough for stress knots to form across Madeleine's shoulders. The pain was immediate, as though the weight of the world crashed onto her, which—in a way—it had. Right now, her world consisted of this room and the wrath of one teenager. "Honey, you know I'm not exactly comfortable with the idea of—"

"Mum! Honestly. You're so—yesterday." Savannah rushed out of the living area, taking care to slam her bedroom door as she disappeared behind it.

Madeleine tried to suppress a sigh. Failed. She used to be a perfect mum, back when she did not have children of her own. Back then, she used to know the answer to every parenting conundrum (yes to vaccinations, no to the myth of Santa Claus, at five they're old enough to empty the dishwasher, no dating till they're sixteen, or perhaps twenty-six). The good old days.

Now Savannah was fifteen, almost sixteen, and all her friends had boyfriends. And tonight—tonight all her friends were going to a party with alcohol and no adult supervision.

Yes, it was the alcohol.

Yes, it was the no-supervision.

Not to mention that Savannah was planning to go to party while Aiko—one of her best friends—was in hospital, prognosis of recovery still unknown.

Most of all, though, it was the choking fear that Aiko's overdose had been orchestrated by someone who had meant to hurt Savannah instead. It's not as though the girls looked alike or shared a room, but emotions were stronger than reason. Madeleine had been warned to cooperate or else. Was Aiko's misfortune the "else"? And would Savannah be next? Although there had been no recent communication from the drug gang, Madeleine's blood ran cold every time her phone chimed.

Ashton emerged from his study and knocked on Savannah's door. "You know the rules, Sav. Love and respect. Please come out and apologise to your mum."

Her daughter returned to the lounge, as if reined in on a magic ribbon. "I'm sorry, Mum."

Just like that. Madeleine could shout, bribe, or offer the silent treatment—all to no avail. Ashton just needed to ask. He was so much better at being a parent than Madeleine, even though she was the one with all the teaching qualifications and managerial experience.

Here was an uncomfortable truth: the world simply favoured men. As clichéd as it was, a man who issued a command was authoritative, while a woman exhibiting the same behaviour was bossy. A man who left a board meeting early to attend his child's swimming gala was a hero, a woman doing it was irresponsible and not committed to her job. A man who screwed around—

She let the thought go.

Savannah took a big breath. "But Mum? Could you please explain why you're being difficult about the party?"

She couldn't. "There's a cyclone warning for Auckland," she said. It wasn't a lie. "The Transport Agency is advising to avoid all non-crucial journeys."

"Well, Mum. Fortunately, the journey to this party is absolutely crucial. And if the weather turns to custard, I'll just stay overnight."

And the boys, how will they get home, Madeleine wondered. They'd have to stay overnight, too. At Vincent's house. With the girls and without parental supervision.

Madeleine knew how to run a boarding school with no internet. She knew how to manage a clique of queen bees, the Ministry of Education, and bitchy parents. She had no idea how to handle her own teenage daughter.

"Let her go, you're only young once," a voice said from the doorway.

When did her mother-in-law get back home? Madeleine had assumed she was still in the city with her friends, hitting the casino or catching up on shopping.

Savannah turned to give her grandma a hug. "Thank you, Granny Smith. Thank you for always being on my side. I love you so much."

The message was clear: let me do what I want, and I'll love you back.

Funny how Madeleine was a completely different person at work. There she was always in charge, a figure of authority, admired and esteemed. At home, she was a doormat to the kids and a first-aid kit to her husband's emotional demands. To her mother-in-law, she was nothing.

At least the twins still loved her. At five years old, they thought their mum was the centre of the universe.

How long before they flipped on her, too?

"Dinner," she said, because it was an easy way out of the situation. Only it wasn't.

William spat out his chewing gum into his fist as soon as they all sat down at the table. On automatic pilot, he handed it to Madeleine, who wrapped it in a tissue and put it in her pocket to join the other three such parcels collected over the course of the day.

At least Savannah didn't spit out her gum and expect her mum to deal with it. No, Savannah would spit out her problems, real or imaginary, and expect Madeleine to solve them.

Not five minutes later, her daughter found another of Madeleine's buttons to press. "This gravy is disgusting."

"Savannah." Even Granny Smith was taken aback. "Don't talk like that about your mother's cooking."

"Never mind," Madeleine decided to make light of the situation. "No offence taken. It's one of those instant jobbies, just add hot water. I didn't make it from scratch."

Granny pierced Madeleine with a stare that was very much like her son's. "That's not the point, and you know it. Savannah should learn to be kind, polite and tactful."

"You want to teach me to tell lies, Granny Smith?" An innocent, too innocent, smile flickered on Savannah's lips. "That's what being tactful is."

"And what of it? You're telling me you've never told a lie at school? To your friends? To a boy?"

Savannah had the good grace to avert her eyes and stare out the window. Madeleine had just returned to the gravy—which in fact tasted not too disgusting—when Savannah screeched.

Madeleine's heart stopped. "Sweetheart? Are you all right?"

Her question mingled with Granny's "Goodness gracious, child" and Ashton's "What is it, Sav?" The twins continued to throw green peas into each other's plates, totally oblivious of the commotion around them.

"A face!" Savannah's voice was an octave higher than usual, and at her maximum volume. "A man's face in the window!"

Madeleine's heart stuttered. Someone from the gang? She fought for composure. "Honey, it was probably a bird. Or a cloud. Nothing to worry about."

"Ugh, Mum, stop invalidating me. It was a face."

Ashton scraped his chair back. "I'll go outside to check. You guys carry on eating. The sausages are delicious." He kissed Madeleine's cheek as he walked past her, and a wave of warmth passed from his lips all the way to her toes. She was one lucky woman to like her husband this much.

Be careful, she thought.

A few minutes later, he was back, bringing with him the smell of wild jasmine and a burst of the cicada tick-tick-tick song. "It's just the wind picking up, Sav." His smile was wide and carefree. Too wide. Too carefree. "Your mum is right to be worried about tonight's weather."

"*Et tu, Brute, contra me?*" declaimed Savannah, her hand on her sternum, her eyes cast upwards.

Madeleine felt such a ridiculous jolt of pride for having insisted on all English classes choosing Shakespeare last year, she almost forgot Ashton's carefully carefree smile. Almost, but not entirely.

"What?" she whispered when dinner was over, and the twins were pretending to stack the dishwasher.

"I found a set of footprints," Ashton took out his phone and opened one of the photos. "Right outside the dining room window."

"Footprints?" The word didn't make sense. Then she looked at his phone. A pair of large impressions in fresh soil. Left foot. Right foot. Next to one another.

Somebody had been standing in Madeline's perfect garden, staring through the window of her perfect family home at her imperfect and precious family.

The scream started deep in her belly and stayed there, trapped like an implosion, both crushing and slicing. She wished she could force it out.

I'm going to fix it, she thought.

It would be nice if she knew how.

As though on cue, her phone thrummed. It was that police officer. *On a Saturday night, really?*

"Good evening, Constable," she said with an ever-so-slight emphasis on the word *evening*. "How can I help?"

A thought right at the back of her mind: even if she wouldn't help the police, perhaps the police would help her.

The Girl's Dad

What he was doing right now was completely insane. Not to mention criminal. A respected professional reduced to trespassing. But he had been so sure.

When he'd learnt about Arcadia High Boarding School, he knew instinctively it would be the ideal hiding place for any teenager whose mother didn't want her found—in the middle of nowhere o'clock, between the northern end of Auckland and the rugged vastness of Northland, with no internet.

Someone had almost caught him this time, and he was pretty sure he'd left footprints on that freshly watered soil under the dining room window. And for what? It's not like he'd recognise his daughter if he saw her, anyway. Certainly, in this household, the teenage girl looked unfamiliar. The two boys were roughly the same age as Courtney when he'd last seen her, and that affected him more than he'd ever care to admit.

So, the teenage girl was a stranger.

The woman though, her mother? The woman he'd recognised.

Constable Zero Zimmerman

The school swimming pool was the standard twenty-five metres length, but the utilitarian rectangle had been disguised by oval wading areas added to the sides, like symmetrical book ends pushed out of line. The water twinkled promises of holidays and swimming sports. It remained silent about the recent death inside it.

"The shape allows swimming galas without compromising the aesthetics."

Aesthetics. Zero contemplated the difference between her own tidy blouse-skirt-combo and Madeleine's business attire. Madeleine's looked like sea foam, airy and soft. Her own felt plastic and cheap in comparison, like a Styrofoam cup next to bone china. Except that bone china was transparent. Madeleine Smith was proving anything but.

Zero believed herself to be an excellent reader of body language, yet the Arcadia High principal was still eluding her. Right now, for example, Madeleine Smith looked like she was about to say something important: her eyes intense, her whole being focused.

However, all she had said so far was the bit of trivia about the aesthetic shape of the swimming pool.

"Madeleine?" Zero made her voice gentle. "Is there something you'd like to tell me?"

There! That wild-bird-in-a-cage expression. That micro-movement of her limbs, as though poised for flight. Madeleine opened her mouth, closed it again.

Zero waited. Silence was often the best interrogator. People rushed in to fill it.

Madeleine opened her mouth again. "Not sure what I can add to what you already know. The incident took place three weeks ago, just as the school year started. We haven't used the pool since … since it happened. We had a Māori elder perform a *whakanoa* to remove the restriction and clear this area spiritually, but it still doesn't feel …" she trailed off.

"The death was ruled an accident?"

"Of course. It couldn't be anything else." Madeleine Smith sounded convincing, until she added, "Could it?"

Zero had read the case file. Parvati Patel, 25, single, female, a graduate teacher specialising in geography and history at secondary school level, Arcadia High Boarding School was her second position, her first being St Alban's Boys High a few kilometres from Arcadia. St Alban's was where Miss Patel completed the first year of her two-year certification process. She had been friends with everyone and, at the same time, with no-one at the school.

"You tell me," Zero said to the school principal. "What else could it have been?"

Again, Madeleine looked panicked and relieved in equal measures. Again, she opened her mouth. And then closed it.

"Do you know what happened to Miss Patel's belongings?" Zero asked when it was clear Madeleine wasn't going to speculate on the drowning.

Madeleine nodded. Together they turned their steps to the admin building. The sun was beginning to set now, the long hot day finally nearing the end. As they walked, Zero spotted something glinting in the sun's rays at the very periphery of the garden, beyond the apple orchard. A greenhouse, that's what it was. The school probably grew its own herbs and vegetables, although the prospectus failed to mention it.

The interior of the admin block was dark after the intense sunlight sheen outside. When Zero's eyes adjusted, she glimpsed a large key in the school principal's hand.

"You keep your door locked?" Zero asked. "With the security guard at the gate and the remote location, I wouldn't have thought it necessary?"

"We have the students' personal information on file in my office."

"Surely there aren't many strangers lurking on the school premises?"

A dark-green suitcase fell out of Madeleine's outstretched arms, narrowly missing her head.

"Careful now," Zero said automatically.

"This is it." Madeleine righted the suitcase on its base, her hands still shaking. "Parvati's bag."

Inside were a few books in a language Zero didn't recognise, a small statue of the Buddha, a mobile phone, and a pack of cards—though not the type you might use for poker or blackjack. Tarot cards, for fortune telling—Zero recognised them from her childhood. Their intricately decorated jackets had always made her think of the oriental rug hanging above her bed in the gypsy wagon, and their sight now made her feel both safe and nostalgic, even though she would never, ever, want to go back.

What was a high school teacher from India doing with a pack of cards associated with a European occult philosophy?

Zero drew a card at random. The Star, the herald of renewed hope, represented by a naked woman kneeling at the edge of a pool, pouring water onto the earth to continue the cycle of fertility. Back in Romania, barely more than a toddler herself, she had told customers this card would bring them a baby. Now she thought it fitting that the card reminded her of Miss Patel's tragic fate.

"I'm sorry," Madeleine said. "We gave away her clothes and toiletries to charity. The rest we kept for the family, but we're still trying to track them down. It's not very much, I'm afraid. Teachers' rooms come fully equipped with furniture and appliances, so our educators tend not to bring a lot when they move in."

With Auckland rentals barely affordable on a teacher's salary, schools that provided accommodation for staff could probably pick the very top applicants.

Zero gloved up, reached for Miss Patel's phone, and powered it up. There was no passcode, and the battery was at twenty-one percent. Not too bad for a couple of weeks' worth of lying switched off in a suitcase. The contents, however, were disappointing.

The device hadn't been set up as a smartphone: there were no social media accounts, no browser, no Uber or Uber Eats apps. The list of contacts contained Madeleine Smith's particulars, a hairdresser, a nail bar, a local pizza restaurant, a taxi service. A boomer's phone, even though Miss Patel must have been closer to Gen Z—a testament to a lonely life and evidence that simpler wasn't necessarily better. At least there was a camera on the phone, and the album app counter was sitting at over a thousand photos.

The text messages were all mundane: one from the dentist about the annual check-up, another about a facial. The history of phone calls registered a few from registered charities, no doubt asking for donations. The most recent outgoing call was to Madeleine Smith at the beginning of February.

"Miss Patel phoned you a few days before her accident?"

"What?"

Zero looked up and waited. Madeleine lifted her chin, narrowed her eyes, bent her lips into a patient smile. "Sorry, I don't remember. Couldn't have been important. Something to do with her first day, maybe?"

So this is what a lying Madeleine looks like, Zero thought slipping the phone into an evidence bag. But the school principal was right, it probably wasn't important. Except that she had just lied about it. So?

So it was low priority.

"Madeleine, a few more questions." She motioned to the sitting area in the foyer. "Do you employ many teachers who don't yet have their full certification?"

"It's a good idea to get them while they're enthusiastic, unspoiled by the bureaucracy."

It wasn't exactly an answer. "Is it usual for teachers to change schools during the certification process?" She knew that it wasn't.

"It happens."

"Why did it happen in this case? Was Miss Patel unhappy in her former school?"

"We covered this at the time of the incident, with the first lot of police officers."

"No, you didn't." Zero had specifically looked for the information in the police file.

"We have a good relationship with St Alban's. Sometimes we

swap our staff members if we feel it'll help their personal development and growth."

That sounded a bit like bullshit. "Did Miss Patel dislike the other school?"

"No."

"They wanted to get rid of her and you did them a favour?"

"It wasn't like that."

"How was it?"

"You're probably aware of the shortage of secondary school teachers in Auckland, so you'll understand how glad we were to welcome Miss Patel, particularly as her cultural background helped us enrich our offering to the students."

Another partial answer—a lot of detail, not much substance. "Why did the boys' school wish to let go of a culturally diverse asset like Miss Patel?"

Madeleine shifted in her seat, uncrossed her ankles. "I believe they found her—distracting." She paused, then, when it became clear that Zero wouldn't fill the silence this time, she added. "Parvati was young and, well, beautiful. Hormonal teenage boys …" she trailed off.

That would do for now. "Tell me why parents choose your school for their daughters."

Madeleine's response sounded automatic, a sales pitch to a prospective customer. "Our small size. The roll ranges between two hundred and three hundred students, all teenagers, so everybody knows everybody else. It's like a true village, the one that's meant to raise your child."

"What else?"

The headmistress passed a quick hand across her eyes, as though removing a mask. "To be frank, the whole no-internet policy is a bit of a gimmick, a hook to make us noticeable in the sea of other private schools. Though of course we genuinely believe that removing electronic devices has a positive impact on learning."

Zero wasn't going to argue. She was no expert on education or pedagogy, but she'd read articles about screen time causing ADHD in children as well as in adults.

"And just think of all the time saved by not replying to emails, not posting on Snapchat, not checking your feed on Twitter."

"Sounds like bliss," Zero said, thinking back to her own cluttered inbox. The amount of admin a police constable had to churn through would frighten the most bureaucratic government official.

"Bliss is exactly what we're aiming for in this school. One of the reasons we employed Miss Patel was to help us create a school program to teach our students how to be happy. We believe that happiness, emotional intelligence, balance, confidence, and self-esteem—in other words, feeling good about ourselves and our place in the world—is the foundation on which great lives and great achievements are built."

Zero couldn't argue. Modern life brought a lot of conveniences, such as she would never have dreamt possible during her childhood in poverty-stricken Romania, but the technology-rich lifestyle had quite a few drawbacks. Stress, anxiety, depression, loneliness—all diseases of today's society.

Madeleine was still talking. "Our school has rehabilitation gardens where students can practise mindfulness and heal social connections, sometimes through meditation, and sometimes through purposeful work outdoors caring for plants and beautifying community spaces."

"Could you say it again, in English?"

Madeleine raised one of her perfectly shaped eyebrows, acknowledging the sarcasm. "Physical work, especially outdoors, is good for children. It gives them purpose, a sense of community and a healthy dose of oxygen. It also occupies them so that they don't have time to mope."

Zero couldn't agree more. Back in Romania, when she had tended the horses, foraged in forests for berries and mushrooms with her gypsy family, helped to catch crayfish in crystal-clear lakes and wild rabbits in traps, she had never once felt anything but deeply grateful to be alive.

Madeleine Smith

She had chickened out. There was a time in the conversation when she almost—almost!—told the constable about the Mekong Dragons, the threats, and especially the latest batch of photos. But would the police be able to guarantee her family's safety? It's not like they would assign a permanent bodyguard each to Savannah, the twins, Ashton. Would they put them in a witness protection programme? Would Madeleine's family even qualify for that, and if they did, would Savannah agree to leave her friends behind and start in a new school in a different city? Knowing Savannah, she wouldn't be happy away from the big shopping malls of Auckland, all the teenage activities like go-karts and *Snowplanet* and the night rides at *Rainbows End*, or the promise of nightclubs when she turned eighteen.

Nightclubs and shopping malls didn't trump personal safety, of course, but Savannah would never forgive her. Simple as that. Also, how good was the witness protection programme anyway? What if the Mekong Dragons had a cop on their payroll? And what if Madeleine told, and the police simply locked her up, no immunity and no protection for the family?

She could tell Ashton. In fact, she should. He had the right to know their family may be in danger. All she had told him so far, was that she was getting the loan sharks off his back. In retrospect though, she should have realised her intervention would change their marital dynamics. The activity that had got Ashton into debt was—or at least could be seen as—manly, a characteristic associated with hegemonic masculinity. Having your wife protect you from big bad guys with big knives and bad intentions—was not.

No. She was on her own.

Bobbi Kentwood

Vincent's party is a blast. Loud music, no adults, yes alcohol. Xander is on his third bottle of beer. I'm not an idiot—I won't let him drive me home. The more he drinks, though, the easier it'll be to escape his roaming hands. It started in the car on the way here, I swear he was like an octopus, and it's a miracle he didn't drive us off the road.

The party's fab, but poor Vincent is in a state. Nobody told him about Aiko when it happened. Like, he fully expected her to be here tonight. The fact that she's not, coupled with the reason why not, has made him morose and withdrawn.

On the one hand, I'm glad I don't have to watch his interaction with Aiko, or see his eyes following her every move, or worry whether they'd end up slow dancing together. On the other hand, I feel his pain almost as acutely as though it's my own.

I also feel a pair of hands under my top.

"Xander, no," I tell my date for the umpteenth time. "Let's go check on Vincent."

Xander raises the beer in a mock toast. "Vincent's fine. He's processing."

"He's processing too much beer in the process of processing Aiko's accident." I'm black-mouthing Vincent, but it's Xander I'm talking about.

"Let him be, Bobbi, for real." His mouth grazes my neck, and I shift away.

Suddenly, a different hand lands on my shoulder. A shriek escapes my throat, drowns in the music.

"Bobbi, a word." Savannah pinches my flesh between her thumb and fingers and propels me towards one of the bedrooms.

Shit, when did she get here? Right now, I'm not sure which of the two I'd rather not be alone with: Xander or Savannah, my almost-boyfriend, or my ex-BFF.

"So your mum let you go out tonight, after all?" I ask. A dumb question, stating the obvious, but anything to postpone the real conversation. "DK is looking for you, by the way." He isn't, but anything to distract her.

"Don't want to talk about my mum. Or DK. I want to talk about Aiko."

"Nothing to talk about. We're cool," I tell her.

"We're not."

Annoyance builds up inside me. I feel its hard spikes in my throat and have to fight to keep it down. "FYI, I spoke to that cop. Didn't tell her a thing."

"Did you mention my name?"

"What the hell, Savannah? Of course not. Now, let's get a drink, have some fun. It's a party!"

I catch Xander's eye, and he trots over, obedient as a puppy. "Beer," I exclaim, as if I've never seen alcohol before. "Magic!" I grab the sweaty bottle and take a swig, then hand it to Savannah. "Let's dance," I command, and the three of us join the small crowd in the middle of the room, passing the drink around and giggling.

Two hours later, Savannah is snoring softly on a bean bag in the TV room, her breath beery but stable. I've read about alcohol poisoning, and I'm relieved that I haven't seen any hard liquor tonight. Still, she drank at least two bottles of Speights, and she's a cheap drunk, so rather safe than sorry.

Xander is sticking to me like a shadow. This is exactly why I wanted him to be my date, but seeing as Vincent hasn't even noticed, what's the point?

"Time to head home," I tell him. "I'll call my dad. He can give you a lift too, and you'll fetch your car tomorrow."

"Why are you being such a tease?"

"Wait, what?" I'm genuinely confused.

"Dancing with me all evening. Leading me on. You clearly want to hook up."

I feel like saying *wait, what* again, then I remember what I let him do while I play with his phone at school. Suppose he has a point.

"You are so hot," he whispers, his hands gliding over my arms, finding their way under my bra. "I've wanted you since the day we met."

His dick is digging into my belly button, hard and hot. Part of me marvels at how much power I have over this boy. He's a head taller than me, and even his muscles have muscles, yet he's totally at my mercy. I can make his day with one *yes*, crush his ego with a *no*.

The rush feels more intoxicating than beer, or that puff of weed I had in Aiko's room at the beginning of the year.

Poor Aiko, I think, as Xander pulls me to the carpet of the TV room, right next to Savannah. And, just like that, the high recedes, and I'm just a girl lying on the floor under the weight of a boy who's half-stupid with hormones.

The big clock on the wall has a hand that moves around measuring seconds. I watch it and listen to Savannah's breathing. When it's counted off seventeen ticks and Xander reaches between my legs, I push him away.

"No," I say, loud and clear, just like they taught us in health lessons during *Mates and Dates* when they talked about consent. "I don't want this."

St Alban's School must have had the same lessons, because Xander stops. Almost immediately. It's like watching a logging truck full of timber from the North skid to a stop while white smoke curls under the wheels.

"Cock tease," he says without looking at me.

This hurts more than the sex would have.

When he leaves, I check on Savannah once more, then rush down the corridor and fling open a random door. The tears blur out the detail and magnify the furniture, but I instantly realise where I am. Theo's room. Vincent's older brother who took his own life last year. Six months ago. An accident that was no accident. Just like Aiko's.

It's creepy. Everything is as he had left it: his school bag, his rugby medals, a pair of white socks spilling out of the sports shoes that are lying on their sides by the window, Theo's multi-use water bottle by the bed—I have one, and so do all my friends. We are the generation that cares about the environment. About hurting ourselves—not so much.

I wonder what Vincent makes of this room. Does he come here to feel close to his brother? Or does he envy him the place Theo will forever hold in his parents' hearts?

I also wonder which of my stuff I would like my mum to keep, to be remembered by. Not a pair of dirty socks, that's for sure. My poems? No. Old ballet trophies? Meh. Shoes? Maybe those gorgeous red ones.

But seriously, when you're dead, what do you care about the shrine you leave behind, or what they say at the funeral? What do you care about anything?

Constable Zero Zimmerman

There was no change in Aiko's condition: the girl was still in Starship Children's Hospital, the Intensive Care unit, stable but unresponsive. This time, however, Zero was allowed into the hospital room.

Zero took one look at the tubes and the monitors and decided that she desperately didn't want to remember the sight. The girl was too young, the prospect of her never waking up (or waking up damaged) too grim.

A diminutive woman sat in the only chair, watching Zero's every move, the eyes dry yet desolate. "You are with the police." A statement, not a question.

Zero tried to put together everything she remembered about the Japanese people. Excruciatingly polite and humble, respectful towards others. Football fans cleaning the stadium after a game. Killing whales and dolphins. Prisoner of War camps and kamikaze pilots. None of it hung together. None of it made sense.

"Mrs Hamasaki?" Zero asked.

A nod.

"I'm Constable Zimmerman."

Another nod.

How was she supposed to question the mother, Zero wondered, while the husk of her child listened in unconscious?

"Can we talk, Mrs Hamasaki?"

"Yes."

Zero tried to order her questions by priority. "Forgive me for intruding, but I'm told that your daughter is at a boarding school because of difficulties at home?"

Silence.

"Mrs Hamasaki?"

The dark eyes glinted like obsidian. "All the girls at Arcadia are there because of difficulties at home."

"How do you mean?"

"It's like a military academy without the military. You have a uniform, you have rules, you have discipline. There is only one entrance to the property, guarded day and night. When parental correction doesn't work, you end up in Arcadia. If you're lucky."

That was unexpected. Zero had somehow believed that Arcadia was an exclusive finishing school, and that being part of its alumni network would be a badge of honour. The way Aiko's mother said it, it sounded like the boarding school was a place where the rich sent their daughters when they wanted to be rid of them yet keep them locked up.

"Aiko and your husband don't get along?"

"Teenage girls do not get along with their fathers, as a rule. When they are little, they adore their dads, but as they grow up, they cannot forgive their idols for not being perfect." Aiko's mum recited the words without emotion, as though she had repeated them so many times before, they had lost their meaning. "Then—they rebel. They are disrespectful. Contrary. Confused. All part of growing up."

Zero thought back to her own dad. Had she ever been rude to him? No. She'd always been too bloody grateful for having been adopted.

"But your husband is not Aiko's biological father, right?"

Silence.

"Where is her biological dad, Mrs Hamasaki?"

A shake of the head. "Dead." She didn't seem to be too cut up about it.

"And the stepfather?"

"We will not talk about that."

Zero decided to explore another avenue of enquiry. "Does Aiko have a boyfriend?"

"No." Fast, no hesitation.

"Closest friends?"

"Bobbi and Savannah."

"Savannah?"

"Savannah Smith. The school principal's daughter."

Interesting.

"How did Aiko act in the last few weeks? How did she sound when she called home? Same as usual? Sadder? More cheerful?" Sometimes, Zero knew, people suffering from chronic depression actually seem happier when they decide to go through with a suicide plan.

"She didn't try to kill herself. I gave her everything she wanted. Put her in the school of her choice. Respected her decisions. Even got her that lamp with a special light to induce good mood."

Getting everything you wanted didn't necessarily make for a happy child. What was Mrs Hamasaki trying to compensate for? What did she feel guilty about?

The woman closed her eyes, as though settling in for a nap. "You will find the person who did this to Aiko," she said. Not a command or a request, just quiet certainty.

Zero couldn't find the strength to talk to Mrs Hamasaki about the secret Jackson had discovered on Aiko's phone.

Bobbi Kentwood

I can't find Vincent. He's the one person I want right now. I text and DM him, all with no result. Eventually I even stoop low enough to give him a call—like a Boomer—but the connection goes straight to voicemail. I don't leave a message.

His parents are back from wherever they'd disappeared to for the night. They must know where he is, but I'm not that girl. I won't ask.

Xander is in no state to touch the steering wheel, plus he's mad at me, so Vincent's mother gives me a ride. "Did you have a good time?" she asks.

"Yes, thank you," I say automatically. "You have a beautiful home." The second part is true enough, the house must have been designed with parties in mind, all high ceilings and indoor-outdoor flow, a spa pool and love swings under a gazebo, a sound system that pours music straight into your body. And yet the most unforgettable space in the entire mansion is Theo's old room.

The first part of my reply, though? That's a lie. I didn't have a good time, of course I didn't. Vincent is in love with someone else. Savannah likes Aiko more than she likes me. I did a lot of stupid stuff with Xander while trying to make Vincent jealous. Stupid. Stupid. Stupid.

Mrs Linden compliments my dress, and then we run out of things to say. Any other mum would keep the conversation flowing by asking me about my favourite subjects at school and what I want to be when I grow up. With Mrs Linden, though, it's different. As our school counsellor, she knows all this. At least I hope she doesn't need her notes to remember that my favourite subject is history, and the answer I give whenever somebody asks me what I want to be when I grow up is *psychologist*. The true answer to what I want to be when I grow up is: *not afraid anymore.*

The weather is playing up. Mrs Linden's car passes under trees that sway in the wind. The road is already littered with loose leaves and small twigs. If it gets any stronger, it'll be branches blocking the way.

"Sorry you have to go out in this storm, Mrs Linden," I break the silence inside the car. Most teenagers call adults by their first names, but our school has this stupid rule about etiquette. One day, when Vincent and I get married, I'll call her by her first name. Emmanuelle.

Perhaps I'll shorten it to Emma. Em. Or Elle? No, Emmanuelle suits her, the proud cheekbones, the very full lips. Vincent has the same mouth. It's friendly yet exciting at the same time, and when his lips move, your eyes fasten onto them as though hypnotised.

Vincent's mum is staring into the night ahead, all her attention on the driving conditions. "No problem at all, Bobbi. It's still perfectly safe to drive for the next couple of hours. The wind's quite unusual, though, for this time of the year."

The lower part of Mrs Linden's face smiles her trademark tell-me-your-secrets smile. Her eyes, though, the eyes are always sad.

"Mrs Linden?"

"Yes?"

"Vincent was really upset tonight. Is there anything I … we … can do to help?" No, that's too easy to dismiss as hollow politeness, so I add, "I really mean it. It'll make me feel better if I can do something."

Vincent's mum opens her mouth, and I can already see the *thank you* forming on her lips, then she changes her mind. "Perhaps when the weather calms down tomorrow, you could go to the movies? To distract him and give him something else to think about?"

"Perfect," I tell her.

You know what they say—the best way to get over a girl is to get under another one. If Vincent needs to get over Aiko, I'm happy to oblige.

As if reading my mind, Mrs Linden says, "Will you come see me on Monday? I'm free before classes start, then again during the third and fourth period."

No way am I going to discuss the boy situation with her, and we've already dealt with Aiko's pill-popping, but the idea of spending time with Vincent's mum is alluring.

"Thank you, that's a good idea." I remember my manners just in time. "Before school on Monday will be splendid."

Madeleine Smith

Madeleine offered her heartfelt thanks to the parent who dropped Savannah off at home and turned her eyes to her daughter. "Fun party?"

"Mm."

Was that alcohol on her daughter's breath? "Glad you got home before the storm. I was worried when I couldn't get hold of you."

"Battery low. Switched off the phone."

"To conserve the battery in case of an emergency? That's good thinking."

"Mum. Stop it. You're being condescending. I'm tired and all I want is sleep."

Savannah's tone was exactly what you'd expect from a teenager if your idea of a teenager came from American TV shows. Madeleine's expectations couldn't be more different. She often wondered whether TV merely reflected reality or helped shape it. As in, children saw bratty teenagers shout at their parents in the TV world, and thought they had to do the same in real life.

"Savannah. Let's try it one more time." She was hoping her school tone would do the trick. Ashton was asleep already and she'd hate to wake him, mainly because of how it would show up her lack of authority.

The teen's face was an open battlefield of exhaustion and contrariness. Exhaustion won. "Sure, whatever. The party was a lot of fun. Sorry you worried when you couldn't get hold of me. It's late so I'll say goodnight now. Speak in the morning." Even the tone was perfect. The defiance was all in the eyes.

Her bones heavy and her brain begging for bed, Madeleine chose to accept form over meaning. "Good night, sweetheart. Sweet dreams."

She'd deal with her daughter tomorrow. Probably. Maybe.

She'd deal with the drug gang tomorrow, too. Definitely.

By the time she managed to fall asleep, the wind outside howled as though its most urgent desire was to strip off the top layer of the city, toss it into the sky, then smash it back down.

Constable Zero Zimmerman

Back at the police headquarters, Zero entered Aiko's case into the computer system as an active investigation. This gave her an official number to which she could book her time and forensic jobs, but she knew that come Monday her sergeant would put pressure on her to wrap it up and move on. She needed something, anything, to point towards foul play; otherwise, she would not be able to continue the investigation.

And yet, everything she touched turned to more reasons for suicide: the stepfather situation, the conversation with the school's mental health counsellor, the secret she found on Aiko's phone.

The secret on Aiko's phone. Was it all so simple?

No. It didn't feel right. For one, Zero didn't see any suicide plans in Aiko's notes. The girl's browsing history, even when undeleted in all its glory by Jackson, didn't contain any websites depressed teens tended to visit. Comparing this case to the suicide she'd worked on just a few months before, she was almost sure this was different.

Almost totally sure.

She logged into the computer, fired up the medical report. Because this wasn't a fatality, thank goodness, the doctor wasn't obliged to stipulate what time Aiko had ingested the pills, but he or she had been scrupulous enough to postulate that the medication must have been taken over a period of about an hour, with the initial dose already in the patient's system (judging by the state of unconsciousness), and with some of the chemicals still undigested in the stomach contents and discovered during stomach-pumping.

How had that played out? Had Aiko swallowed some pills, waited, grown impatient, increased the dose? Why not just take all of them at once?

The timing was also curious. Why do it in the morning, not the previous night, or the following evening after going to bed? Aiko must have known that the headmistress would come looking for her. Was this a staged cry for help that had gone too far?

Zero didn't think so.

There was one other thing. Zero had noticed how Madeleine had reacted when she joked about strangers lurking on the school premises. Combined with Madeleine's defensive—no, protective—behaviour the day before, something was definitely rotten in the state of Arcadia. What, she couldn't imagine. For a school built on sound philosophies like fresh air and no internet, though, Arcadia was experiencing an unusual number of problems.

With the case in limbo for now, she shifted her attention to the Mekong Dragons. The gang (some reports were calling it a cartel) consisted of mainly Vietnamese citizens operating in Auckland and the rest of the upper North Island. One of the members had been caught growing cannabis on the outskirts of Auckland and put in protective custody in exchange for information on the Le brothers. Quan and Hai Le had dealings with people who worked for 14K, but 14K was a powerful crime syndicate involved in importing pseudoephedrine and selling it to New Zealand gangs, such as the Head Hunters and the Hells Angels, for distribution. It didn't make sense for the Mekong Dragons to bother with cannabis.

Zero sent an email to Kath Taipari. Last year, Kath had been Zero's boss, but she had since been seconded to the National Drug Intelligence Bureau. If anybody had more information about the Mekong Dragons, it was the NDIB.

Her phone rang. Jackson. "We need to visit a house party on the North Shore. Neighbours say the teens are out of control. They already called Noise Control, but the kids refused to listen."

"How can they listen with all that noise?"

"Very funny, Zimmerman. A few of them got aggressive. It's not looking pretty. I've booked a car. See you downstairs."

This wouldn't normally be their duty, but—Saturday night. Lots of callouts. Most of them, ironically enough, to the pricier suburbs of Auckland. The poorer side of town didn't like to involve the cops in trivial matters such as a pub fight or domestic violence. And if a party were too loud, they'd simply join in or break it up themselves.

"Any flags on the NIA?" Zero asked as she got into the car.

The NIA, police's National Intelligence Application, was a database used to, in official lingo, *manage information needed to support operational policing*. In layman's terms, it was a collection of records about offences and incidents reported to the police, plus any additional intelligence observations. Records typically contained information about vehicles, people, and locations, with the functionality to link them to each other. Whenever a car was deployed to an unfolding incident, the responding officers would be updated with advice about any flags of the person or location involved, notably if there was any history of assaulting police.

Jackson shook his head. "Newbies."

His grin made the corners of her own mouth lift a fraction, despite her best efforts to restrain them.

They crossed the city in record time because there was no traffic.

All club goers would still be queueing up to go in, the theatres were in session, and the restaurants were serving main dishes. As they approached the Harbour Bridge, Zero turned back to admire the lights of the city reflected in the still calm water. The sky was overcast, but there was no sign of the approaching storm. She wondered how many people had chosen to stay home in case the forecasted weather bomb hit earlier than expected.

Campbells Bay was a suburb of water-facing manors, with opulent gardens, swimming pools and an occasional tennis court. Newer money than in the eastern parts of old Auckland on the business district side of the bridge. Here, you expected well-toned women of indeterminable age clad in camel-coloured cashmere sipping sherry on the outdoor sofas. You expected classical music in the background and soft murmurs of polite trivia.

You did not expect a brightly lit house, swaying teenagers, blazing music with four-letter words, empty bottles and goodness-knows-what in the darker corners. You didn't expect it, but perhaps you should have.

Zero, for one, didn't expect to encounter so many disrespectful young people at once.

"I'm not turning down the music," said the teenage hostess. "It's my house."

"You paid for it?" Zero demanded.

The girl, dressed in a headband for a top and a smaller headband for a skirt, shrugged to show just how unimpressed she was. A disk in her earlobe—one of her many earrings—was so shiny Zero could see her own reflection in it.

"We have our rights, you know," said a young man in an accent so posh and a breath so saturated with alcohol, Zero fought the urge to raise an eyebrow. "You can't encro- encroach, see, on my freedom to party the way I want to."

That whole freedom argument, Zero mused, was warped. It overlooked one simple fact: the rights of an individual should not go against the greater good of society. Perhaps parents who sent their daughters to Arcadia High Boarding School had a point: far away from the spoiled rich brats of Auckland's North Shore, far away from drugs, isolated from internet influencers.

Jackson strode over to the boom box and silenced it with a few clicks. A pair of handcuffs glinted in his hand. Just for show, Zero knew. "This party is over. Nobody is driving home, though. Call your parents or an Uber."

"Why, Captain my Captain," one of the teenagers said. "Look at your big handcuffs." She giggled. "Would you like to use those on me … upstairs?"

For heaven's sake, the girl was—what? Sixteen? Seventeen? Zero wasn't interested in having children, but if she ever had the misfortune to parent a teenager, she'd be signing them up for Arcadia as soon as they were born, regardless of their gender.

Another teenager approached Jackson from the back, raised a half-empty bottle of what looked like aged scotch. Without turning, Jackson reached behind him and grabbed the boy's wrist. The bottle tumbled to the ground.

"Ouch, ouch, ouch," the boy wailed. "A policeman assaulted me! You guys are all witnesses. He hurt me. It's police violence, that's what it is. Just like in America. It's—it's racist."

The scene before her eyes—a black policeman being accused of racial profiling by a white youth—was so comical, Zero couldn't suppress a smile. She tried to turn it into a scoff, but she wasn't holding her breath for the result.

Jackson's face remained blank. "Constable Zimmerman," a nod

at Zero, "will take you to a holding cell now. Please place your hands in front of you, wrists together."

"Mum!" The girl who'd flirted with Jackson just a minute ago turned towards the staircase leading to the upper levels of the mansion. Her face crumpled. "*M-u-u-u-m!*"

Her parents were at home? The mind boggled.

They let the boy off with a warning. His mum and dad came to fetch him, but neither they nor the hosts seemed to think it was a big deal.

"Teenagers need to let off steam," one of the mothers said. "You're only young once. And the poor kids are under so much pressure to perform well at school, and they have to do all these extracurricular activities to get university scholarships—"

Zero stopped listening.

When they finally left the Shore, she noticed that the wind had picked up. As the car climbed up the Harbour Bridge, Zero had to fight the steering wheel to stay in her lane. She hoped the engineers who'd designed the bridge in the 1950s had made the railings strong enough.

They certainly made them tall enough to discourage jumpers. A small comfort.

Chapter 4

Last Sunday

Madeleine Smith

Madeleine woke up before dawn. Her head felt like an eighties disco, complete with noise and blinding strobe lights and cigarette fog.

They were supposed to be going to Sunday mass, but the weather warning had turned into a stage-two cyclone. The school was safe, so far, and the access roads were all driveable, but some areas of Auckland remained without electricity. At the risk of appearing melodramatic, Madeleine thought, the storm outside was eerily symbolic.

No new messages on her phone. The Mekong Dragons still hadn't contacted her. And yet she couldn't shake the feeling that Aiko's poisoning was a warning from Luck Long, the boss whom she'd only seen once, but whose persona had taken on sinister overtones since the sex slave photos. Her dilemma was amplified by her inability to research the drug gang: no Google hits on Luck Long, very few on Mekong Dragons and yet the extent of their operations made it unlikely that they were a new player. The fact that they'd eluded publicity unfortunately implied that they were very good at their job.

She'd had no idea what she was getting into when the two professional-looking businessmen knocked on her office door two years before. Slim bodies, sharp eyes, Asian skin. One was wearing wire-rimmed glasses, the other sported a wispy goatee. They'd shown her copies of money receipts signed by Ashley. The one with the goatee pulled out a serrated knife with a wooden handle, the metal of the blade decorated by a wavy pattern.

All she could see was the knife, the whole world consisted of nothing except that knife. Glasses selected three pencils from the holder on her desk and passed them to Goatee. Goatee rested the bunched-up pencils on Madeleine's desk and sliced them into six separate cylinders with one cut. The slash left a deep groove in the polished surface.

"It goes through bone and muscle just as easily," Glasses said. "Your husband's fingers are approximately the same thickness."

"So is his dick," Goatee added. "Though possibly only as thick as one pencil, not three."

Their command of English was excellent.

Madeleine found the words at the back of her throat. They slid out with a sob. "I don't have the money."

"We can help you make some. Your school is built on excellent soil."

That's how it had started.

Now, she needed to fix the mess she'd caused when she agreed to grow cannabis for the Mekong Dragons. She had to protect her family. Actually, as Arcadia High's principal, she had to protect everyone at the school, but if she prodded deep enough, the ugly truth was that she'd throw the whole world under the bus in order to save her children and Ashton.

The police? No, they would probably stick her in the same cell as Luck Long and throw away the key. Last week, she'd seen a news article about a man who got caught growing cannabis and was sentenced to four years in prison. The article helpfully supplied the number of the plants in his greenhouse: 1067. Madeleine knew that she currently hosted almost five times the number in the school's garden. Would that mean five times the jail sentence, twenty years? Or were these things not linear?

"Why can't I have a tattoo?" Savannah asked as soon as she emerged from her bedroom, smelling of sleep and digested beer.

"Because it's a form of self-harm," Madeleine said without thinking. Then her acquired skills caught up with the inborn impulsiveness. "Whoa, back up. Sorry. Let's start again. Why do you want a tattoo?"

And just like that, instead of discussing last night's party and curfew and the beer on Savannah's breath—they were fighting over something new: Madeleine's values clashing with her daughter's need to conform to the crowd.

"You're a racist." Savannah's eyes pierced straight through Madeleine's sternum into her heart. "You don't want me to get a tattoo because that's too Māori for you."

"Honey. That doesn't even make sense. Your dad's Māori. How could I ever be racist?"

Savannah was quick on the uptake. "Exactly. You hate that I'm half-Māori and you don't want me to embrace my heritage."

"If it's about your heritage, then all right. A Māori design. Not Chinese symbols or hearts or a boy's name."

Chinese symbols. Something stirred in Madeleine's memory. The gang leader, Luck Long, had Chinese writing inked across his neck and a colourful picture of a long, snake-like dragon tattooed onto his bald skull.

"My body, my choice, Mum. Piss off."

Madeleine's headache surged. "Language!"

"*Piss* is not a swear word."

How she wished she could send Savannah off to a boarding school where they would teach her manners and respect. The irony wasn't lost on her. "Sweetheart," she tried. "Let's get some perspective. One of your best friends is in hospital—"

"Only because she was incompetent." Savannah's shrug was theatrical, but her words couldn't have felt more real. "When I kill myself, I'll do it properly."

Madeleine knew Savannah was just trying to get attention. Still, all the parenting articles she'd read about teens and suicide advocated for treating attention-seeking in the same way you would a potential danger. *Take it seriously and don't dismiss it as acting out or teenage drama.*

The articles reminded parents to show their unconditional love. Pointed out that talking about suicide didn't plant suicidal ideas in their heads. Went as far as saying that the person talking about suicide didn't necessarily want to die—they simply needed to talk about their feelings. Even the conversation starters were provided: *I had no idea things were so bad for you, help me understand what's going on.*

What the articles didn't mention, though, was how the readers should deal with their own feelings of exasperation, and the resulting feelings of guilt for not being a more compassionate parent.

Madeleine swallowed. Planned her tone of voice. Asked, "Are you feeling suicidal right now? Can we talk about it?"

Savannah didn't bother to check her tone of voice. Her eye roll was a perfect ten out of ten in execution. "Mum. You're so ... just so-o-o-o ... Ugh."

All those article writers? Madeleine would bet her last dollar that they never had to deal with real-life teenagers. *I love her more than life*, she thought. *Why do we keep fighting?*

She updated her mental to-do list. One: make enough money to move away from Granny Smith. Two: fix Ashton's depression. Three: repair her relationship with Savannah. Four: don't neglect the twins—they needed her even if they didn't cause any trouble. Five: get rid of the drugs and the Mekong Dragons.

Compared to number three, all the remaining points seemed easy enough. Even number five.

She blamed social media for all the trouble with today's teens. Truly, the world had been a far better place before the internet.

This line of thought was confirmed as soon as she logged on. Her inbox was overflowing, as usual, but her eyes zeroed in on one message.

A name from the past.

She was hoping he'd write again.

Constable Zero Zimmerman

The sound of distant banging woke up Zero.

Knock-knock. Like a lame joke. A pause, then more knocking, then a muffled, "Who's in there? You're taking too long!"

The sound of knuckles against wood continued. Not on Zero's bedroom door. Further back. The bathroom?

"What?" Another voice shouted back.

"You're wasting water!"

"Can't hear you!"

"That's because you're running too much water!"

"What?"

In Zero's experience, New Zealanders sucked at constructive conflict, and this latest occurrence was no exception. Even if they did progress their grievances all the way to a confrontation, they conducted it through a closed door and drowned out by the noise of water hitting the shower floor.

Sleep gone, Zero pulled the curtain open, then quickly closed it again. The cyclone was such an unusual weather event for Auckland that she didn't know what to do. Tie down outdoor furniture? She didn't have any. Keep pets indoors? Ditto.

She padded to the kitchen, where Amelia and Rachel glared at one another across the breakfast counter, their eyes harsh above mouths twitching in passive-aggressive smiles. Rachel's hair, weighted by the water from the shower, hugged her buttocks and stopped mid-thigh, like a sleek dark jacket.

"Electricity's just gone out," Amelia was saying. "No coffee. No eggs for breakfast. And now, no hot water thanks to someone who showered too long. No offence."

Zero opened the fridge and took out a plastic container of vanilla yogurt. Didn't people realise that as soon as you said *no offence*, people would take offence? Or was that precisely the idea?

Rachel tilted her head. "Can't help it, hon. I have a lot of hair."

"Rachel, darling, you know we love you." Amelia turned up her smile a notch and Zero detected desperate notes in the tone of the voice. "So I was just thinking, maybe you'd find a shorter hairstyle more practical?"

Rachel nodded. "Maybe."

That perhaps meant *maybe* to Amelia, but Zero knew better. This *maybe* meant *no*.

Amelia turned her eyes to Zero's cloud of red hair, opened her mouth, then closed it again. She knew well enough that Zero showered at the gym.

"I'm sure I had a packet of biscuits in the cupboard," she said instead. "Has anybody seen it?"

Jackson, Friday night, the Tim Tams. Zero knew how to spot a liar, and that made her a good liar herself. "Can't say that I have," she replied.

Rachel shrugged. "Keith, maybe? Why don't you ask him?"

The smile that spread across Amelia's face reached all the way up to the eyes and down to the suddenly relaxed shoulders. "I think he's still asleep."

"He sleeps a lot."

"He's depressed. It's his way of dealing with the divorce."

"It's his way of escaping his problems," Rachel corrected.

Zero didn't think sleep was a particularly good solution, but then, who was she to judge? Her own way of coping was to pretend her problems didn't exist.

Millie, she thought. She had to visit her sister. She owed her that much. And she had to find a way to talk to her parents about the whole Millie situation.

A movement by the window caught her eye. A small bird flitted into the house.

"Shit!" Rachel's hand shot to her throat. "A fantail!"

Zero didn't understand. Fantails were perhaps the most common native birds, and there were plenty of them in the garden. If Rachel were a small moth, she might have been in danger of being breakfast, but fantails were notoriously skittish and posed no threat to humans.

"What about it?"

"They're bad luck indoors," Rachel's voice came out weak and grainy. "In Māori mythology, the piwakawaka is the forerunner of death."

Bobbi Kentwood

I want to be happy. But what does it even mean?

In critical thinking class last year we learnt about different takes on happiness. Aristotle thought that being happy was the whole point of it all, the very meaning of life, though he didn't exactly leave an instruction scroll on how to achieve it. Plato maintained that in order to be truly happy we must be moral: restrained in our desires, courageous and some other shit. Except I get a weird feeling that he placed more value on the morality than on the resulting happiness. Socrates said that the secret of happiness was to learn to enjoy what you have, which sounds totally self-righteous. And I forget who came up with the dodgy idea that the journey to find happiness is in itself happiness, but that's such a copout.

Last night's storm continued in the morning but didn't knock out electricity in our area. Vincent saw my message, the invitation to go to the movies, yet didn't respond. I mean, who does that? I hate him. Hate him, hate him, hate him.

Where is everyone? How's this for irony: I'm in the family room, but I'm all alone. Re-watching *The Avengers* on the big TV all by myself.

Savannah asked me once, before Aiko arrived on the scene and we were best friends still, what superpower I'd want. Back then, we couldn't agree what was better: flying, reading other people's minds, or seeing the future.

And now? I already have one superpower: I'm invisible. Reading people's minds is too scary for words: I honestly don't want to know what Savannah thinks about me, or what Aiko thinks, or whether Vincent likes me in a non-friend way. Seeing the future? Why-ever-for? The future sucks. Flying may be the answer, though. If I could have one superpower, it would be to fly. Fly. Fly away. Yeah.

The superheroes are trying to prevent the end of the world. And, you know what? Why bother? Everything sucks. If humanity is erased from the surface of the earth, the earth will be all the better for it. Humans are selfish. Humans are evil. We destroy the earth with every selfish kilometre we drive, with every piece of beef steak; we choke the ocean with our plastic packaging … all this while knowing there is no Planet B.

And even though we suspect there is no future for our generation, we're still under this enormous pressure to make a success of our lives: get good grades at school, be all-rounders, appear to be fit and healthy and team players. Meanwhile, the cost of housing in New Zealand means our generation can study as hard as we can, work at prestigious companies, and still not be able to afford a mortgage on an apartment or even to rent one in Auckland.

I just want to kill myself.

Adults think that the social media are to blame. That's why parents like our school and its no-internet policy. Idiots. They don't understand that failure on Instagram doesn't translate into real life. In real life, the number of likes doesn't hurt. The reason there is a correlation at all is this: people who get upset about things on social media, will also get upset about things outside the computer.

I don't care about Savannah's online behaviour. I care that she's ditched me in real life.

My phone pings with a message. Vincent!

"Hi."

"Hi," I type back.

"Not up to a movie, sorry. Also, the weather."

I think for a long time before I come up with, "Yeah."

"Want to talk?"

Hell, yes. But I can't say that. Play it cool. "If you want." That comes across callous, so I add a "Sure." Ten out of ten for eloquence, Bobbi.

It takes a while and many back-and-forth phrases, like a ping pong game, but the gist is this: Theo's birthday is coming up. He would have been eighteen, but now he will remain seventeen forever. Vincent will catch up with him this year. In a year's time, he will get older than his older brother. He can't get his mind around it.

Strange how I never think of Vincent in terms of his older brother and of how Theo's death must have affected him. Vincent had always worshipped Theo, copied his hairstyle and his mannerisms. To suddenly lose his role model must have been devastating and yet, if you knew Vincent, you would never have guessed. Perhaps that went to show that you didn't know Vincent at all.

"What does your school's mental health counsellor say about it?" I ask.

"I don't believe in that shit. We got psychoanalysed for breakfast at home, and a fat lot of good did it do in Theo's case."

"You can't blame your mum for Theo."

"I'm not. Just saying psychotherapy doesn't work. For me anyway."

"Okay."

"You know what else doesn't work? It's like my parents don't care about me. I can misbehave all I like; I don't get into trouble anymore."

Oh, Vin. "I'm sure it's not like that." Should I tell him his mum cares about him so much, she's asked me to suggest going to the movies? No, that'll make it sound like I'm only doing it for her.

"They want me to follow in Theo's footsteps," he says. "To become just like him. Well, you know what? Fuck that."

"Fuck that," I agree. "Don't change. I like you just the way you are."

There, I've said it.

"Thanks, Bobbi. You're a good friend."

And just like that, the dream world I dared to construct while we chatted shatters around me into sharp shards of nothingness.

Constable Zero Zimmerman

Sunday usually meant a big lunch with Zero's parents, and today was no exception, although they did make her delay her journey till the wind had died down altogether.

Even though she was here, and Millie was not, Zero still felt she was the less important daughter. Millie was a happier person, softer around the edges, a person with a more interesting life—or perhaps just someone who could talk about mundane things in a fascinating way.

"Asparagus!" she exclaimed when they sat down at the dining table. Time to address the elephant in the room, or take it by the horns, or whatever the metaphor was. "Millie's favourite. Hope she gets to taste some this season."

"It's also your favourite, darling," her mum said. "Isn't it?" Her eyes looked less sharp than usual, as though painted with watercolours instead of oils.

Zero put on her most reassuring smile. "It is," she lied.

Dad didn't look up from his plate. "Dreadful weather last night. Climate change is no joke."

He was trying to change the subject, but Zero wouldn't have it. "I admire Millie so much for taking part in the protests. Remember her slogan, *Modern technology owes ecology an apology*? And, speaking of apologies—"

"Speaking of technology," her mother interrupted, "isn't it astounding how we can now read any book we want, see any movie, by just clicking a few buttons? Though I do worry that all this instant gratification ..."

The problem with taking the elephant in the room by the horns, of course, was that elephants didn't have horns. Clearly, her parents were still avoiding the topic of Millie and what happened last year. Was it because Millie's involvement in selling babies to childless couples was an unforgivable crime in their eyes, or because as a once-childless couple themselves they saw nothing wrong with her actions? Either way, the fact that Zero had figured it out and arrested her own sister had intensified the shock. Her parents hated that Millie was in prison, still awaiting her trial and sentencing, as though it was also Zero's fault Millie couldn't be remanded on bail even though it was due to the homicides the other perpetrator had committed.

"This was an excellent meal." Dad kissed Mum's hand the way he did every day ever since Zero could remember. "Are you girls all right to clean up?" His voice wobbled slightly on the word *girls*, no doubt thinking about Millie. "Time for my little nap."

The *little nap* was a new addition to the family routine. Before Millie's arrest, time after the weekend meal was for a family walk if the weather wasn't too dreadful, and board games or charades otherwise.

Dad was getting old, Zero realised, her heart clenching.

When her dad retired to his man cave, Zero joined her mother in the kitchen to help scrub the pots that were too big to fit into the dishwasher.

"Mum," she tried as soon as they were alone, but no chance.

"How's work, darling? Tell me all about it."

"The boarding school's environment struck me as artificial," she told her mum as she attacked the baking tray with bits of lasagne baked into it. "The rustic eco-friendly image was awesome, and I wanted to treat it like any other school, but I don't know. No boys.

No internet. How weird is that?"

"No internet? I say, *Alleluia*! We could have done with far less Internet when you," just the slightest pause in her mum's voice to indicate she was thinking about her other daughter as well, "when you were growing up, that's for sure. But the whole single-sex education, I don't know. School is meant to prepare you for life, not only teach you the three Rs. Dealing with the opposite gender surely has to be one of the most important skills you can learn in life? Here, squirt some Mr Muscle onto that burnt patch." No break in the flow of words this time.

"Mum, you shouldn't say *the opposite gender* nowadays."

Her mother hmphed.

"In fact," Zero was struck by a sudden revelation, "learning to deal with the new gender definitions and accepting those students into your community should be part of any school's curriculum. As you say, preparing for life in today's society."

"Teach them to say *please* and to sew on buttons first. Even when you girls were at school," here was the first explicit mention of the other daughter, "most parents concentrated on violin lessons and karate, and not so much on teaching responsibility for household chores or how to use public transport. Swimming lessons, now that's a useful skill in a country surrounded by water, but table tennis? Cheerleading? Quiz club? When do these kids have time to sit down and feel content with their lot?"

"You know what," Zero remembered, "this school has something called a Happiness Garden."

"Happiness Garden, my foot. All teens are miserable from time to time. Why is it the school's job, or the parents' job for that matter, to provide an uninterrupted stream of entertainment and feel-good situations?"

"Wait, what? Surely parents want their children to be happy, right? Mum, right?"

Her mum stopped polishing an already dry water glass. "Sure. But the idea is not to rush in and create artificial Gardens of Happiness. The idea is to teach them how to live with everyday stress and frustrations. They have to learn to handle setbacks, to accept they can't have their way all the time, and they can't necessarily get stuff as soon as they choose to desire it. By providing constant happiness in the now, parents fail to equip their children with tools to create their own happiness later." She paused. "Sorry, that was a mouthful."

"It made sense, though. You're a wise woman, Mum."

"Not that I'm an expert on raising children."

"Mum. Don't."

Long after she'd devoured dessert and taken the westbound train home, Zero thought about her mother's words. Had Arcadia High Boarding School got it all backwards? Did the best solution to teenage problems lie in unwrapping them from the protective layers of Madeleine Smith's cotton wool and throwing them into the troubled waters of boy uncertainties, social media and solving your own problems? Not by raking sand in the Happiness Garden, but by dealing with real life?

Something to think about, for sure, if she ever decided to do a Master's Degree in Psychology. Meanwhile, was it useful in Aiko Hamasaki's case? Probably not.

The most important information about Aiko's state of mind was held by those around her. Her mother, Madeleine, Bobbi, and the teachers hadn't been much help. She had to talk to Savannah.

As fitting to an overworked professional, Zero's evening routine usually involved multitasking. Brushing her teeth, she simultaneously browsed through the photos on Miss Patel's phone. Hundreds of them were of the ocean in its many moods: sunny, stormy, steely. There were creamy seagulls surfing the breeze and black tui birds warbling in pohutukawa branches. There was a sequence of photos seemingly out of place: a delivery van, people carrying black rubbish bags. She zoomed in, paying attention to the details. The dirt track and the vegetation could have been anywhere in New Zealand, at Arcadia High or Stewart Island way down south. The people looked like people—one of them had a colourful tattoo on his head, not unlike the one she'd seen during a domestic disturbance callout earlier this month. The van's number plate was on an angle and blurry—was it a V or a Y?—but Zero made a note of its possible combinations. She would run it through the motor vehicle database next week.

She scrolled on. There were close-ups of kowhai flowers, and—hello, what did we have here?—a seven-fingered green leaf with jagged edges. Zero was no expert, but this sure looked like a cannabis plant.

CHAPTER 5

The Last Day of the Summer Holidays

Bobbi Kentwood

What I want, what I really, really want, is to make Aiko disappear.

We all meet at Long Bay beach by the ice cream stand: Savannah, Aiko, Xander and Vincent. Three girls to two boys. Anybody could predict this will turn out to be a bad idea: awkward at best, disastrous at its most likely.

The love triangle is not complicated: Xander likes me, I like Vincent, Vincent likes Aiko. Aiko likes nobody. So perhaps it's not a complete triangle, after all. Especially given that Aiko and Vincent were an item for a while last year. Not official boyfriend and girlfriend, the level before that, but it still made me jealous as fuck.

And Savannah—who knows. Before Aiko, Savannah liked me—not as in "liked" liked, but we were best friends. Now sometimes I think she prefers Aiko.

The five of us often meet up and go places like movies or the beach because, on the surface, we're all "just friends," so of course it's not weird. And because we're "just friends," we girls can splash around in bikinis, and the boys can buy us ice cream, and it all means nothing. Just a group of mates, the Tight Five, having a good time. Move along, nothing to see here.

At least, that's what I'm telling myself.

By the time we girls arrive at the ice cream stand, the boys are finishing their cones.

"Yo, wanna ice cream?" Vincent addresses the question to all three of us, but it's obvious he's only interested in Aiko's reply.

"Matcha is my favourite," she says. "You know? Green tea flavour?"

"They have vanilla, dark chocolate, Hokey Pokey …"

"Nah, in that case, I'm good."

Vincent grins at her. "I know you're good. I'm asking what ice cream you'd like."

"No thanks."

The air is humid and sticky, and I would have liked nothing better than the sweet coldness of ice cream in my mouth. Now that Aiko has declined, though, I'd look like a pig if I went ahead.

Savannah threads her arm through Aiko's. "No thanks," she echoes. Her lips move close to Aiko's ear. I can hear the smudged sound of whispered words but not the meaning. It's like the two of them have forgotten I'm there.

"Let's go swim," I suggest, already heading down the steps. "It's too hot to live."

Xander walks next to me, carrying my beach bag. He tries to keep the conversation going, but I'm only listening with one ear, because Savannah and Aiko are giggling like mad behind us, and I'd like to be in on the joke. Vincent brings up the rear, keeping a bit of distance, and I wonder whether he's feeling excluded, or whether he's taking this opportunity to look at Aiko's bum. Seeing that we're all mates, and all. Yeah, right.

A shadow falls across the sand. A man. My heart jumps into my throat, its frantic beat so loud in my ears, I'm surprised the others don't hear it. I taste adrenalin on my tongue.

Run!

Then the stranger moves away, and my body slumps.

"You okay?"

"Yeah, Xander," I lie. "Totally."

The first touch of the glittering water is a shock to the senses. The water almost sizzles on my skin, stinging with its cold droplets, hugging me with a liquid shroud. I dive into a wave, tasting salt, and float face down looking at the kelp at the bottom, its strands like long wet hair of girls who had drowned their sorrows in the ocean.

There is silence here, a cool shelter from the summer's heat, an escape from the memories of how Savannah hugged Aiko hello and how Vincent's eyes stayed glued to the pair of them. I watch the bubbles of air escape my mouth and wonder what to do when they stop. Shall I come up for air or breathe in a mouthful of tangy brine? Would it hurt? Would it be over quickly? Is Vincent worth it? Is Savannah?

A movement below me. Riptide? A shark? No, just Xander swimming to position himself right underneath me. He flips onto his back, his eyes wide open, locked onto mine. And now he's kicking upwards, forcing my body to rise with his, up, up, up, all the way to the sunlight.

He surfaces, coughing and spluttering. I'm not even hungry for that first gulp of air, but when I do take it, my lungs thank me, and when I thank Xander, I really mean it.

He's grinning, but it's an embarrassed sort of grin. "Your, er," he points.

Oh, hell. My bikini top has come undone, and my boobs are protruding in all their naked glory. My arms shoot up to fold over my chest. I feel my face go warm, and hope nobody's noticed my blush in the harsh white light. "Now you've seen everything," I quip.

"I mean, not quite *everything*," he counters. His cheeks are turning red too, and it's totally visible despite the sunlight.

"Oh. Good."

Savannah places herself in front of me, like a curtain, while I adjust my swimming top, but there's no need. My nipples are doubtlessly etched into Xander's eyeballs forever, and Vincent is watching the sea droplets running like mercury down Aiko's neck so intently, I'm pretty sure he's not even aware of my wardrobe malfunction.

After the swim, we go to my house to watch *Heartbreak Island*. It's like *Survivor*, only about dating, not about making fire without matches. The boys make fun of us and pretend not to look at the TV screen. We make fun of them and pretend not to care.

The first rule of *Heartbreak Island* is that popularity means power in the game—not so different from real life. The reality show is aptly named: hearts and egos get broken here. The ranking process resembles emotional bullying. "One of you was not chosen by any of the guys," the presenter says to a gorgeous brunette. "How does it feel to be the most unpopular girl on the island?"

What a dick. How does he think it must feel? Honestly, I have no idea why anybody would go on this show, prize dollars or not.

Xander leans into my ear. "I choose you," he whispers. "I always choose you."

It means less than nothing. It should be Vincent choosing me over Aiko. It should be Savannah choosing me over Aiko. What Xander chooses … well, okay, I guess it would be worse if he also chose Aiko.

We binge-watch five or six episodes, I lose count. But I discover that the second rule of *Heartbreak Island* is that being skilled at challenges is more important than being pretty or fun. And that, I know, is bullshit in real life. In real life, popularity is everything. Just look at Aiko: her smile dimples her cheeks and that's enough for people to want to do her bidding.

The third rule of *Heartbreak Island* is a contradiction: you can choose to win the prize money, or you can choose love, but you can't win without love. I guess the show is trying to make some moralistic comment about real life. It fails. Love is totally overrated. And so is money.

People say that although money can't buy happiness, it's more fun to mope around a luxurious mansion than around a poky apartment with mould on the walls. They have a point. What they don't understand, though, is that when you're depressed in a luxury mansion surrounded by designer furniture and dressed in Italian silks, people don't tend to relate. They think you have no excuse.

They have no idea.

"Hey, Bobbi," Savannah's voice brings me back to my TV room. "I'm starving."

"Shall we make popcorn?" I ask. "Or toasted cheese sandwiches?"

There is a general chorus in favour of toasted cheese sandwiches, *lots of them*, but nobody is moving to help. Aiko and Savannah are giggling over something on one of their phones, neither of them thinking to share it with me. Vincent and Xander are also on their phones, separately but united by the nature of their activity.

As usual, I'm disconnected from the group. Excluded. Alone.

Mrs Linden would say that people who feel a sense of love and belonging are those who feel worthy of love and belonging. Or she'd say that my need to fit in has sabotaged real belonging.

Whatever.

I end up frying the frigging cheese sandwiches for them. Not sure whether this makes me the bigger person or the biggest loser.

Madeleine Smith

"Your coffee, madam."

"Mm." Madeleine opened one eye and sat up in bed, her hand reaching for the cup. The aroma of dark roasted beans was already in her nostrils. The first sip was warm foamy milk, made sweet by the steaming process. *Micro-foam*, Ashton called it. The second taste brought in the oily brew of pure caffeine. "Delicious. Your talents are wasted on the domestic front. How do you feel about a career as a barista?"

Ashton sat on the bed next to her. Winked. "A barrister? Why not? Lawyers get paid well enough, and we could use the money."

That much was true. Before the conversation got into the dangerous territory, however, Ashton took her empty cup and placed it on the side table. His tongue sampled the inside of her mouth.

That was the advantage of second marriages, this ability to skirt around uncomfortable topics, to take only the good and ignore the bad. First relationships are trial runs and training exercises, they make you and then ultimately break you, the battle scars too deep to heal, the cracks too wide to mend.

Not that her second marriage was without problems, Madeleine thought. The money, of course and—more to the point—what might happen if they don't repay it. That toothy knife made of patterned metal—Madeleine now knew it was called Damascus steel—made regular appearances in her nightmares.

They owed two hundred and fifty thousand dollars—not a huge sum to anybody who owned a house in Auckland, where an average three-bedroom house cost a cool million—except that they didn't own a house. Granny Smith didn't own her house outright, either. It belonged to a trust fund, to be used as a family home by her, Ashton, and Ashton's descendants, but never to be sold.

Then there was Ashton's depression, and the stupid-stupid-stupid reason money was evaporating from their bank account like water from a rock pool on a sunny day.

The kiss turned into something more and Madeleine stopped thinking altogether.

When she woke up again, she didn't feel better. Silence filled the house. Savannah was off with her friends for the day, and she would be staying for a sleepover at Bobbi's house, so that she could go to school the next day with Bobbi's family, not with Madeleine. Madeleine understood. It would be humiliating enough for any teenager to be seen with their mum on the first day of the new school year—but when the mum was also the school's principal, the world would simply have to end to hide Savannah's embarrassment.

Although this was the last day of the summer holidays, a few girls had arrived at the boarding school already, some even as early as a week in advance, and the duty teachers worked hard to engage them in mind-expanding trips to the observatory, the Museum of Transport and Technology, sailing courses and etiquette workshops (which sadly offered a lot more fashion tips than guidance on how to treat people with respect). Glorified babysitting, for which parents were prepared to pay a premium. From time to time, Madeleine would watch another BMW pull up to the school, spit out a teenage girl with her suitcases, and spin its wheels in the haste to get away. On those occasions, she'd wonder how it was possible for those parents to cherish their daughters so little.

On the occasions when Savannah acted up, Madeleine empathised.

Anyway. Savannah-The-Attention-Seeking-Teen was away, which gave Madeleine a rare opportunity to spend the day with her sons. William and Watterson had turned five the previous October and had completed two months of Year Zero at the local primary school, so they didn't consider tomorrow's start of the school year a big deal at all.

Still, when she delivered a plate of fresh blueberries to the playroom, she tried to steer the conversation in that direction. "So, an important day tomorrow," she said, in a tone that promised a celebration filled with ice cream, trained tigers and zip lining.

The twins didn't fall for it. Watterson put a kind hand on her forearm. "Mum. School is boring. We've climbed every tree. Looked in every cupboard. There's nothing more to discover."

"It's still the holidays," William added. "School only starts tomorrow."

Madeleine gave him a high five. "Right. So what shall we do today?"

Incomprehension in the twins' eyes. "We're building a fort in the garden," William said, his expression patient.

"You are?" As far as Madeleine could see, they were taking turns to jump from the beanbag onto a pile of dirty laundry.

"We're on a break."

"Right. Can I join you? Have some fun together?"

The twins exchanged a complicated look. When William addressed her, his tone was coaxing, the very copy of Ashton's parenting tone. "Why don't you go work on your computer, Mummy?"

Is that what her sons thought? *Mummy always works on her computer?* Fair enough, she usually brought work home at night. That was the deal: she contributed the money, Ashton looked after the household. Granny Smith, Ashton's mother, lived with them, and her main job was to meddle. Division of labour.

No, that wasn't fair, of course it wasn't. Ashton's mum didn't live with them—*they* all lived with her, in her house. Madeleine and Ashton would never be able to afford property in Auckland. Not even here, on the very edge of where Auckland stopped and Northland began. Not even on Madeleine's income. Not with Ashton's … illness … swallowing a large portion of their finances on days when he lost the plot.

Where was he, anyway? "Ashton?" she called out. It was like having one more child, an overgrown adult child who should know better. She checked the lounge, the study. In the kitchen, she picked up an empty coffee mug from the breakfast counter, rinsed it and placed it in the dishwasher. She swept a few crumbs of Hubbards Amazing Cluster Cereal (raspberry and cacao flavour) into the palm of her hand. Ran the kitchen sponge over the counter and rinsed it out in bleach. All of that to take her mind off the obvious fact that the kitchen was totally empty. No husband in sight. Her apprehension deepened. "Ashton?"

Granny Smith appeared in the corridor that led to her wing of the house. "Ashton is helping the twins build the fort in the garden. It's high time he paid attention to *his* children."

Without the emphasis on *his*, the Granny Smith's comment would have been just an ordinary sentence. As it was, the barb found its mark. Granny Smith never let Madeleine forget that Ashton had married a single mum—a woman older than him—and raised her daughter as his own.

Madeleine itched to point out that the twins were in the playroom, not outside. She resisted.

Her mother-in-law continued. "This project of theirs calls for a hammer and a lot of nails. You sure are brave to let them play with those."

Another barb. This one didn't land. Madeleine's beliefs about letting children play with real stuff couldn't be shaken. Not by someone whose mothering raised a chronically depressed porn-addict, anyway.

"Thank you," she said, pretending to interpret her mother-in-law's words as a compliment. Now that she listened for it, Madeleine could hear the irregular whack-whack-whack of the hammer. She relaxed. As long as Ashton was outside, close to nature, working with his hands, interacting with people, he was all right. The trouble usually came when daylight grew shorter and the world became a soggy sponge of rainwater, when the only entertainment came from the computer's clutches.

Perhaps she should sell up, pack up the family, and move them all up north. Bay of Islands? Kerikeri? Doubtless Bay?

Everyone except Ashton's mum, of course.

Without thinking, she went to her laptop and opened a new window. "Houses for sale Kerikeri," she typed.

Before she could look at any of the hits, her email pinged.

Constable Zero Zimmerman

They all gathered in the living room: Zero, Amelia, Rachel, and the newest addition to the household, Keith, who'd replaced Kevin a few months back. "At least it'll be easy to remember," Amelia had joked after they'd interviewed him as a potential flatmate. "Keith, Kevin, small diffs."

Now it seemed as though they should have been less enamoured with first names and done a background check on Keith's finances.

"I'm skint," he repeated. "Broke the budget. Can't come up with next week's rent money."

"Right," Zero said, when it was clear nobody else would. The police detective in her wanted to find out what he'd spent his money on, but that would be rude. "What about the rent the week after?"

"I'm not sure." Keith's tone made it clear that he was satisfied with his answer, but Zero's stare must have made him add, "The thing is, I have a daughter, and I pay maintenance to her mum. We decided to let our baby have swimming lessons this summer, so that was an expense we hadn't initially considered when doing the budget."

Amelia's face softened. "How old is your daughter?"

"Eighteen months."

Zero's phone vibrated. Her mum. She let it go to voicemail.

Keith reached into his pocket. A rustle of fabric, a snap of a phone cover. "My daughter. Her name is Koru."

Zero wondered why parents were always so insistent on showing off photos of their kids. She made herself lean closer. Took in the toddler face split by a wide smile. The photo left her cold. Not an iota of maternal instinct woke up to raise a question mark. Not surprising, that. Zero had always known she was not cut out to be a mother.

What surprised her was how young the child looked. Eighteen months sounded old until she saw the baby face and the stubby legs. Now she wondered whether eighteen months was a bit too premature to start swimming lessons. She and her sister had been older, but then, at eighteen months, Zero had been living in a Romanian forest, nowhere near swimming pools or the Pacific Ocean with its treacherous waters.

Then she paid attention to the other thought that was competing for her attention. Keith was lying. Zero could usually pick up on the body language, the change in vocal pitch, the undefinable something she'd come to accept as intuition, but could simply have been a skill at reading people.

She considered confronting him. It would achieve exactly nothing.

"So what's your plan?" she asked instead.

Keith flashed them a smile—boyish, self-conscious yet confident. "If you could just bear with me? The thing is, stressing about money is not great for my mental health. Last year I ended up on antidepressants."

To Zero, that sounded exactly like emotional manipulation. Amelia and Rachel, however, were eating it up. She wondered whether they'd flip a coin to see which one would be the first to try curing his sadness with sex. It was that obvious.

"Nothing wrong with antidepressants," she observed, knowing her efforts would be futile. "My mum's mood has lifted significantly ever since she started taking them. She's now well enough to work with her therapist on the root of the problem. Say, would you like the contact details of the clinic? They're very good."

The hurt look in Keith's eyes might have looked genuine to Amelia and Rachel. Zero saw right through it.

I'm watching you, buddy, she thought.

"If the three of us chip in," Amelia said, "surely we can cover Keith's share of the rent?"

Zero didn't want to chip in. Her constable salary was barely enough for her portion of the living expenses, transport to work, and student loan repayments. But there was no way to refuse it without damaging the flatmate relationship.

Back in Romania, she had learnt to be assertive and pushy, qualities much needed when selling her fortune-telling tricks to passers-by. Adopted into New Zealand, she'd had to acquire a new way of fitting in, based on diplomacy and democracy and never ever speaking her mind.

Flexibility and adaptability outperformed survival of the strongest every time.

"Of course," she said, making her tone sound genuine. "We can cover for Keith."

It's not that she was a heartless monster, it's just that she speculated over why he was lying. Just to get out of paying? Or was it something more sinister?

The voicemail icon on her phone blinked, distracting her from the conversation. She clicked. Her mother's voice filled her ear. Dad was still not quite himself; he could do with a bit of her company. Translated into not-New-Zealand-speak *please come, your father needs you.*

"My shift starts in an hour," she texted back. "I'm on nights this week. Can I come for breakfast after?"

She was already in her office when she got the reply. "Never mind, baby girl, have a good shift and then get some rest. Don't worry about us."

Zero didn't worry. Her parents always managed to solve her problems when she needed them to, and they never had any problems of their own. They were—Parents—with a capital P. They were all-mighty and all-knowing. Back when she was a teenager, Zero had watched her friends crap all over their parents, calling them stupid and out of touch—often to their faces. She had never felt that way. While other parents were losing their feet of clay, Zero would hoist her adoptive parents higher and higher on their pedestal.

They would cope. They'd always managed to in the past.

Having put her family out of her mind, she fired up her computer. She had criminals to catch.

Bobbi Kentwood

While I'm making the toasted cheese sandwiches, I google *friends who exclude you*, and here's what I find:

1. Break off the toxic relationships *now*. Don't waste time or space on people who don't value you. Make new friends who care.
2. Take control of your life. Have opinions, even if they don't agree with those of your crowd.
3. Nobody should make you feel bad. Don't allow your friends' words or actions to hurt you.
4. When people make fun of you, don't laugh along with them. Explain how you feel, and if they continue their behaviour, stop hanging out with them.

Yeah, right. It's not that easy. I don't want to stop being friends with Savannah. Ideally, Savannah would stop being friends with Aiko. Perhaps if I could show her that Aiko's a toxic friend? Deep inside, though, I know that's not true. Aiko is just Aiko. Fun, smart, content to be in our friendship group and equally content to be left alone with her art.

The last batch of sandwiches is ready, each of them a perfect uniform golden brown in colour, crisp in texture. Pity the toaster cuts out when they're hot—it would be justice to have the edges charcoaled.

"Bobbi!" Aiko's arms encircle my waist. "You're amazing."

And just like that, I'm back under her spell, hypnotised like a tui in the presence of a cat. With the corner of one eye, I see Vincent looking in our direction, but I know he's watching only her. To him, I'm just a pillar of see-through nothing taking up the coveted zone in Aiko's embrace.

Madeleine Smith

The emails arrived one after another. Today's teenagers, Madeleine was sure, would be using direct messaging or some such, but for her, email was a perfect compromise between proper letters and the speed that came with technology.

The latest exchange, though, resembled a dialogue instead of love notes.

"I would die for another night with you," her ex said.

"You'd die a disappointed man. Three children later, I'm a shadow of the real Madeleine. I'd fall asleep before my head hit the pillow."

"You're a better lay asleep than most women are when they're awake."

Having sex with a sleeping woman was totally unacceptable from the point of view of consent, and yet the words sent a shiver of pleasure down her vertebral column and into her blood vessels, all the way to her heart. Words were cheap, she knew that. It wasn't her fault she could never resist a smooth talker.

Just as well this was all online.

Because there was no way she wanted something like that in real life. No. Bloody. Way.

All she wanted was …

She paused. What did she really want?

What had she ever wanted in life?

Grow up to be a school principal? No: she'd wanted to become a doctor, your regular GP who showed kids how to blow their nose and prescribed pain killers to busy mothers. Her parents had persuaded her out of it: it would have meant too many years at university incurring student debt, too much hard work, too much of giving to others. Not the giving kind, her folks.

Had she ever wanted to be a mother? No: as much as she loved her children, she had never heard her biological clock tick. Her first husband had wanted a child, and so—Savannah. The twins had been an accident—a wonderful accident, as she now knew, but not something she had desired at the time.

What about Ashton? Yes: him she'd wanted at first sight. Her mouth had gone dry, her heart had performed a complicated dance in her throat, her hands had ached to touch the square lines of his jaw. Still, he had been the one who approached her, asked for her phone number, leaned in for the first kiss. She had simply let him.

All her life, she had drifted wherever the current had taken her, not once curious enough to grab the oars and paddle in another direction.

And now? Now she did *not want* to have an affair with an old boyfriend.

But she still wanted his emails.

This here, however, was an email she didn't want. Sent from an anonymous address—it was always anonymous, always different, and always disestablished after a single thread of conversation.

"Your science labs," the unwanted email said. "Glad to see they are well-equipped. Perfect for students and teachers alike."

On the face of it—innocuous. It could be a prospective parent keen on their daughter's STEM education. But Madeleine knew better. A shudder crawled down her spine, fat and twisty like a creamy *huhu* grub inside rotten wood.

The people to whom Ashton owed all that money were tightening the net. It was bad enough when they made her grow cannabis plants on the school grounds, but Madeleine could live with that. Cannabis could be used for medicinal purposes, and the government was talking again about making it legal. Plus, it's just weed, right? A bit of fun, a bit of a naughty thrill for a school principal and a mother of three. Meth on the other hand was a depressant in the short term, a killer further down the road.

There was also another aspect to consider.

If Madeleine were to agree to a meth lab, what would the Mekong Dragons demand next?

In retrospect, she should have made a different choice—sell Arcadia High, her car, Ashton's bike. But back then she had been full of optimism, she had truly believed she'd be able to clear the debt and keep the school of her dreams—all by growing a few plants.

How wrong she'd been.

CHAPTER 6

First Day of the School Year

Madeleine Smith

The next morning, Madeleine woke up worrying about Savannah. Her daughter and Bobbi used to be such awesome friends. Siamese twins, she'd call them. Inseparable like a pair of albatrosses, birds that were famous for mating for life.

But also, she remembered, for being a metaphoric dead weight.

Then Aiko had come along, Aiko with her glossy hair, and easy manner, and problems at home she needed to escape. At the time, Madeleine's heart had gone out to the poor girl. Now she wished she had stuck to the school's waiting list policy. Because Savannah had changed. Perhaps it was just the hormones, but the onset of her challenging behaviour corresponded with Aiko's arrival.

After the early morning shower, Madeleine sat in front of the mirror. She had to put herself together, bit by precise bit. Only when she looked perfect, did she feel confident and in control. The makeup came first, subtle and subdued. Then the hair mousse. A gold chain around her neck. A silk business suit, lightweight and appropriate for the summer heat, was already waiting on the bed.

Midway through dabbing perfume on her wrists, she powered

up her laptop. Couldn't help herself. The euphoria caused by talking to an old boyfriend was more addictive than chocolate. She opened her emails.

Meet me.

Wait, what? Spending the better part of yesterday exchanging memes and memories was one thing, meeting him in person was a no-go area. It would be too easy to fall into the habits of old. It would be all wrong. She had Ashton now.

"Mum! Where are my school shoes?" Watterson? No, William. Their voices usually sounded the same. Except that Watterson was super-organised, while his twin relied on the universe to look after his schedule and his belongings.

School shoes found, and Ashton left in charge of the breakfast pancakes, Madeleine returned to her bedroom to finish dressing.

Her phone buzzed. Parvati Patel. The new teacher. What could she possibly want at seven o'clock in the morning, on the first day of school? Madeleine had met the staff two days ago to finalise the plans and smooth out any kinks. So why?

"Miss Patel, good morning. How are you?" She always made a point of addressing all teachers in a formal manner.

"Mrs Smith, so sorry to bother you. This couldn't wait."

"Of course. What can I do for you?"

"Are you aware—sorry, I'm sure you aren't. It's just that … This might come as a bit of a shock."

Madeleine suppressed a sigh. "Go on," she said in what she hoped was an encouraging tone.

"I've seen some suspicious activities on the school grounds, Mrs Smith. Shady characters arriving in vans."

Ah, that. Madeleine could deal with that. "Oh dear," she said to the young woman. "Gosh, that's totally unacceptable." She paused to gather her thoughts. "In what way are they shady?"

Silence. Then, "I apologise, Mrs Smith, I wouldn't want to presume or typecast. But they looked like gang members. The patches, the tattoos. They collected large bags and drove off. I'm sorry to say, it reminded me of a drug pickup."

"Well, if that's the case, at least they collected the drugs and drove off, right?"

On the other end of the line, Madeleine heard Miss Patel took a noisy gulp of air. The young teacher clearly couldn't take a joke. "Sorry, that was in poor taste. Thank you for alerting me to this issue, Miss Patel. You did the right thing. I'll take it from here." That last bit wasn't a lie.

She disconnected the call, dialled another number.

"To what do I owe the pleasure?" the property caretaker asked.

"Hep. We have a problem."

"The secret garden?"

"Not so secret as it turns out. Parvati Patel witnessed last night's transaction."

"Fuck. Move the plants from the greenhouse?"

Madeleine didn't hesitate. "The garden itself is well concealed. But move the full bags somewhere safe. Really safe this time. And let's do the drop-offs ourselves. No more pickups at the school."

"I thought that the new teacher would be trouble, Mads, the way she walks the length and the breadth of the school grounds, her nose always in everybody's business."

"Yes. Well. I'm sure I can come up with an explanation that will satisfy our curious Miss Patel. Rubbish collection or something."

"And if you can't?"

Madeleine didn't answer.

"Right, Mads. I'd better get onto it."

Madeleine disconnected the call, stole a glance in the mirror. Yes, perfect. A simple look for a complex woman, a woman who owned a school for growing girls as well as a secret garden for growing pot, but one who would say no to a meth lab.

Hopefully.

Her phone pinged. WhatsApp this time. Honestly, there were days when half of her stress ensued from continuously switching between all the communication channels: email, SMS, WhatsApp, Facebook's Messenger, Instagram on weekends when Savannah chose that way of drip-feeding information to her.

She opened the message. A clip from a newspaper article.

The family of a five-year-old Chinese girl abducted from a well-to-do area of the New Zealand city of Auckland has made an impassioned appeal to the kidnapper to return her safely. Ma Xinxin was riding her bicycle on the footpath of Corricvale Way, Albany, about 12.30 pm on Monday when a masked man driving a silver-coloured car stopped, grabbed her, bundled into the boot of the vehicle, and sped away.

Madeleine remembered the incident. Luckily this one didn't end in tragedy—after a week of anguish the girl had been found alive. She did a quick search on *Ma Xinxin* and confirmed her suspicions: the kidnapping had been linked to a drug gang called 14K, not to the Mekong Dragons, but the message was clear.

Your child could be next.

Should she tell Hep? Of course she should.

Would she? Of course not.

Bobbi Kentwood

"Depression is nothing to be ashamed of," Mrs Linden tells me. "It's like having a migraine or a head cold. In other words, not your fault."

She's way off. Thing is, I'm not ashamed of being depressed. I just want her to help me. I try again. "I feel like I'm doing something wrong. Living my life wrong. Going through my day all wrong."

Mrs Linden nods. It's not an *I-agree-you're-doing-something-wrong* nod. It's an *I'm-listening-please-continue* nod. I like the way her eyes are on my face, her whole body turned towards me, tweaked to my words like a flute to a tuning fork.

There's a haze of greyness in my brain and hollowness where my chest should be. "It's like I'm wasting my life on living it. Nothing matters. I have no purpose. Like, on the one hand I'm looking forward to this school year, and at the same time I couldn't be bothered to get up in the morning."

"So what I hear you say is that your life is lacking meaning at the moment. Do you feel that way often? Or only every now and then?"

"Always."

"Tell me more about it."

I don't know what to say. The thing with Aiko and Savannah is too raw after yesterday, and I don't want to talk about it, not yet. If she weren't Vincent's mum, I could have told her about my body image issues. It's not like she's going to tell him, but still—I can't. Just can't.

"It's nothing. People settle for a level of despair they can tolerate and call it happiness."

The tips of her teeth show briefly between her widening lips. Her smile makes me think of Vincent. Everything makes me think of him today. "Kierkegaard said that, Bobbi. You know what else he said? That a man assumes his happiness lies outside him, but when he finally turns inward, he discovers that the source of happiness is within him."

Great. So now it's my fault. But there's something else I can fight her on. "A man may do that, sure. What about a woman? Why is everyone so bl—", I catch myself in time, "so blindingly sexist?"

She doesn't take the bait, tries the silence game, then when it's clear I'm not going to play, she changes tack. "Bobbi, are you close to your parents?"

How to answer that? I settle for a non-committal mmm-hmm. Adults joke all the time about teenagers grunting and not talking in complete sentences. May as well prove their point.

"Would you say that your mum is a good mother?"

"Definitely."

Mum. Hair that smells of herbal shampoo. Cool hand on my forehead to check that I'm not running a fever. A voice in the dark casting away my demons. She never nags the way Savannah's mum does. I know all about that. Savannah told me. Back when she was still my best friend.

"What about your dad?"

What about him? I'm thinking about Savannah, so it takes me a moment to remember Mrs Linden's previous question. "You mean, is he a good mother?"

"Bobbi, please."

"Sorry. Yeah, he's a good dad. Buys me what I want. Doesn't shout. Drives me where I want to go. Always has time for me. He's good to my mum. I've seen worse." I honestly have.

"Do your parents love you and accept you? Or do they criticise?"

I just shrug.

"Have you heard of self-hypnosis, Bobbi? Sometimes if we keep concentrating on the negative, telling ourselves that everything is pointless—"

What does she think I am, five years old? Of course I know about self-hypnosis, the power of positive thinking and that I'm supposed to do affirmations in the mirror while brushing teeth. If she starts talking about mindfulness and being in the moment, I'm going to throw up.

"Mrs Linden," I interrupt her. "When you tell me that what I'm experiencing is the result of negative self-talk or hormonal imbalance, it's like you're invalidating my emotions."

Verbalising it all makes me feel a bit better. Not enough, though.

"So what I hear is that if we attempt to discover the source of your negative emotions, it's the same as invalidating them?"

Put like that, it's silly. "No. What you're doing is blaming my mood on something external: my parents, my self-talk, teenage hormones."

"What should I be doing instead?"

"Accept that my emotions come from me, not from my hormones or my thoughts."

"And who are you, Bobbi? Who is the *me* giving you all these emotions?"

That's a bloody good question. Who am I? I discovered the answer in my science class. I'm like a white object. If you shine red light on me, I appear red, and if you shine blue light onto me, I'll be blue. I change depending on the people around me.

But Savannah is a red object, and if you shine blue light onto her, she'll appear black. It's physics. Simple. Beautiful.

And Aiko? Aiko is a black object—she absorbs all light and reflects nothing back.

Constable Zero Zimmerman

After her shift, Zero fired up her phone and noticed two missed calls from her parents, plus one voicemail. Strange, she had seen them for lunch only the previous day, played chess with Dad, then watched a Netflix show with Mum while Dad took a nap. What could be so important?

As it turned out, nothing. She listened to the recorded message, her mother's voice unusually high and upbeat, asking about Zero's day. Then, right at the end, "We haven't heard from your sister in a while. Next time you speak to her, could you remind her to call home?"

So that was it. Mum didn't really want to speak to her younger daughter, after all. She wanted Millie. Millie the favourite child. Millie the champion swimmer. Millie the clever one. Not Zero who'd started a promising career in law, then switched to being a cop. Even after what Millie had done, after all the bad choices she'd made, everything was always about Millie.

To distract herself from the unwanted thoughts, Zero browsed her phone. The news feed showed her a headline: "Police Minister Stuart Nash has admitted that New Zealand has a gang problem." Zero Zimmerman looked out of the train window. Yeah, enough time to skim the article before her stop: "Gangs have become a lot more sophisticated and organised, predominantly because of their control over the methamphetamine trade," and "Inter-gang warfare is increasing in New Zealand—and fast—as Australian groups infiltrate our shores," and "The Government has done a lot to tackle the gang problem, including putting 900 more police on the street."

The trouble, though, was that without handling the country's poverty problem, the crackdown on gangs was pointless.

New Zealand must be the only developed country in the world where educated people worked white-collar jobs and still couldn't afford meat for dinner, Zero thought as she left the train station and headed for the supermarket,

It was her turn to do the grocery shopping, and she was staring at the refrigerated shelf of lamb shanks, lamb legs and lamb steaks at the local supermarket. Unaffordable. Even though New Zealand had more sheep than people, her and her flatmates' budget did not stretch to lamb dinners. And now Keith wasn't even paying his share. Zero glanced longingly at the more-reasonably priced pig snouts on the next shelf. In her childhood home, this would have been a delicacy, but she knew better than to try. Keith would assume it was a dig at him and his freeloading, while Amelia and Rachel would have been disgusted by the idea of eating something that looked like an animal part.

After much deliberation, Zero bought a packet of soup bones (lentil soup today, pumpkin soup in a couple of days), a pack of pepperoni for tomorrow's pizza, and all the trimmings for a Mexican dish vegetarian style.

Perhaps she should cash in on that dinner rain check with Jackson, after all.

Zero was a qualified lawyer now training to be a police detective. Salary: above the national average, but not by much. Amelia did marketing for an insurance company. Rachel worked as an auditor, studying towards some qualification: chartered accountant, or perhaps one up from that? Zero couldn't recall. Keith worked for the government—he always said it with an exaggerated wink, his tone ominous when he reached the word *government*. Was that his pickup strategy, she wondered, *my name is Bond, James Bond*?

All of them fully employed. They shared one house and cooked together to save money. They wore jackets and gloves indoors rather than switch on the heater. And every week, their money barely stretched to a bottle of the cheapest wine.

Ludicrous.

All this made it totally feasible that Keith was out of money because of a toddler's swimming lessons.

Zero still didn't believe him.

Before she went to sleep, she made a note in her calendar to visit Millie.

Bobbi Kentwood

"When shall we three meet again," I intone, "in thunder, lightning, or in rain?" We did *Macbeth* at school last year, and that's probably when our obsession with spells and magic began.

"Well, I can do next Tuesday."

Aiko's words are jarring, disharmonious with the mood, like a knife on a china plate in the school's posh dining room.

"Aiko." This single word from Savannah and all is good again. Savannah has that effect on people.

Aiko mutters a *sorry*, and something about quoting Terry Pratchett. She's an uber-nerd, still, people love her—most people most of the time, anyway. Plus, she's got the candles: four red ones and two white ones, made of real wax, so we forgive her.

We've had the whole summer to search online for the best love spells and to put them to action. Like, we met on the shortest night of the year to pick nine different flowers, which we then placed under our pillows to dream of our future lovers. And for Christmas, Aiko got her parents to give her tarot cards and a book on how to interpret them.

Tonight we're using white magic to attract a deep and lasting soulmate love. We sit in a circle in Aiko's dorm room and light the candles. I sure hope this works better than the nine flowers—that night, I didn't have visions of Vincent, or even Xander. Instead, my dreams were filled with exam papers I couldn't read, and a headless monster who chased me down a hill towards a tsunami wave and having to read the news on national TV. A psychologist would have a field day.

"Soulmate," I start, "I invite you into my life, to share our secrets and our time and our future." Vincent, I think. Vincent.

"Soulmate," echoes Savannah, "If you're hot and have a sense of humour, I am ready to meet you and to love you."

Aiko waits so long, I worry she's not going to go through with it, but eventually she whispers, "Set this thought in his mind, set this thought in his heart, set this thought in his life that we shall never part."

Does she have somebody specific in mind, I wonder. Before I can ask, Aiko opens her arms as though her soulmate has just materialised in our circle, and she's rushing to embrace him. One of the candles falls over, its flaming wick lapping at the carpet.

Like every school, we've had fire drills. They started with an alarm. Now there's no alarm. Just a spot of golden heat, growing and leaping with every second.

CHAPTER 7

Second Day of the School Year

Bobbi Kentwood

After last night, I'm ready to talk about the friendship issue. "It hurts that I don't have a best friend." *Anymore*, I want to add. I don't have a best friend ever since Aiko glammed Savannah away from me.

Mrs Linden looks at me as though I were a fish with legs. "Why?"

What does she mean, why? Isn't it bloody obvious? The stupid school system is all about giving obvious answers, and I'm beginning to get the impression that mental health therapy is going to be much the same. Aloud I say, "Not having a best friend makes me feel stupid. Incompetent. Everyone has a best friend."

"So do you want a best friend for yourself, or for others? For the sake of appearances?"

"I guess a bit of both."

"Because you have to be perfect?"

That's easy. "Yes."

"Why do you feel the need to be perfect, Bobbi?"

I like the way Mrs Linden says my name. Not exactly in a foreign accent, because the o-sound is as short and round as when all native-speakers say it, the end rhyming exactly with *movie*, and yet in her mouth, my name soaks up some of her charm and glamour.

"Bobbi?"

Why do I want to be perfect? It's something so obvious it can't be explained. But she's waiting for me to say something, so I settle for, "I? Don't? Know?"

"Imagine yourself on an island. No other people. Just yourself. What would your life feel like?"

Automatically, I want to say, *lonely*, because that's the answer she's expecting, but that's not right. "Fantastic," I hear my voice. "It would be fantastic. I'd be able to breathe."

Mrs Linden doesn't break the silence that lasts for what seems like hours while I try to figure out what the hell. So, an island all to myself. Nobody there to look at me, to want stuff from me, to make me feel guilty, to judge me. Yes, that's it. Nobody there to judge me. I could eat ice cream all day long and put on weight. I could have a best friend, or not. My family situation could be as effed up as it pleased, and it wouldn't matter one bit.

Best of all, I would be safe.

"I think I want to live on that island," I say. But I don't *think* I want to live there. I *know*.

"Good news," she says. "You already do."

Of course she would say exactly something like this. Challenging. Nonsensical. That's counselling for you. Always playing with words, twisting them, throwing them back in your face. Smoke and mirrors.

It's my turn to stretch the silence until she adds, "It's your choice which people you invite to visit you on the island. Whose opinions you choose to value above your own. Whom you allow to pollute your pristine paradise."

I know she's talking metaphorically. It's not that I shouldn't have any friends and be a hermit. It's that I should not let people hurt my feelings. Still, one thing is certain. I would not invite Aiko onto my island.

"Bobbi?"

"Yes, Mrs Linden."

"How do you feel about what happened last night? The fire in Aiko's room? The fact that she has to live in a different wing now?"

Good, I think. *I feel really good about it.*

Madeleine Smith

Last night, after the fire damaged Aiko's room, Madeleine moved the girl to one of the empty dorms. Right away, Aiko complained the room was too small and the window faced the less glamorous part of the garden—the orchard and the vegetable patch.

Her mum was on the phone to Madeleine in the morning, first thing.

"It's because of the light," Mrs Hamasaki said. "The room faces south. In Japan, that's a good thing. But here in New Zealand, down under, the sun's position is reversed, you know."

Yes, Madeleine did know.

"South is cold and dark. Aiko gets unhappy in gloomy rooms. Sometimes even," a small pause, "depressed."

"I'm very sorry to hear that, Mrs Hamasaki. Unfortunately, all the north-facing rooms are occupied."

"Perhaps someone would be willing to swap? I'm happy to pay."

Madeleine allowed herself a smile, knowing that Akio's mother couldn't see her. The students all came from well-to-do families— money would hold no appeal to them.

Mrs Hamasaki must have come to the same conclusion, because she continued, "Perhaps one of the teachers?"

"I'm sorry," said Madeleine again. "The teachers have their own bedroom wing. No students are allowed in there. Besides, I'm sure Aiko would prefer to stay closer to her friends."

"Friends," Mrs Hamasaki began.

Madeleine knew where this was going. Savannah was one of Aiko's friends, but she was also Madeleine's daughter. Well, tough. Madeleine was not going to make Savannah give up her school bedroom because a client wanted it.

"Mrs Hamasaki, I'm terribly sorry," Madeleine apologised for the third time, "but I have to go. There's another matter that requires my immediate intervention. Not in Aiko's class," she added so as not to cause alarm. "We shall speak again very soon, I'm sure."

That afternoon, a courier dropped off a large parcel addressed to Aiko. Inside was a sunlight therapy lamp, its box promising to combat seasonal mood changes associated with winter months in sun-deprived countries.

That's overprotective parents for you, Madeleine thought. *At least this time Aiko's mum solved her own effing problem.*

Constable Zero Zimmerman

Another text from her mum. Dad, doctor, diagnosis, depression.

Zero didn't know what to do. A problem solver by nature, she knew she wasn't qualified to prescribe treatment. Should she phone her mum? Of course she should. And say what? She wasn't good at small talk, or empathy, or listening for the sake of making the other person feel better.

She ended up texting: "Thanks for letting me know. Visit soon?"

Then she spent the rest of the day thinking about her dad: the gentle soul who always loved everyone else better than he loved himself, and whose mental resilience couldn't withstand it when

Zero's sister had made a few bad life choices—New Zealand-speak for *fucked up her future.*

Zero had always wanted to make her parents proud. That's why she worked all those insane hours and didn't have a lot of time left over for them—first studying hard to get into law at university, now doing overtime to make their city a better place.

This is how she showed her love and gratitude. Pity they didn't understand. They loved Millie more, Millie whose language was words and hugs not hard work and fighting for justice.

Was justice being served by holding Millie in custody for her crime of enabling childless people to enjoy the joys of parenthood? Was justice being served by having their dad lose his will to live? Was it justice that no matter what Zero did, she was always a massive failure?

Oh, screw it all to hell and back. Pity party over.

Her phone chimed. A callout to a domestic argument—the neighbours thought the woman might be in danger, because they heard shouting and swearing in the house next door. Normally the General Duties Branch, the colleagues in uniform, would handle it. They must have noticed something suspicious to have alerted the Criminal Investigation Branch.

Zero checked her mobile phone. The NIA database raised three flags for previous domestic incidents at the same address.

"Do we need backup?" she asked Jackson.

"You *are* my backup, Zimmerman."

That didn't worry her, as there were no flags on assault of police officers. Most of the time domestic violence callouts didn't yield any results: either the woman (the alleged victim was usually a woman) would shrug it off and insist it had been nothing, or the man would calm down upon seeing the uniforms and the wife would refuse to lay charges. Zero understood the psychology of abuse well enough not to blame them.

This one was different. As soon as Zero and Jackson walked through the front door, she saw an Asian man—probably Vietnamese judging by his surname and appearance—with wrists cuffed behind him, a sure sign that the uniformed constable had deemed him a threat. A tattoo of Chinese characters necklaced his throat, which didn't make sense given his supposed nationality. Neither did the brown-and-gold dragon tattooed across his head, with the paws stretching to the eyebrows and the tail curling down the spine.

"My wife," the man said. "My right to hit if she disobeys."

A tight ball of anger bloomed right inside Zero's chest. "That's not how the law works." She wanted to add, *in New Zealand*, but that would be patronising.

"Detective," the uniformed cop said, granting her the rank she hadn't yet achieved, "a word outside?"

Jackson motioned towards the handcuffed man with an *I've got this* gesture.

"The thing is," the other constable said when they were out of earshot, "this is a residence of interest. Guys from the Organised Crime Unit are staking it out and they have a court order to install listening devices."

"Okay," Zero said.

"This is a good opportunity to do the installation. We can hold the guy overnight if she presses charges, take him to the station for a talk if she doesn't."

"Okay," Zero repeated. "I'll talk to the wife. Get her to go somewhere else for the night."

Or for a lot longer, she added silently.

Unfortunately, getting the woman to leave proved harder than she imagined.

"No, no, no," the woman kept repeating.

"Ma'am, you and your husband shouldn't be together tonight." *Make that, ever.* "Please. You don't want to be here when he gets back."

"I have no other family. No friends."

"There's a shelter nearby, especially for women," Zero said. "They will help you come out with a safe plan, a restraining order should you want one."

The woman shook her head, lips clamped tight.

Zero could see it from her point of view. The shelter would only be able to accommodate the woman for a few days. And then what? Where would she live? What job could she get? Would she be safe? The restraining order couldn't keep the husband away if he wasn't scared of legal consequences.

In theory, there were processes and benefits and safety nets. In practice, they didn't always work.

What would an ideal system look like? A world without men? A world without violence and anger? A world where restraining orders were enforced via microchips embedded inside our bodies?

Zero shuddered. No microchip implants.

What then? Perhaps you could start with making kindness compulsory, until it became a habit, like brushing teeth and not leaving the house naked?

"At least let me drive you to a motel. Just for tonight. Somewhere with room service."

Something flickered in the woman's face. "Room service? And a large TV?"

"Definitely."

They drove the woman to a four-star motel in Mission Bay, close to the beach. A spa pool, room service, Netflix. Zero paid with her own credit card. She knew she wouldn't be able to claim it back, but it didn't matter. In the overall balance of generosity given and received, she owed the universe—as well as her adoptive parents—a big one.

"Zimmerman? You ready to roll?"

Conscious of her new resolution towards kindness, she offered him a smile. It was easy to be kind to Jackson, even if he did get annoyingly chauvinistic and one-track minded at times. The real trick was to be kind closer to home: answer Millie's phone calls, visit her parents more often, be more patient with her flatmates.

Easier said than done.

Bobbi Kentwood

Tarot cards are like little paintings, each one a piece of art. When I look at the card called the Page of Swords—that's *page* as in a *messenger boy*, not a *sheet of paper*—I always think of Xander, with his longish blond hair and his distant gaze. Mind you, that gaze was anything but distant three days ago when my bikini top slipped off in the water.

The Emperor card reminds me of Vincent, the way he's always in control, always the centre of attention—why couldn't it have been Vincent who got to see my boobs?

The Lovers card, my favourite, features a magic cauldron with two kissing silhouettes intertwined in the steam.

I wish there were a Friendship card in the pack, something to tell me what's going on. Savannah and I are best friends; supposed to be anyway. Yet for the last few months, it seems that Savannah lights up whenever Aiko walks into the room. Aiko is fun, I get it. It's just that, before she came to our school, it was Savannah and me, me and Savannah, always.

That's the way it should be.

"Read my future," Savannah demands, and Aiko shuffles the tarot deck a few times before instructing Savannah to do the same.

"Which one would you like? Past, Present, and Future? Success? Love?"

Savannah's voice deepens. "Love," she says. "Always love."

"Draw three cards and put them face down in a row."

I watch my two friends as they sit side by side at Aiko's temporary desk, their shoulders touching, Savannah does as she's told, and Aiko turns over the first card.

"Ace of Wands in the Current Situation Position," she says, even though we can all see. "This suit stands for ambition, desire and risk-taking. The Ace means a fateful step, one that will unleash a chain of events leading towards your goal. You are experiencing a new beginning, you are totally focused, keeping your eyes on the prize."

Savannah is listening, enchanted.

"Wands, hey?" I tease. "Rather phallic, like." This particular brand of humour is not me at all—I'm just trying to get my best friend's attention.

I fail.

"Bobbi, please," Savannah doesn't even shift her gaze from the card. "It's not funny."

"It is a little funny." Aiko is always the one to make peace, or try to make peace, at any rate. "Now let's see what we have in the Obstacles location." She flips over the second card. "The Queen of Cups, an empathic, omniscient woman who offers unconditional love. Her caring nature caters to your emotions and needs, but it also stands in the way of your goal."

"My mum, that's for sure," mutters Savannah. "Mum is standing in the way of my love life. Aiko, you're a genius."

Her admiration for somebody else hurts. Hurts so much I have trouble understanding the third card, the one that is supposed to guide Savannah. Some Moon or other, advising her to listen to her instinct and to trust her intuition. If I were doing the reading, I'd advise her to trust and listen to old friends, not new ones.

"Your turn, Bobbi." Aiko pats the seat next to her, miraculously vacated by Savannah. "Come sit with me and choose your cards. Shall we all do the love reading?"

I want to say no. No to love. No to a reading of any sort. No to the second fiddle seat she's offering me in our friendship. But her smile is infectious, and I don't know how it's happened that I'm sitting in the chair still warm from Savannah's jeans, Aiko's hair smelling faintly of Savannah's perfume. It's a sweet and spicy fragrance, painfully familiar and reminiscent of old times when it was just the two of us. It brings sour remnants of dinner right up to my throat.

"Three cards, Bobbi."

Fortune telling is all nonsense, of course. There's no way tarot pictures can know anything about your future, or your past for that matter. But just to be safe, I pluck the top three cards from the deck. There. You can't say I was directed to them by some spiritual inspiration.

"So, the Current Situation." Aiko turns over the first card. It's the Lovers.

Savannah hoots with laughter. "Bobbi has a boyfriend!"

Kind of true, but not really. Not the boyfriend I want, anyway.

Aiko, meanwhile, taps the card with her index finger, her forehead creased. "This card only stands for sex and lovers in pop culture," she says. "Its actual meaning is a decision to be made, a crossroads. It could be a choice of romantic partners, but also one between a path of pleasure and a path of spiritual growth."

Honestly, where is she channelling this from? Quickly, before Savannah can make a comment about pleasure in the context of lovers, I reveal the next picture, even though custom dictates that whoever is doing the reading should handle the cards at this stage of the process. "Judgement," I call out. "Upside down. Can't remember what it means."

Aiko can, of course. "You are hindered from achieving your goal by the lies and deception that surround you."

Lies? Deception? My throat is tight, there's a whooshing noise in my ears.

Meanwhile, Aiko is zooming ahead with the reading. "King of Cups is your Guidance card tonight. A powerful ally, a father figure, he will bring you advice. You won't untangle the lies or make the right choice on the crossroads without him."

A father figure?

Unsure how to react, I'm glad when Savannah comes to my rescue. "How does that relate to choosing boyfriends and finding out the truth? Who is this guy, the one that Bobbi is supposed to consult—her dad?"

I make sure I laugh the loudest. Then I pass the deck to Aiko. "Your turn." I want to be the one reading her fortune, and I'm already sitting next to her.

The first one is the Sun, reversed. "You're depressed," I tell her.

Aiko shrugs. "Nothing to be depressed about when I have you two, right?"

"Not even the fact that the holidays are over and we're back to the grindstone?" I ask without thinking, then do a mental head slap.

Aiko's situation at home is far from idyllic. She's probably delirious with happiness to be back here.

My fingers find the next card. "Let's see what the challenge is. The Pope. Also reversed. OMG, what's with the reversed cards?"

Savannah is looking it up in the book. Any normal school, it would be her phone. Blast the stupid rules about the internet. "It means breakdown of family values, or abuse of power."

Honestly, she shouldn't have read it out. If that interpretation doesn't spell out a violent stepfather, I don't know what does. Aiko's second shrug seems a bit too elaborate, a little too desperate. Now it is Aiko who's reaching for the Guidance card, unauthorised.

It's the Death card. In this edition, the picture is not of a hanging man—it's a female figure, bent over backwards, with butterflies flying out of her abdomen. Eerie. Terrifying. Savannah and I exchange panicky glances.

Aiko shrugs for the third time. "It's also reversed." Her voice is steady. "It means a change of perspective, that what you thought was a fact, may not be true after all."

I'm not taking it in. My mind can only focus on one thing.

The Death card.

CHAPTER 8

Third Day of the School Year

Bobbi Kentwood

Although it's against the school rules, we ended up having a sleepover with Aiko last night. Aiko's temporary room, the one she landed in after the fire, is loathsome. Dim and dispiriting. I asked why she didn't brighten it up with her posters and things, and she said it would be wrong to tarnish her things. And so dim and dispiriting it is. At least her sun lamp helps a little. The true saving grace, though, is the view of the garden.

Last night, while Aiko and Savannah were having a laugh about something in the corner, I saw the caretaker, Mr King, unlock a narrow door concealed in a brick wall behind some shrubbery. Just like in that book, *The Secret Garden.* More bored than curious, I climbed out of the window and followed him. The door—he didn't lock it behind him—led to a patio-like hall with a glass roof, a glasshouse nursery of sorts, full of plants growing in pots. I'd seen the TV series *Weeds* so I knew what the plants were. Plus, I could see a thin tendril of smoke wafting from a tool shed in the corner of the hall. I've smelled the smell before—sweet, but not pleasant. Mr King must have been sampling the harvest.

Pot plants, hahaha. Get it? *Pot*?

I pulled off a handful of leaves to use at the next party and tiptoed out. I'm sure he hadn't seen me, but if he had, hopefully he'd put it down to cannabis-induced hallucinations. When I got back to Aiko's room, I hid the leaves under the mattress. Maybe it'll get Aiko in trouble.

The other girls hadn't even noticed my absence. Deadwood, a hanger-on; that's what I've become.

So that was last night. This morning, when I wake up, Savannah is already gone, and Aiko is on her way to the shower. I'm brushing my teeth in the window when whom do I see if not Mr King again. This time, he's not alone. The woman with him has her back to me, her arms around his waist, her face in his chest.

Even though I can't see much of her, she looks familiar. At first, I assume it's the headmistress, because of the hair, and the long neck and the shape of her legs, but I'm wrong. When she lets go of him and turns, I see the darker colouring and the face I know like my own.

It's not Mrs Smith.

It's her daughter.

Savannah.

My forever-best-friend Savannah. Correction: my former best friend.

Oh. My. Holy. Shit.

I have to do something to protect her. My thoughts are in a jumble. Confront Savannah? What if she gets mad at me? The embrace looked heartfelt, nothing coerced about it. So, tell her mum? Tell the school's pastoral care dean? Tell Mrs Linden? What if Savannah denies it?

"What the hell?" Aiko has crept up on me so silently, I start at the sound of her voice.

"Exactly."

"We should tell someone."

"And that will help how?"

We argue back and forth for a while. Suddenly Aiko snaps her fingers. "I have an idea," she says.

She won't say what it is, and I pretend not to care. It's all about power games and control. On the way back to my room, I see the school cat skulking with something in her mouth. I distract her by snaking a dead leaf of a cabbage tree along the path, and when she drops her prey, I see it's a puriri moth, leafy-green, as big as my hand. It flutters away, slow but unhurt. Legend has it that these moths are spiritual messengers from our ancestors. In this case, the message is clearly: *You don't matter, Bobbi.* Received loud and clear.

"Roxie," I call. "Come, kitty cat."

It's against the rules, but I take her into the dining hall and give her my slice of breakfast bacon.

Madeleine Smith

When Madeleine had decided to run Arcadia, she'd never realised what she was signing up for. A boarding school principal was more than a manager of teachers: the role stretched to embrace preparing a budget, knowing the rules around suspending students for bad behaviour, understanding property issues such as boilers, leaky roofs, and asbestos. It meant having to deal with fire in one of the dorms and a mother who objected to a less prestigious room.

Today, it also meant having to handle a complaint of a disturbing nature.

"Are you sure that's what happened?" she asked again.

"Yes."

"You didn't misunderstand? Misinterpret the situation? Sometimes something may appear one way—"

"I did not misunderstand anything," Aiko interrupted. "Mr King acted inappropriately. I was walking to class, and he brushed against me as he walked past, then he pretended to stumble, and he put his arms around me so that my breasts touched his chest."

"Sounds like an accident to me. You said yourself that he stumbled—"

"Pretended to stumble."

Madeleine hated what she had to do next. She took out a form. "Would you like to make an official complaint?"

Aiko nodded.

As the girl dictated, Madeleine considered what she was writing down on the form. It didn't make sense. For example, Aiko said the incident had occurred on her way to class, which would make it around eight fifty, because the bell went off at eight fifty-five. And yet, Hep had been in this very office from half past eight till well after the nine o'clock bell.

Also, Aiko was short for a teenager—calling it five feet would be generous. Hep, on the other hand, was a big man, six foot four. If Hep were to stumble and embrace Aiko, the girl's breasts would end up nowhere near his chest.

Most importantly, though, Madeleine knew that what Aiko was implying was simply impossible. Hep was not into schoolgirls.

"Right," she asked. "And where did it take place?"

"By that brick wall facing the window of my temporary room."

The answer made her heart grow cold. When she trusted her voice again, she said, "Come show me the exact spot."

Once they got there, her fears became reality. The secret gate was visible through the vegetation. Not in an obvious way, but certainly there if someone looked.

Madeleine dismissed Aiko and combed the grounds in search of

Hep. She found him by the beehives.

"Hey," she said, "we have a problem. Two problems."

She told him. Then she put her hand on his shoulder. "I'll take care of it," she promised.

And then she wondered how.

Bobbi Kentwood

I'm the one who loves the tarot card paintings, but it's Aiko who can make them speak. They divulge their secrets, obedient like the sheep that graze on our soccer field.

Mystical.

Magical.

At lunchtime, several girls queue up for *a reading*, the word said in a lowered voice, with emphasis and reverence, but just a touch of a giggle to suggest that no, of course, they're not taking it seriously at all.

Savannah wants to listen in, but I tell her the girls will be more forthcoming with Aiko alone, and we'll get all the dirt afterwards. The truth is, though, that I want Savannah to myself.

My arm around her waist, hers draped over my shoulders like a shawl, we stroll towards the Garden of Happiness, because it's usually quiet there. The popular girls think it's a stupid place, so their cliques and wannabes stay away. The brainy girls are in the library, the sporty girls on the basketball courts or wherever it is they disappear to between lessons.

"So who is he, Savannah?" I ask when I'm sure we can't be overheard.

She stiffens but doesn't take her arm away. "Who?"

"The guy. Come on, you wanted a *love* reading last night."

"No one. That's why I wanted the reading. To see whether

someone would arrive on the scene. It sucks to be in a girls-only school."

"What about that guy you met when you went camping? Shane?"

Savannah sighs, her chest swelling up as she breathes in, then not quite deflating when she breathes out, as though she decides to keep a bit of the sigh in her heart. "I miss him. But, you know."

I do know. He's in a co-ed school in a different part of Auckland. Savannah can't Snapchat or Instagram him during the week. Theoretically, she could phone or text him in the evening, but boys are not into words. "Are you going to see him this weekend? It may not be such a bad thing, a weekend boyfriend. Sports and studies Monday till Friday with no distractions, then a date Friday night."

"Maybe."

Can't tell whether she's considering it, or just humouring me. "I'm seeing Xander on Saturday," I tell her.

"Why? Thought you weren't that into him?"

"I'm not. But he has friends." Vincent, I think. Vincent. As far as I give a damn, Xander has only one friend who counts. A year ago, when Savannah and I were still best friends, I would have said it out loud. All I add now, though, is, "And they're planning a party soon. I'll ask him to invite you as well."

"Not sure Aiko is into parties."

I don't tell Savannah that actually I had no intention to include Aiko. But before I can respond, I hear quick footsteps and Aiko appears behind us. "Miss Patel confiscated my cards," she calls out. "Hell and damn, damn and hell."

Swearing on the school premises is grounds for expulsion, and even though we sometimes pretend that we'd welcome expulsion as it would mean a different school and boys and the internet, the reality is, none of us would risk it. So instead of proper swear words, we use these old-lady cusses. Totally useless in getting the bad energy out.

Savannah once asked Aiko why she didn't use Japanese to swear, and Aiko said she didn't want to be reminded she was any different from us. She's not even taking Japanese as a subject, even though it would give her easy credits.

"What do you mean—confiscated the cards?" Savannah asks. "She can't do that."

"She told me off for offering advice, like which boyfriend to choose and what career path to take. Talked about the responsibility that comes with fortune telling. Said people should make up their own minds, not rely on cards to instruct them what to do."

"Stupid cow. It was just for fun."

I keep quiet. When Aiko and Savannah talk, I feel worse than a spare wheel. A spare wheel comes in useful if you have a puncture, but I'm sure they wouldn't need me if they had a flat tyre or even an accident. When Aiko and Savannah are together, I'm made of air. May as well not be around at all.

"But wait, you haven't heard the best part." Aiko pauses, making sure she has Savannah's full attention. She even glances at the invisible me. "When she took them, the pack split, and three cards fell to the ground. As though she had selected them for a reading. I picked them up for her, of course."

Of course. Old fashioned manners rule in Arcadia.

"Did you look?" Savannah asks.

I'm still on mute.

"Yes."

"And?"

"Well," Aiko stretches the suspense just enough. "They were all the Suit of Swords. Anger, guilt, harsh judgement. Power and oppression. Spot on, right?"

"Or death," Savannah's words drip with glee.

I've so had enough of this topic. "What are we going to do tonight, now that we don't have the cards?"

"We can start a sex club," Savannah says. She would do it too, given the opportunity.

Aiko wrinkles her nose, as though smelling something unpleasant. "Or a poetry club," she suggests.

Savannah won't give up. "Or a poetry club that is a sex club in disguise."

I think fast. "Or a sex club that is a poetry club in disguise."

"Word," the others say in unison.

We bump fists.

Constable Zero Zimmerman

It was after dinnertime and Zero was still stuck at work. Her eyes hurt from reading reports, her brain sweated.

Another case of aggravated robbery in a corner shop in South Auckland—the owner defended himself with a baseball bat and rendered the assailant unconscious. A baseball bat against a knife? Yeah, Zero could see that. It would be nice to think that the law wouldn't punish the shop owner for his actions. Knowing the law, Zero didn't harbour much hope.

What else? Fraud in a government agency, two officials accused of taking bribes in the form of luxury travel, restaurants, and gifts. That surprised her, given how many hoops she had to jump through to claim back a lunch expense or replace a broken laptop mouse.

Phone scams: thieves calling unsuspecting grandparents to tell them their grandchild had been in an accident, asking for a credit card number to pay for a taxi to drive them to the hospital because the ambulance was stuck in traffic. If the victim refused, the second call would be from the thieves pretending to be the police, praising them for not falling for the scam, and asking for their credit card details to make absolutely sure no money had been taken.

A new drug gang operating north of Auckland, with an as-yet-unestablished source of cannabis, was trying to expand its operations into hard drugs. One of the police informants in the gang's outer circle signalled that a university or a high school lab may be involved in the production.

Zero rubbed her forehead, stood up from her desk and walked the length of the corridor to the police quarters cafeteria. Jack Jackson stepped away from the coffee machine.

"After you," he said. "I've just given it a good clean."

The coffee tasted better than a few hours before, which suggested Jackson's good clean really did help. "What are you working on?" she asked.

"Death in a school swimming pool."

"I haven't seen it."

He shrugged. "It hasn't come in yet via the official channels. I got it from an ambulance response system."

Jackson and his famous hacking abilities. Zero knew better than to ask how many laws he had almost broken for the information that would likely appear in the next police update anyway. "A kid?" she asked with a heavy heart.

"A teacher."

That made it only marginally better. "Are they going to involve us?"

"Probably just someone from the local station. They're thinking an accident at this point. Say, Zero, have you eaten yet?"

"Yes." She'd eaten lunch. Or maybe breakfast. But she had eaten.

No way was she opening the possibility of having dinner with Jackson again. The only time they had tried it, they would've ended up in bed, had it not been for an unexpected development in a case they'd been working on.

And now they had no case to distract them.

"Fancy some dessert?"

"No," she lied.

Madeleine Smith

The call came just as day three of week one was ending. Madeleine Smith was still in her office, going over the five-year budget. She glanced at the caller ID. Hep.

"Yes, what is it?" she asked, irritated at the interruption, trying her best to sound upbeat and eager instead.

"Mads, you have to come down to the pool," Hep said.

His tone should have alerted her, but her brain was still in the spreadsheets. The money wasn't looking great.

"Can it wait till tomorrow?"

"No. Haven't you heard the sirens?"

She hadn't. Her office was well insulated, and she had shut the window against mosquitoes. The gate and the pool were on the other side of the school grounds.

"What's going on, Hep?" *Sirens? The police? Had someone discovered their cash-cow plants again?*

"There's been an accident, Mads. One of the teachers. Come now."

Madeleine imagined a broken wrist, a twisted ankle. Not … not what awaited her.

An ambulance was parked on the grass.

Two paramedics packing away a defibrillator, no haste in their movements. *We should get one of those*, she thought.

A body was lying by the side of the pool, covered by a sheet.

"Who— who—?" She couldn't get the words out.

Hep put his hand on her shoulder, gathered her into his arms. "It's Miss Patel. She must have been taking an evening swim."

"Is she—" Madeleine broke off. *Of course* the poor teacher was dead. "Isn't there anything they can do?"

"Sorry, Mrs Smith."

The *Mrs Smith* coming from Hep's mouth, all official, helped to ground her. That, his arms around her, and a small flask of whisky he passed to her.

It was Hep who'd found Parvati's body. His caretaker duties included rolling out the swimming pool cover for the night, to keep the sun's heat in for the early morning squad training.

He'd called 111 and performed CPR for the twenty-two minutes it took the ambulance to get to the school. Then he'd called Madeleine.

Bobbi Kentwood

A sex club that is actually a poetry club. Or the other way around. We settle on a poetry club with a sex theme. In other words, dress up hot and make your words sizzle.

To begin with, we assume we'd invite other girls, make it a feminist gathering with chocolate and revolutionary ideas about bursting through glass ceilings by reclaiming sex for women and woman power. Aiko, though, is keen to invite boys. Can't figure out why, seeing that she doesn't even like Vincent in that way, but whatever.

At least I get my way, in that Vincent and Xander are bringing a third guy, because the dynamic of having just the five of us together sucks. And maybe, just maybe, the third guy will divert Aiko's attention from Savannah.

We meet in the clearing by the fence of our school. The air smells of crushed moss and sun-warmed tea trees. It's after dinner, but there's still daylight till past nine o'clock. The boys arrive by car, each of them in a separate vehicle, because they are too young to drive passengers. The third guy turns out to be a geek with wavy dark hair and black-rimmed glasses to match. His name is Dakota. DK. He makes no impression on me at first, but then he writes:

resting my head here
on your breast I can see
the Milky Way

I start paying attention.

DK composes by hand, even though the boys' electronic devices aren't restricted the way ours are. His poems spill from the pen with such speed and surety, that I think he must have them memorised.

"Hey," I challenge. "Can you write something to order?"

His eyes behind the cool glasses look away. "Like what?"

"Like say one thing but mean another. Write about a peppermint."

Within minutes, he pens a poem in which the best part of a meal is the peppermint after. It's full of sexual innuendo, but at face value he could still be talking about a family dinner.

I may be falling for DK a little.

Savannah may be falling for DK a lot. It's in the tilt of her head, the suddenly throaty voice, the way she doesn't look at him. Well, that's too bad. She can't have Aiko as well as DK.

Vincent and Xander type their poems into their phones, and we girls use lined paper from a book of refill sheets. We all share our creations, the boys competing to see which one can come up with the rudest imagery, the girls teasing them back by writing about feelings. I notice that Aiko holds back a page, crumples it into her pocket, shares the next poem on her writing pad. I don't say anything.

The boys get tired of poetry before we do.

"Who's your science teacher?" DK asks the others.

Vincent's voice does complicated things to my heart. "The new blonde one. She's pretty. Young."

I'm jealous. Stupid, stupid, stupid. But it's Vincent. Vincent!

"Yum, did you say?"

"Dakota!"

DK laughs. I like the sound, and that confuses me. So, Vincent or DK? DK or Vincent? Is it possible to like two guys at once? From a purely rational and self-serving perspective, DK makes more sense.

Then Vincent speaks again, and my heart is all his once again. "She's hopeless at keeping discipline. So you know the cow eyeball we're meant to dissect, right? Xander put it in a plastic glove and chucked it around the lab. And then he turned on the gas and lit a match right next to it with the gas running. The whole thing just went whoosh."

"Cool! Did you get into trouble?"

Xander smiles. "Yeah. The whole S block could have blown."

So Xander is a bit of a bad boy. Great. Now I like all three.

Probably means I'm not serious about any of them.

That's fine. Totes.

Not like I need a boyfriend or anything.

I just want Savannah back.

When it gets too dark to see, we hug the boys goodnight—I still like hugging Vincent best—and sneak back to the rectangles of light shining from the school buildings.

"Uh-uh. Trouble." Savannah stops before we reach the dormitory wing. She points towards the swimming pool. Behind the trees, a flash of red and blue lights.

"An ambulance?" Aiko guesses.

I know better. "No, their lights are red. This is the police." My instinct is to run.

"Shit, you think they've noticed we're gone? Are they looking for us?"

"What—in the swimming pool?"

We giggle, relax, tiptoe past the Matron's room, sneak into our own bedrooms. Not five minutes later, there's a scratch on my door and Aiko's face pops into the gap.

"I need to tell you something," she whispers.

It's big, what she did, the lie, but also inconsequential, in a weird kind of way. After all, we both definitely saw Savannah with Mr King in an inappropriate situation. And so Aiko told the headmistress about it, except that she'd changed up the cast. To protect Savannah, Aiko put herself on the stage with Mr King. He'll be disgraced and fired. Simple. Brilliant.

"I also reported him to the police," she says. But I'm not listening.

When Aiko leaves, I don't think about Savannah and Mr King. I don't think about the lie Aiko told to get Mr King fired. I only think what a powerful tool she's gifted me to alienate her from Savannah. If I wield it right, I'll get our friendship back to normal.

Aiko may be thinking that she's doing Savannah a favour. I know my ex-best friend, though. She's stubborn and self-assured and impossible to manipulate. If she and Mr King are doing anything, Savannah's the one calling the shots.

So yeah, he's old enough to be her father, but he's fit. Strong body, cool tatts. More mature than boys our age—he wouldn't be throwing a cow's eye around the science lab, and he definitely wouldn't brag about it to get a girl's attention. And it's not even an abuse of authority thing, because Mr King is not a teacher. Not like he'd mark her assignment down if she refused to jerk him off, or anything.

I almost forget, but I don't. Before I go to sleep, I unfurl Aiko's crumpled page of poetry, the one I slipped out of her pocket while we were hugging the boys goodnight. She probably thought one of them was copping a feel of her bum.

The lines are beautifully centred, every word a masterpiece of calligraphy. The message, though, hits me like a hammer between the eyes. This is bigger than my friendship with Savannah or my jealousy over Vincent. This is a real issue.

You ask for a label
You want to summarise me
In a single word
So let the word be
Hot or brainy or geek
There's no need to put me
In a box with a gender tick

Holy fucking shit!

Aiko has gender identity issues?

I stare at the paper, at the handwriting that can be identified as Aiko's as surely as a selfie. Fate has just handed me a weapon. Wielded correctly, it can bring me back my Savannah. And even if it can't exactly win me Vincent's heart, at least it can make him more open to new love interests.

It's not that gender classification is a big deal, it's just… Yeah, okay, so it is a big deal. To some people. Savannah is one of those people, even though she pretends she's not. She'll find another angle, like she'll be mad at Aiko for keeping it a secret from her, and that will be her excuse to end the friendship.

And Vincent?

I don't know.

There's another thing I don't know—whether I'm the type of person to expose a secret like this one.

CHAPTER 9

Fourth Day of the School Year

Madeleine Smith

It was this morning of all mornings that Madeleine realised just how seldom she felt her own emotions. She was usually as happy as her saddest child, as loving towards Ashton as he was being to her, as calm as her mother-in-law at any given moment. A true emotional chameleon.

Despite the tragedy at the school pool, when the twins climbed into Madeleine's bed for morning cuddles, she basked in the state of utter bliss generated by hugging two identical heads that smelled of lavender shampoo.

Then Ashton woke up in an uneven-keeled temper, and his mood rubbed off on Madeleine. She arrived at the school frazzled and found Savannah waiting for her inside her office.

"How are you, Mum?" her daughter smiled up at her from the depths of the principal's desk chair.

"All the better for seeing you," Madeleine replied truthfully. Savannah's presence in her office was such a rare and happy event, that Madeleine forgot to filter.

"Eew, Mum, so lame."

That's when it hit her—Savannah was right. She was lame. Whenever someone asked her how she was, Madeleine would run a mental checklist: are the children healthy, are they struggling with friendships or homework, is Ashton on top of his depression? When teachers asked about her weekend plans, those would be filled with driving the twins to soccer or swimming or music, shopping for jeans with Savannah, cajoling her family to do a day's hiking in a kauri bush or have a picnic at the beach. Even the annual Christmas newsletter to her parents and sister read more like a principal's report to the Board of Trustees than a reflection on her year as Madeleine Smith, person.

Who was Madeleine Smith, person, anyway? She was Madeleine Smith, mother. Madeleine Smith, wife. Mrs Smith, headmistress. And that was—that. Who was she when she stripped away the layers of career and family ties?

"What can I do for you, honey?" she asked. She would deal with her identity crisis later. Make that, never.

"Is it true about Miss Patel?"

"I'm afraid it is. So sorry. It must be hard for you. Such a tragic accident."

Savannah didn't look like someone who's sad. "Are you sure?"

"Sure about what?"

"That it was an accident. That she wasn't," Savannah paused for effect, then stage-whispered, "murdered?"

The word was like a white-tail spider: a roving hunter seeking a prey to envenom. It hit the target, but Madeleine managed to keep her composure. "Why would you say that?"

Savannah shrugged and slunk off to class, leaving Madeleine on the battlefield.

A murder on the school premises would be more than a tragedy for Miss Patel and her family, it would also be fatal to Arcadia. No parent would want to send their kid to a place where a murder had taken place—an accidental drowning was probably the limit of parental tolerance.

The challenge was to frame the accident in the right way. Damage control had to start with the students. Madeleine left her own office and knocked on the office door that led to the school counsellor's office.

"What am I supposed to tell them?" Madeleine felt out of her depth, and the sense of ineptitude made her even more uneasy.

She looked across her desk at the school counsellor. Informing a hall of teenage girls that there'd been a death on the premises—that was Mrs Linden's area of expertise.

Mrs Linden leaned towards her, her expression as comforting as a downy pillow, the hand that she placed on Madeleine's firm and steadying. "Don't tell the students that you understand how they feel. Chances are, they aren't feeling much beyond dismay and curiosity. Most of them didn't even know Miss Patel. Don't make them guilty for not experiencing sadness or grief. It's a shock, for sure, but three days was not long enough to forge bonds between the teacher and any of the girls."

This didn't make Madeleine feel any better. "So what should I do?"

"Leave it to me. I'll talk to them and make individual appointments for those girls who'd like to have a session. Meanwhile, how can I be of help to you? Would you like me to talk to Miss Patel's family? Sort out her things?"

It was tempting to say yes. Madeleine had more than enough on her plate. Unfortunately, this too was all her responsibility, damn it. "That's very kind of you, Mrs Linden, but no. I'll manage just fine.

In fact, can I be of any help to you?"

She didn't have to spell it out. They'd had this talk when Mrs Linden returned to work after her older son had taken his own life. Back then, the counsellor had said it would aid her recovery to be able to continue her job. *I wasn't able to save my own son*, she'd said, *so perhaps at least I could help save someone else's daughter.*

Now, though, here was a young teacher whose death was currently being viewed as an accident by the police, but it may as well have been a suicide. Surely Mrs Linden could see the parallel?

Mrs Linden's sad eyes met Madeleine's. "Thank you, Mrs Smith. I'm all right. Perfectly all right."

Bobbi Kentwood

We're all numb.

Miss Patel drowned in the school swimming pool last night. The police say it was an accident. But why was she swimming at night, all alone, in the first place? And how does one drown in a swimming pool, where there are no riptides or waves even, and the water is so warm from the February sun that you couldn't possibly get a cramp? That's what I can't wrap my head around.

It's just my ugly personality and my wishful thinking, but I can't help wondering whether Aiko had tried to get her tarot cards back and … and what, Bobbi? Held Miss Patel's head under the water? Ridiculous.

In a normal school, we would have set up a Facebook Memorial Page. In Arcadia, we have a whiteboard with messages. Some are simple, like "We'll miss you." Others attempt to show off.

"The best teachers teach from the heart, not from a book."

"Death is not the opposite of life, but a part of it."

"It is not the length of life, but the depth."

The truth is, though, we hardly knew Miss Patel. This was her first week with us. Of course, we all got introduced to her at the first assembly, and we had classes with her for three days. So far, she seemed like a good teacher, fun and engaging. Aiko was besotted with her until the tarot cards incident.

The emotions we're feeling are complex. The shock of someone in our school community dying, mainly. Sadness that we're not sadder. Also, disappointment that the headmistress is now teaching Miss Patel's classes. I mean, Savannah's mum is all right, but she *is the headmistress.*

Earlier today, Mrs Linden went into each individual classroom to offer us pointers in grieving and told us she was available 24/7 if we wanted to talk to her one-to-one, or as a group.

Because looking after your mental health has become fashionable in our school over the last year or so, several girls have made appointments. Savannah, Aiko, and I, meanwhile, gathered in Aiko's room for our own group therapy session.

I want to sit next to Savannah, but she flops onto Aiko's bed, taking up all the space. "You'll never get your tarot cards back now that Miss Patel is dead," she says.

Seriously?

While I wouldn't dare say it out loud for fear of offending Savannah, Aiko has no such worries. She tosses her head back and stares Savannah right down. "Can't believe you've just said that. My mum can buy me a new pack of cards, but nothing will bring Miss Patel back to life."

Savannah is trying to save face. "Dead or alive, it's just a matter of how you look at it," she jokes, patting Aiko's duvet cover with the Schrodinger cat slogan on it. Because she's lying on it, the effect is comical, and for the moment the tension dissipates.

"That reminds me." Aiko points her finger, like a conjurer pointing at a top hat, then shifts her duvet with Savannah still on it. Savannah's not a big girl, but even so, Aiko's movements are effortless as she lifts the mattress. I remember the poem and the gender tick box. With all that's been going on, I haven't had a chance to decide what I think I should do with that.

"What shall we do with this?" Aiko asks.

Shit. I totally forgot. The marijuana leaves that I secreted under the mattress lie limply in the palm of Aiko's hand.

I make my eyes wide. "Not weed, surely?"

"Yes weed, surely. I thought we could smoke it." Aiko raises her eyebrows at us. It's more a dare than a question.

"I think you can smoke it," I retort. After all, the idea behind planting the contraband under her mattress—it was to get Aiko in trouble.

Savannah's not keen, either. "Somebody will smell it for sure—in the room, or in our hair. Plus, we don't have the equipment."

Plus, we've already set one room on fire.

"What, then?"

"We could eat it. You've heard of hash brownies?"

Savannah runs to her room to get a slab of Whittakers, and we each eat a few crumbs of the illegal leaf with a double row of milk chocolate.

Then we wait. And wait. Nothing happens.

"You know it's called *puha* in Māori?" I say to break the silence.

"*Electric puha*," Savannah's voice resembles her mother's: a teacher's voice that makes me bristle.

Aiko shifts on the bed, sending the pillow to the floor. "DK is cute." She says it in a way that makes me suspect she's trying to avoid confrontation.

"Yeah, he is. You can't have him, though. Vincent is your guy." Savannah is on the floor, trussed up in the duvet. We can't see her face from our perch on the bed.

I bristle some more. Vincent is mine, mine, mine.

Aiko makes a pouty face. "Don't want Vincent. Want DK."

"I'll have Vincent," I say quickly. I'm both offended and relieved she doesn't want him.

"I want DK," Savannah says at the same time.

"But he likes me." Aiko states this with such conviction I'm sure she must have heard from him somehow.

Savannah echoes my thoughts. "How do you know?"

"Because he kissed me."

"What?" Still Savannah. I'm just a spectator. "When?"

"Last night. He didn't go back to his school."

"He followed us here?"

Aiko nods.

"To your room?"

Another nod.

"Aiko? What the hell? You let him in?"

"Didn't want the matron to see him."

It's only because I know Savannah so well, I notice how she's struggling to maintain composure. "Then what happened?"

"I told him I liked his poetry. He told me he liked me."

"And?"

"And then he pulled me closer, and we kissed."

"With tongues?"

Aiko blushes. "I don't want to talk about it."

Savannah jumps up, bunches up the duvet and throws it at Aiko. Misses. "Bobbi, let's go," she calls out, already halfway to the door.

I follow without as much as a glance at Aiko.

"How dare she?" Savannah fumes all the way back to our corridor. "How fucking dare she?"

A small part of me is whispering DK was fair game. We all met him at the same time, none of us called dibs. And yet, it feels so good to have Savannah back, I agree with her. "Aiko's a bitch," I say.

"I'll tell you what else Aiko is," Savannah replies when the door to her room closes behind us. "She's in my way. And I want to get rid of her."

Constable Zero Zimmerman

It happened sooner than Zero had anticipated. She arrived home later than usual, after a farewell party for her supervising officer, and as she closed the front door behind her, she saw Keith tiptoe out of Amelia's room.

"Shhh," he whispered, his finger raised to his lips in an over-dramatic gesture. "Don't tell a soul."

Four people lived in the flat: Zero, Amelia, Keith, Rachel. With Zero, Amelia and Keith already in the know, there was only one soul she wasn't supposed to tell. Even so, it made her feel uncomfortable. Zero Zimmerman was not good with secrets.

And yet, there was a secret she had been keeping from her flatmates, her old school friends, and anybody at work who didn't absolutely have to know.

Jackson knew, but he never said anything. Since that particular baby-selling case on which they'd worked together last year, he had never mentioned her sister.

Bobbi Kentwood

"Get rid of her?" My throat is dry and itchy. Fear? Excitement? The weed eaten with chocolate, now taking effect? I can't tell. I suppress a cough. "What do you mean?"

"We could drown her in the swimming pool," Savannah's eyes look darker than usual, her mouth is larger than her face. "She can keep Miss Patel company."

That sounds really, really scary. It's the drug talking, I know it, and yet I don't like this new Savannah.

I don't like the new me, either, for I giggle in response, even though I'm frightened out of my wits. I try to control the laughter, but it comes anyway, springing up like volcanic lava from my stomach right into my mouth.

"Or we could shave her head," Savannah takes a fistful of her own ponytail and scrutinises it. "Wow. All these colours. Blonde and dark brown and even copper." She looks and sounds mesmerised.

Is that what being drugged looks like? Why am I not affected?

"Shave her head?" I repeat, barely able to force the words out of my wooden mouth. "Why?"

"So that DK won't find her attractive."

Aiko's crumpled up poem, the one about not ticking the gender box, bubbles in my head. That would be something far more powerful than a shaved head.

A bridge too far?

A blow too low?

I giggle at the rhyme. "A blow too low," I say out loud. Only I don't. Nothing comes out.

Before I learn to shape sounds in my mouth again, my best friend—how I love the sound of that term, *best friend*—has a new idea. "Let's cast a spell."

From under Savannah's bed, out slide the printouts of internet pages we browsed over the holidays. Incantations for finding the love of your life. Magic oils for winning lotto. Potions for making someone fall in love with you …

"This one's funny." Savannah lies down flat on her belly, her chin resting on her stacked-up fists. "*To make someone fall in love with you, carry a piece of bread in your armpit for the whole day, then crumble it into his wine…* Does DK drink wine, you think? He strikes me more as a G&T kind of guy."

I try to imagine what the bread would smell like after a day in someone's armpit. I giggle again on the inside, yet nothing comes out.

"Right, I found it. There we go. How to get rid of a rival."

Get rid of arrival? My head is spinning.

"*To vanquish your love rival,*" Savannah reads in a foreign accent. "*You need a plate, a sharp knife, black pepper, oil and vinegar, three candles …*"

Not candles again, I think.

While Savannah is off searching for a plant with thorns that's not a rose, I let my heavy eyelids fall. It seems like only a second passes before Savannah wakes me up and it's morning. The air smells of artificial wax and black pepper. A dirty plate sits discarded on the floor.

"It's done," she tells me. "The spell is cast. Goodbye Aiko. And good riddance."

CHAPTER 10

Fifth Day of the School Year

Bobbi Kentwood

I feel like shit, so I end up telling the school counsellor. Not about the drugs or the tarot cards or the magic spell, of course. Just the stuff with Aiko and Savannah both liking DK.

"So I know it's disloyal, but a part of me really wishes that Aiko starts going out with DK," I say.

Mrs Linden doesn't ask the why question, but it's out in the open, hanging in the air, waiting.

"That way, the guy who likes Aiko might stop liking her and notice me instead."

"How do you know he likes her?"

I do a mental shrug. Is she for real? How can she be this dense? Aloud I say, "It's the way he looks at her."

That shuts her up for a few moments. Her brows and eyes do this frowny focus, like she's thinking. What is there to think about? Surely she knows what it's like when a guy looks at a girl he's interested in? If she were anybody else, I'd be creating mental jibes about how she's never seen that particular expression, but she's Mrs Linden, so I muzzle my inner Mean Girl.

"Bobbi," she finally brings her attention back to me. "This guy who likes Aiko …"

I can't tell her it's her son. I just can't.

"… does she like him back?"

I don't hesitate. "As a friend, sure. Not in a romantic way."

"All right then. So," she pauses, taps her finger to her mouth. "So. So. So. If you really want this guy to notice you, what are some ways in which you might achieve that?"

"They're all lame."

"No judging at this stage. Just brainstorming."

With my left hand, I tick off the ideas on my fingers, one by one. "I could talk to him on weekends when I have access to the internet. I could throw a party and invite him. I could ask him to help me with my maths. I could sneak a laxative into Aiko's food so that she has to stay at home while the rest of us go to the movies this Saturday."

The next one I don't say out loud, just think it: I could flirt with Xander and hope to make Vincent jealous.

When I get back to class, Savannah and Aiko are sitting together, whispering, and snickering behind their hands, as usual. Looks like the DK crisis is over, and all's forgiven.

So much for casting spells. Aiko hasn't gone anywhere.

I sit in the desk behind them and try to keep the tears inside my eyes. They are sharp like broken glass.

Constable Zero Zimmerman

This Zero hadn't anticipated. She usually slept through the night without interruptions, but something must have awoken her. On her way to the toilet, she bumped into Keith just as he was leaving Rachel's bedroom.

As though re-enacting the scene from the previous night, he placed his index finger on his mouth. "Shhh," he said. "Don't tell."

That made a lot more sense. Don't tell Amelia about Rachel. Don't tell Rachel about Amelia. Got it.

Madeleine Smith

Another message from another number her phone didn't recognise.

We'd like to arrange a date for a school visit in the near future. When are you available to show us around? We're particularly keen to see the science department and your school's lab equipment. Would next Monday work for you?

Madeleine threw the phone across the room. Its screen was made of gorilla glass, so it didn't shatter.

A few hours later, an email with the horrid sex slave images landed in her inbox.

Her first impulse was to tell Savannah's dad; he had the right to know. But her instinct to protect his peace of mind trumped her desire to share. No, she had got them all into this mess when she thought it was cool to be Cannabis Queen, and now she was going to get them out.

CHAPTER 11

The Day the Girl Ceased to Exist

The Girl with a Rubbish Bag

The day the girl ceased to exist started with raised voices. Not unusual in itself: her parents were hot-tempered at the best of times, and the last three months had not been the best of times.

The unusual came in the form of black plastic bags.

"What are they for, Mummy?"

"Put your favourite toys into one of these bags, all right, baby girl? This one."

That didn't make any sense. "But all the toys are my favourite." Then she noticed the tears. "Mummy, don't cry. We can fix it."

Mummy shut and opened her eyes a few times, very fast. "Better to cry because something is over, than to cry because something is still continuing."

The girl didn't understand, but the words had a nice ring to them, and she tried to memorise them. "Better to cry because something is over, than to cry because something is still con- con- what was that word, Mummy?"

Mummy wasn't listening. She was emptying the cupboard and

throwing the girl's clothes into another bag.

"Mummy! Don't put my pink dress in the rubbish!"

"We're not, honey. We're packing to take them to our new house. Our perfect new house, where we'll be happy."

The girl still didn't get it. "So what are we throwing away?"

A smile lifted the ends of mummy's mouth. Pretty. Even her eyes looked less puffy.

"Daddy," her mother replied. "We're throwing away Daddy."

"I don't want to."

"Shh, honey. Mummy knows what's best."

Five Years Ago

Chapter 12

Christmas Season

The Girl with a Rubbish Bag

She wasn't called Courtney anymore. Most of the time, she couldn't remember ever having another identity, another house, another dad. For a while, whenever she heard her old name, even just the first syllable, *court*, she'd twitch and look up. But even that had stopped.

Mummy was still Mummy. Always had been, always would be, even though her hair was short now, and a different colour. What stayed the same was the terror in Mummy's eyes, every time there was a knock on the door, every time the landline rang, every time a car drove past the garden.

"Time to decorate the Christmas tree," her dad said. Her new dad, the one whose voice never made her scurry away to hide under the bed. "And when we're done, we're going to write a letter to Santa."

"Dad. There is no Santa."

Her dad placed his hand across his chest. "How can you say that? Every time a child says there's no Santa, Mrs. Santa Claus cries."

"There's a Mrs. Santa Claus now?"

"Course there is. How else would he keep track of all the

presents? Who would remember to feed the reindeer? And how else would he manage to be so jolly and so *ho-ho-ho* every Christmas?"

"You need a wife to be jolly?"

"You bet, Princess."

"And to *ho-ho-ho*?"

"Especially to *ho-ho-ho*. How's the new school? Different from all the others, right?"

The girl thought about it. "Different but the same."

"You like it?"

"I think so. If I keep on liking it, can we stay? Please. It makes me sad to move houses and schools."

"It is sad to say goodbye to friends and to places we know. But you know what? No matter where we live, we'll always be a family. We'll always have each other. And we'll have our traditions to keep us happy. Writing letters to Santa is part of our family tradition."

Dear Santa, she wrote. *What I want for Christmas is that everything stays the same. Same house, same school, same Daddy. I don't want to move anymore. And I want Mummy to stop being scared.*

Her dad put the letter in a big envelope decorated with reindeer, then he handed her the Christmas tree angel. "Remember, in our tradition, this goes on first. Right at the very top, so that she can look after us."

She fluffed up the angel's skirt, straightened the wings, looked into the ever-smiling face, and planted a delicate kiss on the porcelain cheeks.

"Happy Christmas, Angel," she whispered. "Please keep us safe here."

The Girl's Dad

He was still looking. They hadn't moved overseas, he knew that, because as soon as he'd seen the empty shelves in their closets, he applied for a court order preventing his daughter's removal from New Zealand. As a lawyer, he'd known to apply for the order *without notice*, meaning it would be implemented right away, not giving his wife a chance to respond.

He didn't bother with the police. He knew he was smarter than them.

Five years had passed. His daughter would be ten now. What did ten-year-old girls like? Fairies? Ponies? Ballet? He had no idea and nobody to ask. Not that he'd had much of an idea before they left—he'd been working all hours, and when he came home he didn't know how to talk to a little girl who still lisped despite the fact that she was already at school.

Nevertheless, his wife had no right. Louis had given her a big house, a clothing allowance and diamonds every anniversary. Any other woman would have been grateful. Any other woman would be guessing his every wish before he'd even realised he had one. Any other woman would have stayed.

As he hung meaningless baubles on the purple Christmas tree (Courtney's choice five Christmases ago), he reviewed the assumptions he'd made.

One, they were still in the country.

Two, his wife wasn't on a single-parent benefit, nor on an unemployment benefit—he knew enough hackers to obtain this kind of information. Neither was she paying taxes—same government database, same hacker. Therefore, she was either flying under a fake name, or leaching off another sucker.

Three, his daughter wasn't being home-schooled. Another

database and another hacker, but they had checked out all the families who'd applied for permission to home-school in the year Courtney had disappeared, and he continued screening the new applicants. Therefore, she had to be at a school somewhere, and every school had an extensive student roll that could be his for a few hundred dollars. What proved tricky was keeping track of the new enrolments. The student lists as such were useless, assuming his daughter went under a fake name now. He needed lists of students who were new to the school, and such lists didn't exist.

Four, his wife and daughter would avoid small towns where people knew each other from Adam and would be inherently suspicious of newcomers. So, urban centres like Auckland, Hamilton, Christchurch, Wellington. Dunedin or Tauranga at a pinch.

Five, his wife loved playing bridge and doing yoga. By now, she'd probably feel secure enough to join a social bridge club, to attend yoga classes. These records were not in any database, so as he moved from city to city, he would spend most of his after-work time visiting bridge clubs and fitness centres. There weren't many bridge clubs around, so he created an online persona of a thirty-something mother of two who was desperately hoping to connect with bridge players around New Zealand. He checked every response with meticulous determination, but so far, nothing from his wife.

Fitness centres and yoga classes presented the opposite problem: there were too many, often without a website. No way of predicting which one his wife would frequent, on what day, at what time.

Still, he wasn't going to give up. He was going to find them. If it took all his money, all his energy, and all the time in the world, he would find them.

A Year Ago

CHAPTER 13

Last Easter

Madeleine Smith

New Zealand's cannabis season typically stretched though the summer from November to April. This year's crop was flowering now that the days were getting shorter. Inappropriate as it was, Madeleine felt a sense of satisfaction as she walked through the secret part of the school garden among rows upon rows of greenery. Each plant was covered with small pinkish flowers, like cake frosting applied in messy patches.

As human beings, we're meant to work the land, she thought, to put seeds into black soil and tend to them as they grow.

Before she got into this business, she had imagined that you rolled up smoked cannabis leaves to get high, but it was the flowers that had the highest concentration of tetrahydrocannabinol, the psychoactive component of the marihuana plant. The leaves could be used in salads and smoothies, and to brew tea, but the idea was strangely repulsive—smoothies and salads were wholesome things, while cannabis, its medicinal properties aside, was *weed*.

The pistils were turning brown. Soon it'll be time to harvest the flowers and dry them in the roof cavities of the school buildings. The roof cavities were too small to act as attics—they were designed to provide additional insulation not storage space—but they would do as dehydrators for her crop. Then her team would trim them, cure them, and send them on their merry way. She was looking forward to the winter months, the school premises untainted once more.

That night she received a phone call. A burner phone, as usual, the number different every time.

"We can't afford to have a season of no grow," the voice said. Madeleine didn't know whether this was the man with a tattoo on his skull, but the accent was Vietnamese. "It's time to build a greenhouse."

The Girl with a Rubbish Bag

If somebody were to say *Courtney* now, she wouldn't even notice. Over the years, she'd been friends with two other Courtneys and one Courtlyn. Not once did she get confused. She had her own name, a new name that didn't start with *court.*

"How's school?" Her new dad stopped the supermarket trolley in front of a gigantic display of chocolate eggs.

"Fine".

"You like it?"

"It's okay. School's school."

"You like it enough to keep going to it for a few more years?"

Panic rose like lava inside her throat. "How do you mean? Do we have to move? Has Mum—" she wanted to ask whether her mother had been acting weird again, but if she voiced the fear, it would become real, she knew that much. It'd happened before.

"Don't worry about it, honey, I'll talk to Mum."

The lava sank down to her stomach, churning and burning, but not coming out of her mouth. "Okay then. Shall we get the chocolate kiwi for her?"

"Of course. And a bunny for you, as usual?"

Quickly, before he could talk about how traditions were what made a family a family, she added a chocolate kiwi bird and a chocolate rabbit to the mountain of food inside the trolley. She looked into the ever-smiling face of the Easter Bunny; his chocolate smirk covered by golden foil. Sometimes, just sometimes, she wanted to smash her fist through that stupid grin.

Back home, she looked for a good spot to hide the chocolate kiwi bird for her mum to find, while her dad was making a big show of hiding the chocolate bunny for her in all the obvious places like the fridge, and the pantry, and the oven drawer. Traditions. They didn't make a family, the girl knew, but little routines helped to keep her mum from getting worse.

The girl pulled down the fold-out ladder that led to the little attic above the corridor. A few years ago, she'd play with her friends here, or climb up with a book and an apple, but lately she couldn't be bothered. This would make a good hidey-hole for mum's Easter treat.

She was at the top of the ladder, the upper half of the body already inside the attic, when she noticed the two rucksacks to the left. Her hands clammy, she opened the smaller one, knowing what she'd find, hoping against all hope that she was wrong.

She wasn't wrong. Inside the smaller rucksack, rolled up tight, was a pair of her tracksuit pants, three T-shirts, three pairs of socks, three pairs of knickers, one bra, a hoodie. The larger rucksack had the same clothes in her mother's size, plus protein bars, packets of nuts, two bottles of water and two solar-powered flashlights.

Mum had been spiralling again.

At least the rucksacks were a step up from the black plastic rubbish bags.

The Girl's Dad

He was still looking.

Now

CHAPTER 14
Monday

Madeleine Smith

Monday. It was not going to be a good day.

Whenever Ashton was feeling well, Madeleine liked Mondays. Weekends were littered with family obligations, with chauffeuring the kids to soccer games and singing lessons and playdates, with grocery shopping and parties. Mondays meant going back to the routine she craved, in a quiet office at school, away from Olivia Kentwood's disturbing presence in the house next door.

Olivia Kentwood was a cliché. A Scandinavian-looking woman with creamy skin and buttery hair, their neighbour's wife, the one whom Ashton coveted with his entire being.

Had he done more than covet? Madeleine couldn't be sure. She was fairly sure, however, that she would have preferred him to have an affair and get Olivia out of his system, rather than have him fantasise about Olivia while in his marital bed. Experience had taught Madeleine that real-life sex was almost always worse than fantasy-sex: real people had sweaty armpits and coffee-breath that tickled your skin, they touched you in the wrong places, not hard enough or not long enough. In contrast, fantasies were perfect.

Be that as it may, Madeleine was happy to note that today Olivia Kentwood wasn't sunning topless on the porch or pruning grapes in her impossibly tight white shorts or standing in the kitchen window chopping vegetables. Her car was gone, too, which broke the usual pattern for the household next door. Olivia Kentwood's Mondays were for laundry and gardening. Olivia only left the house on Thursdays to do grocery shopping, and on every first Friday of the month to attend the school Board of Trustees meetings. Madeleine knew all this because on several occasions she had slipped back to the house to spy on her husband, back when she had suspected something was going on between him and Olivia.

And yet today the laundry room was empty—Madeleine could see that much through her binoculars—and there were no sheets bulging with the breeze on the washing line. The neighbours' garden was empty except for the three egg-shaped swing chairs, a covered spa pool, a picnic table under the gazebo, some picturesque debris. A flawless garden for a flawless family.

In contrast, today was not going to be a good Monday for Madeleine's far-from-flawless family. Just one look at Ashton told Madeleine that his mood was out of control. Sometime during the night, bleakness had wrapped itself around her husband like a python. Getting out of bed would have felt pointless to him. Clearing the twigs and branches that still littered their yard after Saturday's storm would have felt pointless. The future would have loomed before her husband, every day stretching from here to eternity, one as pointless as the next.

"Do you know how annoying it is," he asked her in response to her *good morning,* "to wake up next to someone who's always upbeat?"

She wanted to throw the question back at him, ask how he thought it felt to wake up next to someone so negative. Instead, she chose to leave the room. Ashton's mood had nothing to do with her energy. It was caused by neither the trouble the school was in, nor by the twins pelting each other with milk soaked Nutrigrain at the breakfast table. Periodically, ill humour would seep into Ashton, irrespective of how well or badly his life fared at the time.

People around him had tried to understand and failed. Depression was like drowning, but not in sadness. It was drowning in numbness. When Ashton was in one of those moods, he said it was as though he were numb to emotions, to hope, to life. Madeleine had tried to understand and failed, too.

Normally on a Monday, Ashton would attend to his online business. Madeleine knew that even on a good day he would only do enough to make it look promising, without letting it blossom into a full-time occupation. When not working, he would most often get lost in the sticky web of online porn, each adventure more expensive than the previous one. It was obscene that loneliness online could make such a lucrative business proposition.

Though, to be fair, it wasn't only the online club subscriptions that made up the debt, it was the interest rate the Mekong Dragons had exacted. When Ashton signed up for a 17% interest rate, it looked good to him compared to the 20% credit card companies were charging, particularly as all the banks had cancelled his cards. What he failed to spot in the fine print, was that the 17% interest rate was charged monthly, not annually.

Their friends assumed that Ashton had married Madeleine for her money, the typical *toy-boy and cougar* setup. Many must have thought him trapped when the twins arrived. What the friends didn't realise was, back when they'd met, Ashton had been the one with the money, and he had been shrewd enough to invest most of it in the charter school Madeleine had converted into Arcadia High Boarding School. Plus, he'd had the foresight or the sheer luck to tie her down by getting her pregnant.

And now the money was all spent on Ashton's quality porn experiences and loan repayments, and they were living with his mother in order to cut costs. Granny Smith doted on her boy, spoiled her grandchildren, and tolerated Madeleine.

In return, Madeleine couldn't tolerate her mother-in-law. She hated the fact Granny had known Ashton since birth, remembered his little-boy dreams and understood his every facial expression. In a way, she was more jealous of Granny Smith than of Olivia Kentwood. Ironic and twisted—yet no less true.

Madeleine also suspected Ashton's mother was the reason he wasn't getting on top of his depression. Pedagogy textbooks talked about snowplough parenting, and even though Auckland had never seen snowploughs (the last snow flurries a decade ago had melted as they were hitting the ground), Madeleine understood the metaphor. Granny Smith was like a machine moving in front of Ashton, clearing any obstacles in his path to success. Sure, it's a parent's job to protect the children with their adult wisdom and experience, but if the children never suffer failure, how would they cope in the real world?

They coped exactly the way Ashton did, that's how, which translated to *not very well.* At thirty, he still had his mum organise his hairdresser appointments because he didn't like talking on the phone, and he let her deal with the Inland Revenue Department because he couldn't be bothered with all the paperwork.

And his depression? Granny Smith would spend hours talking to her son about his doom and gloom. What if all that constant validation had the perverse outcome of aiding him to wallow in self-pity?

One part of Madeleine's brain knew that wasn't how it worked. Depression was not caused by a sympathetic ear. And yet, she couldn't help but wonder whether some types of depression couldn't be cured by having to get off your backside and doing a hard day's work. People fighting for their livelihood seldom had the time to analyse their feelings.

Ashton had plenty to value in his life. Two women who competed for the privilege to love him, a hot next-door neighbour with an air of mystery about her, a constant supply of quality porn more expensive than Krug champagne, two sons who worshipped him, a teenage stepdaughter who didn't use drugs or cut herself and listened to him from time to time.

It was a pity Ashton's depression didn't want to appreciate it all.

What Madeleine wanted right now was to raise enough money to be able to move her family far from Granny Smith, and even further from the drug gang. Preferably to a spot without internet access, where Ashton could work with his hands, jog on the beach, and heal.

Catch 22. To move away, she needed money. To get money, she needed the drug gang. To cook meth was unthinkable. To lose Savannah would be worse.

Constable Zero Zimmerman

Monday morning, and the first email Zero read was from Sergeant Malhi. It had no body, the message contained in its entirety in the subject line: *Reminder: The Arcadia High report today please.*

He even added a *please*. Coming from Sergeant Malhi, it was exactly that. A polite reminder—polite for now. She should really move on. The Mekong Dragons weren't going to investigate themselves. She was already spending too much time on the Arcadia High case, which wasn't even a proper case yet, and might never become one.

What did she have, really? Two recent deaths in the school community, if you include the sister school. A water bottle that could have been used to dispense the overdose. A symbol associated with a religion that prohibited self-harm. An unfinished book. A secret which might have made Aiko a target for haters. Not nearly enough. She knew what Sarge would say if she talked to him now: *dispense with the case immediately unless you find compelling evidence it's a homicide.*

As tragic and heartstring-tugging as the situation was, Auckland was full of other wrongs to right.

Zero was halfway through memorising a dossier on Quan and Hai Le, wealthy Vietnamese brothers whose business partners included confirmed members of the Mekong Dragons, when Jackson stuck his head into Zero's office, bringing with him subliminal messages of coffee beans and cocoa. "Yo, Zee. You working that cult school case?"

Was she still working the case? "It's not a cult school, Jackson. Just a private school with no internet. And yes. Sort of. Why?"

"Couple of reasons. One, are the-powers-that be type-casting you?" This referred to a case last winter, when Zero was asked to investigate a series of suicides in another private school. On that occasion, she had unearthed a toxic environment full of bullying and impossible parental expectations, but no foul play. "Two," Jackson continued, counting off on his fingers, "we have a missing person report. A parent at the school. A Mrs Olivia Kentwood. Thought you might like to tail along to interview the husband."

Mrs Kentwood, Bobbi's mum.

Zero wasn't sure whether the surge of adrenalin was thanks to the case, or the prospect of Jackson's company. She nodded. "Let's go."

"Dibs on driving." Jackson's impossibly white teeth gleamed in a sudden grin. "But to avoid being called a chauvinist, I'll let you be on top the first time we have sex. Deal?"

It sucked how much she wanted to say yes. Settled for, "In your dreams."

"You're not wrong there, Zimmerman."

The Kentwood family's garden was covered with debris from the weekend's windstorm, lending a neglected, abandoned look to the whole house. Nobody had bothered to clean up.

The man who opened the red door in the navy-blue house looked like he'd slept in his clothes. He led them to the same chocolatey sofa Zero had occupied on Saturday, and, like his daughter two days before, didn't offer coffee. Zero couldn't hold it against him.

This being a Monday, Bobbi had to be at school. Probably left earlier this morning or last night. Did she even realise her mother was missing? Or had she spent the weekend seeped in a typical teenage oblivion?

Jackson got the preliminaries out of the way. Name, age, mobile number of the phone the missing woman was not answering.

"She just took off," Blair Kentwood said. "Her overnight bag is missing, so she must have packed it and left. She usually picks a direction on the motorway: north or south. Drives until she gets tired, then stops off at a motel."

"*Usually?*" Zero and Jackson said in unison. Zero waved to indicate that he should take the lead.

"My wife, she doesn't deal with stress very well. When life gets too much for her, she sometimes needs a change of scene. A few hours alone out on a hiking trail, or a night in a motel … it just clears her head to be somewhere else."

Jackson drummed his fingers. "Did she leave a note?"

"No."

"Does she *usually?*"

"Sometimes."

"More often than not?"

The husband spread his arms in a gesture of helplessness. "Don't know. Fifty-fifty, maybe?"

"And it doesn't bother you, her disappearing like that?"

"It does. That's why I called you."

"I mean the trend. You're fine with the fact that your wife just takes off and goes to a motel from time to time?"

The implication was clear. Blair Kentwood shifted in his seat. "It's not like that. It's just that she needs to be alone. You know women."

Zero imagined that Jackson knew women very, very well. She bit down on the thought. She was not going to get jealous.

Jackson ignored the comment. "What's the longest your wife's been away, sir?"

"A night."

"So three days, today being the third day, is out of the ordinary?"

"I'd say."

Jackson raised his eyes from the notebook. "You worried?"

"Not especially." His face belied the words. He pressed the tips of his fingers into his temples, then repeated, "You know women."

"I don't actually." Jackson shrugged. "I'm gay."

All light and oxygen got sucked out of the room for an instant, before Zero realised that she didn't believe it. This was Jackson lying. Why would he lie?

Blair rubbed his forehead. "You may be onto something there, mate. Women are …" he trailed off. "Excuse me." His voice was ragged. "I'll just …" He left the lounge. Zero heard his footsteps grow faint deep inside the house.

"Looks like he is worried, after all," Jackson said.

Zero ignored his comment. "What was that about you being gay?"

"Why? Are you disappointed?"

"Why would I be?"

"Because we still have unfinished business. The rain check, remember?"

She remembered.

"And guess what, Zimmerman. It's not raining right now."

"Jackson, really? We're on duty."

"So that's your only objection? That we're on duty? Cool."

Zero was still blushing when Blair Kentwood returned, clutching an A4 printout. "Here's the most recent picture of Olivia. She hates being photographed, says the camera always makes her look ugly. I caught her unawares in this one."

Madeleine Smith

It was like a nightmare on repeat. Bobbi failed to turn up for her first class, and her absence was reported via the usual channels to Madeleine. Just like Aiko last Friday.

Ashton and his depression forgotten, Madeleine approached Bobbi's dorm room, her stomach already knotting. Foreboding sucked air from her lungs. She fully expected to see Bobbi stretched out on her bed, a bottle of pills nearby.

She held onto the door handle, caught her breath, knocked. Entered.

Bobbi's room was empty. As in, no Bobbi Kentwood. It was certainly not empty from a materialistic perspective. The wardrobe leaked denim onto the carpet: white jeans, light pink jeans, faded blue jeans, black jeans laddered along the thigh, white denim shorts, light pink denim shorts, faded blue denim shorts, black denim shorts laddered on the bum—the after-class clothes the students were allowed to wear in the evenings. There were iPhone cases in a loose heap on the desk (who needed more than one phone case, especially when the phone was locked away most of the time?), mingling with perfume bottles, crumpled tissues with traces of lipstick, and a lacy bra.

In the old days, kids who ran away from home used a long stick and a handkerchief to carry their belongings. Today, they would need a theatre curtain in place of the handkerchief. And they'd spend all day packing.

Madeleine was certain Bobbi hadn't run away. Fairly certain. But this last straw was not something she could carry by herself. With hands less steady than she would have liked, she dialled Ashton's phone from the Starred Contacts list and listened to it ring. Damn. No reply.

Her palms sweaty, her lower jaw numb, Madeleine knew she was seconds away from a panic attack. The last one had been years ago, when the twins were sick, and their high fever wasn't responding to Pamol nor to cool damp flannels. Friday's incident with Aiko had propelled her into action that averted a potential panic attack: dial 111, answer the operator's questions, follow instructions.

Today, though, she was crashing. All she could do was curl into a ball, pull Bobbi's blanket over her head and ride it out.

When she was done, she noticed a voicemail on her phone. Bobbi's teacher. She played it back, almost apathetic now to the news that Bobbi was safely in class, with an absence note from the mental health counsellor.

She was putting Bobbi's blanket away when something under the bed caught her eye. A piece of paper, folded over, and bearing signs of having been crumpled up in the past:

You ask for a label
You want to summarise me
In a single word
So let the word be
Hot or brainy or geek
There's no need to put me
In a box with a gender tick

What the hell? Was Bobbi questioning her biological gender? What did that mean for Arcadia High? This was a school for girls—granted, an outmoded concept in today's woke society—but it was what it was: ill-prepared to handle someone who wanted to be treated as a male. Would she have to move Bobbi to a different wing? Would they still be allowed to have her—him?—on the school's all-girl netball team? What about the toilets and shower rooms—the unisex toilet versus the liberal cry defending an individual's right to use whichever toilet the individual felt the most comfortable with?

It was all doing Madeleine's head in, not least of all because it sounded so—tempting. Never before had it occurred to her that the gender she had grown up with, the one assigned to her at birth, could be returned and exchanged like a dress that didn't fit when you tried it on at home.

Would Madeleine want to be a man given the option? Maybe. Not in the physical sense because—penis envy? Nah. With the biological equipment that the good Lord had given her, she could get as many penises as she wanted, whenever she wanted. And yet, not having to prove herself every time she took on a task and not having her decisions questioned, would be nice. Liberating.

New Zealand was the first country to give women the vote, she thought. It was lagging behind the rest of the developed world in terms of giving us unbiased treatment.

Suddenly Madeleine felt a yearning to do something un-female. She knew she shouldn't. She knew she would. Quickly, before she'd get a chance to come to her senses, she scrolled through her phone's longer, non-starred Contacts screen and selected another name. This one did not go to voicemail.

"All right," she said instead of a greeting. "Let's meet." She named a busy café on the state highway, one that all locals avoided because of the tourists, the mediocre coffee, and because they supported Chris and Chris, the couple who ran the tearooms in the nearby village. "Is now a good time?"

"It's always a good time to see you," he said. A cliché, but a much needed one.

Life was a collection of stories. Marrying Ashton had been the fairy-tale Madeleine had been telling herself for years. Louis was from a totally different narrative: a bad boy you lusted after but would never settle down with. This didn't excuse what she was about to do, but it went some way towards explaining it.

The state highway café turned out to be noisier than she'd anticipated. The only unoccupied table was jammed between a group of mothers with babies, and a software company's team meeting. Fortunately, she knew nobody from either group. The professionals were probably touring the vineyards in Matakana, and the mothers … hopefully on their way to the honey centre or the goat cheese factory, not to the vineyards.

"I know—so much judgement. I would never judge other mums."

"The paradigms are shifting in the client-centric approach."

"Not sleeping through the night yet. Unless midnight-till-four-thirty counts? Then he wants the boob."

"Going forward, we should spreadsheet the core competencies in our team—"

"Madeleine." Louis's voice barely made it through the white—and not so white—noise of the coffee machine.

He said something else.

"Sorry? I didn't catch that."

"I said I missed you."

He'd got fat since she last saw him. Not just pleasantly padded like a content middle-age CEO, more like somebody who ate unhealthy food—and lots of it. She wanted to ask and found that she couldn't. It would have been socially acceptable for him to comment on her own declining weight but not the other way around. You didn't comment about plus sizes for fear of being accused of fat-shaming.

Louis moved his mouth to her ear. "Let's go somewhere quiet."

"So we can talk?"

"So we can fuck."

The directness took her breath away. She should say no. "You have a condom?" she asked instead.

"Always have one handy."

Oh, the hell with it. "I think we'll need more than one."

As he disappeared inside the motel while she waited a few moments for the sake of any watchful eyes, she wondered what cruel life's twist had resulted in his weight gain. Back when they were teenagers, he was broad-shouldered but slim. Had he suffered a physical illness, something to do with his metabolism? Or did he simply not love himself enough to care? It was weird to see the old Louis hidden underneath a bodysuit of lard. Worrying and mystifying, but not a put-off. In his motel room, she turned to him and found the inside of his mouth with her tongue as easily as all those years before, and with even more urgency.

The kiss itself wasn't earth moving. Madeleine refused to contemplate whether she was getting too old—no, she wasn't old as in *elderly*; but perhaps after a few years you simply outgrew sexual activities the way you outgrew late-night parties and experimenting with LSD?

The *concept* of the kiss, though—the *doing* something for herself, with selfish disregard for everyone else—that was pure bliss. Why would anybody need antidepressants or anti-anxiety medication when you could have an affair instead?

Bobbi Kentwood

I almost don't keep my appointment with Mrs Linden. Yesterday's fug, the post-party depression, is still with me, and experience has taught me not to speak to mental health counsellors when I'm depressed. They only make it worse. Who needs to dwell on bad things, past or present? It's like probing a sore tooth with your tongue: it only keeps reminding you the pain is still there. It's better, much better, to concentrate on whatever makes you happy.

Today, though, I realise that there is something I could discuss with Mrs Linden without bringing Vincent into the conversation: I could talk about Savannah and Aiko. My emotions are similar: Aiko is distracting Savannah from being my best friend in the same way she's distracting Vincent from noticing my breasts. Perhaps the solution for the one I can talk about will be of the one-size-fits all variety.

I've mentioned friendship issues to Mrs Linden before, we discussed my need for having a best friend, but this is the first time I spell it all out.

"The worst thing is," I say, even though I don't consider it the worst thing, I'm just pretending to care, "the worst thing is that now Aiko is in hospital, and I feel like a bitch—like a bad person—for even minding how she came between Savannah and me."

Mrs Linden reassures me, says all the right things, before moving on. "Have you spoken to Savannah? Told her how you feel about the fact that now there are three of you in the friendship?" she asks.

"Yeah." Like, duh!

"And?"

"She said I was imagining it. That nothing's changed. That we're still best friends."

"But it doesn't feel that way?"

My voice is louder than I intend, and I can't control the volume. "Savannah's face lights up when Aiko walks into the room. They're always exchanging in-jokes I don't get. Or dancing together." There's more but my throat tightens, and I know words won't be able to squeeze through.

Mrs Linden's expression tells me she gets me totally. She's a good therapist that way. "You feel that you're third-wheeling?"

I spread my arms in a what-can-I-do gesture.

Mrs Linden delivers a mini-lecture on the nature of three-person friendships, and how the balance changes over time, the power shifting from one friend to another, and how there are six relationships within that dynamic, and I keep thinking that this isn't a useful parallel for the Vincent-Aiko problem.

Suddenly Mrs Linden changes tack. "Of course, things would have shifted on Friday."

That's the thought that's been banging around in my brain the whole weekend, yet when I hear it spoken aloud, I'm alarmed, because it cuts to the heart of the issue: without Aiko around, my life is a lot better.

"Bobbi?" Mrs Linden's voice brings me out of my head. "How has Savannah been acting towards you since Friday?"

This makes me pause because I have no idea. My mind was so full of Aiko, Vincent, Xander, and family stuff, that I never even noticed Savannah's attitude towards me. Vincent—I did notice how Vincent was treating me on Saturday. I sigh a deep, sob-like sigh.

"Best friend relationships can be a bit like romantic relationships, just without the romance," Mrs Linden says when it's obvious that I won't be answering her question. "You want to be exclusive. You get jealous. You grow apart. And—if you're lucky—you grow closer again. But if it's not meant to be Savannah, Bobbi, there are lots of fish in the sea."

I can see myself with girl fish who are not Savannah, but I can't see myself with any boy fish other than Vincent. So much for friendships being like romantic relationships.

I'm still gathering my courage to address the Vincent issue, in a round-about-no-naming-names way, when there's a knock on the door and Savannah walks in.

"Am I early?" she asks. "Shall I come back?"

My feet have already moved towards the door. "No need," I tell her. "Thank you, Mrs Linden. I'm done."

As we pass each other, Savannah shoots me a glance and pretends to wipe a tear off her cheek. She's whistling the tune of *Cry Me a River*.

"Hilarious," I whisper. "Think it up all by yourself, did you?"

I'm not sure she hears me.

Schoolwork is the last thing on my mind, I realise, when instead of in class I find myself in the tranquillity garden.

At this moment, I'm so done with everything. School. Aiko. Savannah most of all.

Not Vincent, though. No, never Vincent.

Constable Zero Zimmerman

"I need coffee," Zero said when they got back to Jackson's car.

"Coffee? I thought we'd pay a visit to the cult. The missing woman is a parent there."

"It's not a cult."

"Yeah, right. Just a super weird school."

"You're intrigued, Detective. That's good. The coffee shop is on the way to Arcadia."

"*The* coffee shop? The one and only?"

"Yes, Jackson, the one and only. We're in the rough country here. It may be called Auckland by the width of a hair, but there's no coffee culture. Luckily, they know what a cappuccino is."

Jackson flashed a set of perfect teeth, all the whiter in contrast with his mocha skin. "Do they know what a long black is?"

Zero felt a wave of heat in her cheeks. *Do not go there, Zimmerman.* "I believe it's a tall glass of coffee without milk," she said, hoping her voice didn't betray her. Here she was, falling for dirty talk. "Now drive before things get ugly. I. Need. Coffee."

"Yes, ma'am."

Jackson drove way over the speed limit, but the road was wide and straight and empty. Plus, they were in a cop car. That provided the additional benefit of parking outside the coffee shop, right on the yellow lines.

"Don't look," Zero said as soon as they went inside.

Jackson looked. "What, where?"

"I said, *don't*. Pretend you're reading the menu on the wall and use the mirror below. See that table to the left? The woman wearing a dress made of ocean waves? That's Madeleine Smith, the headmistress."

"And the fat guy with her?"

Zero shrugged. "Don't call people *fat*."

"Just a word, Zimmerman. Relax. I'd have no problem with you describing me as black. Or dark-skinned. Or, of African descent. Those words are not offensive when used without prejudice."

"Right."

Jackson pretended to study the menu while keeping his eyes on the couple. "I can't figure them out. Would be interesting to get hold of their mobile phones. Read the messages, check the photos."

"I'll tell you one thing, Jackson. They're definitely not married."

"Yeah?"

"It's in the body language. They're into each other in the taboo-sex way, not in the couple-sex way."

"And what about you, Zimmerman? Are you into me in the taboo-sex way? Or in the couple-sex way?"

The only thing Zero could think of saying was *yes*, so she turned her attention to the waitress. "A large latte please. With a muffin. To go."

"Thought you drank your coffee without milk," Jackson whispered into the back of her neck once he'd placed his own order.

His breath warmed her skin. She cleared her throat. "Lattes are more substantial. I'm hungry."

"Hungry? I know just the—"

"Jackson. Don't." And yet the thought made her head spin. In a good way. "Look," she said to distract her mind from going *there* again, to the place in which she and Jackson might be a thing, for a night or for more than just one night. "Madeline Smith is leaving. With her alleged non-husband."

"I'll follow them. You wait for the order." Jackson disappeared before she could respond. But that was all right. She was curious where Madeleine was heading, and Jackson was the obvious choice for the tailing job, as Madeleine had never met him.

When Zero stepped outside with the coffees, Jackson was there. "They didn't go far. The motel across the road."

That sounded about right. That taboo-sex thing and all. And yet, something wasn't quite right with the picture. Taboo sex yes, but not … she couldn't put her finger on it. Taboo sex, but not taboo? No. Taboo but not sex? Not quite.

Perhaps it was just that her faith in humankind had suffered a knock. Madeleine Smith had not seemed the sort to have an affair. Cook the books a little maybe, or push boundaries on the tax return form, but not cheat on a loved one.

"Isn't she worried someone would see them? She's well known in the community."

"Madeleine waited a bit before following him in. She used that time to put her sunglasses on."

Zero gave the motel a final once-over. There was a black BMW X5 in the parking lot. She squinted. The same number plate as the car that drove past the school on Saturday morning—she could trust her memory for numbers on that. Coincidence? After all, it was a rental car, so it made sense the driver would be staying in a motel.

"Guess there's no point going to the school with the headmistress occupied elsewhere."

Jackson turned towards the car. "We should interview Olivia Kentwood's daughter. And I could do with your muffin."

"*Excuse* me?"

Jackson pointed at the brown bag in her hand. "You snagged the last muffin. Can I at least have a bite?" His smile broadened. "Why, what did you think?"

"Oh, stop it."

He laughed. It was a good laugh. A great laugh in fact. Sexy. Heart-warming.

Jackson's voice pulled her out of her reverie. "What does she see in that guy? The headmistress?"

Zero bristled. "What? Because he's large?"

"No. It's just that she has a business in which her reputation is everything. Also a family, a husband and three kids. What? Why are you looking at me like that? I've done a background check. So why risk losing it all for an hour in a three-star motel?"

Zero shrugged. She couldn't fathom it.

"I mean it, Zimmerman. What does she see in him? What would tempt you to go to a motel room with someone?"

You, thought Zero. Jackson could tempt her to do anything. It was just as well her mobile pinged.

"Message from the sarge," she told Jackson.

"Let me guess. Sandy wants you to put Aiko Hamasaki's case to bed and work on a gang shooting."

"Close. *Sergeant Sandeep Malhi* wants me to put Aiko Hamasaki's case to bed. And do last month's admin if I'm not up to the task of progressing the Mekong Dragons investigation."

"And?"

"I'll text him later that there was no signal in Arcadia. Let's go, Detective. We have detecting to do."

"Shouldn't you pay some attention to the Mekong Dragons?"

"Yes," Zero sighed. "I really should. Later."

Bobbi Kentwood

They come to my maths class. It's the same red-headed cop that I saw here on Friday, the same one I talked to on Saturday. This time, though, she's with a guy, and he's hot. The way his lips contrast with the hardness of his jaw makes me wonder whether maybe Vincent is not the only guy in the world, and I get so distracted I don't realise I'm being asked a question.

"Sorry, what?" We're standing outside the classroom, and the other girls are gaping through the window.

"Your mum," the hot guy cop says. "Any idea where she might have gone?"

"Nope."

"When was the last time you saw her?"

"When I got home on Friday night. We had dinner, watched Netflix."

"You, your mum and your dad?"

Like, duh. "Yeah."

"And the next morning?"

I glance at the redhead, who hasn't said a thing yet. Constable Z-something. Will she get into trouble if I mention our chat on Saturday?

She takes the lead. "Did you see her at all, Bobbi? Either before or after I came to speak to you at your house?"

I shake my head.

The hot guy keeps a poker face. "Bobbi," he says, and I like the sound of my name inside his mouth. I like it despite the anxiety burning the lining of my stomach. *Where is she? Where has she gone this time?* "Bobbi, do you know anything that might help us?"

Like, duh. But I say nothing.

The female cop takes over. "Listen. We want you to know that we'll find your mum. We're getting data from traffic cameras, questioning motel staff, her phone provider is letting us look through her call history. So don't worry. We're just asking these questions to speed things up. Okay?"

It's not okay, and I am worried, but I nod.

"Did she leave a note? Text you? Call you?"

"I texted her. Didn't get a reply."

"What did you text her about?"

"Money. I needed to buy a few things for the party on Saturday."

"You had a party on Saturday?"

"Nah. I went to one. Wanted to get some … chips and stuff."

The redhead breaks the rhythm of the exchange between me and the hot cop. "And by *chips and stuff*, you mean alcohol?"

"Well, yeah. Not like it's against the law."

"Actually, it is."

"Lady, I'm sixteen. I can have alcohol." Okay, almost sixteen. But still.

"Young people aged sixteen or seventeen can drink beer, wine or cider with a meal if it is bought by an adult and they are accompanied by an adult," the redhead one recites this in a voice that makes it clear she agrees with every word. "Under the *Sale and Supply of Alcohol Act*, the minimum legal age for the purchase of alcohol in New Zealand is eighteen years." She sounds like a law book until she asks, "Where do you buy your alcohol, Bobbi?"

"I don't." Truth. I don't buy alcohol. Xander does. His fake ID isn't very good, but the liquor store guy doesn't care. No way am I telling them that.

The redhead changes the topic. "So, about your mum."

No way am I telling them about my mum, either.

"Just find her," I say. "Bring her home. Please."

Madeleine Smith

At the end, she couldn't go through with the sex. After a few kisses, her body refused to cooperate. It was like trying to have another bite of pizza once you've already had three slices too many.

They managed to laugh about it, she and Louis. The laughter was also a good antidepressant.

"Want to get high instead?" she asked. Not waiting for the reply, she pulled out a few buds and rolled a joint. Her own stash, from her own farm. Sampling the merch.

Cannabis was not an antidepressant, certainly not in high doses. Still, Madeleine knew from experience that a few puffs would relax her, and sometimes that's all you could hope for when your children were acting up, your job was going to hell in a handbasket (whatever that meant) and it felt like your husband still lived at home with his mother, while you were an unexpected guest overstaying her welcome at their house.

"Anyway," Louis said while the tension in her shoulders released like a bunch of stretched elastics. "Sex was not the only reason I rented a motel room close by."

"Oh yeah?" She was too relaxed to feel curious.

"Yeah. I was hoping you could help me."

"Kay."

"I'm looking for my wife and daughter. They disappeared a few years ago. Wondered if you knew them. My girl, Courtney, is fifteen now. She might be a pupil at your school."

Alarm bells sounded in Madeleine's head. Muffled, as though they were ringing for another woman, in a different country, in a galaxy far, far away.

"No Courtney at my school," she slurred. Why was she slurring? Her head was as clear as the blue waters of Kai Iwi Lakes.

"She may have changed her name."

"To what?" Her joke was hilarious, and she hiccupped through her giggles.

"Madeleine. Look at the picture. Please. Does this woman look like anybody you know?"

Madeleine looked. "Wait. Is this Courtney, your daughter? Grown up already?" She slapped her thighs in mirth. So funny! She was being so fricking funny!

"Maddie, come on. Be serious. That's my wife. Do you know her?"

She wanted to answer, she did, but at that moment, drug-induced inertia spread through her veins like liquid concrete. She couldn't move a muscle. Even her tongue lay at the bottom of her mouth as useless as a slice of Christmas ham.

When the paralysis passed, another wave of laughter cascaded through her. She chuckled and chortled and even snorted. Tears stung her eyes and threatened to stream down her face.

"My wife is sick, Madeleine. She needs my help. If you know her, if you've ever seen her, you have to tell me."

His words were ice. Madeleine sobered up. "You're wrong," she said, her fingers already twisted through the straps of her handbag, her feet almost at the door. "I don't have to tell you anything."

She knew she shouldn't drive drugged up, so she called a local service to deliver her and her car home. Half-reclining in the passenger seat, her mind still on the poem she had discovered in Bobbi's room, Madeleine googled transgender students in New Zealand schools.

The legal side was simplified to this layman interpretation of the students' rights: "Transgender students have the right to an environment that will not damage their mental health. Schools need to, as far as reasonably practicable, eliminate risks to their mental health or if that is not possible, minimise those risks. A school can discriminate on the basis of sex when deciding to admit a student to a school but not after a student is enrolled."

But what if the student decided to … how did one phrase it? *Change gender? Transition?* Even the terminology eluded her. She scrolled on. One article caught her attention, about an exclusive all-boys school that was helping one of the students stay on as a female. "Our school's values—particularly respect and compassion—have guided us throughout this matter," the deputy principal had said.

What were Arcadia High's school values? Madeleine suppressed another giggle. Arcadia High—*High*, get it? When she could think straight again, her mind went back to the school values. Other than the no-internet rule, there were the usual slogans: holistic development, integrity, diligence, achievement. Individual happiness even.

What about compassion and kindness? What about respecting people's rights? Such things hadn't seemed important when she was starting up the school.

And now?

Now she was sure she'd missed something important. Not only kindness as a school value. Something bigger. Puzzling.

Then it came to her. Why had Louis shown her a picture of Olivia Kentwood with a wig on?

Constable Zero Zimmerman

Zero watched Bobbi's bouncing ponytail as the girl disappeared inside the classroom.

"What do you make of her?" Jackson asked. "You with your gift for reading people?"

She was going to deny it. Or tell him that she didn't read people the way a psychic or polygraph test might—more like a fake fortune teller, attuned to the nuances of clothes, body language, reactions to the things you said to them.

"How do you know about that?" she asked instead.

"Word gets around."

"Jackson."

"I've seen you in action, Zero. With colleagues, with people we interview, with me even. You know when someone fibs, you hear things that haven't been said. Like right now, quick, what am I thinking about?"

"Sex," Zero supplied automatically. Then she tried to backtrack. "That's what men usually think about, right? Plus, it's what you talk about all the time."

"Only when I'm with sexy constables, Constable. So, what do you make of Bobbi?"

She's hiding so many things, Zero thought, I don't even know where to start unravelling her story.

"I'll tell you what to make of Bobbi," a voice said.

The man who stepped out of the garden's shadows was large in a healthy, strong way. His naturally darker skin was browned deeper by the sun and the wind. Blue ink covered his biceps. His head was shaved, exposing a ridge of bone around the skull.

"And you are?" Jackson asked.

"Hep King's the name. Property manager."

"What's that when it's at home?"

"I fix stuff around the school. Not me personally. With fifty acres of land, that would be a tall order. My responsibilities include telling contractors when to prune the fruit trees and which bits of roof to fix first. Order new sports equipment. Check the lawn's been mowed in the right places by our woolly lawnmowers, and make sure their poop is removed in a timely fashion so that the students don't get it on their shoes."

His voice didn't match his athletic silhouette. It came out raspy, as though he suffered from a head cold, or from a habit of too many cigarettes. Given the summer weather, Zero thought the head cold was the less likely option.

She judged it was time to join the discussion. "Mr King. What did you want to say about Bobbi?"

"The only time she doesn't lie is when her mouth's closed."

That didn't strike Zero as particularly accurate. Sure, the girl hadn't been forthcoming with answers, but that hardly qualified as pathological lying. "You know her mother's missing?" she asked as a way of deflecting the conversation away from Bobbi's value as a potential source of information.

Hep King spat on the ground. "Again?"

They knew it already, but confirm and re-confirm, that was the bulk of detective work. "Happened before?"

"Sure."

"Mrs Kentwood would just leave her family and disappear?" Zero still couldn't wrap her head around it. She remembered her own mum's eternal motto: *Happiness is a Journey, Not a Destination.* Even when life had turned on its head last year, when Zero's sister had caused so much trouble, their mum had remained the calm centre of their household and their universe, holding the family together. The idea of Mum abandoning the family when the going got tough didn't even compute.

Jackson's reasoning took a slightly different track. "Mr Kentwood puts up with it?"

Hep King gave him a long eye. "Ever been divorced, son?"

"Nope. Why?"

"If I can give you one word of advice, from a man who's made that particular mistake already: don't. Don't get a divorce. Don't move out when your woman pisses you off. Don't wish for peace and quiet, because, son, there is nothing worse than peace and quiet." Hep King pointed an earth-stained finger at Zero. "When you two get married, and this one gets bitchy or nag-nag-nags at you, just do yourself a favour and picture another man sleeping in your bed every night, drinking coffee from your mug in your kitchen, watching your TV with your daughter. No amount of pride is worth that much, and it won't keep you warm on lonely nights, either."

With that, the property manager did an about-turn and melted into the shrubbery, before Zero could correct his misconception about her and Jackson's pending nuptials.

"Well," Jackson watched the maroon-coloured plant, still swaying from Hep King's passage. "He might have a point there."

"That a bad relationship is better than no relationship?"

"Not a *bad* relationship—an *imperfect* one. But that's not what I meant. He might have a point about us getting married."

Zero thought she'd misheard. "Sorry, what?"

"I'm not proposing right here right now. Just that it might be an idea to consider it. For the endgame."

"As opposed to what? A one-night stand?"

"Exactly. Think about it, Zimmerman."

"What I'm thinking right now," lied Zero, "is that it's time to see the Garden of Happiness."

Jackson's eyebrows shot up. "Is that some sort of a metaphor for having sex?"

"Nope."

Tucked away between the tennis courts and the native bush surrounding the school grounds, the Garden of Happiness was an oasis of scents and soothing sounds. The white-pebbled path wound through patches of mint, lavender, and something citrusy—lemon balm, perhaps? The whisper of a miniature waterfall blended in with the rustle of leaves in the trees nearby. A reflection pool shimmered silently in a far corner. Zero wondered how they stopped it from becoming a breeding ground for mosquitoes.

"A good spot for secret meetings," Jackson's tone was—for a change—matter of fact and not in the least suggestive. "You can see and hear it if people approach."

Zero searched the perimeter. "It's a dead end, though. You can't run or hide. Not a good spot if you don't want to be seen together."

"So where would you go if you wanted to meet a boy?"

"Why would I want to meet a boy?"

"Come on, Zimmerman. It's an all-girl school. You'd want to meet a boy for variety if nothing else."

Zero retraced their steps along the white-pebbled path, walked along the fence. Jackson followed. When they reached a narrow gap concealed by the vegetation, only Zero was small enough to fit through. The lonely path wound through the dense native flora, and after fifty or so steps she came upon a tiny clearing, tapering into another path on the other side. That path took her to a bush track leading east and west. Her map app showed her that eastwards lay deeper bush, but west would take her to the main road and to St Alban's Boys High just twelve kilometres away.

As she walked back, she scanned both sides of the path. She knew the sort of items she was likely to find: beer bottles, used condoms, hypodermics. What she found instead—less than half a metre from the path—surprised her. By the look of it, it hadn't been placed there too long ago.

Among the broad leaves of wild ginger lay a plastic lunchbox shaped like R2D2. Zero didn't hesitate as she snapped it open. Inside rested a folded piece of paper. It wasn't the same kind of paper as the one found in the pink envelope in Aiko's room, and the handwriting was different too—not Aiko's, by now Zero was familiar with the girl's calligraphy-like lettering—but she'd bet her last dollar the lunchbox formed a set with Aiko's Darth Vader water bottle and was now acting as an unofficial letter box, a throwback to a time when teenagers passed notes made of paper, not pixels.

The message was not punctuated, the words untidy. It read like a letter but was formatted like a piece of poetry.

No cap
I'm thinking Vin is catching feelings for ya
We should talk

Zero felt a million years old. Just the other day, it seemed, she had been a teenager. Now she had no idea what the words meant. "No cap"? What the hell? She tapped her phone, couldn't find a signal. Bloody Madeleine Smith and her no-internet gimmick.

Still, food for thought, to be sure. Who was Vin? And who had written the note? That it had been meant for Aiko went almost without question.

Something pulled her eyes deeper into the brush. She wouldn't have spotted it if she hadn't detoured from the path in order to pick up the lunchbox, and if she hadn't been standing there trying to decipher the message.

The something was a rough shack, almost totally concealed by the vegetation. Made mostly from the trunks of silver fern trees and insulated by woven flax leaves, it housed a roll of what Zero assumed was a sleeping bag, a thick foamy ground sheet and several blankets.

She sniffed: clean with no sign of mould.

A chill went down her spine. Was a serial killer using the shack to stalk and kill his victims in Arcadia High and St Alban's?

When she squeezed through the fence to where Jackson was waiting, she asked him to call it in.

"We can't," he said. "Not a shred of evidence this is connected to Aiko's poisoning or Olivia Kentwood's disappearance."

"Can't do it off the books, either. I'm fresh out of favours with the forensic team."

Jackson sighed as though he were acting on Broadway, pulled out his phone, selected a number. "Hi, long time. Yeah, yeah. Yeah. Listen. Yeah. Listen. Can you do me a solid?"

Constable Zero Zimmerman

When Zero got back to the police headquarters, she did what she had promised Bobbi: she requested data from traffic cameras on highways nearby Arcadia, while Jackson worked his magic with the Vodafone staff.

Jackson hit the jackpot first, A negative jackpot, anyway. Olivia Kentwood's phone disappeared off the grid on Saturday morning and hadn't been switched back on since.

He had requested the phone's history too and must have charmed somebody to get onto his request pronto, because here they were: all the texts and calls for the last three months. Jackson had already imported them into a spreadsheet and sorted by frequency. Zero felt the first drops of disappointment settle in her stomach: all Olivia Kentwood's texts and phone calls for the last three months had been to and from her husband, her daughter, the school office, the local GP, Madeleine Smith's mobile phone.

"No friends," Jackson stated as he handed the spreadsheet to

Zero. "No other family. Who lives like that?"

Zero scrolled through her own phone's history, then compared it to the spreadsheet and to the original printout. "No hairdresser, no beauty salon, no contact with fellow mums. She's a hermit."

"Or she's trying to hide something."

"Or she's trying to hide."

Jackson rubbed the right angle in his jawline. "Mm. No social media presence, either. Not under her own name, anyway."

They hit the camera footage next. The first lot was from ATOC, Auckland Transport Operation Centre, which monitored multiple traffic cameras across Auckland's motorways. By the end of the day, Zero spotted the white Ford Fiesta registered to Bobbi's dad but driven by Bobbi's mum across the Harbour Bridge on its way to South Auckland.

I must remember to chase up that number plate from Parvati Patel's photograph, Zero thought.

Before she could send herself a memo, though, another camera picked up the white Ford Fiesta at one of the airport's car parks.

Auckland airport was where the trail grew cold. Olivia Kentwood did not appear on any flight manifest, domestic or international. She had not cleared passport control, nor had she hired a car. She could have used an airport bus to get back into the city. More likely, though, she'd booked a domestic flight under a fake name. In theory, you had to produce a photo ID on request. In practice, nobody ever checked.

Airports also had cameras: security cameras. One phone call from Jackson, and fifteen minutes later they had the recorded footage from last Saturday. Nothing.

Zero stretched, massaged her stiff neck, then returned to the computer screen. "We should have software for this," she grumbled as she viewed waves of people walking through the airport.

Meanwhile, Jackson scanned footage from the airports in Wellington and Queenstown. No luck. What next? Nelson? Christchurch? Invercargill?

Jackson brought her a coffee. It was just right, but she didn't allow herself the luxury to take a mini break. She opened another link, calculated the earliest possible time Olivia could have landed in Christchurch. Scanned, scanned, scanned.

"Gotcha," she muttered under her breath when she spotted the now familiar figure.

"Where?"

"Christchurch airport. Why?"

Jackson's fingers danced on his laptop.

"Okay, now what?" she asked.

"Give me a second."

It took more than a second. It took less than a minute. "No Olivia Kentwood, or Olive Kentwood, or Liv Kentwood, doing anything in Christchurch throughout the history of the internet," he said. "No record of house ownership or rental, nothing in the local papers. A few Kentwoods on the Electoral Roll, but I doubt she's gone there to visit her in-laws."

"What's her maiden name?"

Jackson made the computer keyboard tap-dance. "Weird," he replied. "Can't find it. There is no record of Blair Kentwood marrying anybody."

"How about an Olivia Kentwood marrying Blair Somebody? He could have taken her name."

"Already checked. I'm all modern and woke like that."

Zero laughed. The term *woke* coming from someone like Jackson—very dark skin, for sure, but the least politically correct person she knew—produced an unexpectedly comical effect. "Touché.

So what's left? How about: some couples choose not to go ahead with the official mumbo jumbo, opting for living in sin?"

"Mm."

It wasn't the way he said it that tipped her off. It was that she'd said *sin*, and he didn't take up the bait. "What?"

"No record of Bobbi Kentwood being born, either."

Bobbi Kentwood

I tell the matron I have to go home for the night. She doesn't question it. Guess by now everyone knows my mum's missing.

Blair picks me up.

"How are you holding up, Bobbi?"

"Meh. You?"

"About the same. Want to stop in Albany Village for ice cream?"

I shake my head. We drive home in silence.

When we get there, I send Blair out for takeaways. I opt for Nando's Chicken because the closest one is a fifteen-minute drive away, and they're usually busy, so there's always a wait.

As soon as his car leaves the driveway, I go upstairs and into the main bedroom. They have a huge bed, super king size, and when I was small, we'd watch TV while lying on their bed under velvety blankets and spilling popcorn everywhere. Mum's side is the one further from the door, and I know her well enough to understand her conscious or subconscious decision to have the bulk of Blair between her and the dangers of the outside world. For years, I'd drag my desk chair to block my bedroom door every night before going to bed. I don't do that anymore. I refuse to be a victim.

This need to be in charge of my life is driving my actions now. One by one I open the drawers in my mum's nightstand. Fortunately, I don't find anything gross. Just a packet of Disprin, a tub of rose-scented hand cream (I sniff it as it's almost as though she's right here in the room with me), a wheat bag for cold winter nights, photos.

Mum is one of those people who actually composes photo books online and gets them printed. I open one at random: our train trip from Auckland to Wellington last winter. Another one is from our whale-watching holiday in Kaikoura a few months before the earthquake. Stewart Island. Hobbiton. Ninety Mile Beach which is apparently only fifty-five miles long, but still the most beautiful and terrifying thing I've ever seen—all that emptiness got into my head.

My friends ask me why we don't go overseas, not even to Fiji. I tell them there's enough to see in New Zealand, and that I want to explore the rest of the world by myself, without the parents as chaperones. The truth, of course, is that I can't apply for a passport.

My mum's overnight bag is not in her walk-in closet. From what I can tell, though, all her clothes and cosmetics are here. That freaks me out so much I almost forget to look in the attic. But when I do climb up the ladder, both get-away rucksacks are still there.

The Girl's Dad

He phoned his contact. "Have anything for me?"

"Not yet."

"Try harder."

Constable Zero Zimmerman

Just before midnight, so technically still on Monday and therefore within the deadline, Zero sent an email to Sergeant Sandeep Malhi.

Subject: Report for the Arcadia High poisoning. Body of the message: Still working on the report, sir. Possible links to two other deaths in the same community (teacher and another student), working theory suicide pacts or serial killer. Escalation as another member of the community (school parent) reported missing. Permission to continue with the investigation?

She had omitted the fact that Olivia Kentwood had been located in Christchurch. That would only de-escalate the situation without providing any clarity. Particularly as Olivia Kentwood didn't seem to exist.

Just before she went to bed, she remembered the Mekong Dragons file.

Tomorrow, she promised herself.

CHAPTER 15

Tuesday

Constable Zero Zimmerman

Zero's working day started with a reply from her superior officer giving her permission to commit *a limited amount of time* to the Arcadia High case and requesting an update on the Mekong Dragons by midweek. Midweek sounded reasonable, except it was already Tuesday.

Blair Kentwood and Olivia were not officially married, Olivia Kentwood didn't exist anywhere in the official paper trail under that name, and neither did Bobbi Kentwood.

All of which was unusual but didn't explain what happened to Aiko. Nor why Olivia had disappeared, only to arrive in Christchurch. Nor what had happened to her once she'd left Christchurch Airport.

After the tragic earthquake in February 2011, the city of Christchurch faced many challenges, one of them being crime spots that had sprouted up virtually overnight. As part of the rebuilding programme, ten new council-owned security cameras had been installed in Riccarton, Addington, Merivale, and New Brighton, bringing up the total to sixty-eight. Zero had been secretly glad the number wasn't one more, because Jackson would have been sure to comment.

"The cameras are monitored 24/7 at the Christchurch central police station," Jackson said the previous evening, before they left the office. "The thing is, though, they're located in the trouble spots. If Olivia Kentwood doesn't visit Addington or New Brighton, we're screwed. Also, if she wants to avoid security cameras, it's easy enough to google their position. And I believe there are signs on the ground informing the public the area is being monitored."

Zero thought for a bit. "Banks and some shops will have their own surveillance footage, surely."

"Yeah. Sourcing it, though? Forget it. We're talking hundreds, thousands. Most of their cameras will be looking inside their own building, anyway. They wouldn't record foot traffic just passing by."

"And, just on the off-chance they *did* pick up something interesting," Zero hazarded, "could you—"

"Sorry." He really had looked sorry. "They're all stored on their own networks. Not connected to the web."

They had parted with quick goodnights, and Jackson hadn't suggested anything inappropriate. Zero told herself she felt relieved. This morning, she hoped to catch up with him at the compulsory mental resilience workshop every police employee had to undergo on an annual basis, but Jackson must have been scheduled for another time slot.

During the coffee break, Zero overheard the workshop instructor talk to a group of cops about research into teenage girl self-harm. Zero stood to the side, listening. Aiko's doctors hadn't reported any cuts on her arms or thighs, but self-harm could have manifested in other ways. Like taking too many pills, for example.

The years 2006, 2009 and 2013—according to the instructor— each saw a disproportionate increase in suicide attempts by young teenage girls. Those calendar years corresponded to the invention of the "Like" button on Facebook, and other social media developments.

"Whether the correlation is causal or coincidental," the workshop instructor said, "the fact remains that girls get attacked on social media more often than not. And even if they happen to be free of cyberbullying, their social media experience will likely leave them with feelings of jealousy, inferiority and being excluded."

Nods all around. Most of the cops present were parents and grandparents. One or two were young enough to be barely out of school, and they were probably nodding from personal experience. Still, Zero wondered whether social media was to blame in Aiko's case, seeing that there was no internet in Arcadia. Would regular weekend exposure have been enough?

As far as compliance exercises went, today's workshop wasn't too bad. Instead of mindfulness, it talked about the amygdala, and the four make-you-feel-good hormones, and the parasympathetic brain responses. It didn't make anyone participate in stupid group activities of the pair-share-dare kind, and Zero wondered why the de-stressing techniques they'd learnt weren't being offered at schools around the country as part of the curriculum.

Before she drove to Arcadia, she stopped off at Starship Hospital, a facility dedicated to children and young adults. The nurse in charge confirmed that there was no change in Aiko's condition: she had described it as *stable*. The girl's mother was still at her bedside, but this time she was looking through a large folder. An art portfolio, Zero realised.

"See here," Mrs Hamasaki said without a preamble. "This picture. And this one. And this."

Zero looked, but she didn't see. "Yes," she said. "Remarkable. Aiko is a very talented—" she almost said *girl*, but corrected herself, "artist."

"No," Aiko's mother said. "Not that. Look again."

The likeness of every portrait was remarkable. There was Bobbi, her face almost life-like despite the odd choice of colours: purples and violets and all shades of pink except flesh and nude. Looking closer, Zero realised that there were miniature hearts hidden all over the drawing: in Bobbi's irises, in the shadow of her collarbone, in the strands of her ponytail. Some of the hearts looked full, others shrivelled up or broken.

Savannah's portrait was an orgy of orange, mandarin, and grapefruit hues. She looked as though the sun were rising out of her cheekbones, but her eyes reflected human skulls, like matching warning signs. Her lips were made of skulls and her skeletal fingers held a skull-shaped cup.

"This," Mrs Hamasaki pointed at Bobbi's face. "A good friend. But this one," the finger jabbed towards Savannah, "double-faced. One face hidden, one face a mask. Aiko's art talks in symbols and colours."

Indeed, now that she looked closer, she realised that the panda-like shadows around Savannah's eyes looked like a cartoon mask of a villain.

She really, really needed to speak to Savannah.

"What does this one mean?" Zero flipped through the papers and gestured towards a drawing of a boy—a young man really—with curly hair and glasses. His colours were variations of blue and his features hid words and phrases: *moon tiger, jigsaw, laws of love* ... or was that *lore of love?*

Was the boy the author of the cryptic note Zero had found in the *Star Wars* box on the school footpath? Or of the poem in Aiko's room? Or both? The forensic experts would have their say in due course, but the current wait time was a week at best.

Mrs Hamasaki snapped the folder shut. "Trouble," she said.

"Who is he, Mrs Hamasaki?"

"Not important who. Aiko has school. No time for boys."

"How does Aiko feel about it?"

"Same. Every time a boy is interested, Aiko tells him the same thing."

"Which is?"

"That she has enough friends already. No need for more."

Zero pointed to the picture. "So how is he different?" But she knew. Even without the word *love* daubed over his eyelids, the very fact that Aiko had drawn him would have sounded warning bells for any parent.

What must have been even harder for a parent as overprotective as Mrs Hamasaki, was the fact that the boy in the picture was naked.

Madeleine Smith

Miraculously, Madeleine didn't have a cannabis-induced hangover, so the morning started like most mornings, with the dawn full of tui song and Ashton's snoring. She touched his shoulder. The snoring stopped for a few seconds, only to pick up again, louder this time.

She slid her foot down his leg, the feel of lean muscle on those long bones a visceral reminder of why she had fallen in love with him. Or, if she was being honest with herself, why she had fallen in lust with him. The feeling of love came later, when she'd shown him the pregnancy test and seen the incomprehension in his face morph into joy, when he'd brought her sparkling water and fruitcake as she sat up in bed breastfeeding the twins, when he'd gotten up in the middle of the night to change nappies and serve bottles and bounce the twins to sleep one baby bundle in each arm.

That was before he'd started snoring. Or had she been so tired, she'd never noticed the snoring back then?

Her arm across his waist, she trailed her fingers downwards. Ashton murmured and shifted away. The snoring continued. A typical married morning.

When the alarm sounded, they both got up grumpy, her husband's face stamped with that expression of detached desolation she'd learnt to dread.

"I just want to die," he whispered, pulling the pillow over his eyes.

Frustration fizzed in Madeleine's veins, burst into her chest like hot lava. She was so fed up with all the drama. She'd heard it all before, and this morning, of all mornings, she didn't have the energy.

"I want to kill myself," he paraphrased.

Madeleine channelled her inner Eastwood: *Go ahead*, she thought, *make my day*.

Then she immediately felt remorseful. This was Ashton. Still the love of her life. As much as she hated pharmaceuticals, she wished he'd take something—anything—to lift his mood. This morning, the urge to have the old Ashton back was so strong, that she started researching antidepressants on her tablet computer while brushing teeth, the high-fluoride toothpaste dribbling from the corner of her mouth onto the silk of the dressing gown.

"*... you might see depression explained simply as a "chemical imbalance" or a "serotonin deficiency." Unfortunately, it's not that simple. We really don't know what causes depression or how it affects the brain. We don't exactly know how antidepressants improve ...*"

"What the fuck?" Ashton's voice, inches away from her right shoulder, startled her so much she dropped the toothbrush. "Why are you reading that?"

The foam in her mouth splattered into a myriad of miniature blue puddles on the creamy white carpet. "Ash—"

"You're not going to drug me!" He gripped her arms, spun her around so that he could shout directly into her face. "Fuck off! I hate you!"

"Let me go." Somewhere in the bowels of the house, the twins were getting ready for breakfast. She steadied her voice, lowered the volume. "Let go, I said."

He pushed past her, slamming the bedroom door on the way out. The worst aspect of the altercation, Madeleine reflected as she dabbed a face cloth into the toothpaste stains on her dressing gown, was how little it had affected her. She felt neither shocked nor hurt, as though her feelings had grown a thick skin a long time ago. She was low-key hoping (Savannah's phrase) that the boys hadn't heard, but then again, it was nothing they, or their half-sister, or Ashton's mother, hadn't heard before.

Bad example. They were setting a bad example for their children, and it had to stop. Would she be a better mother by walking away, or by staying and healing their family?

Perhaps she should just get a doctor to prescribe the antidepressants for her, and then sneak them to Ashton, without his knowledge, in the reusable eco-friendly water bottle he took to the gym?

The thought was so jolting she dropped the toothbrush for the second time this morning.

Is that what had happened to Aiko?

But no. The pill bottle had been lying right there. Madeleine had seen it. Aiko—it had to have been an accident.

Or, as much as she feared to admit it, even to herself, a suicide attempt.

She was already at the front door, going through her daily checking routine (handbag—check; laptop—check; lunch bag—

purposefully left empty in the pantry) when she heard Ashton's footsteps. His face looked caved in, collapsed on itself, his eyes glistened wet.

"Don't leave me," he said. "You're the only one who makes my life bearable. Never leave me."

No apology. Not that she would have forgiven him had he told her he was sorry, but at least it would have been a gesture of sorts, an acknowledgement that he'd done her wrong. Instead, there was just another demand. Like a vampire feasting on her time and her emotions.

She wondered how it was possible to love someone, despise him, and feel indifferent towards him all at the same time.

In sickness and in health, that's what they had promised one another. *In sickness and in health*. But was Ashton's conduct attributable to sickness, or bad manners, or jerk-like personality? And if she stayed, would she be supporting her husband in need, or enabling his abusive behaviour?

With a shudder, she realised she was analysing her husband's actions the way she would Savannah's; as though he, too, were an insolent teenager in need of guidance and connection. This shouldn't surprise her at all, really: the truth of it was that in age, her husband was closer to Savannah than to Madeleine.

Constable Zero Zimmerman

Jackson's call came just as Zero was getting into her car, ready to head for Arcadia High. "The sergeant says we have to talk to Blair Kentwood. Ask what his wife's real name is."

"Don't we want to play it close to the chest?"

"Apparently not. I'll pick you up in ten?"

"I'm on the road. *I'll* pick *you* up in ten."

"Ha! You think I'm easy, Zimmerman? You'd better give me a

good pick-up line, or I won't cooperate."

Zero refused to admit she'd spent the entire time between the hospital and the police station thinking up pick-up lines. But when Jackson swung the passenger door open and paused expectantly, all she came up with was, "You're getting in, or what?"

Not her best work.

A broad grin split his face. "Are you coming on to me, Zimmerman?"

"Wait, what?" She replayed her words and gritted her teeth. Honestly, Jackson could make even a *good morning* sound like double entendre.

Zero didn't think. She just floored the accelerator, and the car door handle flew out of Jackson's hand. She stopped a hundred metres down the street and waited for him to catch up. It felt good.

They rode to Blair Kentwood's house in silence, apart from the background noise of Jackson's music selection emanating from his phone.

"Sorry," he said as they waited at the red door.

"Good."

The door swung open. Blair Kentwood's face looked like he hadn't slept in a week. This was Jackson's case, so Zero waited for him to take the lead.

"Mr Kentwood," he began.

"Have you found Olivia?"

"Yes and no, sir. We don't know where she is at the moment, but we know where she went when she left home. May we come in?"

Blair Kentwood led them back to the living room. The sofa swallowed them into its chocolate embrace. Jackson explained about Christchurch and the security cameras.

"Your wife didn't fly under the name Olivia Kentwood. We're

busy cross-checking the aeroplane's manifest with the voter roll," he told Blair. "Might work out her assumed name by process of elimination. But it would speed things up if you could tell us what her maiden name was?"

Blair was still for a few seconds. "We're not officially married."

"So what's Olivia's last name?"

"I'm afraid I don't know."

They waited.

"Look, she came into my life with baggage, all right? A past she didn't want to talk about. At night, she'd wake up screaming. By daylight, she'd watch the shadows. A few months into our relationship, we were in a restaurant, and she disappeared between the main course and the dessert. Climbed out the bathroom window and didn't come home that night. Bobbi must have been five or six at the time. I paid the babysitter to stay the whole night in case Bobbi woke up and wanted her mum. In the morning, Olivia walked into the house with a bottle of milk and fresh bread rolls, as though she had just popped out to the shops."

"And you've never asked?"

Blair's shoulders slumped. "Of course I've asked."

"And?"

"She said it was safer if I didn't know."

"Safer for you?"

"For all of us."

Bobbi Kentwood

Just like I see Vincent as Vincent—not the younger brother of a guy who committed suicide, I never think of Mrs Linden in terms of Theo. To me, she's my mental health counsellor and also Vincent's mother. Always Vincent's, never Theo's.

I can't even comprehend her loss, although, when I catch my own mum looking at me, sometimes I almost get it. The way my mum looks at me, it's like I'm the centre of the universe. Like she's playing violin in the orchestra and I'm the conductor.

Should make me feel special.

It makes me afraid.

She's the parent, but in our relationship it's like I'm the one in charge. If I'm happy, she's happy. If I hurt, she coils in pain. She wants to fight my battles before I begin them and bulldoze over obstacles I haven't even noticed yet.

Perhaps all mothers are like this.

But I bet you nobody else's mum disappears.

And I bet nobody else's mum has two rucksacks permanently packed with essentials and stored in the attic.

Mum has never been gone this long and I'm worried that I will end up saying way, w-a-a-a-y too much to Mrs Linden when I see her at my emergency appointment. Today, the world is grey even though the weather is a hundred percent sunshine. Today, I have a giant hand around my chest, squeezing the breath out of me with every passing minute. Today, Mum is all I think about.

That's why I make an error of judgement.

"Have you any idea where your mum is?" Mrs Linden asks. She has this way of posing questions—like a doctor, not like a police officer. You want to tell her everything so that she can prescribe a pill to solve all your problems.

A pill … My mind hovers around Aiko and the sleeping pills. Did she think they were a solution? A shudder builds up between my shoulder blades, shoots upwards into my neck.

"Bobbi?"

"Sorry, Mrs. Linden. I was miles away. No, I've no idea where my mum is. But I'm worried—" I break off, force myself to swallow the rest of the sentence.

"Bobbi?"

I shake my head.

"If you know something about your mum, you have to tell the police."

"No way. He has friends in the police. He'll find out."

"Who?"

My lips are hurting from pressing together, my tongue feels glued to the dry roof of my mouth.

"Bobbi—"

"No!"

"Listen to me. We have to find your mother. What if she's in danger?"

I know the answer to that one. I don't say it aloud, but it forms in my head one perfect word after another: *That's an* if. *But you know what's not an* if? *That she'll be in danger when he finds her.*

Constable Zero Zimmerman

Sitting in the school's reception area once again, Zero wondered whether Madeleine Smith's entire wardrobe was stitched out of sea water. So far, she'd seen her in variations of turquoise and greyish green. Today's green was flecked with gold splotches, as though sunlight were sliding off the ocean's waves. Would Madeleine's black dresses look like the ocean in moonlight, Zero wondered, the matte black of diving beneath the surface at night, or the black sheen of an oil spill?

Jackson, sprawled in the armchair next to Zero, stood up and waited for Madeleine to settle down before he returned to his seat. He didn't seem distracted by the principal's apparel. "Please accept our apologies," he'd said after introducing himself, "we should have contacted you sooner." He flashed his super-white teeth at Madeleine in what Zero knew to be a grin calculated to charm and disarm.

It worked. The woman smiled back with her eyes as well as her mouth, before Jackson's words turned into meaning inside her head. "Why should you have contacted me sooner? What happened? Is Aiko …? I spoke to the hospital this morning …" She stopped talking, her gaze turning from Jackson to Zero and back again.

"No news of Aiko," Jackson replied. "Sorry. However, Bobbi's mother is missing. Has been since Saturday. We came by your office yesterday." He left it there, a statement, not a question.

Madeleine shifted in her seat. "Yesterday?" Playing for time. She was impenetrable like the ocean portrayed by the colour of her clothes. A pair of eyeglasses appeared in her hand, seemingly out of nowhere, and she perched them on her nose.

The rectangle of the window reflected its blue sky off the lenses, making it impossible for Zero to see the expression in the headmistress's eyes. She suspected they were just a fashion accessory, intended to make Madeleine look more like an education specialist, hiding her true self.

"Let me get this straight," Madeleine's voice was back to normal—professional, in control. "Mrs Kentwood has been missing for four days? That's simply awful. Does Bobbi know?"

"She does."

Zero and Jackson had decided not to reveal the camera sighting of Olivia Kentwood in Christchurch. The facts of the case remained unchanged: a woman left her home, her husband, her child— without as much as an explanation. She wasn't reachable by phone. Her whereabouts in Christchurch were unknown. Added to that, she didn't even exist, and neither did her teenage daughter.

"Poor Bobbi." Madeleine sounded as though she meant it. "How can I help?"

Jackson tapped his lower lip with his index finger, as though contemplating the question. "Do you know anything that could shed light on this incident?"

A pause. "Can't think of anything offhand."

"Do you know Bobbi's mum well?"

Another pause. "Better than most."

"Why do you say that?"

Zero observed the involuntary blink behind the headmistress's eyeglasses. "Bobbi's been at our school for several years. Her mum comes to every parent-teacher interview, helps with school functions, sits on the Board of Trustees. I have more contact with her than with other parents."

So, nothing about Bobbi and Madeleine's daughter being friends. Was that simply a mother's instinct at play, the need to protect her child? Or was she deliberately concealing something?

Jackson flashed Madeleine a melt-on-the-spot smile. "That's perfect! Please tell us everything you know about Mrs Kentwood."

"What can I possibly tell you that will be helpful? She's lovely. A good person. Kind-hearted. A bit shy—likes to stay out of the spotlight. Wouldn't even pose for our annual Board of Trustees photo. She's devoted to her daughter, that's very clear when you see them together. Child-raising experts say—" She broke off. "Sorry. I'm gossiping."

"This is a missing person case, Mrs Smith."

"Of course, I understand that."

"So what do child-raising experts say?"

"It's just that, well, it may not be in the child's best interest to think that she's the centre of the world."

"Bobbi is a spoilt little princess?"

Madeleine Smith adjusted her spectacles. "I'm not putting this very well. Sometimes Olivia—Mrs Kentwood—acts as though she doesn't have a life of her own. Everything is about Bobbi's needs."

"For example?"

"Bobbi gets facials and massages, practically every weekend. She wears designer clothes to parties. Does horse riding—that's a rich person's sport in Auckland. Her mum attends every night of every school play. When Bobbi didn't understand trigonometry, her mum hired a private tutor, even though our teachers offer lunchtime and after-school help with their subjects."

"So what would make her leave Bobbi without warning? Tell me, as a mother."

Madeleine spread her arms in a universal signal of helplessness. "To protect her daughter somehow? Sorry, that's all I can think of."

"From what?"

This time the helpless gesture appeared less genuine. Zero took out her notebook and jotted down her observations, more for show than out of a real need. "All right," she said when she was done. "Perhaps there's something else you can assist us with. I have a few more questions, although they're unrelated to Mrs Kentwood's disappearance. Probably only marginally connected with the events leading to Aiko's hospitalisation. Please bear with us as we attempt to clear them out of the way."

Madeleine nodded.

"Our society is beginning to recognise transgender and pangender persons," Zero said and observed a slight shift in Madeleine's posture, a squaring of the shoulders as though she were bracing for a blow. "How does an all-girl school deal with someone who was born male but is transitioning to becoming a female, for example? Or the reverse?"

"I really don't see how it's relevant."

Liar, Zero thought. Aloud she said, "As I explained, it may not be." She wasn't going to tell the headmistress what she found on Aiko's phone.

"It's complicated." Madeleine's index finger tapped the wooden armrests of her chair, one-two-three, as though she were typing three exclamation marks into an emotion-filled Facebook post. "The law is of no help when it comes to gender-fluid issues. The Ministry of Health has guidelines on making schools safe for transgender students, and how to support students of minority sexes and sexualities, but in reality, there is no law that says a girls-only school should enrol someone who is transitioning from being one gender to another. A lot of it is guided by the school community, the students as well as the parents. You might remember a …" she hesitated, looking for a word, "a lively discussion in the media a few years ago about the use of school toilets?"

Zero and Jackson nodded in unison. A male student in one of New Zealand's schools was transitioning to becoming female and wanted to use the girls' toilets, instead of the unisex ones. Because the common areas of the toilets also served as a changing room, a few girls felt uncomfortable undressing in front of someone who looked like a teenage boy, irrespective of what gender the person identified as.

"Schools overseas are a lot more advanced," the headmistress continued. "We're still playing catch-up here."

Zero thought for a moment. "Right, so here's a hypothetical for you. Let's say that a student transitioning to a female applies for admission to Arcadia. How would you handle it?"

"We have very strict admission criteria here, and a long waiting list."

Zero raised her eyebrow. "Meaning what?"

"Meaning that, to be completely honest, I'm afraid the easiest course of action would be to fail such a student on their CV. Find something in the behaviour record, or give preference to a student with a better academic history—"

"For real? Didn't an all-boy school recently accommodate a pupil of theirs who decided to transition to a female?"

"It's not me, and it's not personal," Madeleine said quickly. "It's just … working with teenage girls is difficult enough. You're dealing with body image issues, maths confidence issues, boy issues, emotional bullying. You're dealing with their very real embarrassment of changing for a PE class in front of someone who looks like a boy. Also, girls excel at excluding people from their cliques, and the idea of a transgender student trying to fit into that environment is just heart-breaking." She paused, took in a long breath. "Is that enough of a hypothetical, detective?"

Jackson took that one. "I'd like to have a look at all of Miss Patel's emails, please. Her online history, too. May I take a look at the device she was using while employed by your school?"

Madeleine lifted her eyebrows as though taken aback by the sudden change of topic but she went with it. "Certainly. If it's password-protected, though, I won't be able to help you."

"That's all right."

Jackson stood up when Madeleine got to her feet, and he remained standing until she emerged back into the reception area carrying a black laptop case. "Thank you, Mrs Smith."

Zero also rose. "Can we see Aiko's room again?"

"Of course. But … please don't think I have any objections, it's just—why? What are you hoping to find?"

"Need to check something."

Jackson gestured towards the laptop case. "I'll stay here."

Constable Zero Zimmerman

The previous time Zero was at the school, they had cut across the sun-drenched courtyard, straight to Aiko's room. But now raindrops dripped from the sky outside, straight onto a huddle of black sheep, so Madeleine Smith led Zero around the terracotta-tiled courtyard and along two corridors. As they walked, Zero paid attention to the doors on the left and the right.

"Why isn't Aiko's room together with those of the other students?"

Madeleine stopped. "There was a fire in Aiko's room at the beginning of the school year. The smell was unbearable. Still is. We had to move her."

"A fire?" Zero thought. Another accident? Arson? Had somebody attempted to kill Aiko weeks ago? "How did it happen?"

"Oh, it was just carelessness. The girls—Aiko and her friends—lit candles in her bedroom. A moment of clumsiness was all it took. Our carpets are natural, pure wool, and unfortunately very flammable. Would you like to see Aiko's old room as well?"

"Please."

The front of the school building overlooked fields and parkland, while the bedrooms at the back faced the ocean. The view from Aiko's old bedroom took Zero's breath away. It made her think of a painting: a rolling meadow, waves on the water, a few boats. She almost exclaimed when a jet ski cut a white line of seafoam across the landscape. Why would anybody need the internet if one could just look out the window?

The smell in the room contrasted sharply with the picturesque landscape outside—the acrid stench of burnt fabric mixed with the corrosive smell of the fire extinguisher. No wonder Aiko had to move out. There were photographs on the walls and Zero moved across to have a look. She felt a little nosy and self-conscious. Undamaged by the fire, the photos were attached to a golden grate by tiny golden pegs. They were made to look like the self-developing photos of the 1980s, stiff with a huge white border, except that these were five times bigger and a million times higher resolution.

Zero thought back to the photo she'd found in Aiko's reading book, the one with the guy who could have been her dad. There was no sign of him in these images. She wondered what Aiko's stepfather looked like, but she couldn't find him in any of the pictures, either. Not even at the Christmas dinner with mum and grandparents. Perhaps he was the one behind the camera lens? Zero counted the set places around the table: one for Aiko, one for her mum, two for the grandparents. All present and accounted for, the photo must have been taken on a timer. So where was her stepfather?

She quickly checked the cupboards and drawers. All empty. The photo display was the only item left behind, possibly because Aiko didn't have a wall hook in her new room, or because she wanted to believe that the move was temporary.

"Constable?" Madeleine prompted.

"Sorry, yes. Thank you. Can we go back to the room Aiko occupies now?"

As soon as Zero walked into Aiko's temporary room, she realised something had changed. She looked at the book, the gold chain, the walls, the bed. Ah, the bed. The duvet cover was as white as ever. The black writing on it, however, was different. Zero read it again. "Schrödinger's cat is alive," it said. She was convinced last time she'd seen it, the writing proclaimed the cat to be dead.

She tilted her neck. Right. Depending on whether she was reading the inside or the outside of the letters, the black or the white, the words spelled out "dead" or "alive." Just a matter of perspective, depending on how you looked at it, but also—inadvertently—an ironic parallel to Aiko's present condition.

For a fifteen-year-old girl, it was a super nerdy cover. "How do the students keep up to date with music, and the celebs, and teenage trends?" she asked.

"We don't restrict their internet activities when they're back home on weekends and holidays."

Still, Zero mused. No internet to check the lyrics of *The Louvre* or whether koalas were true bears. The girls at Arcadia High must feel really disconnected. Isolated. Frustrated?

No wonder Aiko had all those non-fiction books. *Surely You're Joking, Mr Feynman*, a thesaurus, *World Mythology*, a few books on genetics, and—yes, that's what had been bugging her: a book on tarot card readings.

No tarot cards though. She quickly double-checked all the drawers, but she already knew. Aiko's tarot cards were currently in Miss Patel's suitcase.

Zero moved on. She re-discovered a drawer full of art supplies, just as she left it after she'd searched the room on Friday. This time, though, she knew what she was looking for. More drawings.

She only found three. One was an incomplete landscape of the school grounds, with a green sheep in school uniform grazing on ultra-green grass, cutting the letters *Baaah* into the lawn in blood-red—a no-brainer in terms of its symbolism. The other was of Aiko herself, one half of her face exactly like her face, the other with a moustache and a five-o'clock shadow, all in charcoal. Zero angled this one in such a way that the headmistress couldn't see it—the gender deliberation was Aiko's secret, after all. The third drawing was of a young-looking woman standing next to a swimming pool.

"It's Miss Patel," Madeleine said. "Oh dear."

Oh dear was right. The drawing, sketched in a watery-blue medium like pale ink, featured Miss Patel, although Zero doubted that Miss Patel's breasts had in reality been bigger than her head. The other silhouette was that of a teenage boy reaching up from the bottom of a swimming pool, his hand sticking out of the water, holding out a heart. A real human heart, with ventricles and blood vessels.

"Do you know who the boy is?"

Madeleine shook her head. "The drawing of the boy is much too small to see any detail. Sorry."

Although Madeleine had a point about the size—most of the paper was taken up by the drawing of Miss Patel—Zero wasn't going to let her off the hook. "But you have your suspicions?"

"Not facts."

"This is not a court of law, Madeleine. I don't need evidence. A wild guess will do."

The headmistress pressed her lips together. "I wouldn't know."

This was another untruth for the constable's notebook. And another photo of an artwork for her phone's collection of images.

Madeleine Smith

When she said goodbye to the cops, Madeleine's thoughts kept swirling back to Olivia Kentwood. She assumed she understood why a mum might have wanted to grab the car keys and drive off into the sunset for a few hours. Teenage girls were tricky to get along with, their storm of adolescent hormones mixing dangerously with your own imperfect premenopausal storm, their instinct telling them exactly where to attack you to deliver the most impact.

So as a mum you'd drive to a beach and take a walk, or drive to a motel and spend the night, but you wouldn't be able to stay away longer than that. At the very least, you'd text. Four days of no contact—that was unthinkable. Surely Olivia would realise how much Bobbi worried.

Madeleine hesitated, then fished out Constable Zimmerman's business card from her desk, punched in the number. Phone or text? She wasn't sure what to say in it either. Phone then.

"Hello, Constable." She knew her tone came across hesitant and imagined herself addressing an assembly hall full of parents. "When you have a moment, I'd be grateful for a return visit. There's something I'd like to share with you."

"We're still on the premises," the cop said. "Be with you in ten."

What were they still doing here? What if they found the crop? It had been careless of her to let them walk around unsupervised, though, to be fair, the secret garden was hidden well enough to protect it from students roaming the school grounds. She was just being paranoid.

Still, when the copper-haired constable returned to the reception, Madeleine offered silent thanks to Olivia Kentwood for the distraction she would provide. Selfish? Yes. Heartless? Maybe. Effective? She could only hope.

"As I mentioned before, Constable, Olivia Kentwood is on the school's Board of Trustees. She also happens to be my next-door neighbour. We're not close friends, but we socialise in the same circles and have got to know one another over the years. A few Christmases ago, a barbecue get-together got out of hand." She replayed that last sentence in her head. "In a good sense, I hasten to add. We all had fun, drank a bit too much, passed the rude-joke stage to the confessions stage. Olivia told me that she and Bobbi were hiding from her husband—that's Olivia's ex-husband, obviously."

Madeleine paused, glanced at Zero, but couldn't read her. "She never explained, but I got the impression it wasn't anything like," she stumbled over the next words, "child abuse or domestic violence." Not that Madeleine could claim to be an expert on either. "He could have been a drug lord maybe?" Okay, she could claim some expertise in the drug lording department. "Or a spy? Does New Zealand have any spies, Constable?"

"You mean like intelligence officers? Or counterintelligence? We do indeed. Probably have more drug lords than spies though."

Madeleine couldn't force a laugh. She nodded instead. "Sounds about right. Olivia told me that she lived in constant fear for their lives. The two of them, Olivia and Bobbi, ran from place to place, never settling anywhere for long, lying low, moving on before he'd get a chance to find them."

"Do you think Mrs. Kentwood ran away?"

"No. She wouldn't have left Bobbi."

"Right. Okay. I can tell there's something you're not saying."

Madeleine paused. "The story of hiding from her ex has always sounded too melodramatic, like something you'd binge-watch on Netflix. I'm not sure I believe any of it. Or, more accurately, I used to be not sure."

"And now you are?"

"Now that she's missing, I'm convinced she was telling the truth."

It was a good hour after the cop had left that Madeleine suddenly remembered something else. Louis and his questions and the photo of Olivia Kentwood wearing a wig.

Constable Zero Zimmerman

Jackson was waiting for her in the car with Miss Patel's laptop. One email was already opened, spanning the entire width and height of the screen.

I greet you, it said. *I have bad news for you. I hacked your operating system and got full access to your account. It is useless to change the password, my malware intercepts it every time. I looked at the sites that you regularly visit and came to the big delight of your preferred resources. I'm talking about sites for adults. You are a big pervert. You have unbridled fantasy! I strongly believe that you would not like to show these pictures to your relatives, friends, or colleagues. I think $50,000 is a very small amount for my silence.*

Zero looked up at Jackson. "What the hell?"

"The weird thing is I've checked this laptop."

"Let me guess. No history of visiting adult sites?"

"None. Parvati Patel's online presence was limited to communicating with her family back in India. She didn't seem to have a boyfriend or any friends."

"So this email is—what? A scam?" Then her brain caught up with her ears. "Wait, what? What do you mean? No boyfriend or friends? For the whole two years she was in New Zealand?"

"This laptop is almost brand new. Parvati Patel must have been using a different laptop when she worked at St Alban's."

Zero opened her mouth but Jackson beat her to it. "I know, Zimmerman. Can I be a lamb and find out what happened to the computer Parvati Patel used at her previous place of employment? Yes, I can. I can be a lamb. Or a tiger. Whatever you like. Do you prefer lambs or tigers in bed?"

"Neither. I need to talk to Savannah now."

Jackson glanced at his phone. "She has science right now. In the lab building. That's separate from the classroom building, north-east of here."

"Jackson, for crying out loud, how should I know where north-east is?"

But she was teasing. She had always known how to find her way out of the deepest forest, out of the crinkliest back streets in Bucharest and Auckland alike, out of lies straight into the truth.

What she didn't know yet was how to find her way in the current mystery.

Bobbi Kentwood

I see Constable Zimmerman as soon as I walk out of the science lab. Savannah must have assumed it's bad news, because her hand goes to mine and squeezes. The pressure shoots up from my fingers into my chest.

"My mum?" I say through a throat that doesn't work.

"She's in Christchurch somewhere," the policewoman replies. "We've identified her face on a security camera at the airport. Any idea why she would fly there without letting you know?"

My heart slows down enough for me to regain my wits. I shake my head. "No, sorry," I add for emphasis.

No way am I telling her about the false breadcrumb trails Mum lays for my biological father a few times a year. Besides, this feels different: her usual Hansel-and-Gretel trips are shorter.

The constable gives me a long, steady look. She can spot the lie, I'm sure, but she lets it go. "All right. I don't want to keep you girls from your next class, but can you answer a few questions?" She doesn't wait for us to reply. "First of all, was Aiko religious?"

Savannah and I look at each other.

"Not in an uncool way," she says. "But yeah. Church on Sundays. Big into Christmas in a non-commercial spiritual way. That sort of thing."

"Do you think her faith would prevent her from trying to take her own life?"

I haven't considered that, and I see neither has Savannah. "I mean ..." She shrugs.

Exactly. Who knows, right?

"All right. Can you tell me whose lunchbox this is?" Her hand holding the phone is positioned exactly halfway between me and Savannah, the curves of R2D2 unmistakeable.

"Aiko's," we chorus. We could have rehearsed it.

"And this handwriting?"

Another photo, this one of just two words on a piece of paper: *No cap*. With a capital N and no punctuation.

"Not Aiko's," I say at the same time as Savannah pipes up: "Not mine."

"And not mine," I add for good measure.

"All right." This time the constable's steady gaze stays glued to my face. "Who has a crush on Aiko?"

I can't bring myself to say Vincent's name. Savannah is also silent. Out of loyalty to me? Because she doesn't want to mention DK and she doesn't know about Vincent's feelings?

The constable pinches the photo on her phone, shows us the screen again.

No cap
I'm thinking Vin is catching feelings for ya
We should talk

"What a douche bag," Savannah lets go of my hand and rushes off. I know that tell-tale curve of her shoulders—she's crying.

"Who wrote that, Bobbi?" the constable asks.

"DK, at a guess. He's the only guy I know who'd say they should *talk*. Guys don't talk."

"So why is Savannah so upset, Bobbi? Does she like DK? Or Vin?"

I shrug. Shake my head.

"What does *no cap* mean?"

Guess I could tell her that. "Means, like, it's serious, no kidding. That sort of thing." Makes me feel good to know something she doesn't. Perhaps I could study to be a teacher.

"Why does it mean that? Is it short for something?"

I go back to a shrug accompanied by silence. Maybe I don't want to be a teacher, after all.

"Never mind," the policewoman says. "I'll google it. Now, perhaps you can tell me who this is?"

I stare at another photo, this one of a piece of art. No point denying it. "Definitely DK."

The drawing style is Aiko's for sure. And from the twist of his mouth, I'm sure he must have posed while she worked.

DK.

Posed.

For.

Aiko.

Without.

His.

Clothes.

Poor Savannah, I think. And I mean it.

But I'm also a little glad. We feel the same pain, she and I. She over DK, me over Vincent. Like being best friends again. Twins.

"Bobbi?"

"Yes, ma'am?" The damned school etiquette again. I long for the freedom to say "What?" or "Yo?" to an adult.

"We found this in Aiko's room. After she took the pills. Any idea who might have written it?"

The policewoman swipes the screen of her phone and points it at me again. It's a photograph of a poem. The world spins around me in a brown *whoosh* that blocks out her questions. The school bell pierces through my shock. I use it as an excuse to run off.

Madeleine Smith

Should she tell the police about Louis? Absolutely. But what would she say? The events of the previous day swam in and out of her memory like drunk butterflies: transient, flimsy and unrealistically psychedelic. Which bits were authentic, and which conjured up by cannabis smoke scrambling her brain?

She picked up the phone. Put it down again. This wasn't like her. Her normal self was decisive. She picked up the phone again, glanced at the screen.

Shit.

Shit—shit—shit.

Her normal self was totally aligned with her daily schedule and her to-do list. Yet here it was, a calendar reminder for an appointment she was nearly going to be late for. For Madeleine Smith, mother and principal, such forgetfulness was unthinkable.

She didn't feel like going for her mammogram today of all days, but she was not the type of woman to cancel an engagement, break a promise, or quit something she had started. As soon as the lessons were over and the girls had congregated in the cafeteria for their afternoon tea, she drove out the school gates and headed south towards Auckland.

Despite the heat, she kept the windows rolled down, choosing the humid country air over the iciness of the car's air con. The smell of the sea and sun-drenched vegetation accompanied her all the way to the state highway, where petrol fumes took over.

That's why she hated going into the Big Smoke. Over the years, she'd become more and more of a suburban queen: shopping at the local food market, going out to the local coffee shop whose manager had graduated from Arcadia a few years back, having her hair cut at the local hairdresser who worked from home.

The women's clinic was decorated in muted blues. She filled in a short form, put on a linen dressing gown and was escorted to the torture chamber. No matter how much they told you it wouldn't hurt, it always did. Always.

"Now lean into the machine like this," the technician said, splaying her right boob on the hard, cold surface. A little more. Feet closer. That's the way. Now, is it all right if I touch your head? Sorry, I have to ask in case of cultural or religious objections."

Political correctness gone mad. *You've already touched my breast,* Madeleine thought with unusual sarcasm, *so I guess it's all right to progress up the intimacy levels.* She didn't say it though. The protocols were what they were, the signs on the walls claiming the right of both the patient and the medical staff to be treated with respect. Respect. She liked that. Perhaps she could hang such a sign at home. What would it say?

Both the parents and the children have the right to feel loved and respected. Would she extend the sentiment to include Granny Smith? She doubted she'd ever feel that magnanimous.

In this house we practice kindness and forgiveness. Madeline could just imagine Savannah's comment: "Mum! That's so passive-aggressive!"

Was calling someone passive-aggressive, passive-aggressive in itself? Or was it just aggressive?

How about something more inspirational? *Mental wellbeing is a process, not a destination?* Please. Too many people nowadays, especially teenagers, were being handled with kid gloves. How many mental health issues would just go away if they weren't so damned fashionable?

"Ouch." Madeleine gritted her teeth against the pain of her breast flattening between two gigantic presses.

"You're doing very well," the technician told her, removing her boob from the machine. "Now the other side, please."

Oh joy.

The only upside of today? Still no word from the drug gang.

Constable Zero Zimmerman

Jackson had already paved the way at St Alban's Boys High, so Zero Zimmerman wasted no time in securing interviews with Dakota Young and Vincent Linden.

Dakota, or DK as Bobbi had called him, was first. Zero had set up shop in an empty classroom that smelled of whiteboard markers and boy sweat. She tried for a balance of authority and approachability, perched on the edge of the teacher's desk with her feet on the ground.

The young man who knocked on the door sported an unruly mop of hair and Bill Gates spectacles. "I'm DK, and my pronouns are he/him." He didn't offer to shake hands and flopped onto one of the desks before she could ask him to sit.

Zero decided to steer towards more formal. "Dakota Young?"

"DK."

"I'm in charge of looking into last week's incident at Arcadia High."

He waited.

"Do you know Aiko Hamasaki?"

"Yes."

"Did you know she's in hospital?"

"People talk."

"They sure do. What do they say?"

His hand shot up to his glasses, pushed them up, weaved itself through his hair before settling back on the desk in front of him. "That she tried to kill herself."

"And what do you think?"

"That's not like Aiko."

Zero waited and DK filled in the silence. "That's not what Aiko is like."

Not much of an explanation, then. "What *is* she like?"

"Cute. Smart. Serious. Normal."

"*Normal?*"

DK raked his hair again, adjusted his glasses. "Most girls are crazy. No offense, ma'am. But they shriek when they see something exciting or scary, they cry for no reason, they stop talking to you for weeks then blame you for ignoring them. They get depressed or anxious or whatever. Aiko is nothing like that."

Zero showed him a photo of the message she found in the *Star Wars* lunchbox and saw DK's shoulders relax. "You found it in the bush?"

"Yes." Briefly, she wondered why it was important to the boy. Then she understood. Of course. "You were worried that she did something stupid after she'd read the message?"

DK held completely still. Then he nodded.

"*Were* you going to break up with her?"

A half-hearted shrug. "Don't know. Probably. Vin is my best friend, you know? That's more important than scoring a chick. We talked, Vin and I, and he mentioned he wanted a chance with Aiko. He didn't know that she and I—" DK broke off. "Still doesn't know.

Please don't tell him. It means so little to me, and so much to him."

Zero showed him the painting of the nude figure next. Even without DK's reaction she could see the identity of the young man in Aiko's artwork.

DK stared at the photo in Zero's phone, his cheeks slowly darkening. "Oh fuck. This is private."

"You would think. But I found it in Aiko's art folder. And her mum has it."

"Fuck," he repeated.

"Language," Zero said, then bit her tongue. That single word made her sound exactly like her mother. She quickly swiped her phone's screen to reveal the painting of Miss Patel and a boy at the bottom of a swimming pool holding out a human heart.

"Ffff-far out." DK moved closer to the screen. "May I?" He zoomed in. "That's our teacher from last year. Miss Patel."

"What does the painting mean, do you think?" Zero was curious what someone Aiko's age would make of the art's symbolism.

"Somebody was into her."

"Into Miss Patel?"

"Yeah."

"Who?"

DK jutted out his chin, moved it from side to side as though chewing on the question. "Many of us had a thing for her last year. She was hot. Sucks that she's dead."

"Yes, it does suck." Zero waited a beat. "What's the boy doing in the swimming pool?"

"Drowning?"

A smart-arse answer if she'd ever heard one. "An astute observation, DK. Why do you think Aiko drew that?"

"Because," DK's tone was patient, talking slowly, like a teacher to a particularly dim-witted student, "Miss Patel drowned in a swimming pool. So the drawing is ironic. Reversed, like. Poetic licence, do you see?"

"Not really. But then I'm not into art."

DK's face said *your loss*.

The last photo Zero showed him was that of the poem she found in Aiko's room next to the pills.

"Don't know."

"Do you write poetry?"

"Sometimes. But it's not mine. Nor Vin's."

"You sure?"

"Positive. Not his writing. Not his style."

"Okay, thank you. Please send him in. Oh, and DK?"

"Yeah?"

"You mean, *yes ma'am*?"

"Yes, ma'am?"

"You happen to know about a shack in the bush right by Arcadia?"

"No, ma'am."

Vincent was the visual opposite of DK: a well-sculpted body and a buzz cut. His swagger was so ostentatious, it preceded the boy into the classroom with the way he swung his legs and stuck out his elbows. Posturing, making himself bigger than he was, puffing out his chest like a tui bird in his mating song.

"The girls had this poetry club," he said when Zero showed him the poem. "We met up a few times. Did a bit of writing. I don't recognise this one. Not one of those that got read out loud. But all you need is a sample of everyone's handwriting. There are these apps that can compare and match."

Another one for Jackson. Her debt to him was expanding at an alarming rate. What's worse, she was still no closer to knowing whether she was even chasing a failed murderer.

"Who's in the poetry club?"

"Me, DK, Xander. Bobbi, Savannah, Aiko."

"Who's Xander?"

"Xander Foreskin. I mean, sorry, Fiskin. His surname is Fiskin. He's in my form class."

Seeing that Zero's real name was Zara, she knew enough about school nicknames to let this one slide. "Tell me about Aiko."

"How is she?"

Zero tried to put a positive spin on things. "Progressing."

"Has she woken up yet?"

No way to spin that one. "Not yet."

Vincent looked close to tears.

Zero asked gently, "You really like her, huh?"

"To be honest, yeah. But my man DK got there first. So no hard feelings."

That last bit she didn't believe. You didn't have to be a human polygraph to realise that Vincent was still very much invested. Didn't he know that DK had stepped aside?

Zero spared him the drawing of his naked friend. Showed him the Miss Patel one though.

"Did Aiko do this one? She's so good!"

"Why do you think she drew that?"

"Don't know. The proportions are all wrong. Unrealistic. The female figure is much larger than the swimming pool."

That was a good point, Zero thought. In the drawing, Miss Patel was too large to fit into the swimming pool, certainly too large to drown in it. Wishful thinking? Had Aiko tried to rewrite the past? She asked, "And that signifies what?"

Vincent looked at her with incomprehension. "How do you

mean? It's just art. Doesn't signify anything. It's like trick photography. Playing with perspective?"

Clearly, Vincent was even less into art that Zero was.

"There is a shack, like a tent made from fern trees, right by the girls' school. Can you tell me anything about it?"

The boy squirmed. Actually squirmed, moved his frame side to side as though trying to wriggle out of his own skin. "It's like a joke, you know? Or wishful thinking?"

"How do you mean?"

"Xander built it. For Bobbi. In case she agreed to," his Adam's apple slid down when he swallowed, but he soldiered on, "to hook up with him. He worked on it Friday night and Saturday morning. To be honest, I thought it would have blown away in the storm Saturday night."

"It hasn't."

"Ah."

Zero didn't know where to go from there, so dismissed Vincent and wondered whether there was any merit in interviewing Xander Fiskin, but she didn't know what questions she could possibly ask. *Do you have feelings for Aiko?* Probably not, if he'd built the shack for Bobbi. What then? *Do you think Aiko took the sleeping pills on purpose? And if not, who would want to do her harm?*

Just then, a message from Jackson arrived on her phone. "Miss Patel's old laptop is now a wide-opened sesame waiting for you."

Yeah. A much better way to use her time.

She let it go.

Bobbi Kentwood

I'm sitting in class, and I don't even know whether it's maths or English. My brain superimposes the photo of that poem everywhere:

on my book, on the whiteboard, outside the window.

I can guess what the cop was asking: do I know whose handwriting it is? Indeed I do. It's mine. The words are scorched inside my heart.

so

you jerk me

back and forth

hot then cold

then silence

so

you speak poetry

woven with nothing

so

what do i

actually

mean to you?

How on earth did Aiko manage to get hold of my poem? Is that why she took those pills? Did she realise that she was the reason Savannah was jerking me around?

Is it all my fault?

Constable Zero Zimmerman

Outside St Alban's Boys High, Jackson was leaning on a wood-carved sign that said *Per Scientia ad Astra*. Zero remembered just enough Latin from her university days to understand it translated to *Through Knowledge to the Stars*.

"Jackson. Please tell me you bring me knowledge and insight."

Jackson pointed to the sign. "Sure you wouldn't want me to put stars in your eyes instead?"

"Ugh! What does that even mean?"

"Not everything has to be dirty talk, Zimmerman. Just want to see you happy, you know?"

The emotions rushing at her now were too complicated. "You said you found something?"

Jackson patted a laptop case swinging from his shoulder. "This is the teacher's old device, the one she used at St Alban's. It was passed on to Miss Patel's replacement, with the hard disk reformatted, but they didn't do a professional wiping job. I've already recovered the old contents. Haven't had time to read it. Want to get a coffee and have a look?"

She did.

Reading emails and documents recovered from a formatted hard disk was exactly like reading normal emails and documents. Zero was surprised it was all there: lesson plans, student reports, exemplars. Because the boys' school had internet, there were also lengthy email exchanges between Miss Patel and her students.

One boy in particular seemed to be more diligent than the others. Theo Linden emailed her every day for a period of almost four months, including the July school holidays. Parvati Patel's subject must have been history at St Alban's, because the emails went back and forth about the causes and consequences of using the atom bomb in World War II, as well as the effect of the Springbok Rugby Tour on New Zealand in the 1980s.

"Boring." Jackson's finger on the touchpad moved faster with each email. "Back in the States, we did the Second World War to death at school. We were the good guys, of course, being American, atom bomb and all. That had no consequences on the world, nor on the good people of Hiroshima and Nagasaki, of course."

"Of course."

Jackson kept scrolling. "He sure seems to like history. A lot."

"He sure seems to like Miss Patel. A lot," echoed Zero. "Look how he asks for movie and book recommendations in-between all the schoolwork questions. And here, asking about her weekend."

"Simply trying to be polite?"

"Hang on," Zero said suddenly. "Go back."

The email that had caught her attention was dressed up with a colourful background, like a meme, except much, much longer. The title was a single word, written with a small letter: *you.*

you must have heard the jangle

of my thoughts

as the poker chips fell

one by one

like my scruples

you must have touched the rustle

of my needs

as the cards unfolded

one by one

like my defences

and then

your steps ebbed

one by one

away

"Hang on," Zero repeated. "Does it mean what I think it means?"

Jackson pulled his mouth into a helpless grimace. "I'm no e.e. cummings. The steps ebbing away, that's someone leaving, right?"

"Yeah. The stuff before, it talks about playing cards, gambling. Gambling with emotions, maybe? Theo Linden bet everything on this one stake, cast aside his scruples and defences, and then she walked away. Left him."

"A bit sexual too, the thing about needs."

Zero play-smacked his arm. "Everything is a bit sexual to you."

"No, Zimmerman. Everything is not a bit sexual to me. Everything is a lot sexual to me."

Yep, she'd walked right into that one. And now his face moved dangerously close to hers, so close she could see the lines on his lower lip.

Her phone broke into song. Literally saved by the bell. Zero recognised the number of the incoming call. She answered with: "Do you have anything for me?"

"Nothing like a stray hair or a drop of blood with handy DNA," the forensics expert replied. "But fingerprints on the items you gave us? There are multiple layers of prints on the phone, and they all match those of Aiko Hamasaki, which, as a mum of teenagers, I find quite unusual. Girls tend to bite their parents' heads off if they go near their phones, but they do let their close friends look at photos or messages from boys."

"Right." Zero wasn't going to go into lengthy explanations of the internet ban at Arcadia High.

"The envelope and the poem, however, are both devoid of fingerprints."

"Wiped clean?"

"Perhaps, although studies indicate that only roughly fifty percent of the fingerprints present on paper are of good enough quality to be of use. It all depends on the composition and amount of sweat left behind, as well as the physical qualities of the paper itself."

"In this case?" Zero prompted. She understood the need for forensic experts to be as factual as possible, but couldn't they just cut to the chase?

"In this case, I'd lean towards the fingerprints being wiped clean."

Yes! So not a suicide attempt. Now she could put this finding in her report to Sergeant Malhi and finally be allowed to investigate the case officially.

"Of course, whether by a person or through natural contact with soft surfaces such as bedding, towels or clothes, I couldn't say."

Of course not.

"Now. The pill bottle does contain fingerprints consistent with those of Aiko Hamasaki. However—"

Please, not another however.

"—the angle and the force with which the prints were made on the bottle make it highly unlikely that the victim—I mean, the patient—actually held the item in question. It looks more like she rested her fingers on one side. Or like the bottle rested against her fingers."

Zero made sure her sigh wouldn't be audible on the other end of the line. "Are you saying someone wiped their own prints, then tried to imprint hers?"

"You are the detective. I'm just here to interpret the data."

"But if you had to speculate?"

"Then I'd have to say the fingerprints are consistent with the following scenario: the bottle, which was devoid of any other prints, was positioned next to Aiko Hamasaki's hand in such a way that her fingertips brushed the surface of the bottle. Whether accidentally or on purpose, I cannot hazard a guess."

By the time Zero terminated the phone call, Jackson had finished stabbing and swiping his own phone. "Get this," he said before she had a chance to share the fingerprint scoop. "According to the coroner's database, Theo Linden was the St Alban's boy who committed suicide last year."

Chapter 16

Wednesday

Constable Zero Zimmerman

Like most office workers, Constable Zero Zimmerman was in the habit of checking her work emails during her morning commute. The smell of coffee escaping from take-away cups held by most other passengers waiting for the bus from Kingsland into central Auckland tickled her nostrils, fraying her under-caffeinated nerves. She didn't want to waste money when she could have free coffee at work but delaying this particular gratification did nothing for building her character. It simply released her inner bitch.

The bus was almost full, and the only vacant seat was a narrow strip of a double bench, mostly occupied by one woman. Not fat by any means, but not petite either. Auckland bus spaces were designed for passengers of more Lilliputian proportions, so Zero perched on her fraction of a seat, anchored her feet into the floor and opened her phone.

Another text from Sergeant Sandeep Malhi. All in capitals, and no *please*, which meant trouble. *COME SEE ME WHEN YOU GET IN*. Damn. If the sarge pushed to close the case, she would never get justice for Aiko. Or for Miss Patel, if her drowning turned out to be less than accidental. Or for Theo Linden.

But hang on. Yesterday's findings about wiped fingerprints surely made it likely that Aiko's poisoning was an attempted homicide. So why?

Would more experienced officers now need to take over responsibility for the enquiry? Shit. Shit—shit—shit.

Her bad mood deepened when she came across an email from Arcadia High Boarding School's local police station. Sexual assault? The hell? She checked the date—they sat on that report for weeks, since the beginning of February. And she was only getting visibility of it now. Bloody bureaucracy.

Technically she was in the clear as far as the sergeant's request went because she only stopped at the office to collect a police car before she set off north.

It was a mistake. Using a car in Auckland's rush hour traffic was not for the impatient at heart. Roadworks everywhere—whoever was manufacturing those plastic orange cones could retire a millionaire. Crawling past Victoria Park on the way to the Harbour Bridge, Zero regretted not having that cup of coffee. When she finally left the city and the North Shore suburbs behind her, the sight of green hills covered with fern trees hit her like a tranquiliser.

She told her Google Assistant to dial Jackson's number. Voicemail. She left a brief message to tell him where she was going and why. Then she called her sergeant.

Sergeant Sandeep Malhi came straight to the point. "Under normal circumstances, given the wiped fingerprints and the possible connection to the Mekong Dragons, a more senior officer would be assigned to the Arcadia High case. However, given the current staff shortages," he paused, "congratulations, Constable. You are it."

"And Jackson?"

"Jackson is the lead on the Olivia Kentwood case. If they turn out to be related, he will lead both."

"Understood. Thank you, sir."

Madeleine Smith met her outside the office building, on the loop that was convenient for cars, but which now reminded Zero about the circle of life, about beginnings and ends, about the futility of it all.

"Constable. Good morning." The headmistress locked eyes with Zero for the briefest of moments. "May I interest you in a cup of coffee?"

A bloody mind reader. Zero wanted to refuse, didn't find the strength. "That's very kind of you." Normally she would have added something about bribing the police force with caffeine, but she wasn't in a jokey state of mind.

The coffee from the Nespresso machine in Madeleine's office was probably good, but Zero gulped it too quickly to form an opinion. "I'm going to come straight to the point," she said as she set down the cup next to a deep gouge in Madeleine's desktop and wondered briefly why the Arcadia principal didn't have the desk repaired or replaced. "Earlier this morning, I was made aware of an anonymous complaint made to *Crime Stoppers* several weeks ago. The complaint concerns this school."

The headmistress paused with her own coffee cup halfway to her lips. Today's outfit was a sand-coloured pantsuit with a layer of sea-blue lace camisole. "I don't understand," she said, her words slow, as though spoken under water. "*Crime Stoppers*?"

"The website where members of the public can report crimes anonymously."

"I know what *Crime Stoppers* is." Madeleine shook her head as though dodging a fly. "But I fail to see …" she trailed off.

Zero waited, but there wasn't anything more. She filled in the silence. "Somebody reported inappropriate sexual behaviour of one of the staff members towards a student at Arcadia High."

Madeleine's body relaxed, the coffee cup travelled up towards her mouth. "Oh," she exhaled, "that."

"Why? What did you think it was about?"

"I … I'm not sure. Just, you know, the word. *Crime*. That sounds serious, like fraud or theft or …" The headmistress paused again. "It gave me a fright, that's all."

Zero could tell that wasn't the whole truth. "Sexual assault is a serious crime, ma'am."

"Madeleine."

"Sexual assault is a serious crime, Madeleine."

"Yes, but that's not what it was."

"What was it then?"

Silence. Madeleine's hands folded loosely in her lap, the pose radiating calm. The coffee cup neatly back on the saucer, the saucer centred on the desk in a perfect illustration of outer and inner order.

Zero decided to take the lead. "The student reported uninvited sexual touching. Are you aware of that?"

"I don't know what to tell you, Constable. I investigated the matter at the time and found it unsubstantiated."

"Unsubstantiated simply means *without evidence*. Doesn't mean it didn't actually happen."

Madeleine shook her head. "Such allegations—especially against teachers—are easy to make, and once they become public, they're almost impossible to put to rest. People say there's no smoke without fire. Reputations get damaged, lives destroyed."

"What about lives destroyed through sexual abuse?"

"There's no sexual abuse at my school."

That sounded true. Zero trusted her in-built lie detector, the skill she must have been born with, then heightened by learning to read people's reactions when her gypsy grandmother read their fortunes in the cards or in the creases of their palms.

And yet, the headmistress was hiding something.

Zero stood up, the change in position allowing her to dominate the conversation. "All right," she said, making her voice official and police-like. "What aren't you telling me?"

Madeleine folded into herself, the fight whooshing out of her with every breath. "The person named in Aiko's accusation was our property manager, Hep King. He—he and I used to be married. In name only. His preferences ..." She trailed off.

Zero wasn't having it. "Your ex-husband was accused of sexually interfering with a student, and you hushed it up?"

"It's not like that. Hep is gay. We were best friends growing up, and we married to conceal his sexual orientation. His family is very conservative. They don't know to this day. Savannah doesn't know either, though I doubt she'd mind. Having a gay dad is probably cool nowadays. It's Hep's parents and brother he's concerned about." Madeleine shot her a pleading glance. "I hope you can keep it confidential? Please?"

Zero nodded. "As long as it isn't connected with the case."

"Of course. That's how I knew Aiko's accusation couldn't have been true. Hep is not interested in women. Especially not in someone his daughter's age."

"He must have been interested in women, at least once, to have a fathered a child."

A grimace twisted Madeleine's lips. "That's what turkey basters are for."

"Pardon?"

"Like in that movie, *Magik and Rose*? Oliver Driver? No? Maybe before your time."

Zero shrugged. "Haven't seen it. But you don't have to draw me a picture, I get it."

She would talk to Hep King, watch his reaction, document his reply and her own assessment in her report. Just to be thorough and do everything by the book. Her own mind, however, was made up. Madeleine was telling the truth.

Zero consulted her notes. Ah, yes. "Has Aiko been seeing the school counsellor? Because of the alleged sexual harassment, or any other matter?"

Five minutes later, Zero found herself moving two doors down the corridor, to a spacious room decorated in soft pastels and rounded lines. A few upright books decorated otherwise bare shelves. A gigantic, perfectly see-through vase stood empty in the corner. A small hexagonal tray on the desk held a single pen. Its fat body told Zero that the pen was no standard OfficeMax issue. She recalled the cherry blossom branch Emmanuelle Linden had used during their Zoom call—yes, its minimalism aligned with the ascetic atmosphere of the office.

The school counsellor rose from the pale desk and extended her hand. "Lovely to meet you in person. Please sit down."

Zero got straight to the point. "Has Aiko spoken to you about the sexual assault?"

Emmanuelle Linden blinked. "The … sorry, what did you say? Sexual assault? There's never been a sexual assault at this school, certainly not to my knowledge. Aiko certainly never mentioned anything of the kind."

"Has she ever said anything that might have implied it? Talked about men, or a particular man, with fear or antipathy?"

"No."

"What has she talked about?"

Again Zero expected a conversation about patient confidentiality. Again, the counsellor must have decided that it was all part of the investigation into the suicide attempt.

Mrs Linden opened an invisible drawer and took out a cardboard file. "What would you like to know?"

The next hour was a sharp learning curve. Zero absorbed phrases like non-binary gender, intersex, disorders of sexual development, gender not being defined by genitalia, gender not being defined by the XX or XY genetic makeup.

From reading people's opinions on social media, Zero knew this was not as simple an issue as the counsellor suggested. Many people believed that there were only two genders: those with a penis and those with a vagina, case closed, no matter what science may have to say about it.

"So Aiko is what?" she asked eventually. "A transgender person? A natural female wanting to be male? Or the other way round?"

"Nothing like that. Aiko recognises that there are more than the two traditionally acknowledged genders, and she's happy to identify as neither. She's embraced the term gender-fluid to describe how she feels about her identity. Not male, not female, a bit of both, the proportions unequal and different in various stages of her life. She grew up a girl, with tomboy behaviour and stereotypically male interests in the sciences. Aiko is happy with the personal pronoun *she*, though many gender-fluid people prefer the word *they*. In Aiko's mind, she has no defined gender, she's a mixture of male and female, so pronouns are incidental."

"Okay," Zero said to keep the counsellor going.

"When most of Aiko's peers hit puberty, she lagged behind. Her friends told her that menstruation was nothing to look forward to, and to count herself lucky, but she was impatient, she wanted to fit in and be like everybody else. At her request, her mum took her to the doctor, then to a specialist. An ultrasound scan of the abdomen revealed the presence of both ovarian and testicular matter."

"Meaning?"

"In politically incorrect terms, and I will use the label with all respect and no negative connotations that sometimes accompany it, Aiko's biological gender can be described as *hermaphroditic.*"

"Biologically, she is both male and female?"

"Biologically, she presents both male and female gonads."

Zero tried, and failed, to recall the term from school biology lessons. "Gonads?"

"Ovaries and testicles. Again, the presence or absence of those does not determine a person's gender. A woman who has her ovaries removed is still a woman."

Zero thought about her adoptive mum, who couldn't have biological children, yet was the very quintessence of a woman. Yes, she totally agreed with the counsellor that reproductive organs did not determine a person's gender.

However, if Aiko was somehow both a girl and a boy, might that explain that Hep may have been drawn to her?

The counsellor continued. "Her gender ambiguity is a far cry from Aiko's original wish to fit in and be like everybody else, of course, but she received excellent support from the medical profession, as well as emotional support at home. Her mum and grandma are amazing, both very understanding and accepting."

"Speaking of which. The home situation. A stepfather? What about the father?"

"Aiko's father died when she was in primary school. Mrs Hamasaki never remarried."

"What about a boyfriend?"

A slight shift in the counsellor's position, a twitch of lips, a deeper intake of breath. Her tone was level enough, though. "No, Aiko feels that a boyfriend would be too much work at this point in her life. She wants to explore fully who she is, to be selfish—her word—and to only concentrate on herself. A typical teenager. Exactly at it should be."

"I meant Mrs Hamasaki's boyfriend. The reason Aiko came to board at Arcadia was that she didn't get along with—"

Mrs Linden stopped her with a raised palm. "Aiko really wanted to come to this school, away from the social media, all the noise about gender diversity and potential peer pressure into transitioning to either gender. Arcadia High has a long waiting list, and you can only get priority placement if you plead your individual case to the headmistress. An abusive relationship at home was a story Aiko felt more comfortable with than the gender-identity one. Everybody is sympathetic to survivors of domestic violence or sexual abuse. The world is less forgiving when it comes to not conforming into a binary gender classification system."

"So Aiko and her mum lied?" If Aiko had lied about her home situation, might she have lied about Hep King and the alleged sexual assault?

The counsellor moved her hand up and down as though weighing something. "A white lie."

To Zero, there was no difference. A lie was a lie. But she wasn't here for a philosophical discussion. "From your perspective, Mrs Linden, do you think Aiko is conflicted enough about her gender identity that she may have attempted to commit suicide?"

The counsellor rested her elbow on the desk and hid her eyes in the palm of her hand. "In my professional assessment, she wasn't in any immediate danger of harming herself. Before Friday, I would have said that she just saw herself as a normal person who didn't tick traditional gender boxes, as well-adjusted as any teenager in this day and age. In view of what happened, however …" She paused, swallowed. "Looks like this one's on me."

Zero believed her.

The Girl's Dad

His ex-wife—no, his estranged wife, for they'd never divorced—was in Christchurch. He heard from his contact at Air New Zealand when she bought the ticket and boarded the plane. His computer guy checked the hotel and Airbnb bookings, and hey presto—the Rydges in Christchurch scores a hit.

He booked the first flight out of Auckland.

Madeleine Smith

The constable knocked on Madeleine's door and let herself in before Madeleine had the chance to reply. "Just a few more questions. Is Vincent Linden related to Emmanuelle Linden, your school's counsellor?"

"He's her son. But I don't see what it has to do—"

"And Theo Linden?"

A hollow whooshing sound filled Madeleine's head. "Please tell me you did not discuss Theo with Mrs Linden."

"Why is that?"

"It's still a difficult topic for her. For all of us. Theo—Theo was her older son. He died last year."

"I'm sorry to hear that." Zero Zimmerman didn't seem sorry. Curious, maybe. Imposing, definitely. "How did he die?"

"I don't think that's relevant." A lie. Madeleine knew it was relevant all right.

"Did he commit suicide?"

"Why would you think that?"

The constable counted off on her fingers. "One, because his social media accounts say so. Two, because last year's newspapers reported it. And three, because I've read the coroner's report."

That seemed quite definite, but the constable wasn't finished yet.

"And you knowingly allowed his mother to remain a counsellor at your school?"

The policewoman clearly had no idea about employment law. Not to mention ordinary human compassion. Madeleine drew herself to her full height. It literally felt like she was inserting a wooden rod into her spine, inch by glorious inch. "I find the question inappropriate. Mrs Linden underwent a full post-trauma evaluation prior to returning to work. Her private life has nothing to do with her professional role here in Arcadia."

That was another lie. A convenient bunch of politically correct phrases. The hell Emmanuelle Linden must have gone through would have affected her personality, her outlook on the world, even—according to the latest medical research—the physical shape of her heart.

Bobbi Kentwood

I'm freaking out about Mum. Where is she? Still in Christchurch? Why? She's never been gone this long before. She left on Saturday. Today's Wednesday—the fifth day she's missing. And all this time, not a word from her.

The fire-headed cop is coming out of the school building. I meet her halfway. I want to ask her about my mum, but one look at her face and I know there's nothing new. "I need to tell you something in private," I say instead.

So yeah, I feel like a copy-cat following in Aiko's footsteps. She lied to the police about Mr King. I'm about to lie about Xander. But we've learnt about plagiarism at school, and you can't plagiarise ideas. As long as your words are different, you're safe.

The constable touches my upper arm with her fingertips. It's the briefest of contacts, yet it feels good. Reassuring.

"Would you like a teacher or the school counsellor present?" Her tone of voice matches that touch: encouraging and warm, establishing a connection, building trust.

Trust I'm about to destroy.

"No." Want to leave it at that. Can't. Bloody Arcadia High and the manners they've drilled into us. "No, thank you."

"In that case, let's go somewhere we can't be overheard."

I want to be overheard. Want to scream out my version of events, the way I would have preferred them to have unfolded. Instead, I follow her to the principal's office, as though I did something wrong, which, I guess, I'm about to do.

The cop tells Mrs Smith we'll be using her office—doesn't ask, just states it like it's a fact, and the headmistress leaves us alone. Such power is intoxicating, even if it's not mine. Perhaps I should join the police force when I leave school.

"What would you like to talk about, Bobbi?"

And here it is. My greatest fear. The only thing I can think about. The one thing I'm not allowed to tell her. If I tell the police, he— my biological dad—might find my mum before they do. So instead, I come up with a lie that I hope will bring her back. "I'm pregnant."

It's not a good plan, but at least it's a plan. With all the fuss of arranging a pregnancy test, perhaps I can get hold of a phone or computer connected to the internet, I reason. Put this lie on my social media. If Mum is watching my accounts, she'll—

"Bullshit."

I can't believe the porcelain doll has said that. *Bullshit* is not a word I'd expect the police to use, especially not in the principal's office of Arcadia High. I assume Mrs Smith's most icy tone. "Excuse me?" I say.

"Bullshit, Bobbi. You may be many things, but you're not pregnant."

"What are you, a human pregnancy test?" If Mrs Smith could hear me now, she'd have a heart attack, and then she'd expel me. Our school has a zero-tolerance policy for rudeness, just like it has zero tolerance for the internet.

The constable shakes all that red hair. "No. But I am a human lie detector."

"Oh yeah?"

"Yeah."

If I could only beat the cop at her own game, I think, maybe she'd get less confident in her stupid abilities and choose to believe me. "I'm going to tell you two truths and a lie. You'll tell me which is which. Ready? One, my name is Bobbi Eleanor Kentwood. Two, I'm pregnant. Three, I'm responsible for Aiko's suicide attempt. Which one is the lie?"

A cool stare from the constable. "All three statements are lies, Bobbi." She doesn't give me a chance to recover from the shock. "Tell me about your mum. What do you think she's doing in Christchurch?"

It just comes out. "I'm worried it has to do with my dad."

"Is your dad …" she pauses, looks for the right word, "unkind to your mum?"

It's the present tense that does it. Of course, she's imagining my mum and *Blair* fighting. The image is so ridiculous, something like laughter forces its way out of my throat into my mouth. It would have been a full-on giggle if not for the worry that's making the air heavy and thick.

"Not my dad," I explain. "My *dad*." Yeah, I can hear how that may have sounded confusing. "My *biological* dad. He's not a good man."

I end up telling her everything. How we left home when I was five. How Mum covered our tracks, cut her hair and changed our names. How every three months she leaves for a day or two to lay a false trail of breadcrumbs in another part of New Zealand, in case he's still looking. "Sometimes she joins a gym in her previous name. Gets into the video footage of a rugby game and waves when they pan over the spectator seats. Goes to a movie premiere and gives an interview afterwards. Once she started a disturbance in the street and made sure her name was mentioned in the paper."

The constable listens without interrupting. She's a good listener: the more she listens, the more I want to keep talking. "Mum always comes back, always. It's never been this long."

"All right, Bobbi. Thank you for telling me."

"Will this help you bring my mum back?"

She opens her hands palms up in an I-don't-know gesture. "At least now that we know, we'll be able to offer protection—as soon as we make contact with her."

I stand up to leave, but she's not finished. "I'd like to ask you about a fourth lie. The one Aiko made up about Mr King."

"That wasn't a lie," I protest. "It really happened."

"*What* really happened?" She places a lot of emphasis on the first word.

"Mr King acted in an inappropriate way. We both saw it."

"*Who* saw it?"

Again that emphasis on the interrogative word. Yeah, we learn things at Arcadia High, like grammar and what interrogative words are.

I shrug. "Me and Aiko."

"Aiko saw Mr King acting inappropriately towards Aiko?"

She's tricked me. The bloody policewoman has bloody well tricked me.

"Bobbi. Just tell me."

So I tell her how we saw Savannah hug Mr King. "He didn't force her or anything. She really wanted to, and in a way that was worse, because he's so much older and ..." I feel yuck even thinking about it. "Anyway. We didn't want her to have to talk about it. Then Aiko had this brilliant idea to still report it but to change the facts a bit. To protect Savannah's identity, you know."

She nods, but I can see her mind is elsewhere. "Why do you feel responsible for what happened to Aiko?" she asks.

"I don't—"

"You're not to blame, I know that much. But why do you think that you ought to be blamed? Where is all that guilt coming from? You feel it's your fault. Why?"

Words pour out of me like water that shoots up from a geyser in one of Rotorua's thermal parks. The tarot cards, DK, our sex poetry club, the kiss between DK and Aiko, the spell to vanquish a love rival.

Constable Zimmerman laughs, and it's a long, loud laugh. "Back in Romania," she says, her breath still short from her merriment, "I was raised by the gypsies. We'd move our wagons from town to town, telling fortunes and casting spells on demand. We got plenty of money to live on. People's gullibility knows no bounds, particularly if you're desperate to believe that a feather from a black chicken slaughtered at midnight will break a baby's fever or secure the love of your dream man."

Or bring your mum home, I think. But I say nothing.

She carries on with the lecture. "Surely you must realise what a load of nonsense and superstition it is. Gather a plant with thorns that's not a rose, for crying out loud, Bobbi! Magic spells don't happen by candlelight. They happen in chemistry labs when you apply science, and in the kitchen when you cook with love—"

"Love? Is that some kind of an herb?" I interrupt.

"Better than any herb."

"So if you don't believe in spells," I venture, "you won't mind if I put a fertility spell on you?"

"Go for it. I'm not planning to have sex anytime soon."

"You forgot to say and it's all nonsense, anyway."

The cop shrugs. "And it's all nonsense, anyway, which is a good thing, because I'd make a truly lousy mother."

I couldn't agree more.

Constable Zero Zimmerman

Zero walked back to her car, only faintly aware of her surroundings. Yes, the asphalt of the school's driveway felt hot through the soles of her shoes, and the tui in the nearby shrubbery were whistling their haunting melody, yet her senses failed to ground her or provide a mindfulness moment. Yes, she could smell the breeze coming off the ocean and the sunshine baked into the kauri trees in the nearby bush, but it didn't remind her of anything except that it was Wednesday already, and she still hadn't made any progress. Collected many pieces of the puzzle, for sure, but those pieces just refused to fit together.

The car was hot, and she could feel moisture on her upper lip as she dialled the number of the forensic lab. "Any progress on the handwriting?" she asked after she'd identified herself. She knew she wasn't making herself popular by being the squeaky wheel. She didn't care. It took all her willpower not to yell, *I want the results, and I want them now!* But that would be a very old school way—a stereotypical male cop way—of doing things.

Yeah, she would not make a great boss. Or a great teacher. Or a great mother, for that matter. She was deficient in the patience department. Emotionally challenged in the nurturing department. Plus, she had abandonment issues which she'd rather not pass on to a baby.

Zero was still thinking about Bobbi's fertility spell, when her mobile phone rang. Amelia's number. Her flatmates never called and rarely texted. An anomaly. Possibly an emergency.

"It's Keith," Amelia's voice was thick, fracturing like splintered wood.

Zero remembered Keith's silhouette in Amelia's door, merging with the darkness of her bedroom. Don't screw the crew, stated the sacred rule of sharing a house with a bunch of friends or strangers. And yet it happened all the time. She remembered the story repeating itself with Rachel. Had Amelia found out?

"You guys had a fight?"

A long silence. "He's dead." And now Amelia's voice did crack, the rest of the sentence lost in a choking sob.

Zero broke the speed limit driving home. A heart attack? Keith was too young for that, surely? Not a car crash—she would have heard about any road fatality on the public radio, never mind the police one. Did he finally try to trim the totara tree in the backyard and fall off the ladder?

But deep inside, she knew the statistics. The second largest cause of death for non-Māori males, right after heart disease, was suicide.

When she got to First Street in Kingsland and rushed into the wooden villa, Zero discovered that Keith had left a letter. Addressed to his baby daughter. In it he reminded her that he would always love her, and that she was the best thing that had happened to him. He hadn't referred to the suicide.

The cynical part of Zero told her that the always-love-his-daughter part of the letter was a sham. It's easy to promise a forever if you're about to check out of this world. How long did the *always* last in Keith's case? A few minutes? An hour?

The rational part of her was trying to use logic. Why do people feel desperate enough to go through with something like that? A malfunction, an over-active sense of unhappiness? After all, being dissatisfied with one's life usually led to progress and economic growth. Millions of years of evolution caused unhappy sea creatures to seek greener grasses on land, made apes climb down from their vines and trees, pushed *Homo erectus* out of Africa, and made billions of modern humans leave their beds every morning to make money so that they could buy new shiny things.

Zero told her cynical and rational parts to shut up. The rest of her was hurting. Not because she had been particularly fond of Keith, because she hadn't been, but because of the finality of it all.

"He missed his daughter so much," Amelia said through tears that swelled in her eyes yet refused to fall. "Hated not being able to see her. His ex, she made up some stuff about him, vicious lies. The court believed her. He couldn't get joint custody. All his visits were supervised. I thought I was helping him get through it, I really did." Now the tears escaped down Amelia's cheeks, across her jawline, onto her throat. "I thought I would save him. I never thought, never realised, that even though he had me, he still wanted to die."

He didn't want to die, Zero thought. He just wanted the pain to stop. Perhaps he hadn't realised he would be transferring it to his loved ones instead. It would have been bad enough for Amelia to deal with Keith's death had he been hit by a train, but now she had to face complicated issues such as anger, rejection and guilt. Sorting through it would make the healing process all the more challenging.

"We must call the police," she said.

Amelia's forehead scrunched up. "I did call the police. You."

With all the formalities completed and Keith's body removed, Zero concentrated on taking care of Amelia. She tried to reach Rachel, got voice-mail, decided against leaving a message.

"If only I'd checked up on him." It wasn't the first time Amelia said it, but it was the first time her words hit a chord in Zero's soul.

Mental health was complicated, Zero was beginning to realise. The person you might assume to have the most valid reason to be discontented with their lot in life, for instance because of their gender identity, was the one most well-adjusted according to their mental health counsellor. The guy who had seemed happy enough to be skimming off his flatmates and sleeping with his new girlfriend— two new girlfriends—had just committed suicide.

And what about a father whose oldest daughter made some unfortunate life choices and ended up in prison, thanks in part to his younger daughter's policing efforts? How did such a father fare in the resilience department?

As soon as she had put Amelia to bed, with too much cheap gin in her flatmate's stomach and an electric fan blowing ineffectively through the clammy heat of the room, Zero dialled her parents' landline.

"Mum," she said. "Mum. Give it to me straight. How is Dad doing? I mean, really, how is he? No wrapping me in cotton wool. I can take it."

And when she heard that her father only ever got out of his pyjamas on days when Zero was coming over, she left Rachel in charge of looking after the sleeping Amelia. Rachel, who had by now returned home, looked stunned but not emotionally affected by Keith's death. Besides, Zero reasoned, when it came to grief, two was always company.

So she left them in Amelia's room, the pillow probably still smelling of Keith's hair, and drove to her parents' house with her overnight bag and a steadfast intention to listen. She understood that listening was not a miracle cure—it was the equivalent of applying a first aid bandage to a bleeding wound. A lot of work still had to be done by the professionals. But at least for now, it was the three of them—Mum, Dad and Zero—against the blackness.

The three of them. Three. Should have been the *four* of them.

Tomorrow, Zero promised herself, tomorrow she would go and speak to Millie, sibling rivalry and Millie's hostility be damned.

Then she made herself another promise. She would never, ever, ever have children. Just look at the devastation Millie had wreaked on their dad. He was now an old man before his time, a broken human being. He was a shadow of the father who'd dressed up as a pirate—and even as a fairy once—for their birthday parties. He was not the same man who'd driven them up and down the Harbour Bridge to look at the city lights when they were restless in the exam season, stopping at the Wynyard Quarter for soft drinks and hot chips.

Never. Not ever.

And then she read the email Kath Taipari had sent her, the one containing information on the Mekong Dragons. They were more than a straight-forward drug gang: they dealt with money laundering, loan sharking, establishing cannabis growers across New Zealand and conveying the ready product from the farms to endemic New Zealand gangs for retail sales. As far as Kath Taipari understood, their distribution channels and modus operandi were similar to that of the K19 cartel, just cannabis instead of pseudoephedrine. However, Kath had floated a hypothesis that the Mekong Dragons might be planning to expand. That would mean a turf war and potential victims, something the NDIB was keen to avoid.

As Zero already knew, Quan Le and Hai Le were brothers thought to be involved. It wasn't certain whether one of them was the leader of the Mekong Dragons, the feared Lac Long, whose one distinguishing physical characteristic was the gang's symbol on his bald head. When she came across the physical description of the leader, Lac Long (pronounced "Luck" Long), she studied a close-up of the dragon tattoo on his skull and remembered exactly where she'd seen it before. She wasn't yet sure how to use the information, but she knew exactly what she would put in her email to her sergeant: the photo on Parvati Patel's phone that connected the Mekong Dragons with Arcadia High, and the possibility that Lac Long's wife—and domestic violence victim—may be persuaded to contribute information leading to his arrest. The latter would be the purest form of justice Zero could imagine.

CHAPTER 17

Thursday

Constable Zero Zimmerman

This morning Constable Zero Zimmerman wished she had packed more thoughtfully the previous night. The blouse she had grabbed in haste was an old one, once pale blue and now greyed by many laundromat wash cycles, with a small random hole in the left sleeve. At least it was clean. In fact, it still bore the fragrance of her lemony washing powder.

It was shallow and callous to think about her clothes, of course. Keith was dead, her sister was in jail and her dad was on the verge of a complete breakdown. She shouldn't care what she looked like at work.

She did care what she looked like at work. Bloody stupid Jackson.

"Damn," she thought. She may have even said it aloud, because a few of her fellow passengers turned and looked in her direction, without actually looking at her and breaking the unspoken commuter code.

The train from her parents' house to downtown Auckland was crowded, so Zero stood as she held onto the strap hanger with one hand, while scanning the news on her phone with the other. A headline caught her eye. No way!

The offending article was buried between a demand for fewer

cycle lanes and clickbait about hot-desking, so not first page headlines fortunately, yet she now realised how much she had hoped this case wouldn't make it into the media.

The piece was titled "Third suicide in an Auckland private school?" which was incorrect on so many levels: Aiko was alive, it was by no means established how the poison got into her system (Zero blamed herself for not knowing yet), Miss Patel's death had been an accident, and the only suicide had happened in St Alban's, not Arcadia High. Still, she thought with cynicism fuelled by personal experience, when had facts ever stood in the way of a news story?

Surprisingly enough, apart from the misleading and uncreative title, the story was pretty much accurate. Theo Linden's tragic death last year, Miss Patel's drowning, Aiko's pills. Both schools were mentioned by name, although the identities of those involved had been withheld and referenced only as "a teenage student" and "a young teacher".

The hook was that private schools were the epitome of privilege, and spoiled rich teens were more prone to depression because everything came too easily to them, in short, there was nothing in their life they had to strive for. Zero wondered about that. Certainly, growing up poor in her native Romania had taught her how precious life was: when every day is a struggle for survival, your instinct kicks in and you rejoice in every piece of bread you manage to steal. You don't tend to wish you didn't exist—just the contrary, every fibre of your being fights to stay alive.

Did that mean that the human race needed misery in order to be happy?

Zero shook her head. Too much philosophy for one morning. Besides, she was becoming increasingly sure that Aiko hadn't swallowed the pills on purpose.

Was it still too early o'clock to phone the prison and arrange a visit? Zero called the number for the Prisoner Contact team. It was outside their office hours and there wasn't an option to leave a message.

Madeleine Smith

A phone number she didn't recognise was shaking her Samsung Galaxy. Madeleine almost didn't answer it—prospective clients didn't know her private number, and the students' parents usually rang the dean—but what if it was Luck Long on a new phone? The boss of the Mekong Dragons could probably afford to buy a burner phone every day.

She didn't want to answer.

She had no choice.

Hopefully a wrong number, she thought as she answered with "Madeleine Smith, good morning."

"Madeleine, it's Olivia. Olivia Kentwood. Is Bobbi all right?"

"Sorry?" Madeleine composed herself. "I mean, yes, sure. I saw her after breakfast today. She's in class now. Do you need to speak to her? Gosh, Olivia, hello. Where have you been? We're all so, so worried. Are you all right?"

Click.

Madeleine checked the timetable and made her way to English. She had to let Bobbi know her mum was safe. At least, Madeleine assumed Olivia was safe. Weird that she wasn't calling from her own mobile, but she certainly sounded her usual self.

Bobbi first, then that constable. Zero… Zimmer? Zimmerman? Hell's bells, for a school principal, she was dreadful with names.

Before she could find Bobbi, her mobile rang again. Hep.

"I've emailed you a link to a newspaper article that came out this morning," he said. "Not sure what it means for us."

"Wait, you won't believe what's just happened. Olivia Kentwood called me—"

"And she asked you about Bobbi, right?"

Madeleine halted her steps halfway to the classrooms. "How do you know?"

"It's this article. Olivia read it and got spooked. Probably thought it was Bobbi lying there in hospital."

Oh dear. "You mean the newspapers got hold of Aiko's story?"

"Sure did."

Her mind was racing, calculating the odds. With media exposure, there was bound to be pressure on the police to close the case. They might search the school just to look like they're doing their jobs. "It's not worth the risk, Hep. Let's get rid of everything."

"Move the stuff again?"

"Off the premises. Bury it, burn it, sell it in bulk, I don't care. The stress is killing me. The cops keep turning up as if they own the school. It's only a matter of time before they find the greenhouse."

"If we burn the crop, the whole area downwind from the fire will be feeling very mellow."

"Hep."

"Yes?"

"Don't."

And that was exactly why her first marriage had failed, she thought. Even back then, when she and Hep had been best mates pretending to be a couple, she'd had no sense of humour.

"Also, Madeleine? Think of the consequences. Lucky Long will eat you for breakfast."

"*Luck* Long," she corrected him. But damn it, he was right, even though he didn't even know about the threats against Savannah. So

…. So …. So, what should she do?

"Hep, help me think. You're right, we can't destroy the crop."

"You need something to throw the police off the scent, Mads. Allow them to close the case."

What would they need to close the case? A suicide note? No, that ship had sailed. How about a culprit? Was there any way she could throw Luck Long under the bus without implicating herself? The best solution, though? If Granny Smith were to confess and go to jail.

She did not just think that. That's not the kind of person she wanted to be.

"Right, we'll have to risk it. I'll help you move the shipment tonight, everything that's ready. Meanwhile, get some vegetables to put in the glasshouses and the plastic tunnels: cucumbers, tomatoes, radishes."

"Mads, who on earth eats radishes?"

"It's not for eating, it's window-dressing."

"Yes, boss."

Or maybe it was because she'd always been too bossy. Shunting people around as though they were resources. Focused on the goal, not on the journey. Certainly not on making friends along the way. As though she were—a man.

No, that was unfair to men. It was all Madeleine's fault. She was simply a bossy, rude person. A black sheep, unwilling to conform to the flock.

Maybe she deserved everything she got.

Constable Zero Zimmerman

She finally got through to the Prisoner Contact team and booked a visit for the afternoon. The rest of the morning was less successful. When chasing up handwriting experts: *Constable, for crying out loud, there are only twenty-four-and-a-half hours in a day, we're doing everything we can!* Her literal and exact mind wondered where the half had come from. Her experience reminded her that most people didn't make perfect logical sense.

The unproductivity spell continued. When following the trail of sleeping pill prescriptions: no trace of Aiko Hamasaki, her mother or her grandmother anywhere in the national database. *Give us another name, and we'll check it.* Trouble was, she didn't have another name to give them. She'd read the medical report again, noting that the contents of Aiko's pumped stomach didn't include partially digested tablets, only the presence of the medication, meaning that the tablets had probably been crushed or dissolved in something before ingesting. Like in Aiko's Darth Vader bottle. That meant exactly nothing to the case, except maybe to confirm the theory of attempted murder. But by whom?

When saving her reports into the police repository: *The transaction cannot be completed at present.*

When trying to brainstorm the case with her colleagues on Webex Teams, the police collaboration tool—she was still typing her question when another thread popped up: *Saving ducklings today with the boys from the Fire Department.* It was Jackson in his court suit and a borrowed police hat, posing next to shirtless men in a red truck.

Zero clicked, not even realising she was getting distracted, and read about a family of ducklings falling down a deep drain on a motorway. Police worked along firefighters to scoop them out while diverting traffic. Happy ending for the ducks, a good news story for the public, and much needed PR for both departments.

"The duck story must be a real feather in your cap," she messaged Jackson.

"Yeah," he replied straight away. "We gave it a quack and it all went swimmingly."

Oh, brilliant. She already knew that Jackson was a computer wizard and could give any shirtless fireman a run for his money in the looks department. Now she discovered that his sense of humour matched hers.

Other women didn't have the decency to take their comments offline. Right there, on Webex Teams, there were offers of cups of coffee and home-made brownies to reward the duck saver. Sad, really, when you thought about it.

She tried to concentrate on Aiko's case.

Really tried.

Failed.

It was almost lunchtime when Jackson texted her again. "Olivia Kentwood is waiting in Interview Room 2. She's just walked into our building and asked for the officer in charge of the Arcadia investigation."

Both she and Jackson had expected this, ever since Madeleine Smith's phone call earlier. For whatever reason, Bobbi's mother had decided to break the silence by communicating with the school principal. Now it seemed she'd also decided to come back to Auckland.

Jackson was waiting outside the interview room. "I'm not even sure what to ask her."

"Start with *coffee or tea?*"

That got her a smile. A passing police officer shot Zero a look she chose not to decipher. The other woman's jeans were tighter than a Scotsman's fist. Zero fully expected Jackson to turn around for an ogle, but one hundred percent of his brain must have been occupied by the case, because his eyes were on Zero.

"Are you ready?" he asked.

"Piece of cake. If the going gets tough, you can *duck* out and I'll take over."

Jackson's smile got bigger. "Quack-quack. I like your style, Zimmerman. Now let's get to work."

"She's here out of her own free will. We probably won't need to work very hard."

Zero was right.

"I have critical information about a murder," Olivia Kentwood said before they could offer her coffee. Or, indeed, tea.

"Hold on one minute, ma'am." Even though this wasn't a formal interview of a suspect, Jackson went through the routine of setting up the recording device, reciting the date and time, stating who was present, all the legal formalities.

"I'm here to help you catch a murderer," Bobbi's mum said again.

Zero didn't have much of a baseline, but the tone was commanding, firm with a slight downward inflection at the end, the opposite of the forever-questioning way her daughter spoke.

"Who's been murdered, Mrs Kentwood?"

"That girl in Arcadia High. The newspaper said she committed suicide, but that's not true. It was my ex-husband. You have to arrest him. He did it."

The newspaper, Zero was sure, hadn't explicitly stated that Aiko was dead, but she suppressed the need to be pedantic.

"Go on," Jackson said. His tone was a mixture of kindness and curiosity. Coupled with his you're-the-most-interesting-person-in-the-world smile, it did the trick.

"You see," Olivia Kentwood placed her hands flat on the small table—neatly, as though they were decorative cushions on her chocolate-coloured sofa—and leaned towards Jackson, totally ignoring

Zero. "He thought this poor girl was my Bobbi."

Jackson's face didn't reveal any surprise at the notion that petite Aiko's straight black hair and Asian features could be mistaken for Bobbi's prominent nose and blonde ponytail. "Why would your ex-husband want to kill Bobbi?" he asked.

"Because he's a bad man. Pure evil. His greatest desire, no, his only desire, is to own us. He wants a perfect family, with a perfect wife and a perfect daughter. We crossed him—I crossed him by running away and taking our child. So now that he can't have us, he's going to make sure nobody else can."

Zero heard nothing but conviction in Olivia's voice. She had no doubt the woman was telling the truth. Her version of the truth. That was the problem with the truth—it was never absolute.

"We left him ten years ago," Olivia continued. "This is his payback."

"What's his name?" Jackson's fingers moved to his laptop.

"Louis. Louis Harding."

Twenty seconds later, Jackson looked up from the computer screen. Zero could bet he now had access to everything there was to know about Louis Harding, from his driver's licence type to the number of properties he owned and passwords to his social media accounts. But all that could wait.

"Mrs Kentwood," she matched the woman's posture by leaning in, but decided against the splaying of the hands. "Why did you run away last Saturday?"

"Because I saw him in our village when I was out running errands. His car was parked at the local motel. I phoned the receptionist, pretending I had an appointment with a Mr Harding, and she told me he'd already checked in. Such audacity, using his own name. It's a small place, detective, and there's only one school for girls. It was just a matter of time before he found us … found Bobbi."

Zero couldn't keep quiet. "You abandoned your daughter? Ran away?"

"No!" The woman looked appalled. "I protected her. She looks totally different now, after a decade of growing up, and there's no way my ex would recognise her. Me, I'm not so sure. My hair's different, and I have a few more wrinkles …"

None that Zero could see.

"… But I can't change my face. I worried if he were to bump into me … Or go knocking door to door … So I thought, if I just left Auckland, hung around the old neighbourhood, let all his spies report that I'm in Christchurch …" She trailed off yet another sentence before starting anew. "I've done it before."

Like a mother bird, Zero thought, feigning injury and leading the predator away from the nest.

Olivia Kentwood continued. "It worked, too, just took a bit longer than usual. I hired a girl to pose as my daughter, and we enrolled her in one of the schools."

"I'm sorry," Zero thought she'd misheard. "You hired a—"

"A young actress looking for extra cash. The theatres are still quiet this time of the year. With makeup, she could pass for a teenager, especially from afar. As soon as I got word that Louis had arrived in Christchurch, I flew home."

"You *got word*? How?"

Olivia shifted in her chair. "Why are you asking me this?" Her eyes scanned the room, as though marking the exits. There weren't many options. Number of doors, one. Number of windows, none.

Jackson raised his hand fractionally off the table to indicate to Zero that he would take this one. "It's just a routine question."

"Doesn't sound routine."

"Please just answer anyway."

Another scan of the room, counting the single door and the absence of windows. "I have a friend who works … at the airport in Christchurch."

Or for Air New Zealand, Zero thought. Or is able to do what Jackson does with computer systems. But that wasn't too important in the big scheme of things. "Why didn't you let your family know where you were? They were worried sick."

A look of cunning cut across Olivia Kentwood's face. "He has his people everywhere, Louis does. You have no idea what they're capable of. Stealing my phone to look through the list of numbers dialled, tracing my calls with remote gadgets. I can't leave an electronic trail, or he'll find Bobbi. When I read the newspaper article," her voice wobbled, "I worried that he had."

"Ma'am. Do you think you or your daughter are in danger? Would you like to seek a restraining order?"

"No," Olivia's head moved swiftly from side to side. "This way, he'd learn our new names and where we live. But if you arrest him for that girl's murder, we'll all be safe."

"Arrest him for Aiko's murder? She's very much alive, Mrs Kentwood. And Mr Harding is not responsible for her accident."

Olivia Kentwood stared into space, her face getting paler. "What are we going to do?"

"Ma'am, you have a few options—"

Olivia wasn't listening. She stood up and turned to the door, her movements stiff, her expression blank.

"Let me walk you out," Jackson said. When he came back, he plonked two fresh coffee mugs on the table. "I put her in a patrol car and sent her home."

"How is she?"

"Still robot-like. I offered medical assistance—did it look to you like she was in shock?—but she refused. I guess we'd better let her process, then touch base tomorrow. What do you think, Zimmerman?"

"I think it's time to contact Mr Louis Harding. See why he's so terrifying. Where is he? Christchurch?"

"Yep. According to his Facebook page, he's staying in the Rendezvous Hotel. Fancy a trip to the South Island?"

Zero thought about it. A two-hour flight with Jackson, sitting shoulder to shoulder and thigh to thigh. Dinner after work in the hotel restaurant, sharing a double room to save the taxpayer money …

"Why are you smiling like that?" Jackson asked.

"What? Oh. Just daydreaming. Could do with a holiday."

"You can say that again, Zimmerman. Meanwhile, here's the next best thing."

Zero assumed he'd make a lewd suggestion. When he didn't, she wasn't sure whether to be more annoyed at him or herself for the pale sliver of disappointment that flitted somewhere deep in her subconscious.

While Zero was dealing with her emotions, Jackson opened a window on his computer and clicked the mouse button a few times.

"Hello?" said a voice from Jackson's laptop. Zero angled her chair towards the screen now filled with the face of a middle-aged man. Greying temples, a narrow nose, a five o'clock shadow that appeared cultivated. The most obvious characteristic, politically incorrect as it may be to notice, was that he was obese, as though engorged with a despair that—instead of eating him up from the inside—weighed him down on the outside.

She couldn't be certain, but the man looked just like the one Madeleine Smith had met in a coffee shop on Monday.

Jackson must have been thinking the same thing, judging by the quick glance he shot her before directing his full attention to the screen. "Mr Louis Harding?"

"Yes?"

"Mr Harding, this is Detective Sergeant Jackson and Constable Zimmerman from the New Zealand Police, National Criminal Investigation Group. Sir, you're on a video call. May we proceed to talk to you?"

"What is this about?"

"Sir. May we talk to you?"

"Yes. In connection with what?"

"May we record this conversation?"

The man's features grew harder. "No. You may not. What is this about?"

"Your ex-wife—"

"That crazy bitch!" Louis Harding shouted right through Jackson. His neck reddened. "Has she laid a complaint against me?"

Jackson's voice was as smooth as an oyster. "Sir, I will ask you to calm down."

It did the trick.

"I apologise. Have you found my wife? More to the point, have you found Courtney?"

"Who's Courtney?"

"My daughter. She's fifteen."

"Mr Harding, is your daughter missing?"

Never before had Zero seen shoulders sagging as visibly as those of Louis Harding. It was as though a huge bag of sand had dropped onto his neck.

"For a decade."

Courtney Harding? Zero was certain she would have remembered the name, either from the newspapers or from open police files on missing persons.

Jackson must have been thinking along similar lines. "Did you report your wife and daughter missing at the time? Or since?"

An imperceptible murmur. Louis Harding rubbed his face from the cheekbones up with both hands. Sorrow? Hopelessness?

"Sir, could you please repeat that?"

"No. No. I didn't."

"You didn't report it?"

"No." Emphatic.

"Why not?"

"With respect, what would that achieve? What could you have done? There was no foul play."

Ten years ago, Zero mused, New Zealand already had security cameras. The police probably could have found the missing woman and child within days. Not that they would have necessarily encouraged anybody to return to a home that hadn't felt safe. Is that why Louis Harding hadn't contacted the police? Because he had made their home *not safe*?

Jackson was on a roll. "And you didn't worry about your daughter's wellbeing?"

"Hell yeah, I worried!" The noise that came from Jackson's laptop speakers resembled two fists banging together in a steady rhythm. "My wife—we're still married—was ill. When she took Courtney and disappeared …"

"Go on," Jackson said.

"Look, there's no easy way to say this. My wife … she suffers from paranoid schizophrenia. In her case, it manifests as persecutory delusions. While we lived together, she believed that I regularly put poison into her teapot, and also that I employed private detectives to spy on her."

Zero moved closer to the screen. "And did you?"

"No."

Truth.

"Did she get diagnosed?"

"She did, although as with most mental health issues, the process of diagnosing is more of an art than an exact science." Spoken like a lawyer: the choice of words careful to hedge bets. "Nevertheless, my wife consulted several specialists and received a diagnosis. The diagnosis made sense to us … to me, at least." A long pause.

"Yes?" Zero prompted.

Louis Harding closed his eyes. "She refused treatment, unfortunately. Shortly after that she disappeared, taking Courtney with her."

"And that was ten years ago?" Zero asked when it was clear he had come to an obstacle in his tale.

"Yes. I assumed—naively, as it turns out—that she'd be back once she got some space. To work through her issues, or whatever. But days turned into weeks. Then months and years. Sergeant, how I wished I had indeed employed a detective to keep an eye on her. On both of them. I haven't stopped looking."

Truth. Truth, Truth.

Turned out Olivia Kentwood was right in a way, Zero thought. Ever since she'd left him, Louis Harding had been looking for her. Her persecution mania had caused a real persecution.

It felt fitting and unfair all at once.

"What made you decide to look in Arcadia High Boarding School?"

"I've found out recently that the headmistress is an old friend of mine." The way he said it, Zero was sure *friend* meant *girlfriend*. His next words confirmed this. "I was hoping that she'd tell me, for old times' sake, whether Courtney was a current or past pupil at her school."

New Zealand was a small place. Still, wasn't it odd how the scene was full of Madeleine Smith's exes?

Louis Harding continued. "Arcadia was a tough nut to crack. My guys tell me it's impossible to break into the school roll for that place, because they're not on the internet."

Jackson's face said *challenge accepted.*

"Please tell me about Courtney," Louis Harding said. "Is she safe? Can I see her? Where is she?"

In the eyes of the law, he was the girl's father, with no custody arrangements in place because he was still married to her mum. The wife and the daughter had never officially gone missing and there was no restraining order.

In the eyes of what was responsible and morally right, however? It all depended on whether Louis Harding was a dangerous man, or one unjustly accused by his ill wife.

Zero couldn't call it. Either way, it sucked.

"She's safe, sir," Jackson said. "That's all we can disclose at the moment. Thank you for your cooperation."

Constable Zero Zimmerman

Zero was on her way out when somebody from the Prisoner Contact team phoned her back.

"I'm really sorry, Constable Zimmerman. Your sister doesn't want to see you."

Like a punch straight to the throat. It took a few seconds for Zero to find her breath. "I *need* to see her, though, convince her to apply for electronically monitored bail."

"It's a matter for her lawyer."

Zero swallowed a sigh. "The application itself, yes." Even though she was qualified to do it herself, she was too close to the case both as the arresting officer and as the perpetrator's sister. "What I need is her consent to apply for bail."

"Can't help you there, love. But if you write a letter or an email, we'll see that she gets it."

Zero knew the reason behind Millie's obstinance. Being remanded on electronically monitored bail meant that—in addition to wearing a tracking device—you had to have a house address where you could be remanded. Mum and Dad's house was the obvious choice, but Millie didn't want to subject their parents to that. Zero knew there was no money to rent a separate place, but perhaps her flatmates would agree to have Millie stay in Zero's room?

Zero put it all in the email, then added a quick introduction about Dad's mental health and an imploration to Millie to please agree to a visit, either from her parents or from her sister.

Then she put her face in her hands. Tried to cry. Failed.

Bobbi Kentwood

Mum's waiting for me outside the media study classroom as though it's the most natural thing, as though she hasn't been gone for almost a week. The world is a beautiful place once more. I run to her, swallowing big gulping sobs of both anger and relief, and throw my arms around her narrow shoulders. She returns my hug with a fierce squeeze.

"Let's go," she says.

The blockage in my throat loosens. "Go where?"

"Home. We don't have time." She takes my hand and leads me down the hill towards the car park, her eyes darting from side to side like caged laboratory mice.

I still don't get it. In my defence—why would I? It's been years since the last incident, and I always try hard to forget the packed rucksacks in the attic. "Why don't we have time? Do we have plans?"

"We're leaving, Bobbi. Hang on, you're not Bobbi anymore. What fun! You get to choose a new name. Any ideas? Brianna maybe? Or Leigh? It's your choice. And we could make you seventeen if you like."

"Mum." I halt my steps. She tugs at my hand again, her whole body in forward motion, but I stand my ground. "I'm Bobbi. Don't want to be anyone else."

"You will still be Bobbi. Just like you're still Courtney. You'll still have your memories, your personality, your gorgeous smile. A name doesn't define you."

My hand goes into my mouth, and I feel the comforting hardness of my fingernail between my teeth. I'm trying to remember what they taught us about identity in the philosophy classes last year. Something about your identity determining how you understand and experience the world. The question whether you at five are the same person as you are at fifteen—there was a heated debate about that, I remember it precisely because I don't think Courtney and I are the same person, though of course I didn't use it as an example. What else? Aiko was passionately against the idea that the key aspects of identity were gender, sexual orientation, ethnicity, religion. Come to think of it, she was as invested in the discussion as I was. At the time, I didn't wonder why. Now, of course, it all makes sense.

"Bobbi? Let's go."

I don't move. My finger is still in my mouth, waiting for the sweet release of tension that always comes with the first bite through the nail, so I remove it before I say, "If a name doesn't define me, why do I need a new one?"

Her lips part as she expels air in an exasperated exhale. "You know why, baby. It's too dangerous to stay here."

I wonder about that. Over the years, I've gone against my mum on many issues, from politics and abortion to miniskirts and drinking at parties, but I've never questioned her judgement when it came to my other dad.

"Why is it dangerous, mum?" My eyes drill into her face, trying to catch her out, but all I see is fear.

She shakes her head.

"We can tell the police," I venture. My fingernail is back in my mouth, but I'm not biting. It's not going to solve anything. "Constable Zimmerman will help."

Her eyes do that back-and-forth dance. "No honey. No police. He can trace the paperwork back to us."

"Blair can protect us then." Another thought strikes me. "Is Blair even coming with us?"

She closes her eyes for a moment. "I'm not sure."

That means no.

That's when it hits me: I *actually* like my life. Yeah, okay, I still hate the world and all its prejudice towards minority groups; I hate climate change; I hate that Savannah's been a flaky friend. But the world is not going to change if I move schools and become Brianna or Leigh. It's like appendicitis—it's not going to get better when you relocate to a different city. So, to continue with the analogy, if you have a sick appendix, you operate. If you're worried about the climate, you become an activist. You don't change your name to Rose and hope to start smelling all blossom-like—thanks, Will Shakespeare, you were one smart dude back in your day. Unless your poems and plays have been written by someone else; the best theory I've heard was some Italian chick, and it made a lot of sense what with the plays having ties to Italy and featuring girls who dressed up as boys.

So yeah, some things in my life could be better. But if I ever write a play worth publishing, I won't need to hide behind a male pseudonym. Also, we live in a comfortable house with a kind guy who drives me to the mall and is generous with pocket money. Our school is pretty luxurious for a prison and the teachers treat us like adults. The girls are probably no more bitchy than anywhere else in New Zealand, and I don't feel like making new friends elsewhere. And, of course, there is Vincent. And DK and Xander, for sure, but mainly Vincent.

"Mum," I'm surprised at the gentleness in my voice. My words are firm like igneous rock. "We're not going to run away anymore."

There. I've done it. The master of my fate, the captain of my soul, and ten out of ten for Classical English.

I inspect my index finger. The nail is still there. Intact.

Constable Zero Zimmerman

"What can I do to help?" Jackson asked. Just like that. Not *what's wrong*, or, *let me know if there's anything I can do*. Those would have been easier to brush off—a polite gesture between acquaintances, a social form to be completed then disregarded.

It was late evening, and the office was quiet. Most people were at home, enjoying a late dinner with their families, or surfing Netflix alone. Jackson didn't need to be at work, what with his case closed and the disappearing woman no longer disappeared. He could be dancing in one of the night clubs, pulling chicks or whatever it was he did in his spare time. And yet, here he was.

"Come on, Zee. Talk to me."

Keith's death hadn't made the news, but it had been mentioned in the police reports that morning. Either Jackson had put two and two together, or he was particularly perceptive. There was no way he would know about her disastrous attempt to visit Millie.

Still she went for evasion. "Don't know what you mean."

"Liar, liar. Shall I be dousing your pants with a fire extinguisher?"

"And here we are again. You trying—and failing—to get into my pants."

"Constable Zimmerman. Are you attempting to distract me by talking about me getting into your pants?"

"Is it working?"

"Kinda. Is it working for you?"

Zero had to admit that it was. *Kinda.* "No. So what now?"

"Dinner," Jackson said in a tone that meant no negotiations. "I bet you haven't eaten all day. But no drinks—just in case."

"In case of what?"

"In case you succumb to my charms, I want to be certain it's my charms and not sapphire gin."

Zero decided she could live with that. "Fish and chips, and a walk along the waterfront?" she suggested.

"Practical as well as romantic. Zimmerman, you're a real catch."

"I know."

Afterwards, she wasn't sure what had done it: the moonlit beach, the aphrodisiac properties of deep-fried oysters and long thick chips, her need to stop thinking about other people's depression for one night? Or perhaps it was the way Jackson's mouth reminded her of chocolate, and the fact that the sight of his jawline woke up butterflies in her stomach, and that his banter was not too terrible.

The rest of the night happened in short episodes, sharp like a high-res video clip slowed down to replay speed. The Uber ride from the beach to his apartment was a moving painting of liquid lights outside. His lips. Her impatience. Fine grains of sand stuck to his chest. The elevator: his hands electric on her skin.

The carpet in the entrance hall.

"We need protection," Jackson said.

Zero's heart became a hot marshmallow because he used a euphemism. Her inner warning system screamed at full volume: don't get involved, don't get involved!

Tonight she was so not going to let her emotions dictate her actions.

"It's all right, detective." She tried to find reassurance in their usual banter. "You can call a spade a spade. And a condom a condom."

She was going to prattle on, suddenly embarrassed by the reality of what was about to happen. Then Jackson's mouth was on hers again, shutting off her brain. The magic returned with renewed might.

The bedroom door.

The bedroom.

The bed.

And, yep, a gigantic glass bowl full of individually wrapped condoms, like a jar of lollies. And, just like lollies, probably in every colour and flavour, too. But then, what did she expect? She was about to have sex with a guy whose reputation was the worst-kept secret in the force. If policewomen were prone to writing on toilet walls, the female restrooms in the Auckland headquarters would be full of scribbles all amounting to: *For a good time—make it the best time in your life—call Jackson.*

"Zee?" Jackson murmured in her ear. "Are you still with me? You want to, um, go further?"

Despite the sudden sting of jealousy, totally uncalled for, she did want to go further.

So very, very much.

CHAPTER 18

Friday

Constable Zero Zimmerman

Jackson's bed was soft yet firm. Zero woke up to the aroma of his aftershave mingled with fresh coffee. The two scents went together surprisingly well, just like the two of them last night. She could feel the corners of her mouth ride up at the memory as she stretched under the lightest duvet she'd ever encountered.

"Morning, gorgeous." Jackson stood in the door, two mismatched mugs held expertly in one of his large hands.

It must be his morning-after routine, Zero thought as she yanked the duvet up to her chin before sitting up. *Get up early and shower, brew two coffees, make them to-go if he wanted to get rid of the one-night stand with an excuse of an early meeting, or china mugs if he wanted her to stay for another round of Opening the Gates of Mordor.* Ugh. She was beginning to think in euphemisms. All Jackson's fault.

Still, the coffee was excellent, and the sight of Jackson in a sun-coloured towel around his hips was even better. Zero was about to make a not-at-all-subtle reference to kilts, when her phone went off.

"Fuck." She only meant to think it, yet the word escaped her mouth before she could swallow it.

"Is that a request, Zimmerman?" Jackson's fingers were doing something miraculous with her shoulders and neck, and it was making her feel both relaxed and aroused.

"I knew you were going to say that," she lied as she inspected the phone. "And no." She attempted to read the message again, blanking out Jackson to make sure she took the words in this time. "Sorry. Have to go."

"Let me guess. It's work. You're a brain surgeon and they need you in the theatre."

"Almost right. Aiko woke up."

Jackson reached for his jeans. "Let me tag along. Don't worry, I won't take over. You're the lead." He dropped the towel and Zero found it impossible to look away. Most males weren't all that aesthetically pleasing when naked, like a proboscis monkey, but Jackson was in a different league altogether.

She should not be thinking about Jackson, or what he looked like in the nude, and especially not about the fact that he was going to spend his day commando.

On the way to the hospital, Zero allowed herself to believe that now everything would fall into place: Aiko would either confess to taking the overdose, or she'd reveal who'd given her the bottle of pills, or at least offer them an idea why anybody might have wished her ill.

Zero was disappointed.

The first obstacle was the doctor in charge, who was not super keen for the police to go near Aiko, quoting the patient's "physical and mental wellbeing."

The second obstacle was Mrs Hamasaki. "Have you found the person who did this to my girl?" she asked.

"That's what we're hoping to discover here," Zero replied as politely as she could. "Please?"

The final obstacle was Aiko herself. "I don't know," was her consistent answer to questions about what happened and whether she knew of someone who wished to harm her.

"What's the last thing you can recall?" Zero persisted.

"Taking a shower, maybe? Afterwards I came back to my room. Must have."

"Did you get dressed?"

"Can't remember."

Aiko had been found fully clothed and lying on her bed, so either she or somebody else would have had to dress her after the shower.

"Do you remember taking the sleeping pills?"

"I don't use any sleeping aids."

It sounded truthful enough. And it put Zero back on square one.

Madeleine Smith

Madeleine heard a soft knock on her office door.

"Mrs Smith? You wanted to see me?"

Bobbi Kentwood. Time to take that challenge head on.

And yet Madeleine didn't know how to start. *I found a poem under your mattress … no. It's all right to be confused about your gender … double no.*

She settled for "Bobbi, I'd like you to listen to me very carefully. You're a special young individual, and we love having you at the school. We'd hate to lose you, for any reason. Please let me know how the teachers and I can support you through the difficult time you're having."

The girl—was it all right to call Bobbi a girl?—offered Madeleine an uncertain smile. "Credits for all the internal assessments in maths would be awesome."

"A good one, Bobbi, though that wouldn't be productive for your learning outcomes in the long term. But how about something else? If anybody ever bullies you, or excludes you from their group, or makes your life uncomfortable, please let me know and we'll sort it out together. We celebrate differences in Arcadia. You should be proud of who you are."

It made Madeleine's heart swell to see Bobbi's delighted grin.

"Would you like to have a different bedroom, perhaps? One with an attached bathroom that's for your use only?"

"Wow, Mrs Smith, that would be splendid."

"Also, would you like to be a member of the committee tasked with redesigning the school uniform to be more politically correct and on trend?"

Another grin. "You bet, Mrs Smith. I love designing new fashion. Thank you for the vote of confidence."

"It's well deserved. Now, do your parents know about, the," she hesitated, "the situation?"

Bobbi's face clouded. "I—no. Wouldn't want to worry them. Nothing they can do, anyway."

Understandable, Madeleine thought. Still, it was her job to point out avenues of support. "When and if you're ready to talk to them about it, I'd be happy to be a part of the conversation, along with Mrs Linden. Does she know, by the way?"

"Mrs Linden? Yes. I've told her. Most of it, anyway."

"Good. Good."

That was one of the most awkward conversations Madeleine had ever had. Thank heavens it was over. She dealt with it like a woman—with sensitivity and discretion.

No, she told herself, *stop it*. Sensitivity and discretion were not inherently female, just like authority and decisiveness were not inherently male. The world could do with fewer stereotypes.

She consulted her to-do list. Make Arcadia a safe place for transgender students—check. Come to terms with being a woman in a man's world by rejecting the very terminology—check. Next up—repair the cracks in her marriage and deal with the Mekong Dragons. Piece of cake.

Bobbi Kentwood

Standing alone in the school's communal toilet block, I look at the row of basins and the neat stack of linen hand towels, but all I see is the future.

I'm getting my own bathroom. And I have the opportunity to design the new school uniform. Will wonders never cease? I don't know how she found out about the whole Savannah-Aiko debacle, but Mrs Smith's words of support are exactly what I need to forgive, forget and move forward.

Metaphorically speaking. Literally speaking, I don't want to move forward. Don't want to move anywhere. Fortunately, Mum's agreed to stay put for the moment. Blair wanted to get a court order to make sure my biological dad stayed away from us, but Mum's too paranoid about keeping our identities a secret, so that's a no-go, even though I'm sure there must be a legal way around it. We'll install a big fence and a house alarm instead.

The law as a subject to study at uni sounds pretty cool actually. I think about Constable Zimmerman who quotes paragraphs, and about legislation that can keep women safe. Yeah. Definitely something to consider.

Anyway, I might want to talk to him one day. My biological dad. Maybe on WhatsApp? Because, get this, what if she's wrong? What if we have spent all our lives running away and hiding from something that's not even a danger?

An image passes through my mind, a memory long forgotten. The smell of gingerbread. A Christmas tree full of gold and silver and red. A man's voice, not Blair's. *My little girl. My darling little girl. My greatest treasure.* A scratchy cheek against mine, the smell of ginger displaced by the smell of Daddy. In the memory, I'm laughing. For some stupid reason, here and now I seem to be trying hard not to cry.

In other news, Aiko is awake. I don't know how I feel about that.

But also, get this—Xander has built a hut for us in the bush, so that I wouldn't get my uniform green again.

Vincent is still the one, of course. And yet…

Xander.

Built.

Something.

Special.

Just.

For me.

For me! Like I matter. Like I'm not worthless. Like, he really likes me.

Mrs Smith's words come back to me. *You're special. We love having you at the school.*

I catch the eye of the girl in the lipstick-smudged mirror. Today, her ponytail has been pinned up into a bun so tight, it is a miracle she isn't gasping in pain. Without overthinking, I pull the pins out one by one until the ponytail falls back into its usual position. "You are not perfect," I tell her, "but you are appreciated. And that's enough."

It's not much, as far as revelations go, but for me, it's a breakthrough. Mrs Linden will be pleased. Of course, I shouldn't care what people think of me, but small steps.

When I get back to class, the teacher hands me a note. *See the school counsellor during morning tea.* Perfect timing.

As soon as the bell rings, I forego my muesli bar and enter Mrs Linden's office. Straight away, I want to tell her about my lightbulb moment, but protocols have to be observed. "You wanted to see me, Mrs Linden?"

"Yes, Bobbi. Sit." She seems distracted. "I'd like to talk to you about Vincent."

Panic stations. Vincent? Why? Surely, surely, she doesn't know. "Vincent?" The word comes out all croaky.

"Yes. It was a pity that you two didn't end up meeting last Sunday."

She's telling me?

"I'm really worried about him, Bobbi."

I nod, but it doesn't make sense. Why would she be worried about Vincent now, when Aiko's on the mend?

"Do you think you might like to make plans together this weekend? Go to the mall, or to the beach?"

Wait. Is she trying to set me up with Vincent?

Not that I'm not absolutely dying to go out with him, Xander or no Xander. But there's something inherently wrong with the way it's coming about.

I take care formulating the question. "Is that something Vincent would want?" I ask.

Her eyes look angry. "What he wants is not important. I need to ensure he gets what he needs."

Wait, what?

Something's very wrong here.

Constable Zero Zimmerman

"Jackson?" Zero said.

They were in the hospital's café, the chemical stench of medicine mingling with the odour of last week's hotdogs. Even her coffee smelled of Styrofoam. She sucked in a tentative sip, expecting to taste plastic. Fortunately, the liquid's taste did resemble coffee. Not very good coffee, but caffeine was caffeine.

He looked up from a twin Styrofoam cylinder. "Want to talk about last night?"

"So not!"

"Okay."

"Like, it never took place, all right?" The bitter in her mouth was not because of the coffee. Dump him first, before he could dump her. That's the only way she could salvage her pride. The sex had shifted the balance of power between them. Before, he was the one running after her, which was mostly irritating and a little flattering. She'd been tempted a few times, always knowing full well she could take it or leave it. Last night, she'd made the disastrous error of judgement to take it, on the assumption that it would be just a bit of fun. And it was fun. More than just a bit. If she were being honest with herself, she'd admit that … that … Oh, to hell with it. Her personal life could wait. Mrs Hamasaki's *have you found the person who did this to my girl* was weighing her down. "Jackson?"

"Like *what* never took place?" he replied, his face blank.

So that's how easy it was for him to file last night under *shit happens?* Right. It was what she wanted. Exactly what she wanted. "Awesome," she said. She drained her cup, crushed it in her fist, pushed it through a flap into a bin marked *Landfill* together with her feelings of guilt. "I'm hungry."

Jackson indicated the cafeteria's meagre display. "May I interest you in a soggy egg-and-pink stuff croissant? A scone you could probably break a window with? A packet of peanuts?"

In the end, they walked past pairs of parents with identically hollowed-out eyes, straight into Auckland's mid-morning sunshine. They turned right and continued onto the historic Grafton Bridge, closed to private vehicles at this time of day since 2009. Below them, the motorway buzzed to the rhythm of passing traffic, the sound almost hypnotic in its constancy. Ahead of them lay Karangahape Road in all its multi-culture glory: psychedelic graffiti, murals of Pacific Island women with fat flowers behind their ears, drag queens drinking apple tea in Turkish cafes. Karangahape Road—shortened to K Road by all Aucklanders—smelled of incense, cannabis, and fast-food shops. Zero dropped all her coins onto the dirty-pink blanket of a homeless man with a brown Labrador.

"This sushi shop is good," Jackson pointed.

"What? Where? That's an ice-cream parlour. See, Bangkok rolled ice-cream. Whatever that is."

"They pour liquid ice-cream onto a freezing plate, mix it with fruit, then scrape it into a roll. And the good sushi place is behind it."

Indeed, right next to the ice-cream rolls was a small doorway that led into an Asian food court. A tiny Japanese man waved at Jackson, and Jackson called out something that must have been a greeting.

Zero ordered salmon sushi and was surprised to see the chef make it on the spot. A few minutes later, two plates of nine pieces each arrived at their plastic table, complete with a dipping bowl of soy sauce, a green splotch of wasabi, thin slices of ginger, and a cup of complimentary miso soup.

"I'm impressed," she said, her mouth still full. This was the freshest sushi she'd ever eaten. "Delicious."

Jackson nodded.

"So," she said in a pause between piece number five and six. She was already feeling full, yet she wanted to keep eating. "Remember on Tuesday, when we looked through Miss Patel's laptop, the one from last year, the boys' school?"

"Uh-huh."

Jackson was on his miso soup. Zero picked up her sixth piece of sushi and pushed the remainder onto his empty plate.

"Did we finish looking through all the files you recovered? We didn't, did we? First the call from the forensic expert interrupted us, and then you found out about Theo Linden's suicide, which distracted us, and we never got back to the computer."

Jackson gathered the three sushi pieces and put them into his mouth all at once. Then he pulled out his phone, a big model that nevertheless looked tiny in his fingers. His fingers—no, she was not going there.

"What are you going to do," Zero quipped, trying hard not to think about Jackson's hands, "phone Parvati Patel's laptop?"

"Exactly. I can access it remotely using RDP."

"Huh?"

He rolled his eyes at her. "You muppet," he said. He had gorgeous eyes. "The laptop is running something called Remote Desktop. I can log into it from another electronic device."

"Can anybody else?"

"Only if they know my password."

A totally irrational desire to know his password and all his secrets raced through Zero's heart. She had a quick silent talk with herself about the merits of not being an idiot or a fool in love. It didn't help much.

"Here we are," Jackson angled the phone towards her and, as she moved closer to the screen, their heads met. She didn't pull away.

What did that brief physical contact matter, after last night?

She. Would. Not. Go. There.

"Anything specific you're looking for? I browsed through the files a few days ago. There are university assignments for her qualification, tons of lesson plans for the classes she taught, browser history for a million YouTube videos, emails, social media—"

"Let's see her social media posts."

The food court was relatively empty. The sushi shop owner came out to collect their plates and wipe their table. A few shoppers emerged from the Asian supermarket next door, their conversation lost to Zero because of the language barrier.

Jackson trawled through photos of school functions, brunch dishes, iced coffees.

"Friends? Direct messages?" Zero asked.

"Here's something," Jackson said. "One user has been blocked."

"Who?"

"Kiwi_Mind_Soul."

"Who's that?"

"Give me a moment." He played with his phone as minutes ticked away. "It would be easier from my computer."

"Is that a trick to get me back to your apartment, Detective?"

Please say yes, please say yes.

"No." It was a curt *no*. There was no room for misinterpretation. Oh well. That's what she wanted, wasn't it? Wasn't it?

She let him get on with it.

"Got it. Kiwi_Mind_Soul is registered to the Gmail account of one Emmanuelle Linden."

"The school's mental health counsellor? Why would Parvati Patel block her? Wait, this is the old laptop, so that was before she even started working for Arcadia High." Her mind raced. "Hang on.

Naturally, Emmanuelle Linden is also a parent at St Alban's Boys Highschool. Vincent and Theo." Zero could taste the adrenaline in her mouth, her vision narrowed to only the phone's screen, the noise of the café suddenly distant. "Can we go back to the emails? Anything from Emmanuelle Linden."

"They had been permanently deleted before the whole laptop was reformatted," Jackson said.

"Is that a problem?"

"Of course not. I've recovered everything. Just letting you know that Parvati Patel tried to erase them from her inbox."

"Getting rid of evidence?"

"More like getting rid of bad memories."

Zero stared at a string of emails from Emmanuelle Linden. She read them one after another, moving Jackson's finger when he didn't scroll fast enough.

"I'll be damned," Jackson said at last. "Zimmerman, I believe you've done it. Congratulations."

"Screw the congratulations. I need a car."

Bobbi Kentwood

Mrs Linden's office is not a safe place. For years, this was my favourite room in the whole school. Here, I could be myself. Or at least as much of myself as I could ever be with another person.

But now Mrs Linden has an agenda. "I know you don't like Aiko," her words are clipped, her voice sharp. If she were a cat, she'd be hissing. "You've seen how she turned Savannah against you. You know how much damage she can do. Don't you think that she should be put in her place?"

I don't. At least, I didn't. But now the pain and the humiliation are back.

"Yes." It comes out as a whisper.

"So you'll keep Vincent away from her? Make sure she can't hurt him again?"

This is not how a therapist should behave. Yeah, I get it, she's a mum and she's worried about her son, but still.

Suddenly I get it.

And I see that she sees me get it.

The chair falls when I jump up. "I have to go."

"Bobbi? Bobbi!"

The distance to the exit stretches like bubble gum. I run as though in slow motion, and the door moves away with every millisecond that rushes by.

A hand grips my shoulder. I twist sideways and down. Pain. So much pain concentrated in the hollow above my collar bone. Then pressure in the side of my neck. Then blackness.

Constable Zero Zimmerman

The car Zero needed was back in the hospital's parking lot. Together they sprinted back over Grafton Bridge, narrowly missing meeting a navy-and-grey double decker bus head on.

Jackson was a few seconds faster, so he got the driver's seat.

"Don't take K Road," Zero panted as she jabbed the latch plate of her seatbelt into the buckle. "Too many traffic cones."

He turned right and sped towards the interchange between State Highway 16 and State Highway 1, cursing as the red light caught them.

"Second left to go to Arcadia High," Zero sad. "The first left takes you south."

"It's a bloody maze."

It wasn't really, but they were both unfamiliar with that part of town and stupid with too much adrenaline. Jackson saw the second turn to the left at the last minute and spun the wheels to make the tight turn. He should have given way to the cars turning from the other direction, but Zero chose not to comment. They were alive and the car wasn't even scratched.

"Faster," she said when they hit the motorway running north.

"You're kidding, right?"

It was a sunny Friday afternoon, and the entire Auckland population was leaving the city for the white sands and blue waters of the northern beaches. The motorway wasn't exactly standing still, but the big crawl towards the Harbour Bridge took them fifteen minutes. Another ten to get past Albany.

"Faster," she said again.

They were ahead of the traffic now. Most cars must have turned off to go home for the luggage and the rest of the family.

"Imagine making a movie scene with a car chase back in downtown Auckland," Jackson quipped. Now that the road was clear, he was driving twenty percent over the speed limit, his hands calm on the steering wheel, his eyes scanning ahead.

"You'd have to abandon the car and run over the rooftops."

"Plenty of foot chases in movies. Keanu in the *Matrix*? Keanu in *Point Break*?"

Jackson accelerated again and Zero felt her face screw up into a wince. "Keanu in *Speed*?"

"You're funny, Zee, you know that?"

"I do know that. Now shush. I need to think."

She needed a plan for when they got to the school. Other than searching out Emmanuelle Linden, she was plum out of ideas.

Jackson ignored the visitors' parking bays and screeched to a halt on the circle-of-life driveway right outside the admin building. Zero's feet hit the ground when the car was still rocking. She burst through the main entrance—fortunately not yet locked up for the day—sprinted to Mrs Linden's office and flung the door open without knocking.

Emmanuelle Linden was kneeling over a small body crumpled up on the floor, a sofa pillow in her hands.

"Freeze, police!" Zero shouted. It wasn't the phrase she was supposed to use, this one came out of hours and hours of watching *Brooklyn 99*. As phrases went, this one wasn't effective. Mrs Linden froze for only a second, before she sprang up and rushed out the sliding door into the garden.

"On it," Jackson called. "Help Bobbi."

The girl lay on the floor, eyes closed, not moving. "Bobbi," Zero said, shaking her shoulder. "Bobbi, can you hear me?"

Nothing.

Her First Aider training tried to break through the layers of panic. *Calm down, calm down. You're in charge.* DR ABC stood for Danger, Response, Airway, Breathing, Circulation. She'd already ignored Danger—check to see if it's safe to approach the casualty. She'd done Response and Bobbi wasn't responding. What was next? Airway—make sure the airway is open and clear. Zero placed one hand on Bobbi's forehead to tilt the head back and used two fingers from the other hand to lift the chin. B, breathing—the girl's chest didn't look like it was rising or falling. Zero put her ear to Bobbi's mouth and listened. She couldn't hear anything, but she felt a warm wisp of breath tickle her skin.

She placed Bobbi in the stable side position—it was no longer called the recovery position because some victims sadly couldn't recover, and as she monitored her breathing and checked for any signs of bleeding, she cried.

Bobbi Kentwood

Feels like no time has passed, but the very next moment I'm lying on my side, under a foil blanket, and the back of my head feels like it's on fire. But no, the only fire is in the light that reflects off Constable Zimmerman's hair.

"Mrs Linden," I try.

And the cop makes a shushing sound. "We know Bobbi, lie still."

Poor Vincent, I think.

Constable Zero Zimmerman

An ordinary interview room at the Auckland Central police station, the recording equipment running.

Two ordinary women, one on each side of the table.

An extraordinary story waiting to be coaxed out.

"I don't need a lawyer," Emmanuelle Linden repeated, her voice shriller than on previous occasions. Her back was pressed into the chair, her arms folded across her body, creating distance and barriers. "It's all a misunderstanding."

Zero went with vagueness. "We can agree that mistakes were made."

"My behaviour could have been more professional," Emmanuelle Linden clasped her hands into a ball, one of the thumbs moving in slow circles across her skin. "I deeply regret the incident with Bobbi."

"What happened there? Did Bobbi act in a threatening manner?"

"She … I … I believe I thought she was being irrational … a danger to herself. I was trying to restrain her …" Mrs Linden's voice grew softer, faded to nothing.

"How did she act? What made you conclude that she was being irrational?"

"She … she started shouting."

"What was she shouting?"

"My recollection is that she was confessing to trying to poison Aiko."

"And what did you do then?"

"I … I tried to comfort her. I may have reached out to put my arms around her."

Zero closed her eyes to hide the roll. "Okay."

"I'm really sorry if she thinks I was trying to hurt her."

"Okay," Zero said again.

She opened a thick cardboard file and made a show of flicking through sheets of paper. Some were printouts of newspaper articles about Miss Patel's drowning and Theo Linden's suicide. There were witness statements from Aiko's teachers, the matron, even the cook at Arcadia High. There was a transcript from the conversation they'd had with Louis Harding, Bobbi's biological dad, the previous day. There were forensics reports and data dumps from Aiko's phone.

"Now going back to Friday last week," Zero said, tapping one of the sheets, which happened to be one of Theo's messages to Miss Patel. "The morning the ambulance came to attend to Aiko. Please think carefully before you answer," Zero said, employing her usual interview tactic of raising the stress levels in the interviewee. "Is there any reason somebody would have come forward to say they saw you go into Aiko's room that day?"

The question was carefully phrased. Although nobody had seen Emmanuelle near Aiko's room, Zero hadn't lied. She hadn't said there was a witness. She had simply asked whether there was a reason for someone to have come forward.

She really needed a confession. So far, their only evidence was Bobbi's account of what happened in Emmanuelle Linden's office, as well as a handful of emails to Parvati Patel. A defence lawyer would only need to point to Bobbi's subsequent blackout to make her recollection worthless. As to the emails, they could at best support a charge of cyberbullying.

"Mrs Linden? Is there any reason somebody would have come forward—"

"I … may have gone there to talk about her art."

"Why didn't you tell us before?"

Silence.

"You're a good person, Mrs Linden. I can see that. Please help me understand."

Emmanuelle Linden pushed her tongue in and out of her mouth, as though dislodging something distasteful. She looked smaller now, deflated. "What can I say, Constable? Sometimes you do everything right as a mother. You're there for your kids. You listen. You talk to them—at them—about mental health and that depression is like the flu, nothing to be ashamed of, no stigma in asking for help." She drew her elbows closer to her sides, a subconscious attempt at protecting her body from danger.

"Okay."

"But sometimes … sometimes that's not enough. Trying to raise your children to be emotionally resilient is a myth. As a professional I can tell you that it's like walking—you can show them how to put one foot in front of the other, you can hold them upright, but ultimately you can't do it for them."

"Okay." Zero found herself nodding. Regardless of what she thought about couch therapy and probing old wounds, she agreed that ultimately the only person who could make the decision to get better was the patient. "Can I get you a glass of water?" she offered. She could tell from the other woman's slumped shoulders and bowed head that she was close to breaking point. "Mrs Linden?"

A small shake of the head.

"Tell me about Theo," Zero tried next, a wave of empathy rolling over her. Seeing her dad struggle with depression had been heart-wrenching, the shock of Keith's death still crushed Zero's soul like an ever-present boa constrictor of blame, and the combination had messed with her head so much it had propelled her straight into Jackson's bed. No wonder that a son's suicide could send his grieving mother over the edge.

With quick angry brushes of her fingertips, Mrs Linden flicked droplets from under her eyes. "Theo was the oldest, my first baby, born at the end of a long and sticky summer. We had just brought him home from the hospital, three or four days old, when a mosquito founds its way into his bedroom. I don't know how, we were so careful with the windows, closing them as soon as the sun hit the horizon, burning citronella candles in the house. I had just put Theo down in his bassinet after a feed, when I spotted a big fat mosquito on his perfect pink cheek. Couldn't smack the mozzie, of course, without hurting Theo; and the effing thing wouldn't budge when I tried to shoo it away. Eventually I brushed it off and squashed it against the wall of the bassinette. Fresh blood came out, bright red, my baby's blood. My baby's blood. My baby's blood was in that … horrid monster. I went crazy. I smeared the mosquito's remains into the bassinette, over and over again, rubbing it until there was nothing left, all the time wishing with all my soul that the creature would come back to life so that I could hunt it down and kill it all over again. If that's what I wanted to do to an insect, imagine how I felt about anyone who broke my boy's heart."

"Like Miss Patel?" Zero prompted.

Emmanuelle Linden's nostrils dilated. "Parvati Patel. Sounds like a comic book character, the alliteration? Lois Lane. Clark Kent.

Parvati Patel. Poisonous Parvati Patel."

Zero nodded again, murmured to move the story along. "What happened?"

Emmanuelle Linden looked her straight in the face. "I can't go to prison. Vincent needs me."

Should have thought about that before killing anybody, Zero thought, then quickly tried to unthink it. Justice required compassion, not callousness.

"People make mistakes," she said, returning to the interrogation technique of labelling a crime a bad choice. "Now we need to get ahead of the problem. We all want that."

"Yes," the other woman whispered. "When Parvati rejected him, Theo … he couldn't cope with it. I wish I'd realised before … before it was too late. I wish he'd known how magical and special he was, and that he would find love again, real love that's reciprocated." Mrs Linden's eyes were brimming with tears, but her voice remained steady. "I don't remember the funeral, only the sound of the flag at his school, flapping in the wind at half-mast. Afterwards, I sent her emails. So many emails explaining how it was all her fault. She never understood. She didn't want to take responsibility."

"It's tough." Zero paused a few beats. "You blamed Parvati Patel for Theo's death?"

More tears. "That she-devil. Bewitched him, let him feed her ego, then threw his emotions under the bus."

Zero knew better than to ask what Mrs Linden imagined should have happened instead: a romance between a teacher and one of her underage students? As inappropriate as it sounded to most people, would that have been a better alternative than the suicide of a teenage boy and the murder of a young teacher? After all, the French president had had an affair with his teacher when he was sixteen, and the Macron couple served as an example of what could be accomplished if you stop worrying about other people's opinions. "So you met Miss Patel at the Arcadia High school pool?" she prompted.

Theo's mother waved her hand, as though banishing a pesky sand fly. "That's not how it went. When I sent her all those emails, I hoped she'd crumble with guilt and kill herself too. That would have been justice. That would have been … like Romeo and Juliet."

The last time Zero had read the Shakespearean tragedy, the themes were neither guilt nor justice. Her nit-picking nature itched to issue a correction. Her more humane side asked: "What happened?"

"I can't go to jail." Emmanuelle repeated. "Can we make a deal?"

One of the problems with people was that they watched too much television. They thought all your problems could be resolved by the end of the episode. "Striking a deal, that's how it works in America, not in New Zealand. However, the judge will take your confession and cooperation into account when deciding on the sentence."

Nothing.

"I'd like you to look at something," Zero paged through the papers in her file one by one until she found Miss Patel's autopsy report. She pulled it out but held it in her hand, making Emmanuelle Linden lean forward to read it. "See here? That wound in Miss Patel's head? That's something that's been inflicted deliberately." Not a complete lie, just not the complete truth, either. "You will need to explain it in court."

Emmanuelle Linden shrank even further into the chair. Her face was ashen, her eyes exhausted. "It was an accident." Deep, barely audible.

Bingo, Zero thought.

"I was working late that night. From my office in the admin

block, I spotted her—Parvati—on the footpath heading for the pool. Of course, I knew she had transferred to our school, but it was the first time I'd seen her since the funeral. I thought I'd have it out with her, this time in person. Maybe then she'd understand. So I followed her." She swallowed, fell silent once more.

Zero could feel the beating of her own heart. "What happened then?"

"We—we argued. I pushed her into the water—not an angry push—it was meant to give her a shock. I didn't want to kill her!"

"Okay."

"But she must have hit her head and passed out in the pool. I didn't find out until the next morning. I pushed her, and then I turned away, and then I left."

That was consistent with the coroner's report: a bump on the head that could have rendered the victim unconscious but not kill, cause of death—drowning.

"But you know what?" the woman continued, her eyes suddenly bright, angry blotches on her cheeks. "If I hadn't turned away, if I had seen that she—that she was struggling to swim—I still wouldn't have helped her. I would have watched her breathe in the pool water, one gulp after another, until her soul left her body to join Theo's in the afterlife. My boy," her voice cracked, her face split open. "My beautiful boy."

The grief was so raw, Zero was tempted to lead the desolate mother out of the police station and hide her from the legal consequences of her crimes—something she hadn't even considered doing for her own sister when she'd had a chance. Did that make Constable Zero Zimmerman an upstanding fighter for justice or a bad sister?

Zero had to remind herself Emmanuelle Linden had almost

taken another life in her quest for vengeance, this time of a teenager. She made her voice stern, no-nonsense. "What about Aiko?"

Mrs Linden fished a tissue out of her bag, blew her nose, took a few deep breaths. With every word she looked lighter, unburdened. "Vincent had a crush on Aiko last year. Roughly the same time as Theo was in love with … when all that other stuff was going on. They were close like that, my two boys, Vincent always looking up to his older brother, emulating him down to the clothes he wore and the way he parted his hair. So when Theo was crushing on someone, Vincent would find himself a crush as well. Aiko toyed with him, she'd play hot and cold, never saying yes or no. One day she'd act like they were a couple, the next she'd leave his messages on "seen" and never reply. It didn't help that she had no internet access—sometimes Vincent wouldn't know where he stood from one weekend to the next." She paused. "May I have that glass of water now?"

Zero returned with a paper cup, and Emmanuelle Linden continued. "After Theo was gone, Vincent started cutting himself. I sent him to one of my colleagues, one of the best in dealing with adolescents. Time passed and Vincent healed, or we thought he'd healed. But at the beginning of the summer holidays he started talking to Aiko again. I mean, *talking* as in spending time with her online. And hanging out at the beach. And going to the movies. Always in a group of friends—she never wanted to meet him for a date. Then the new school year started, and they carried on socialising on weekends. Every counselling session I had with that girl, I tried to warn her off to stay away from my boy, because he would not survive another breakup."

Zero tried to stay impartial. Found she couldn't. "That's why you tried to kill her?"

"Not *kill*. Just … remove her from his orbit for a while, give him the opportunity to notice other girls. Notice how much girls like Bobbi Kentwood are keen on him."

"Aiko could have died."

"It wasn't a lethal dose, I made sure of that. Also, it was a matter of Aiko's health or Vincent's life. I was protecting my son. For weeks he'd been moody and withdrawn, just like Theo before …" A long pause, then, "I did what had to be done."

Only the truth in Emmanuelle Linden's voice. Because it was the truth? Or because it was the story she told herself over and over until she believed it?

"You forced her to swallow the sleeping pills?" Zero knew that was incorrect, but she had to make sure she was getting a true confession.

"Forced her? No. You think that I'm the kind of person who uses violence?"

Yes, thought Zero, her compassion temporarily pushed aside. *You're the kind of person who kills people.* "So what happened?" she asked.

"Aiko drinks a tablespoon of apple cider vinegar in her water bottle every morning. She told me in one of our sessions that it was her way of keeping her body and spirit healthy. That Friday morning, I went into her room early. I had an excuse ready. I was going to ask her to come and see me at lunchtime about a potential client for her artwork, and when she busied herself with her portfolio, I'd slip the crushed tablets into the bottle. As it happened, Aiko was in the shower when I came, so it was even easier. An hour or so later, just after the first bell, I went back to wash out the water bottle. I also left that poem there and arranged the pills."

Mrs Linden fell silent. Her hands were shaking, and the ice cubes clinked against each other in the plastic cup.

"Were they your prescription pills, Mrs Linden?" Zero could verify it later with the pharmacy database, the question was simply to start Mrs Linden talking again.

"No. They were Theo's. From back when he had anxiety over that bitch of a teacher. I thought that was fitting."

More silence. A small sad smile now graced Emmanuelle Linden's lips.

"Where did you find the poem?"

"Bobbi's file. Bobbi Kentwood. Every week, the girls do journaling for their mental health. It's like a warning system to protect the girls from bullying or self-harm. Meant to be structured, with one highlight, one lowlight, and one wish, but some students like to go off script. Bobbi often submitted poetry instead of a journal entry."

"What about fingerprints?"

"I wiped the door handle and the bottle. And the poem, of course."

That wouldn't play well in court, Zero knew. "Did you try to press Aiko's fingers onto the items?"

"No!"

If Mrs Linden were telling the truth, Aiko's smudged prints must have been the result of the bottle of pills coming to contact with her fingertips. "Did you check whether Aiko was still breathing?"

"I—I couldn't look at her. She was lying very still …"

Zero leaned in, as though confiding a secret. "I thought that's what you wanted? For her to lie there and never wake up?"

Mrs Linden buried her face in a fresh tissue. "That sounds horrible! It's not like I stabbed her through the heart or even pushed her into the pool. I simply dissolved some powder in water. Aiko had a choice whether to drink the water or not. The rest was up to fate."

"And that makes it okay?"

"Constable, let me tell you something. You don't know how evil you are until someone threatens the wellbeing of your child. One day, when you're a mother, you'll understand."

The thought of parenthood changing you into a monster made Zero shudder. It was just as well Zero wasn't planning on being a mother any time soon. Make that, ever.

Madeleine Smith

Madeleine Smith knew exactly what she wanted to do—sell up. Louis Harding seemed so interested in her school the other day—she couldn't quite remember the conversation, but he did ask a lot of questions, so perhaps he had been scouting it out as a possible investment for himself or one of his clients? She'd help them hire her replacement, somebody who would continue Madeleine's dream of an internet-free utopia, while she and Ashton and the kids would move away. Without her mother-in-law, and without the demands of the principal's job, Madeleine would be free to concentrate on helping Ash beat his mental health issues once and for all.

The twins would see it as an adventure. Savannah, though? The same arguments that made it impossible for the family to enter a witness protection program were very valid here—teenagers were notoriously difficult to uproot. Perhaps she could stay on at the boarding school and come home to the new house for the holidays.

As for Madeleine, she would stop being Madeleine Smith, headmistress, and embark on the quest to discover who she really was. She would still be a mother and a wife, but that was all right, she didn't need to shed those labels in order to unearth her identity. In fact, she was beginning to suspect a person's identity couldn't even exist outside the parameters of human relationships.

But apart from being a wife and a mother, who was she? What

movies did she enjoy watching when not constrained by other people's choices? What one-person adventures would she describe in this year's Christmas letter? Scuba diving? Parachuting? Watching turtles lay their eggs on a remote island, or helping in an orangutan orphanage in the exotic Borneo? Writing a book? The world was out there, and she would get to taste it. Savour it. Experience it with all her senses.

Yes, Madeleine knew exactly what she wanted to do. She also knew that she wouldn't. What would they live on? Even if they were to sell their share of Arcadia High, the money would go straight towards covering their debts. Or rather towards not covering their debts.

Also, selling up would feel like running away, and Madeleine Smith prided herself on facing—and crushing—her challenges.

When she got home after school, she didn't notice anything unusual. As it was the end of the school week, Savannah was expected home for the weekend, but for now she must have gone out with friends. In the kitchen, Granny Smith was taking part in a complicated game of one-person chess with pots and chopping boards. The twins were playing in the treehouse—Madeleine knew this because two pairs of sandals lay higgledy-piggledy below, and two almost-identical voices spoke through one another behind the branches.

Ashton was not in his study. Nor in the lounge. Not the garden or their bedroom. His car had been in the garage when she'd parked hers there. His motorbike? She couldn't recall. Just then her phone rang, and she went back into school principal mode again, so it wasn't until dinnertime that she noticed the empty chair and no setting on the table in front of it.

"Where's Ashton?" she asked.

The worry about her husband, Madeleine realised, was her constant companion. Whenever she couldn't locate him, her thoughts immediately turned to the worst-case scenario. His depression was as unpredictable as the weather. But her mother-in-law wouldn't be cooking dinner if something—bad—had happened.

Granny Smith shot her a look while ladling the mac and cheese into bowls. Madeleine knew there would be at least five vegetables hidden in the sauce. Happy kids, happy mother and grandmother.

"He'll be back tomorrow," her mother-in-law said so smoothly, Madeleine was sure she must have practised the tone of voice while grating the carrots. "Talk later," she mouthed, her eyes meeting Madeleine's.

Uh-oh.

"Mum, can we watch the Disney Channel after bath?" William.

"Please, darling Mummy?" Watterson weighed in.

"Pretty please?"

She knew they were buttering her up, yet she couldn't say no.

"Now. About Ashton?" she asked again when the boys had been bathed, pyjamaed and settled in front of the brain-drainer.

Granny Smith thinned her lips. "He is … gone, for the moment. Rethinking his priorities, you might want to call it, though to me it looks like he's ditching his responsibilities and abandoning ship in order to work out what he wants in life. It's a bugger to say it, but family doesn't seem to be a priority at present. I'm so, so sorry. I should've raised him better."

Madeleine didn't know how to respond. To contradict or placate would feel insincere. Most of all, she couldn't believe that Granny knew the word *bugger*. That's why it took a while for the emotions to hit her. Ashton. Gone. He'd left her.

The up-till-now totally theoretical concepts of loss, hurt and rejection came at her like arrows, sharp and sleek and swift, but they failed to penetrate. *It must be the shock*, she thought. The shock was making her numb.

Good. Numb was good.

"Madeleine? Please say something."

She shook her head, hoping to jiggle her disarrayed thoughts into some semblance of a pattern, like in a kaleidoscope. "I don't understand. I thought he couldn't live without me." Not the sort of thing you should be telling your mother-in-law, but it couldn't be unsaid, so Madeleine ploughed on. "He needed me to keep his depression at bay. And he was the one who wanted to have children. He's a great dad."

"Ashton likes the *idea* of having a family. Not necessarily the *reality* of having it. In the old, old days, he'd have been a sailor coming home once a year with precious silks and spices, marvelling at how much the children had grown, then cruising away again before boredom set in."

Madeleine nodded, an empty gesture without any real understanding behind it. She could picture Ashton in a sailor's hat, with a broad collar. Navy blue. Or white? Either way, he'd look smashing.

"I know about his," her mother-in-law hesitated, "online problem."

That made Madeleine blush. She still didn't know what to say, but she said it anyway, just to navigate away from the subject. "When he's had a few weeks to ponder, perhaps we should suggest that he gets help. You know, professional mental health support. A men's group, maybe. Or a counsellor."

Granny Smith opened her mouth, closed it, opened it again.

"What?" Madeleine asked.

"Ash has been seeing a therapist, honey. Every day for the last three years or so. I'm not sure why he chose to keep it a secret from you."

Madeleine didn't react but her brain performed a quick calculation all by itself. An hour a day at two hundred bucks an hour, two-fifty maybe, five days a week … that was a lot of money. Two hundred dollars could buy a week's worth of food for a family on a budget. No wonder their finances were shot. And Ashton would let her believe it was all going to online porn sites rather than admit he was spending it on sorting out his health. Silly man.

"What happens now?" she asked.

"Now we just carry on. Make sure he continues with his therapy while he figures himself out. Meanwhile, he's going to visit the boys every day. And you, of course, if you want to see him."

"What about you?"

"I'll stay here. You are Wonder Woman, my dear, but nobody should be running both a school and a household."

Madeleine tried to process. "So, wait. You're taking my side?"

Granny Smith shook her head. "I'm not taking anybody's side, Madeleine. Simply doing what's right."

Constable Zero Zimmerman

As Zero was falling asleep, a sudden thought jerked her out of bed. The photo of that van on Parvati Patel's phone.

She logged into the motor vehicle register from her laptop. The number plate yielded the make and model of car (Toyota Previa) and the current registered owner. The current registered owner was a company called *Luck Laundry.*

Had Miss Patel been taking pictures of a van collecting the school's dirty linen?

The register of New Zealand companies informed her that *Luck Laundry* was co-owned by Quan Le and Hai Le, the businessmen suspected of running the New Zealand branch of the Mekong Dragons.

And now she had photographic evidence of—what? She couldn't prove that the photo had been taken on the grounds of Arcadia High. Or could she?

She dialled Jackson's number.

"Hello?" he sounded out of breath.

Damn! What if she'd interrupted a sex session?

Not that she cared. At all.

"Is this a bad time? Shall I call back?"

"Nah. Always happy for a break when doing leg exercises. What do you need? Miss me already?"

"Miss your wizardry with electronics. If I showed you a mobile phone—"

"Another phone?"

"Yeah, no password. Could you tell the location and timestamp of a photo taken with it?"

"Sure. Want me to come over?"

"No," she said quickly. "Tomorrow. Or Monday. No hurry."

"As you wish."

Had Jackson just quoted her favourite movie? Zero decided not to go down that particular avenue.

Chapter 19

Saturday

Madeleine Smith

It was another sunny day, a parting gift from the rapidly ageing summer. The humidity was giving way to ocean breezes, not yet cool enough to be called crispy, but with a promise of respite from the heat. The cream-coloured kitchen cabinets gleamed in the morning light with optimism Madeleine was finding difficult to share.

She could hear the twins play with robust enthusiasm in Granny Smith's bedroom. Outside, the garden vibrated with the invasive ticking of a million cicadas. Inside the kitchen, the coffee machine pinged its readiness, and Madeleine began the morning coffee ritual. It was ironic that the more expensive the machine, and the more complex the process, the more difficult it was to get a decent brew at the end.

Coffee was usually Ashton's job. Madeleine measured off the beans into a separate—and hideously expensive—grinder, pressed the button. The noise was reassuringly familiar, the smell of freshly ground coffee intoxicating.

She was battling to tamp the grounds hard enough and level enough when she heard a bedroom door slam. Soon, heavy footsteps approached the kitchen and a cloudy face appeared in the doorway.

"It's all your fault," Savannah said instead of a *good morning*. "Ashton left because of you. You should have tried harder."

Madeleine felt the blow land, absorbed it, ignored the pain. If she had a mental health counsellor, she would probably be told she dealt with things by suppressing them. As far as coping strategies went, it wasn't a shabby one.

Still, she was a mum, and her job was to control toxic behaviour. There were times when she worried Savannah would grow up into someone that hurt people. Other times, she told herself that it's better to hurt others than to get hurt. Today, she couldn't decide. Savannah seemed to both receive and dish out pain in equal amounts.

"Mum? Say something."

Madeleine could do that much, at least. "What would you like for breakfast, honey? Pancakes? Eggs bene? A smoothie?"

"Mum. Are you even listening? Or are you just pretending to be interested in what I have to say?"

"I'm listening. And I don't like what you're saying."

"Typical! You're acting like I'm this huge burden you have to *endure*."

Right then, Madeleine thought. *I'm a failed wife and an ungrateful daughter-in-law. And now also, apparently, a lousy mother.*

She lifted her coffee cup to her lips, not that she could swallow anything, but because the gesture was familiar and comforting. It gave her hands something to do. "I'm sorry you feel this way, honey."

A snort. "That's super passive-aggressive of you. It's not even an apology."

"It's not. You're right there. I didn't mean to apologise. I meant to express sadness that you're upset."

"Mum. You just care about your pride. You don't even love me. You just want to win the argument."

Madeleine was so tired. So very, very tired. Her eyelids felt prickly, grating over eyes that hated to see Savannah's lower lip wobble and curve down, down, down.

"Honey, I love you to infinity and beyond. And what I'm about to say, I'm saying with all my heart—your anger is not my responsibility."

Savannah looked stunned for a second. Her mouth opened, but Madeleine beat her to it. "Ashton is coming over for lunch," she said. "We can talk about the new family arrangements then. Meanwhile, the twins and I are going to the beach for a swim. You're welcome to join us if you like."

Without waiting for a response, Madeleine turned and walked away. It was the hardest thing she'd done in a long time: harder than coping with the murder in Arcadia, harder than dealing with the Mekong Dragons, harder than accepting Ashton's absence and Granny Smith's charity.

"Mum?" Savannah called out. "Mum!"

Madeleine kept walking.

Savannah wasn't the perfectly behaved daughter Madeleine had once assumed she'd have. And that was all good. She loved Savannah for everything the girl was, as well as for what she wasn't. Madeleine was grateful for the opportunity to be the girl's mother. She was grateful for the twins and for their uncomplicated take on life. She was grateful for the years she'd spent with Ashton, even if they were now at an end.

Happiness was—letting go of the need for specific outcomes. Some outcomes were better than others, for sure, sometimes you got what you wanted and sometimes you didn't. Simple as that. Not worth getting upset about.

Madeleine took a big breath. She had her kids. She had her home. She had her work. And no matter what happened with Ashton in the long run—whether they decided to mend their marriage or go their separate ways—her life would all work out.

If fate wanted to throw her a curveball, it was in for a surprise. Madeleine would bounce that curveball right back into fate's stupid grin.

Her phone buzzed with an unknown caller ID. Yet another burner phone, for sure.

"Yes?" she snapped into the mouthpiece.

"About the lab, Madeleine. Now the police are gone, it's time to set it up."

She wanted to ask how he knew. She wanted to tell him to go to hell. But she had a better idea. "When do you want to install?"

They arranged the time and the security code access to the science building. Madeleine promised to inform the guard at the gate to expect a van, as usual.

Then she selected Louis Harding from her list of contacts. Nothing *as usual* about that.

The Mekong Dragons, just like stupid fate, had messed with the wrong girl.

Constable Zero Zimmerman

Zero was on her way to see Millie when her phone buzzed. She recognised the number even though she'd never stored it on the phone's memory. "Madeleine?"

"Constable. I have my lawyer in a three-way conference on this call. Is that all right? Can we go ahead?"

"It is. Who's your lawyer?"

"Louis Harding. I believe you've met."

"Virtually. What can I do for you, Madeleine? And Mr Harding?"

It was Madeleine who answered. "How would you like to catch a drug gang in action?"

"Very much."

"I can help you do just that."

"But?"

"But I have a few conditions." Madeleine's voice was pure school principal.

"That's not my call. Can I pass you to my—"

"I want to deal with you personally, Constable. You can take my offer to your commanding officer or whatever your hierarchy dictates."

"I'm listening. But let me guess," she remembered the photos on Miss Patel's phone and decided to take a gamble. "This has to do with the Mekong Dragons?"

This scoop was going to look good at her next performance review. Ironic. It was just dumb luck Zero was the cop Madeleine knew, just the right girl in the right place at the right time. Weren't careers usually made on dumb luck rather than dumb-ass work?

Auckland Region Women's Corrections Facility was located in South Auckland. Zero arranged the visit by phone, then made her way down the motorway past the chic suburb of Newmarket, past the gigantic shopping mall in Sylvia Park, all the way to industrial Wiri with its steely warehouses and silo-like petroleum storage depots. Greyness descended onto her. It was only partially the result of the gloomy environment.

The prison's perimeter didn't engage in false advertising and did nothing to disguise its purpose—it looked every bit like every prison fence in the movies. Zero forced herself to go through gates and security checks, flashing her ID and the approved visitor letter, making sure she greeted every security guard by the name displayed on their nametag.

They didn't have to, but because she was a cop, they guided her to the private room usually reserved for lawyer visits, away from the crowded area where other inmates received their loved ones. This wing was reserved for those awaiting trial—Zero knew people remanded in custody made up a fifth of the prisoner population—so at least they wore civilian clothing, not the dehumanising prison garb that made people into uniformed non-entities.

Zero waited. Seconds stretched into minutes, minutes into centuries. Eventually the door opened, and a guard walked in, followed by a hunched figure.

"You know the drill, Constable," the guard said as she left them.

Zero almost didn't recognise her.

"Millie," she whispered.

Her sister looked at her with eyes so hard, they were those of a stranger. "So you're going to just sit there? How about a hug for the black sheep of the family?"

Not the best start. The hug went a little better, the unfamiliar scrawniness of Millie's shoulders offset by the familiar scent of her skin. They dispensed with small talk after a few false starts—neither of them was any good at it even in the best of circumstances, and this was not the best of circumstances.

"Dad needs to see you," Zero said. "It's really bad. Like I said in the email—"

"What about Mum? Has she washed her hands of me?"

"They both miss you like crazy." She felt physical pain saying this. Forged on through her stupid jealousy. "Millie. Please listen.

They love you so much. We all do. Possibly more now you're the black sheep or the prodigal daughter, or whatever. Mum's the stronger of the two of them though. Dad's the one not coping."

"Not my fault."

Yes, it was. It was her fault. *Of course* it was her fault. Now, however, was not the time to argue. Instead, Zero dug deep within her soul. "Millie, I'd just like to say that I am so, so sorry." At least that much was true. While she wasn't sorry she had solved that case, she was sorry Millie had broken the law, sorry she was in custody, sorry their parents were hurting. "Are you planning to hold this grudge forever?"

A shrug. "Guess not. So what do you mean, Dad not coping?"

"Sleeping lots. Not enjoying his food or chess or music."

"He's not listening to music?" Millie put the tips of her fingers in her mouth in a gesture almost identical to Bobbi's. "Shit, Zara. I thought if we had no contact, it would be easier on them. They could pretend I was working overseas or something." Millie clicked her knuckles. "Shit."

"So you'll let them visit?"

"I really, really, really don't want them to see me like this."

"Point. It's not about you, though, is it?"

Millie nodded. "Fair. But enough with the lecturing. You're turning into our mother."

Zero's breath caught in her chest. Wait, what? Was Millie paying her a compliment? "There are worse things than being our mother," she said at last.

"For sure."

"I'll bring Mum and Dad to see you tomorrow, all right?"

An overacted sigh to let Zero know how put upon her sister was feeling. "All right then."

"I'll take it as an *all right* then. And you'll let me help you apply for electronic monitoring?"

A promise of a smile flitted on Millie's face. "It's the least you can do."

That kind of justice Zero could live with.

Madeleine Smith

Madeleine made sure that the cop cars came onto the school property before the change of guard at the gate. The officers hid—Madeleine wasn't exactly sure where—in the trees perhaps, or behind other buildings, or inside the walls maybe.

Hep had done an amazing job of getting rid of all the cannabis plants. The Mekong Dragons were now in possession of a large harvest; while the glasshouses and plastic tunnels now housed cherry tomatoes, strawberries, and persimmon saplings. Knowing how much cherry tomatoes cost in supermarkets, Madeleine wondered whether they would be a legitimate business proposition, but she left that thought for another day.

Louis Harding had also done a good job negotiating with the police, although it was Constable Zimmerman's idea to set Madeleine up as an official informer with total immunity for any cannabis she and her unnamed assistants may or may not have grown. As it stood at the moment, she wasn't admitting anything and there was no physical evidence anyway, so it would be her word—the respected school owner and principal—versus that of drug gang members.

She had been told to stay away so she waited in the admin block. The staff lunchroom faced the science labs, but the darkness and the physical distance conspired against her. Hidden behind the curtain, all she saw was the night garden, then sudden spotlights and running silhouettes. There was shouting, though she couldn't distinguish individual words, not even the language in which they were yelled.

Then a gun shot, like a deafening clap.

Then several more.

Constable Zero Zimmerman

Zero's body cramped from kneeling in the bushes. After what seemed like a decade, a light-coloured van arrived. Then another. The second one's number plate was the same as the van in Miss Patel's photo.

Dark figures unlocked the lab and carried packages inside. Zero expected them to switch on the ceiling lights, but they worked with torches. Suddenly her earpiece buzzed with the signal and a countdown. Spotlights came on. People ran out of the building straight into a cordon of officers that magically materialised outside the door.

The memory of Emmanuelle Linden escaping through the floor-to-ceiling window made Zero move her gaze to the side of the building, where the toilets were. She knew that her colleagues would be watching the lab windows, but what about the toilet wing?

Her knees sent painful waves of protest into her brain as she straightened her legs and tiptoed left. Zero counted eleven heartbeats in which nothing happened. On the twelfth heartbeat, one of the windowpanes swivelled upwards and a slim figure half-crawled, half-rolled out.

"Western side," she shouted. "Suspect escaping on foot!"

Six gunshots tore through the air. A bullet punched her in the abdomen and pushed her to the ground.

CHAPTER 20

Sunday

Constable Zero Zimmerman

The day of the funeral was sunny and hot, and the backs of Zero's thighs stuck to the edge of the car seat on the way to the cemetery. Her stomach still hurt where the bullet had struck her Kevlar vest the night before.

Schnapper Rock Road wound through Albany's shoebox housing subdivisions, over what once were strawberry fields and orchards. A swarm of white balloons released by the previous batch of mourners rose up into the impossibly blue sky. *There but for the grace of God go I*, she mused. If not for her protective gear, if the bullet had struck her throat or face ….

I can't do it, Zero thought. *I just can't.*

And then she got out of the car and did it. Looked at the digital photo montage of Keith with his parents, Keith with his schoolmates, Keith with his daughter. Listened to the speeches. Said a few words on behalf of the flatmates. Thought that the ex-wife didn't look particularly sad. Felt sorry for the kid. Nodded to her colleagues and watched them as they invited the ex to accompany them to the police station. She knew they'd be asking questions about the emotionally manipulative texts sent from her phone number, Keith's life insurance policy and the unusually high sum of money involved.

It was a criminal offence to encourage someone to commit suicide. If that's what Keith's ex had done, she'd be looking at jail time. What would happen to baby Koru then? Would having your mum in jail be worse for her or for Vincent? Koru had already lost her dad, Vincent—a brother.

Mothers should really try not to break the law, for their children's sake. Even if it was for their children that they committed those crimes in the first place.

Although it was Zero who'd found the insurance policy when packing up Keith's room, she chose not to go into the office after the funeral. Instead, she headed to the hospital.

Aiko was sitting up in bed, her skin creamy, eyes serene. "Thank you," she said as soon as she saw Zero. "For visiting, as well as for catching the perp. Also, for not telling anybody about me."

Zero didn't trot out the cliché about just doing her job. "You're very welcome."

"It's not that I'm ashamed of who I am, you know?"

Zero thought she understood. "You don't want a label. I get that."

"Yes. No. It's not about labels *as such*. We all have them, don't we?"

Zero nodded. In primary school, her red hair had earned her the unimaginative nickname of Carrot Head until somebody had found a new one—Zero. In time, she had learnt to love both her red hair, as well as the ironic twist of her first name. In a way, it's up to you what your label grows to mean, what story you tell yourself, what play you put on for the world to see. "Right, it's not about a label. What is it then?" she asked.

"When people look at me, I want them to see something more than just the T in LGBTQ. I don't want my gender to be the first, or even the tenth thing they think about. How about smart, sexy, excellent with coloured pencils, kind to friends, compassionate to enemies …"

"Idealistic too?"

Aiko smiled. "I'll take idealistic over other things I've been called."

"Sorry to hear that."

"It's okay. I mean," she said the phrase like a parody of teenage speech patterns, "it's anything but okay, but it's not your fault. Hard enough to deal with those who cling to the belief that there are only two genders. And you know what's worse? Those who insist you speak your truth, those who plaster the label on your forehead in scarlet, then make you live by it, wanting you to be loud and proud."

"Surely there's choice?"

"For gay people, yes. Their choice when and whether to come out. But for people who are gender-fluid, there is this pressure to embrace it, to advertise your pronouns, to consider hormone therapy or surgery for transitioning. The very word, trans, implies that you're on a journey from one gender to another. The idea of being happy in-between genders is still new, even within our community."

Zero got it now. Aiko just wanted to be left alone to be herself: female body, Y chromosome and an aversion to tick any boxes.

"I don't want to be a disadvantaged minority. Don't care that I'm not *gender normal*. But whether you're trans or cis, that just shouldn't be an issue. You shouldn't have to come out or make a special announcement. It's not a big deal. Shouldn't be. Like, people don't get defined by their blood type, nobody says, 'Hey, look at Jane, she's AB positive—'"

That made Zero laugh. It's a bit like ethnicity, she realised. She never thought of Jackson as black. It's not that she was colour-blind, it's just that the colour was not his defining quality. His defining quality was—she felt warmth in her cheeks and her heart—that he was a good person. Underneath the playboy behaviour beat a kind heart. He was a rock, someone she could always turn to. Plus, he was amazing in bed. Okay, now she was probably objectifying him but, as Bobbi would say, *whatever*.

When she returned home, she fired up her laptop and worked on a presentation she would deliver to the students of Arcadia High the following day.

All in a day's work. Cliché intended.

CHAPTER 21

Monday

Constable Zero Zimmerman

Quan Le, also known as Lac Long, the leader of the notorious drug and money laundering gang called Mekong Dragons, died in the intensive care unit of Auckland's Middlemore Hospital thirty hours after he'd been fatally wounded during a shootout in a police sting operation at Arcadia High Boarding School. His brother, Hai Le, died at the scene from a self-inflicted gun wound. Their house, car and dry-cleaning business had been seized by the police. The news item appeared in the online edition of *New Zealand Herald* but didn't make the print version, possibly due to a low click rate.

Quan Le's widow—and that piece of information did not make either version of the newspaper—had to sell her personal belongings, including her wedding ring, to buy a one-way ticket back to Hanoi.

Zero couldn't help thinking that a more perfect justice system would have looked after the widow.

Bobbi Kentwood

Constable Zimmerman visits us at a special assembly. Mrs Smith addresses us first, trying to control the blowout from Mrs Linden's arrest, but she may as well try to control a tsunami, so she hands over the lectern to the policewoman.

The cop says she'd like to put the rumours to rest, but that we will have to wait till the trial to hear the details. She reminds us to call the police if we're ever in need of immediate assistance because of a crime being committed, or the police non-emergency line if we're concerned about something, or Lifeline if we need to talk about mental health.

Afterwards, I wait for her outside the school hall, in the shade of a large pohutukawa tree. Its red blossoms are long gone, but its grey-green leaves provide respite from the heat. The tree trunk is gnarly and weathered. I think that I never want to get old. Then I realise what not getting old implies, and an army of imaginary ants runs down my spine, as though I've teetered on the edge of a cliff. I can't believe a few weeks ago I didn't want to live anymore.

"How are you, Bobbi?"

The cop's voice startles me. I know she means it as an ordinary how-are-you, a greeting, but the question sends me down a self-analysing spiral. How am I really?

A bit emotional.

Frightened of what the future might hold.

Glad we're not running away.

Anxious that my mother will get worse again.

Cut up for Vincent's sake. I mean, it's his *mum*.

I'm not happy. Nor terribly unhappy. And at least I'm not emotionless.

"Well," I say at last. "You know I have mental health issues, right?"

She looks me up and down, like I'm a horse and she a potential buyer. "No. You don't."

Just like that.

I want to argue, but she talks right through me, which in a way is fortunate, otherwise we'd be stuck in an endless loop of "yes I do—no you don't."

"What you do have, is a burden that no teenager should be asked to bear. You have an issue with a mum who—"

"A mum who's barking mad?" I interrupt.

"A mum who needs a lot of stability and care. Are you strong enough to support your stepdad through that?"

"I don't call him that," I say automatically. "Blair is my dad. Louis Harding is nothing right now. Just some guy who made my mum run and hide."

I don't tell Zero Zimmerman that I might give him a chance one day. Instead, I show her my hands. "See how long my fingernails are?"

"You've stopped biting them?"

My nod is a happy one. I'm glad she noticed before.

"That's fantastic, Bobbi. What's changed?"

That's too stupid to dignify with a straight answer. So much has changed. I choose my words carefully. "Here's the thing," I tell Constable Zimmerman. "I've realised that Aiko was not stealing Savannah—Savannah was drifting away from me anyway. She suddenly got it into her head to hang out with the cool girls. Wanted to become more popular."

"Did it work?"

"I guess."

Actually, I can more than guess, I know. As it turns out, Aiko isn't the one Vincent likes. It's—drumroll please—Savannah the cool.

That means Mrs Linden tried to poison the wrong girl. Oh, the irony.

"And you, Bobbi? Do you want to be more popular?"

A no-brainer. "Well, duh. Who wouldn't? But I don't want to hang out with the popular crowd. They're not my people."

The constable raises her eyebrow. "And who are your people?"

"People who like books. And movies that are not about saving the world from aliens. People who care about the amount of plastic in the oceans."

People like Aiko—the reflection pops into my head unsolicited. More irony. And, to be fair, Aiko is both a nerd and popular.

Perhaps we should label people less. Whoever thought that putting individuals in boxes was a smart idea? We're all unique. And, like cats, every one of us needs a separate box.

"Bobbi?"

The next idea is so liberating to think that I decide to say it aloud. "I don't even want to be friends with Savannah anymore. Like, at all." Yep, feels even better to vocalise it.

"Why is that, Bobbi? Has something happened to upset you?"

What happened? I discovered a new philosophy. I used to be a nihilist. Then I got religion—or rather existentialism. Existentialists believe life has no inherent meaning or purpose, other than the purpose we create for ourselves. This purpose is unique to us, and everybody needs to find their own. We have complete control over what we choose. Yes, life is meaningless, but that's not necessarily a bad thing, because it frees us to do what we enjoy.

Also, I used to think Savannah was deep. I longed to strip off the outer layer of the identity she presented to the world, and see what she was hiding, the special self she saved for close friends. Like peeling an onion, layer by layer, to expose new wonders below. Only, when cooking the other day, I noticed that onion layers were all identical. No matter how many you peel off, what you find underneath is more of the same, more onion, smaller and smaller, until all you're left with are watering eyes.

I don't say all that. Instead, I look at the ground and mumble: "Don't know. Grew up, I guess. Need to create my own meaning in life. Can't tie my happiness to Savannah for the rest of my life."

A smile changes the policewoman's face from official to almost motherly. "That's an astute observation," she says. "Happiness doesn't come from other people."

For a moment, I'm sure she's going to ruffle my hair, but then her arm changes direction and initiates a handshake instead. "Goodbye, Bobbi. Make smart choices. And take care."

I will, I think. I'll take very good care of Vincent. Doesn't matter that he thinks he likes Savannah. It's me he needs.

Strange how some things that I felt so strongly about don't matter anymore. Like Savannah.

It's even stranger that other things matter just as much. Like Vincent.

Poor Xander, I think. But then the thought drifts away on a very small puffy cloud, like a ghost of our relationship, over the solitary black sheep grazing on the soccer field.

I can relate to that sheep.

Three weeks later

CHAPTER 22

Just Another Thursday

Constable Zero Zimmerman

Millie was coming home today, to Mum and Dad's house, remanded on electronically monitored bail. She would have to wear a tracker on her ankle, but at least Dad was listening to music again and he had already set up their favourite glass chessboard for an after-dinner game.

And yet Zero wasn't thinking about Millie as much as she normally would have. Instead, she was thinking about Emmanuelle Linden.

Losing your child was tragic beyond words but it still gave you no right to kill another human being, to take away another mother's child. It may be a reason, an explanation—never an excuse. Still, had justice been done in this particular case? Zero had arrested a grief-stricken mother, wreaking havoc in the life of a teenage boy who'd lost his older brother last year. She hadn't met Emmanuelle Linden's husband, but he would be another casualty of Zero's stubborn decision to not let Aiko's poisoning be classified as a suicide attempt.

Really doing well there in making the world a fair place, Zimmerman, she thought.

Her heart went out to Emmanuelle Linden and to all the mothers worldwide—to her own mum visiting her other daughter in prison, and to the biological mother she couldn't remember, and also to the gypsy woman who took her in as a toddler and then gave her up when Zero had a chance of finding a "forever home" in New Zealand.

That all-consuming mama-bear love was scary. Parenthood was scary. The power that parents had over their children's wellbeing, safety, fate—Zero wasn't sure she would ever be ready for such responsibility.

Had her biological mother been overwhelmed by the responsibility of caring for Zero? Is that why she had given up her baby, abandoned her in a park, a cardboard box and a toddler sister the only protection? Had she at least watched from a hiding place to make sure someone would find the children?

The alarm buzzed. Time was up. Zero turned the white stick the right way up and glanced at the results window. The plus sign that must have emerged there a few moments before was identical to the one she had seen the previous night. She bought three more pregnancy tests on the way to work, but she didn't feel like repeating the experiment again. Deep inside, she knew that the outcome wouldn't change.

What would her parents think? How would they react?

Could she still be a cop, or was it too dangerous a job for a pregnant woman? A few weeks ago, Quan Le might have killed her. Tomorrow, a meth-crazed teenager might pull a knife on her.

Had the bulletproof vest been enough protection for the baby? What if the impact had damaged it? No, that wasn't possible, she had been like what—two days pregnant?

Her thoughts were driving her mental. Too many questions and only one answer. She found Jackson in the cafeteria.

"Have this one," he said, extending his coffee mug towards her. "I've just made it."

The smell assaulted her nostrils, made stomach acid rise to her throat. She shook her head. "Better not."

"You? Saying no to coffee?" Jackson's eyes locked on hers. "What's going on?"

Nothing. Or maybe everything.

The silence seemed to stretch like a bungee cord.

"That night," Jackson said at last, his detective face on. "Did it make us pregnant?"

Shirking responsibility already? Zero felt her blood run hot and she regained her ability to speak. "It wasn't exactly *that night's* fault, you know. *It* didn't do the impregnating. And *we* are not pregnant. *I* am. And what *I* want to know is, how? How the hell? We used a condom every time *that night.*"

Jackson looked away. "Yeah, about that."

Zero waited, her eyebrows raised politely, while the rage inside her chest made her thoughts decidedly less polite.

"Shit. Sorry. I should've told you. Didn't know how. I realised afterwards—"

Another detective walked into the cafeteria. "What?" she asked. "Am I interrupting something?"

"No," Zero and Jackson said simultaneously. Then they fell silent, staring at the intruder.

"Riiiiight. I can tell I'm not wanted. Brilliant detective that I am."

When they were alone again, Jackson said, "The condoms were past their expiry date. I only noticed when cleaning up the next day."

"Wait, what? When did you buy them?"

"A few years ago."

"A few years?" It didn't compute. "There are only a dozen per box. And as much as I am for recycling and saving the environment, they are strictly single-use-only items. *Obviously.*"

Jackson shrugged. "What can I say? I wish I were in the habit of having sex more often. *Obviously.*"

Zero felt the world spin. Maybe not the whole world, but the room for sure. Like her sense of reality was about to shatter. "I don't get it. What about your reputation? You're the police force's biggest player."

"Am I?" Something like self-deprecation crossed his face.

"Well …" She was lost for words.

"You know how it is, Zee. You arrive at your first job, and you joke with the guys, locker room talk. They are like, *Hey, you're black, you must have a huge dick.*"

Zero felt an unwanted smile forcing the corners of her mouth upwards. "They weren't wrong."

"They say, *Girls must queue up outside your bedroom. Do you have to chase them away? How many have you had?* And you say *hundreds.* And they believe you. So you're given a label and you try to live up to it. Or down to it, however you want to see it."

"You try to have as much sex as possible?"

Jackson pulled a face. "No. There's nothing as underrated as meaningless sex."

"I thought guys loved meaningless sex?"

"Colour me different. Pun intended."

That made her smile some more. "Why buy all those condoms if you weren't using them?"

"Wishful thinking?"

Zero still didn't get it. "So why not just do it? If you're not into meaningless sex, why not put some meaning into it? The woman who was just here. She's smart and pretty and she'd bang you right on this floor if you gave her half a chance. Why not have a meaningful relationship with her?"

"Detective Yin? She's gorgeous. But not my type."

"What's your type?"

"You."

Zero's heart pumped in her stomach, her throat, her ears. She tried for flippant. "Red hair, you mean?"

"No," Jackson gathered her into a hug. "I mean, you. You can dye your hair blue or shave it off, get a tan, pierce your navel, change the shape of your nose, I don't mind. Physical characteristics are not what make you—*you*."

Her breath caught. "That's the lamest thing ever," she managed.

"Nope. But this might be a contender." With that, Jackson took Zero's hand in his and dropped to one knee. "Zero Zimmerman, will you do me the honour of raising our baby together?"

Acknowledgements

Some of the poems in this book are mine, others were written by Richard H or Karl G. I'm grateful to you both for letting me use your words.

My daughter created Bobbi's diary entry as a work of fiction. I love you, honey.

Inspector Andrew Fabish of the New Zealand Police was patient and kind enough to answer my many naïve questions. Thank you so much!

Constable Zero Zimmerman's interrogation technique is lifted from *The Behavior Panel* YouTube channel—Scott, Mark, Chase, Greg— you guys rock!

Yvonne Eve Walus

You won't believe this, but when I'm not a novelist, I'm a Doctor of Mathematics. A business analyst. A wife and a mother. Most of all, though - I am a writer, hoping to change the world one book at a time.

My heritage is inter-continental. The first twelve years of my life in communist Poland taught me never to trust newspapers, how to play the game within the system, to value uniformity, and to ride in public transport squashed between so many people that my feet didn't touch the ground. The next sixteen years in South Africa's apartheid taught me never to trust newspapers, how to play the game within the system, to value diversity, and to drive the car fifty metres down the driveway to my mailbox. The years that followed taught me that New Zealand is a fantastic country to live in - consequently, I've lived here longer than anywhere else.

Crime fiction is my passion. My childhood hero was, predictably, Hercule Poirot. I've changed my mind several times since, and for a time, I was totally into Harlan Coben's super-rich super-able Win (Windsor Horne Lockwood), but my current favourite is Benedict Timothy Carlton Cumberbatch… I mean, Sherlock Holmes.

www.ingramcontent.com/pod-product-compliance
Lightning Source LLC
Chambersburg PA
CBHW071229300726

48975CB00002B/343